HOW SOCRATES BRAVO
GOT HIS NAME

LESLEY KLENK

How Socrates Bravo Got His Name

By
Lesley Klenk

Published by Eld Inlet Press

ISBN 978-1-7368087-0-2 (paperback)
ISBN 978-1-7368087-1-9 (ebook)

Cover design by wordsugardesigns

www.lesleyklenkauthor.com

Copyright 2021

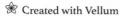 Created with Vellum

Chapter One

I grew up on a cotton farm in northeastern Alabama where three generations of Jeffersons and Ashbys considered the land their own. I was young enough to believe that although there was a wrinkled paper deed to the farm in an old drawer somewhere, the fact that the Jeffersons were Negro and the Ashbys were white did not impact the entwining of our families or the yield of rows of cotton planted to the horizon. A day came, however, when the story of how I came to inherit the name of a Greek philosopher—who lived his life questioning others —pulled us out of the shadows of ignorance and into the harsh light of truth.

"Socrates Bravo, where you at?" Mama's voice boomed from the wide, sagging porch of the big house and echoed across the fields. It was a blistering hot day in early spring, just a few days into the month of March. The heat threw everything and everyone off their normal course. Tree limbs went from brown to green in an afternoon, fields were bone dry when a week before water dripped from a fistful of dirt, and windows in the picker shacks and the big house were left wide open all night. The heat—and my uprising—came without warning or shame.

I shifted my feet trying to keep my hiding place a secret. The thick leaves of the prickly ash copse quivered. The branches were lined with new green leaves and long, curving thorns. One caught in my thick, black hair, and I whimpered under my breath. I heard my brother, Walker, rustle the bushes to aggravate me.

"You gonna get paddled tonight, Soc, and it's not going to be Daddy doing it. Mama means business." Walker leaned into the branches.

"Don't look right at me. They'll know I'm here." I carefully used one finger to wipe the fog off the lenses of my glasses. It was doubtful anyone would look for me in the prickly ash copse. Everyone avoided the bushes during spring when its blooms produced an odor like rotting fruit. I was getting a headache standing with my face pressed into the leaves, but my other choice was staring into the prickly thorns emerging from the canes just inches from my eyes. The longer I stood rigid in the stench and potential impalement, the more I questioned my hasty decision to escape from the tedium of my daily life. I set my lips together and stayed put. It is not every day a boy turns thirteen. I was hiding in plain view; they just did not know where to look.

"Walker, are you still there?" I whispered.

"Yep," he grunted putting his hand to shade his eyes as he looked across the fields. "Daddy's coming. This could get bad, Soc. Why are you doing this?"

I paused while I thought about an answer that would satisfy my brother. "Walker, I'd like just one damn day off from studying."

"Socrates, you are too young to swear." He went silent. "That'd be the death of Mama."

"Socrates Bravo, where are you? We are not done reading the nature poets. Shelley is last. He drowned in the Ligurian Sea, for goodness' sakes," Mrs. Ashby called from inside the house.

"Well, if he is dead, then what's the hurry?" I muttered.

"Who's the Shelley person she's yakking about?" Walker kicked up dirt with his toe. I knew he was pretending he was on a pitcher's mound waiting to send a fastball to the catcher's glove.

"A poet." I squeezed one eye shut.

"Well, that's enough to make a man kill himself."

"Not exactly, Walker." If I had just stayed to do my afternoon studies, I would not be in this predicament. When Mama finally found me, she would manage to paddle me and pester me about Shelley at the same time.

"Come on. Knock it off, Walker." He pulled a baseball from his pocket and stuck it in his mitt.

The screen door slammed, and Mrs. Ashby emerged from the house wearing an old-fashioned, long dress with a high neck and lacy sleeves and a ragged sweater with a handkerchief stuffed in her pocket. Her hair was piled up untidily on her head and held in place with a new, sharpened pencil. She looked up to my mama who was an amazon compared to her. Seeing how my mama was as big as a man, or as my daddy called her, "one tall drink of water," my mama had never had a store-bought dress. She made her own clothes by ripping the seams out of Mrs. Ashby's rejected dresses, blouses, and skirts and refashioning them with added muslin and flour sacks to make them long and wide enough. The resulting wardrobe was colorful with puffed silk sleeves, damask bodices, and long muslin skirts that Mama pulled up and tucked into her waistband when she was hoeing weeds in the garden.

Mama patted Mrs. Ashby's arm and shook her head in slow movements indicating to her that my time would come. I blew out a slow breath. I was in deep.

I observed how the heat hit Mrs. Ashby like an oven when she stepped off the porch. She peeled her sweater off inside out as she walked to the barn. I heard her calling ahead to my daddy.

"William Jefferson, where is Socrates? I've been calling him for ages." I watched her tug on the heavy gray door dotted with flecks of old red paint as it groaned on its rusted hinges.

"You have not. Not ages, at least." I set my lips in a line, deciding what to do.

"Walker, please tell her I'm at the commissary." I felt something scratching on my leg, and I kicked it, hoping it was not a spider. "I want to play ball with you. Come on," I pleaded.

"No, Soc," he said, bouncing the baseball off his arm and catching it in his palm. "Go do your studying and catch up with me later." He walked away and broke into a jog, his mitt tucked under his arm. Soon, I could not see him except for the dust rising in his wake. He had grown again, Mama huffed, and it was not just his pant cuffs that had finally reached their end. At fifteen, his eyes spent more time looking hungrily at the horizon than they did at the farm where he was raised.

While my daddy joined Mrs. Ashby outside the barn, they walked back to the house, their heads bent together in conversation. Something like the fanning of wings brushed the back of my neck, and when I slapped at it, a branch of the prickly ash shook wildly. The motion released the dead fruit scent, and I willed myself not to reveal my hiding place. Daddy must have seen the waving branch because he sat down on his heels in the drive for a moment and peered in my direction. I put my feet in the V of the branch and flinched when the thorns pierced my shoes.

"You know, it's Socrates's birthday," Daddy suggested as Mama and Mrs. Ashby lowered themselves to sit on the porch swing. I could see his toe tapping on the step as they discussed the mystery of my disappearance. I was familiar with the toe tap. A lifetime of watching him keep the peace with my mama revealed that a toe tap meant a series of half-truths were spilling out. "I bet he and Walker went to the creek. Warm day like this? Maybe Socrates forgot his lessons." He took his hat off and wiped his forehead with his forearm. More gray had crept into his hair from the last time I had studied his long frame from afar.

"Oh no, I don't think so," Mama said in a deep voice without a bottom to it.

"Well, I am disappointed in him. This was supposed to be a special day for all of us. I won't be home tonight, so we'll have to celebrate tomorrow." Mrs. Ashby opened the screen door and eased into the house.

Daddy waved his hand behind his back. With a flicker of guilt for the toe tapping he might have to do later, I scuttled out from under the branches and took off.

As we got older, the times that Walker and I could be together were as rare as a night-blooming cereus that unfurls its petals once a year. I was willing to take a chance on a spanking—or worse, my mother's tongue lashing—to be alone with my brother.

I ran down the narrow road built for the field trucks that sliced the farm into three fields. I passed the pickers bent over the mounds of dirt they were making into hills for the cotton seed. If all went well, the upland cotton bushes that grew in northeastern Alabama would produce fat, brown seed pods into cotton bolls the size of plums. Farmers would walk the rows squeezing the palm-sized bundles, waiting for the moment the bolls felt heavy and dry. He would summon the pickers when millions of casings would fall away leaving a field of dirty white down. For the next several months, bolls would mature and bloom in rounds, and if the farmer knew when to hold and when to pick, multiple harvests would happen. About ten years ago, Daddy squeezed seven pickings out of a field, filling Mr. Ashby's bank account and putting food on the pickers' tables all winter, but that was a long time ago—before the boll weevil wormed its way into the heart of the cotton boll.

I had only run ten minutes when I slowed to a walk and pulled my drenched shirt away from my chest. I was not toe tapping when I told Walker I wanted a day off from studying, but I did not tell him all of it. I did not tell him the rest because he could not understand the rest, and neither could my mama or my daddy. They did not know the Socrates Bravo they knew would soon be a memory too slick to hold.

Mrs. Ashby had said to me yesterday, "You are almost ready, Socrates Bravo. You are going to show the world that a thirteen-year-old Negro scholar from Gideon, Alabama, can take the entrance exams at Parson University Preparatory School."

Then she'd patted my back between my shoulder blades. I felt the bony protrusions struggle inside my skin; they were wings uncertain of the rightness of time. Should they stay tucked inside the silence of my body or open deliberately to flap in the sun? It was the contest between the inside silence and the outside flapping that made me risk the horror of the prickly ash, my mama's vigorous tongue lashing, and Mrs. Ashby's keen disappointment. When I dashed under the leaves of the prickly ash copse, despair became the vehicle for deciding whether my wings should remain folded or take flight.

I slid sideways across the lowest field on the farm, leaping over the hills of dirt. "Walker, I'm here," I called. I rounded the side of the wild growth of oak trees, sticker bushes, and boulders that erupted out of the cotton field. It was the Patch.

Tangled and overgrown, pickers attempted to find an entrance, curious about the shady interior, but firethorn with four-inch-long spikes, arching branches of single-petal Cherokee rose, and mostly the kudzu vine, also known as "the vine that ate the South," stood in their way. There was a rule too. Long ago, Mr. Ashby's father ordered my grandfather Louie to send the picker and his family packing if they entered the Patch. Our Mr. Ashby kept the same rule, Daddy said, because it was just easier; only now, it was Daddy who had to tell the picker family to get their things and leave.

"Did you do your studies?" Walker asked, his face red as he sat on a rock in the shade of an oak tree. I raised my arms above my head as I waded through the tall grass, holding them high so the new green blades would not tear at my skin. I bent over and brushed my pant legs, not meeting Walker's eye.

"Heads up." He tossed me my mitt. "I picked it up at home on my way here." He grabbed the bottom of his shirt and used it to wipe his face covered with sweat.

"Happy birthday by the way. You know Mama might give me the paddle too if she finds out you had a plan."

"Well," I said guiltily, "then Daddy will join us, because he's the one who gave me permission to go, sort of." I remembered the waving hand behind his back. "Why are you so out of breath?"

"I'm doing sprints every day, so I'll be ready when I get called up to the Negro League."

He wiped the sweat off his neck and scrambled to his feet. He pulled the ball from his pants pocket. He sauntered into the field to the homemade pitcher's mound.

Mama didn't speak to Walker for a whole week after he had dropped out of country school and got a job at the sawmill in town. As he told the story, he spent his days hauling loads of sawdust out of the mill so they would not catch fire from the saw's sparks. In between moving the towering piles of sawdust that covered him in yellow pine dust, Walker talked about baseball nonstop, not even pausing to groan when he lifted a particularly heavy load.

Walker was crazy about baseball. Mr. Ashby had bought him a ball and a glove when Walker was little, and he'd watched from the porch while Walker and Daddy played catch. Soon, Daddy had to scrape together some money to buy a used glove for himself. Walker threw hard. Even from the beginning, Daddy would hold his glove as a target, and Mr. Ashby told Walker he had to hit the center five times in a row before he could go in. Just to show him who was the one doing the throwing, Walker nailed the target at least ten times, each throw harder than the last one. It might have stayed just a yard game, but as soon as we began listening to baseball games on the radio, Walker leaned in when the announcers talked about pitching. He pictured the pitcher's fingers as they released the ball, and soon, he was throwing fastballs, cutters, splitters, screw-balls, curveballs, and the one he disliked—the changeup. "It's difficult," Walker had told me, "to make yourself throw half as fast as you could just to make an impatient man confirm his place in the world."

There was a reason Walker had begged for a job at the sawmill. Most of the workers played on a Negro country baseball team, and Walker was confident that if they saw him pitch, he could play in real games and throw the ball in a place other than our yard.

When he'd told us about making the team, he acted it out to soften Mama up and make Daddy proud. "Y'all ready?" he stood in the kitchen like it was a pitcher's mound, leaning over so his forearm rested on his knee before standing and pulling his hands into his chest. "Think of this: the saw in the sawmill is always going. Can't sell a board if it is still a tree." He winked at me. "But, when the workers saw me pitch, the saw blade kept going around and around without anything going through it. I threw maybe ten pitches, and they sent the catcher to find out if a fifteen-year-old boy could play on the men's team. The catcher showed them his red hand, maybe it was steaming even a little, and the league had to say yes. What else could they do?" We shook our heads. That was always the question with Walker: What else could he do?

Nothing frightened my brother. When we were younger, Walker had told me he saw things coming when he shut his eyes.

"What kind of things?"

"The future."

"Does it scare you?"

Then he turned to me with one of his breaking smiles that causes a person to stop and stare.

"No, Soc. I'd like to know one way or another."

"You catch first," he said, tossing me the ball and pointing to the home plate we'd made out of a feed bag full of rocks that we'd stashed near the Patch when we weren't using it. "Ten pitches, then we switch."

I took a deep breath and bounced on my heels. It wouldn't be ten, it would be more, but I wasn't much of a pitcher, so it didn't bother me. Walker squared up on the mound and took small, controlled breaths to ready himself.

The pitch came in, but just before it struck my mitt, it broke suddenly over my shoulder. It sailed through the blue sky and dropped into the center of the Patch.

"Damn, Soc. That was our last ball!"

I wondered what Mama thought about him swearing. "You weren't supposed to practice that new pitch on me until Daddy said it was okay," I yelled back.

"Well, the break was pretty high. Sorry. Come on." We fought through the grass and studied the snarled mess in front of us.

"Walker, we're not supposed to go in there."

"What's worse? Mr. Ashby mad that we lost the ball or at least trying to get it back?"

He was right; neither option was appealing.

"There, Soc. You can wiggle through there." Walker pointed to a gap between a rock and a skinny, gray oak tree. "The tree's dead. Let's pull it out." We pushed the tree back and forth, and its brittle branches rained down on us. The root ball popped out of the dirt, and Walker grabbed the lifeless tree and tossed it aside. "You take the ground, and I'll clear the top."

"Fine." I wriggled through the narrow dark gap on my stomach, trying not to yell when the stickers ran a trail of pain along my cheeks. I kept my eyes closed and stayed flat against the ground when I felt Walker swing a large stick over my head. "Be careful," I shrieked under my breath.

"Be quiet, Socrates. You're acting like a baby." I could have said I was the one getting ripped to shreds by the thorns, but I kept quiet. There were not many older brothers who still played with their younger siblings after they got a town job or had to go to the fields, so I had to take what I could get.

I continued my army crawl through the brush and opened my eyes when my fingertips touched the bumpy red stitching of the ball. I pulled away like stung by a hornet; my hand was wet with mud. "Walker, there's water. There's water in there." I tried to get up, but Walker tramped over my head, swinging the stick against the bushes. I failed to drop back to the ground, and the bushes snapped back and hit me in the face. The impact of the thorns slicing my skin stung like a son of a gun.

"Get in here, Soc. You aren't going to believe this." He held out his hand to help me up. "Look." Walker held the ball up, and a web of muddy water dribbled down his arm. He lifted me up to sit on his shoulders, I wrapped my legs around his neck, and he held onto my ankles. There was a wide, worn circle of hardpacked earth in the middle of clearing under a sky of oak leaves. The trees' branches grew thick and tight together overhead and put the whole clearing in shadows. There were pinpricks of sunshine slicing through tiny gaps between the leaves, and the filtered light drifted down like a light-green film. Little flickers of green landed on our skin.

"Walker, people have been here. This is all worn down and permanent." I was afraid the pickers would hear our voices as it was only the walls of the Patch that separated us, but the trees and tall brush blocked all sound. I could not see the steady march of the sun toward dinnertime. I put my finger up to my neck and checked my pulse. I was inside the Patch. I was still Socrates Bravo, age thirteen, Negro scholar of Gideon, Alabama. For just a moment, I had wondered if the boy I knew was also the boy in the clearing.

"Soc, I don't know what to think. We'd hear of it if Daddy had to make some pickers leave, don't you think?" He turned in a circle, holding tight to my legs. "Look here." Walker touched scorch marks on the tree trunks. "Someone wanted this place gone." He carefully stepped over the tops of roots that erupted out of the earth like hard fossils. We looked up into the massive oak branches overhead. I felt as if I was in a church, but not one with boys wearing shined shoes, girls sporting clean dresses, music swelling out the windows, and shouts of amen at the end of the message. No, this church did not need all that. It needed only itself. It stayed sacred by needing no one.

"Where's the water coming from?" Walker let my legs go, and I slipped down off his back. I dropped to the ground and parted some clumps of grass that poked up from the mud. Walker bent over too, and mud started wicking up his pant leg. I smiled to myself. At least, I wouldn't be alone in getting a paddle on my birthday.

"Walker, wait. There might be snakes. Grab some sticks so we can poke the grass as we look." Crawling on our hands and knees, we shoved our sticks ahead of us, jumping when there was a rustle.

The grass closed behind us the farther we went, and

Walker started to panic. He was terrified of snakes. "Soc, let's go."

"Come on. I got this. Walker, don't worry. I think there'd be only ring-neck snakes and they can't hurt you; they'd just sort of fly at us." I kept the possibility that a cottonmouth snake could be there to myself. Ahead, I finally saw a break at the end of the muddy tunnel. "Walker, there. There it is. I see it." The mud ended at the edge of a water hole that crept from under a rock over-hang. The water rippled slightly and drifted away toward a marshy area that seeped sticky, dark earth down a slope. "That's why this corner of the field is always wet."

Dragonflies flitted cross the top of the calm water that was maybe twenty feet across and hidden by low plants and shade. The water swirled gently against the rocks, doubling back on itself, making a curl around the side. The surface was black, and we leaned over on our knees searching for the bottom. "You could walk right by it and not even see it," Walker said, pulling his shirt over his head. "Come on, little brother. Let's go swimming." He slid into the water and hung onto a rock. "Cold, cold, cold!" He shuddered. "Way colder than the creek."

"Hold onto the edge like I am." Walker began pulling himself around in a circle by grasping the rocks ahead of him. "Look at those bubbles behind me." He kicked his feet and pulled himself faster.

"It's a spring coming up from nowhere." I studied the piled boulders and motionless water in the shadows. "I wonder how deep it is."

"Quit yammering and get in here." Walker slid his hand across the water and doused me with a freezing wave.

"Wait. Let me put my glasses down." Mrs. Ashby

would have busted out yelling at me if I lost my glasses. An optometrist came to the farm once a year to test my vision. As the only person on the farm who wore glasses, I was expected to keep them in perfect condition.

I peeled off my clothes and lowered myself into the pool, losing my breath from the cold. I dipped my face and let go of the rock for a moment. The water grew colder the farther I drifted below the surface. I grabbed the rock above me and shook my head to clear my ears.

"This can be our place, Walker. We can hide the opening with the bushes and come out here without anyone knowing." Our eyes shining, we each held onto a rock and stretched our hands. Our fingertips touched for a second before the gentle turn in the water pulled us apart.

I grew bold, splashing and pulling myself around by the rocks. We created a whirlpool that swirled and pushed against us when we tried to go against the flow. The scratches from the prickly ash were gone, my skin was wrinkled and taut, and I knew, from looking at Walker, that my lips were blue and trembling too.

In the back of my mind, I was aware I left Mrs. Ashby and the poor poet, Percy Bysshe Shelley, languishing in the pages of my English book, but the new, unnamed rebellion still burned in my belly. In that moment of deciding whether to feed the fire or to put it out, I threw the whole load of firewood on it.

Walker turned away to yank on a tree root, and I pulled myself out of the water and stood shivering on the edge. I put my hands together in a triangle over my head and dove into the water. I felt layers of coldness rush past my skinny body. I opened my eyes, bubbles frothing in my wake. I had not factored in the possibility of an obstruction on the way down. Too late to stop, my head hit the corner of a boulder. I felt my head crack, my skin rip apart, and my body shudder. Then I felt nothing.

When I came to, my head was bouncing against Walker's naked back as he carried me down the road. A stream of blood ran down his side and into the dirt, and even in my state, I was curious about its origins. It was days later that I realized it was his and mine together.

"Mama, Daddy, Soc cracked his head open." He sounded muffled. Water gushed from my lungs, and I began to cough, spraying the dirt with a mixture of foaming red-and-yellow matter. Walker kept yelling for help. As he left the lowest field to climb the hill to the big house, I lost consciousness again. It was later that Walker told me the noisy chatter inside the picker shacks stopped as he carried me past them. Rocking chairs filled with nursing mamas and old grannies continued to move in a hush on the porch, and all the families stood in the windows watching him struggle. Not one of them offered to help. They knew their place.

When I woke again, I was laying in my mother's lap on the ground, and all I could see was a blur of stiff, red calla lilies in a line rounding the corner of the big house. I felt heavy like the water was squeezing all the air out of my lungs. I wondered if it was a dream until I tried to sit up and waves of pain washed over me. Laying back, I vomited and stained my mother's dress. Putting my hand to my forehead, I watched strings of blood sluice away and drip off my palm.

"Mr. Ashby, please let me take the field truck to town to see the doctor. Soc is hurt real bad," my father panted.

The porch swing creaked on its chains, and the smell of cigar smoke I knew as well as my mother's bacon-grease grits wafted over the grass, making a haze around us. He was mostly in the shadows except for when he stretched out his child-size foot to the porch floor to push the swing into the sunlight.

"Is Walker hurt?" Mr. Ashby asked. My brother stepped forward.

"No, sir. I just swallowed some water. Soc slammed his head on a rock."

"His name is Socrates." He folded the newspaper neatly and laid it down next to him. He stood up and peered over the porch railing to see me. He winced. "Yes, William that does look bad, but you know you can't drive the truck off the farm. Someone in town might think you were taking advantage of me by driving my vehicle. How about Trask take you? Where is he anyway? Bank says he is supposed to watch the farm, but the man is never here. Trask, come here. Trask?" He called around the side of the house, "Trask, the bank says you're to help. So, come help."

His scent reached us before he emerged from the summer kitchen where he was staying for the season. My eyes watered as the odor of rotten eggs engulfed the area, and it distressed me that I couldn't pull my collar over my nose or even hold my breath. To be honest, all I could do then was try not to die.

"Yes?" Trask's face was hidden by a wide-brimmed black hat that shadowed most of his face. He leaned over the porch railing and watched Mr. Ashby rock in the old porch swing. His black shirt was fastened to the top button of his collar, and the cuffs were pulled down severely to cover his arms. The man was so thin his kneecaps and wrist bones protruded beyond his limbs and gave him the appearance of being covered with cabinet knobs. As he stood in the middle of the Jefferson family spilled over the grass next to the house, he did not look at any of us. He pulled out a pair of black leather gloves from his pants pocket and pulled each one on, carefully inserting his fingers and pulling the gloves tight and then fastening small eyelets at his blue-veined wrists using his teeth to ease the latch into the hole. When he finished, he looked up again and said, "Timothy?"

Mr. Ashby stood up from the swing and pointed his index finger at Trask, inches from his face. "You're going to Livingston tonight, aren't you? Go now and drop them in Gideon." Mr. Ashby pointed at us collectively as if we were all parts of one interlocking whole. "You'll pick them up too, mind you. The bank says you'll be here a while. Least you can do is help."

"I do not work for you or Gideon Bank. I work for the Federal Farm Bureau." Trask raised his gloved hand to Mr. Ashby and pointed his black-gloved finger back at him. "And I don't manage pickers."

My daddy's nostrils flared when he turned to look at Mama. We were not pickers. The Ashbys did not concern themselves with managing the farm. The Jeffersons did. Mama slowly shook her head, her eyes steady. They said, *Not now. Do not let the outsider interfere with three generations of Jeffersons and Ashbys living side by side.*

Mr. Ashby fixed Trask with one of the looks he gives people. He had one blue eye and one brown eye. Even with my cheek laying on the grass, I saw Trask pull his hands off the porch rail. The name of the genetic condition, *heterochromia*, floated across the inside of my eyelid, and I imagined myself reaching out and grabbing it by its end so I could say it. In *heterochromia*, the eyes are the same in every way during the baby's development except for a small misfire at the end. One eye settled on one color while the other eye settled on a different one.

Mr. Ashby stared Trask down. His blue eye glared like a hot, August day with an unforgiving cloudless sky, and the brown one scowled like a swollen, churning creek in spring. Trask broke eye contact.

"Then you are fortunate, Trask, because the Jeffersons are not pickers." Mr. Ashby sat back down.

"What are they then?"

"Family." Mr. Ashby tamped out his cigar and laid it in an ashtray. "Go get the truck. I want you gone before Mrs. Ashby sees her boy all bloody like that."

Walker climbed into the bed of the truck, and my daddy handed my limp body up to him. It took Walker pulling and Daddy pushing to get my mama's generous frame over the edge and onto the rusty, metal floor. As the truck lumbered down the drive, although the glimpse I had of his profile did not betray it, I think Trask swerved to hit bumps, trying to knock Walker off the wheel well where he perched. Walker hung on. He would not give someone like Trask the satisfaction of seeing him fall.

My eyes were swollen, but I could tell the difference between sun and shadow by the motion of the tree leaves overhead. We sped through light and dark, light and dark, a comforting pattern, that is, until I caught a look of my mama's stricken face. I turned my head away even though the pain of moving it made my stomach wretch.

"Were you boys at the Patch?" Daddy's voice cracked like a dead tree branch.

Walker nodded looking away.

"What would have happened if Mr. Ashby had found out?" Walker did not respond. "Walker?" Daddy grabbed his arm.

Walker yanked his arm away. "He wouldn't have made us leave. It's our farm too."

"Walker, you know nothing. There is not a piece of paper with our name on it. Only Ashby, that's all." Daddy banged on the window of the cab for Trask to stop.

"It's there up ahead." I saw my daddy squeeze my mama's hand tightly like they were trying to stop a sweater from unraveling no matter how fast it was being knit. I rolled over and heaved a load of water from my stomach.

Trask stopped next to a big garbage barrel where a black cloud of flies was thick in the air. He looked over at a group of men standing one loading dock over.

"Out," he ordered. He put the truck in gear and pulled away while Walker was scrambling out of the back. He had to jump. Daddy grabbed Walker.

Daddy swore.

"William," my mother barked. "Enough. Get some help."

A group of men were waiting for bags of feed to haul home in their old field trucks. They were tenant farmers, poor whites, living on borrowed land and dependent on the success of the crop. They were above a picker, who owned nothing, but far below a farmer, who owned everything. The line between them and the pickers was razor thin while the space between them and the farmer was over the horizon and out of view.

Their hats were pulled low over their faces, and smoke billowed from their nostrils. I heard only snatches of words, but from my daddy's rigid leg twitching next to me, I knew we were the subject of their discussion. My daddy was not a picker, or a farm owner, or a tenant farmer, but they all knew he was the best cotton grower in all of Jackson County. I heard Trask's name said out loud, and I

knew they wondered why William Walker Jefferson
needed a bank man to find out why the Ashby farm had
so many debts.

Another man stood off to the side with his back to the
group. His head was turned enough to hear their talk, but
he stood apart, his body saying he was not a tenant
farmer. I blinked against the pain in my head, and when I
opened my eyes, black boots that smelled of shoe polish
jumped the gap between the landings and walked over to
Walker. Walker turned distant eyes on him. Walker looked
like my daddy, but he was just like Mama on the inside.

The man with the boots sized him up, studying his
muscles and long legs. "What's your name, boy?"

"I'm Walker Jefferson, sir." I felt Daddy stir next to me.

"Your brother?" The man stretched out his toe and
pushed me a little. He was probably checking to make
sure I was still alive.

"Yes." Walker jumped to his feet. "His name is Socrates
Bravo, and he's going to college after preparatory school."
His statement came out with a tone that was colored, just
slightly, with insolence. The tenant farmers looked up,
and the ash on the ends of their cigarettes lengthened.
This was interesting. They waited in the low sunshine for
the stranger to respond.

"Socrates Bravo? I've never heard of it. How odd."

Mama met his gaze. "It's an old family name."

He looked away from Mama. "Wait, Walker Jefferson.
I've heard of you. Baseball, right?" My brother nodded.
Every word that left my brother's mouth opened a door, a
window, or a crack in our family that would leave us
scared of what moved in the dark. "So, you're Ashby's
boy."

"Yes, sir."

"That's too bad. You are about all he's got. Everything else is owned by the bank." He struck a match and held it in his cupped hands. I saw a pointed light, blond beard covering the lower part of his face. "I'm Mr. Grindall. Why don't you come work for me chopping wood for my turpentine still? I'll pay you two dollars a day." I saw my parents' eyes open wide at the amount.

"Thank you, sir, Mr. Grindall, but I'm planning on making the Negro Baseball League and leaving Jackson County as soon as I can." Walker's voice carried, and the men on the other landing came closer. I saw Grindall sneak a look behind to see who all was listening.

"Son," Grindall said in a tight voice, "are you going to turn down a job that white men would be lucky to have?" Walker looked down at the chipped boards of the landing.

"Yes, sir. I don't want the job." The tenant farmers turned away as Grindall rose to his feet.

"Well, that's too bad. You might regret that decision someday." He tipped his hat to Mama. "Hope your boy gets better." He nodded to Daddy and lifted his bag of feed to his shoulder. He walked to a truck parked next to the sidewalk and tossed the bag in back. He paused with his boot on the running board to smooth his pale blond hair over his forehead before he got in. The truck roared to life with an engine that ran well, not like the farm trucks parked around us waiting for their deliveries. He did not leave right away, but when he put the truck in gear, I felt his eyes burn into us.

"Oh, Lord, William, what has he done? Too proud, too proud." My Mama's fear worried a hole in my shirt as she whispered. "William? Where did Walker go?" While my parents had hunched over me, Walker had jumped off the landing and had gone off whistling toward the sawmill. "What was that man talking about?" Mama asked. She tilted her head so she could see Daddy's face. She probably should have been watching his toes.

"Name's Grindall. He's from Chicago. He bought a place out near ours on the other side of the pine woods. Not interested in working cotton. Mr. Ashby says he's working trees." Daddy shook his head. "Don't know what he means."

"Why did he say Walker's all Mr. Ashby's got?"

Daddy sighed. "The farm is in trouble."

I saw Daddy look behind him at the shabby door and the pile of spent cigarettes. The front entrance of the doctor's office was bright white with black shutters, but this back area showed a disinterest in impressing the Negro patients.

"What's going to happen next?" Mama asked.

"I don't know."

Mama started in with her own ideas. "Well, I think—"

"Don't." Daddy's voice was abrupt. He sounded out of patience. "Just let it be." My mama shut her mouth. Even in my bleary state, I saw her biting her lip so little red dots broke through the skin.

Daddy stood up and brushed the dust off his pants. He went to the back door again and banged his fist on it. He raised his foot to strike the door and dropped it. "Annie, I'm going around front. We need someone."

My head hurt like a hand resting on a hot stove by mistake. I tried to pull thoughts together that could stand apart from the throbbing. Mama and I were alone.

"Mama, I did it. Don't be mad at Walker. He saved me."

"Socrates, what if you have died"—Mama hiccupped —"and never known who you were?" She stopped and shifted me on her lap. Even with her ample cushioning, waves crashed through my head.

"What?" The confusion was like a spiderweb all tangled up because someone had smashed through it.

"Socrates Bravo." She heaved a sigh from deep in her chest. "You aren't named after an old relative named Socrates. Mrs. Ashby named you."

I tried to sit up, but the nausea pinned me back to Mama's cushiony thighs. I closed my eyes and remembered Mr. Ashby insist Walker use my whole name.

"We made a pact, Mrs. Ashby and me. When you turned thirteen, we'd tell you what happened when you were born."

"This has to be a nightmare." Mama heard my words and pinched my arm with a little pressure. It was a warning, split-open head or not.

"Mrs. Ashby couldn't hold a baby in her. They always passed. She asked to be there when you were born." Her fingers explored my head, and pinpricks of pain circled my brain like stars.

"Mama, please,"

"Hush, Socrates. This isn't how you were supposed to find out. She asked me to wait until we were in the house together." She turned my head, so I had to meet her eyes. "Are you alive, Socrates? You are all heavy like a sack of potatoes."

"I'm okay, Mama." Her face looked like a mixed-up puzzle. I tried to put the pieces in the right place.

"I labored long with you, and after you were born, the bleeding was bad. Miss Cora had to pack me with rags to stop it."

"Mama, please," I croaked.

"You are just like every man." She swatted at a fly.

"Don't want to hear about how babies are really born. Don't talk until I am done." She took the torn part of her dress and wiped my face. "Miss Cora caught you that day, and there was nowhere to put you but in Mrs. Ashby's arms while she tried to save me. I watched Mrs. Ashby, son. She held onto you tight even though you were all slippery and bawling. I was dying, Socrates. I was. So when I saw her eyes, I knew she wanted to keep you."

Just when I had all the puzzle pieces of my mama's face in the right place, pieces of Mrs. Ashby tumbled into my picture, and I had to start all over again.

"I made a deal with Satan," Mama grunted. "I promised him right there I'd let her think she could be your mama too, if I could just come back to the living world."

"Then it happened. I came back to life, and you better believe I hollered, 'Give me my baby.'" Mama grabbed me by my collar and half lifted me to a sitting position.

"Mama, Mama, oh God, my head hurts so much," I begged.

"Don't you take the Lord's name in vain." She patted my cheek. "She asked to name you after a philosopher, someone from a long time ago that people still talk about, and I knew it was Satan asking for his due. I said yes. All I cared about was you were on my breast and pulling on me in the way babies know their mamas. I've never told her I didn't know what a philosopher was. I didn't want her to think I wasn't smart." She touched my open wound with her finger. It was such a gentle touch I knew it before I felt it. She stopped talking for a moment and then cleared her throat.

"She let me pick the middle name."

"Bravo?" My middle name had been the object of

ridicule by schoolchildren, pickers, and visitors to the big house. When I walked past the kids at the country school, they stood clapping, whistling, and shouting, 'Bravo.' All of them except for Walker. He put at least one of them face down in the dirt to warn the others. He fought without fear. Me? I am ashamed to say I was a runner. Although now, at age thirteen, I am mostly arms and legs, and I am worried I might not get them all working at the same time if it was necessary to escape.

"Remember how violin players come to town and the people watching say, 'Bravo,' because it was a good show? I decided Bravo made a fine name next to Socrates, and Mrs. Ashby agreed. Your daddy didn't say much; he was just glad I was alive. You too."

"It's a fine name, Mama." It's not like I could change it after thirteen years.

Daddy returned with a woman wearing a white nurse's uniform and white pointed hat. She was wearing gloves too, I remember. She looked in my eyes and asked me to look up and down. She held my head sideways and examined the wound.

"Sit up here, young man," she said, and Mama and Daddy helped me sit on a bench next to the back door. She used her fingertips to squeeze all around my neck. Pulling out her stethoscope, she concentrated and closed her eyes while she counted my heartbeats. Her hair smelled of talcum powder, and my nose began to itch. I saw Mama's eyes grow wide until they were as large as eggs.

"Oh, my little man," she cried. "Don't sneeze and hurt your head." She pulled me into her breast where I sneezed all over her dress, bloody snot splattering the fabric. The pain was so horrendous my mouth hung open, and for the life of me, I didn't know how to shut it.

I saw her sneak a look at the nurse's white dress to ensure it was spotless.

The nurse stood up and smoothed her dress. She patted me on the shoulder. "It's too late to stitch it. The bleeding's stopped. I'm sorry we didn't get out here sooner. The doctor was busy with another patient." Mama and Daddy looked around to see where the doctor might be hiding. "It'll be a bad scar, but his hair might grow over it." The flies continued to circle the area above the trash can. "Keep him in bed for a week. He's going to have a terrible headache, and his balance will be off. It's called a concussion. This is a bad one. That'll be ten dollars."

Ten dollars makes you close your eyes. Daddy handed her a pile of coins and crumpled dollar bills. She wrinkled her nose up like the money smelled. It seemed to me that ten dollars is still ten dollars regardless of where it came from.

"I'll pay you back, Daddy," I said.

"Me too," Walker said appearing out of the darkness.

"You could give us the paddle too," I suggested.

"Yeah, Daddy. Even extra swats might be in order," Walker added.

"Socrates, I will deal with you after you heal up." I squeezed my hands together. That voice belonged to Mama, not Daddy.

"Walker, we'll walk and talk." That was my daddy. Those punishments were worse than a spanking. "I'm disappointed in you" was usually part of it.

"I'd rather have the paddle." Walker's voice was abrupt. It shut us out. It said paddle me, but you can't have me.

We waited for Trask sitting against the garage barrels so long my head made a dark circle in the fabric of my mama's lap. I remembered the dress hanging in Mama's closet that morning. It was her Easter dress, new and starched, meaning she'd sewn it at nights. I knew it wouldn't make the rag bag. Mama didn't let things linger if they caused trouble.

When Trask came back for us, he smelled like the sweet, sick odor of the prickly ash, but there was something else too it, a perfume that stayed too long in your nostrils. As soon as he parked the truck at the big house, Walker left to search for my glasses. Mama and Daddy each took one of my arms and carried back to the house.

That day comes to me in my dreams, in the darkness, in the suffocating air of a summer night. It cannot be undone; it was a knife cleaving us from who we were to who we were to become. Trask showed no mercy on the drive home. The poor little truck shuddered as it rounded corners and shook the four of us with its high-pitched shifting of gears. It seemed like Trask was punishing us, the people he visited in Livingston, or even Mr. Ashby.

As for the surprise lurking behind the birth of my name, I closed my eyes in resignation. At least, I knew. The name Socrates Bravo was the marriage of a university scholar and a kitchen maid. I now understood the incomprehensibility of it. The awkward attempt at greatness. The naked error it represented. The disorder it created. The ridiculousness of it all. I could not escape my own truth: Mrs. Ashby held me first.

Chapter Two

A week after my accident, I was summoned to the big house for my return to my lessons with Mrs. Ashby.

"Are you in your right mind, Socrates Bravo? That bump didn't permanently impair you, did it? Let me see your head." Mrs. Ashby explored my skull with her bony, sharp fingers. My head was as swollen as a watermelon after a summer rainstorm. "Is this it?"

I drew a breath as she pressed on the wound. I nodded with tears in my eyes. She pulled her fingers from my hair, settled my glasses firmly on the bridge of my nose, and sat back in her chair at the little table in our classroom.

"I can't believe you showed so little sense. You are too smart for that. We won't speak of it again. I planned on returning to Shelley when you recovered, but he can wait. His story might be a bit morbid right now," she reflected, "what with his drowning and all." She reached for the pencil in her hair. "But luckily, your new geometry books came into the post office yesterday. Mr. Ashby brought them back for us." She put them to her nose and breathed in. "They smell so new and fresh. Smell them, Socrates Bravo." She pushed the book to me. "Let's get started."

When I was four years old, Mrs. Ashby took a dusty sewing room in the big house and made us a classroom. That's what Mrs. Ashby called it. My mama wasn't allowed in it, even to clean or help arrange it. First, Mrs. Ashby emptied it of all its contents—the sewing machine, the heavy velvet drapes, the pictures of flowers on the wall. She dumped them on the porch and told my mama to give it all to the pickers. She didn't want to practice making handkerchiefs or dishtowels anymore. They came out all bunched and snagged anyway.

My first clear memory was not of my parents or my brother, but of Mrs. Ashby opening the door to our classroom. She painted the room buttercream yellow, like my mother's cake frosting. She left the windows bare, and they sparkled from the vinegar and water scrubbing she gave them. Red- and green-backed books marched around the walls of the room, each spine wiped clean of dust. A globe sat in the corner, and a dictionary so large I could not lift it until just last year sat on a table made for it. It was her papa's study all over again, including a book of Plato's writing on Socrates on the corner of the desk. In the center of the room was a table with two chairs. In the beginning, I could barely see over the edge at the books she put before me, but time taught me to twine my ankles around the left leg of the table to still the wobble it made when I shifted in my seat.

I knew every inch of Mrs. Ashby's face from our proximity to one another day after day. When she was younger, her lips were tiny and shaped like a heart, her nose was straight, long, and narrow, and she had a surprising sprinkle of fine freckles that splashed across her nose and cheeks. I remember she'd sometimes pull a strand of yellow hair loose from her sleek, put-up hair and twirl it around her finger while she listened to me read aloud.

That was when Mr. Ashby stopped by and said hello from the doorway on a regular basis. Mrs. Ashby would flush pink and promise to see him soon. Those visits became fewer and fewer the older I became, and soon, they just waved at one another as they passed in the hall.

Nine years later, she was changed. The beauty had sloughed off her like the far wall of the classroom that gamely tried to withstand the glare of the sun streaming in through the front window. At first, I didn't notice the dimming of the paint until it was a blunted white where before it had been a rich yellow. Likewise, Mrs. Ashby's formerly shiny hair had dulled; not washing it didn't help the situation. By the time I was reading the Canterbury Tales in Middle English, pockets had sunk in her cheeks, and her freckles had faded into brown age spots. She had a mole on the side of her face that she'd rub without knowing it, searching for the occasional whisker. She'd have my mama pluck it for her when she found it.

In the last year, I'd grown so fast my wrist bones jutted out of my shirt cuffs and my narrow waist was a translucent map of veins that showed when I stretched my arms over my head. The classroom seemed smaller than it had when I was younger, and now when Mrs. Ashby leaned over my shoulder, her finger following the long lines of numbers, our heads often touched as we worked out a challenging mathematics problem. I worried about spiders or other bugs that could be hiding in her hair. My mama said she would bring Mrs. Ashby a pan of water and soap and encourage her to take a "spit bath" to freshen up. She let my mama help bathe her, but she held the line on her hair. Without washing, it had become a relic that belonged in a museum. It looked like a bird's nest lined with cobwebs, and the pencil perched on the top seemed permanent. My mama said, "Oh no, Socrates, it's fine," but her back was to me when she said it, and I had my suspicions.

Now when Mrs. Ashby pulled on her hair like she had when I was young, chunks of it came out and dropped on the table. She'd brush them on the floor, and when I left at the end of my lessons, they coated the bottom of my shoes until I scraped them off in the grass.

"Most people apply inductive reasoning, but they use it because it is usually true. In geometry there is deductive reasoning. It must be true. You must prove your work now. You will have to work harder. You can do it, Socrates Bravo."

"Deductive reasoning can be written words, symbols, or numbers, Socrates, are you paying attention?" She walked around the table, head down, the geometry book clasped to her chest. "Focus. The modes you choose to demonstrate your reasoning must represent factual implications or hypothetical situations and their consequences." She placed a blank piece of paper in front of me. There were no lines on the paper. She said I didn't need them. "The easiest way to reason deductively is to use an if-then statement. The if is your hypothesis based on facts, rules, and definitions, and the then part is a true assumption that always leads to a true conclusion. You have to know it without a doubt, Socrates Bravo."

I began scanning the text in the book, and my chest started humming like a car put into gear. It was a feeling I knew and liked.

"Socrates, what does being a scholar mean to you?" Mrs. Ashby interrupted my reverie. Gold specks in her eyes looked like drops of amber.

I cleared my throat. "It's a distinguished academic life living for intellectual pursuits."

"I asked what it means to you."

"A scholar is a man of letters."

"Do you want to be a scholar?"

"Yes." My answer was simple. It was explaining it to my family that was hard.

"The longer you stay in Gideon, the harder it will be to become a scholar." I quietly tapped my pencil eraser to the paper. "And, Socrates?" Mrs. Ashby pushed both of her hands down on the surface of the table, so it wobbled. I looked up at her concerned. "Senseless actions will make it harder still. Do we understand one another?" Her words hung in the silence.

"Yes. Mrs. Ashby. No more senseless actions." For a moment, I thought about contending with her definition of senseless actions. What if they were on the road to finding yourself?

She stared out the window, and I began writing, making columns and lists, and drawing arrows that moved ideas into a different order with the swoop of the pencil. I jumped when I heard the screen door on the front porch open and slam against the house. Mr. Ashby's footsteps stomped through the hallway as he made his way to the classroom. Stopping, he stuck his head through the doorway.

"Well, here are two of my favorite people." His face was red, from the heat or excitement I did not know. "Hello, dear wife," he said, kissing the cheek Mrs. Ashby turned up for him. She lifted my books from the table and put them on her father's desk. I could only see her profile, but I saw her swallow as if a lump were stuck in her throat. Mr. Ashby did not often interrupt our lessons, but when he crossed the threshold, we both knew we were done for as long as he wanted. He sat on the edge of the table, lifting his rump over the corner, and pushed my papers and pencils aside. Some sailed to the floor and he didn't pay attention to them.

"Socrates, that's an ugly scar, my goodness. Did it hurt your brain?"

I thought about the energy and vocabulary it would take to explain to Mr. Ashby that a concussion is a person's brain slamming against their skull, and it did, in fact, hurt. "I'm almost better, Mr. Ashby," I said politely.

"Go get Annie," he said, pulling me from my chair. "Wait till you see what I brought home." He clapped his hands together. "I'm going to find William. He will be so excited at my discovery." He stepped into the hall, whistling, and called out, "William? You must come immediately."

"Mr. Ashby, wait." Mrs. Ashby rushed to the doorway to catch her husband before he left the house. "I was thinking Socrates could do a recitation tonight." The delightful breeze that had been filling the classroom died with Mrs. Ashby's words. In the still air, I could feel Mr. Ashby's displeasure dropping around me in unsightly clumps of dirty hair. "He's been working on some exciting pieces, including one from a nineteenth-century transcendentalist." She waited, her head tipped toward the door, the skin on her neck taut and flushed.

"I don't think so, Claire. Another time." The door slammed behind him.

"Socrates, I'm sorry." Mrs. Ashby handed me the book

and my notes. "One of these nights when we are all listening to a baseball game, you can do it then. The whole family will be so impressed." She touched my shoulder.

"In the meantime, take this." She handed me the geometry book. "The first section this week. Check your work." She smiled, the look of dissolution in her eyes. "It must be good, this new discovery, don't you think, Socrates?" She walked away from me, patting her hair absently as if she was astounded it was still on her head. "Annie? Mr. Ashby is quite excited and would like us to see his surprise." Outside the window, Mr. Ashby was struggling with something in the boot of his car. I heard him call for my daddy again.

Mr. Ashby loved the hubbub of the discovery's debut the most. After the big unveiling, during the fleeting moment in which Mr. Ashby was the sole expert, he typically lost interest in the new plaything afterward. Inside the kitchen pantry, an electronic toaster was repurposed to blacken the skin of red and green peppers for canning, and Daddy waited until the cuts on Mr. Ashby's face healed before he had Mama slip him the electric razor to trim and heat seal the bridles for the horses. If Mrs. Ashby got a hold of one of the discoveries, she turned it into a lesson for me. My stomach lurched when I remembered the time she had completely dismantled the family radio and announced that, as a hands-on lesson, I had one hour to make it work again. She had said a little pressure heightened creativity, but she had never felt the heat of Walker's breath steaming on her shoulder minutes before the broadcast of the Philadelphia Phillies and the New York Yankees was due to start.

Although none of us ever asked, we shared one question: How much did it cost?

Mr. Ashby lost interest in many things: his horses, the crops certainly, the windmill his daddy installed years ago for the electricity to run the farm. However, something precious dropped into his lap fourteen years ago, and to this day, he still found it hard to believe that Claire Gannett agreed to be his wife. For the Jeffersons and the pickers, whenever there was a pause in conversation, someone always asked, "Why do you think she married him?" And no one knew the answer. Not even Mama.

Mrs. Ashby knew nothing of sports, having grown up in a family of scholars, but Mr. Ashby got his love of sports from his father, who thought football was a game for men. Although the senior Ashby swore he would never cross the Mason-Dixon line, our Mr. Ashby boarded a train to watch the best football players in Alabama history, the Van de Graaff brothers, play in a game against the North's best, Yale University. The Van de Graaff were notorious for playing outside their positions, kicking field goals, intercepting passes, and bursting through the line for touchdowns. They possessed the easy confidence of natural athletes who think rules don't apply to them.

There was nothing natural about Mr. Ashby. He looked like he was made of extra parts God used at the end of the day. His tiny feet supported spindly legs and a corpulent middle, while whiskerless down grew on a face that sported a wide mouth with a missing tooth kicked out by a horse in his childhood. It was likely the Van de Graaff's dangling ear incident that emboldened him to overcome his fear and cross the Mason-Dixon line so hated by his father.

Hargrove Van de Graaff, the oldest of the three brothers, refused to leave the field during a close game, and in spite of blood spurting from the side of his head, he attempted to yank off his dangling earlobe that had been torn by an opponent. He was forced off the field by the players and the trainers, and they sewed it back on. Mr. Ashby had read later that Hargrove had said, "It would be an honor to go through life with a half an ear if it meant an Alabama victory."

It was at the Yale-versus-Alabama game where the couple met. Mr. Ashby was not a student at Alabama University, but he followed the football team's success, claiming it as his own. Back in those days, it was rare that the South ventured to the North, still suspicious of motives and judgments.

If you met the Ashbys separately, it was immediately apparent that Mrs. Ashby was a sparkling, bold scholar like a diamond in the sky while Mr. Ashby was a sluggish pot of day-old soup that never rose to a full boil.

How the diamond met the soup was one woman's doing. Gertrude Gannett, Mrs. Ashby's mother, should have run for public office even before women were able to vote. While scanning the rowdy crowd attending a pep rally in the stands of her dead husband's college, she'd laid eyes on the timid Timothy Ashby and assessed his potential. Too small to see over the people in front of him, he stood on his seat and was always a second late cheering for a good play. When the university fight song broke out, he moved his lips without knowing the words. He envisioned himself as a leader with information to bestow on his fellow man, but he was a person with tiny limbs who had to tilt his head back until it rested on his shoulders in order to look up at men who towered above him. Mrs. Gannett noticed he tried to speak more quickly like a

Northerner, but his story fell away as it got tangled in his long, slow Southern syllables. He tried to speak to women, but when they leaned down and put their ears to his lips, even he couldn't ignore the absurdity of it all. He carried a book to look intellectual but often forgot it in homes, on trains, and even tucked under his seat at football games.

Several rows away, Mrs. Gannett studied him and made her decision. He needed a wife. Someone he could talk to even if what he had to say didn't amount to much. If Gertrude Gannett had played quarterback that day, she would have given the Van de Graaff brothers something to worry about. She pulled Mr. Ashby through the throng of people until she found her daughter, also a square peg trying to fit in a round hole. The pretty, petite, and remarkably intelligent woman sitting in the back seat of the family car was Claire Gannett, who loved to read— and that was about all. She was holding a book in one hand and a drink with a liquor-soaked cherry wedged at the bottom of the glass in the other. Claire and Timothy sized one another up. She carefully folded the corner of the page to mark her place in the book and stepped out to meet Mr. Ashby. He would do.

"Come in the front room." Mr. Ashby struggled to carry a large package through the door. Daddy grabbed it and placed it on the floor next to the fireplace. We congregated around the box. Mrs. Ashby tucked her legs under her and leaned back on her hand, looking like a young girl with her thoughts elsewhere. Daddy stood in his stockings with a toe emerging from his left foot. Mama ran her hand over the fireplace mantel, checking for dust. I sat on the edge of the rug closest to the door.

"Too bad Walker isn't here. We'll have to show him

how it works when he is done at the sawmill. What time does he get back?"

"Six o'clock, Mr. Ashby," Mama said. "He has chores too, you know."

"Yes, Annie. Fine. There are always chores to do, but there is only one vacuum cleaner in this house." He slid it out of the box and stood it up. "Annie, it is for you. It is made to make a woman's life easier. That what the man said who was selling them in town." He beamed and showed her how it rolled on its back wheels. It was constructed of a waist-high metal tube connected to a square motor with wheels and a rotating brush. An empty fabric bag sagged on the back of the metal tube. A tidy circle of electrical cord hung on the handle. I swallowed with difficulty. Experience had taught us that if Mr. Ashby's discoveries relied on electricity, there was a much greater chance of catastrophic failure.

"It's like a metal broomstick," Mama said, touching it. "What's the bag for? What do you carry in it?" She was intrigued. Daddy and I looked at each other, and Daddy quit trying to hide the hole in his sock. He eased back a few steps.

"Dirt. It holds dirt, Annie." Mr. Ashby turned it over to show us the bottom of the gadget. "This here," he said, moving a line of bristles, "is where the dirt is taken up from the carpet. This here—"

"Mr. Ashby, are you saying my carpets aren't clean?"

"No more beating rugs on the clothesline, Annie. This removes dirt from carpets. It gathers it all up, and then you dump it out."

"Is there a problem with how I beat the carpets? You know I have two carpet beaters I can use anytime I like." She pointed at me. I held my palms up. Of course.

"No, Annie," Mr. Ashby said and waved his hand like he was swatting a bug that irritated him. "Let me show you the other parts, and then we'll plug it in."

"So, it's electric then." Mrs. Ashby unwound the cord. "Does it fit with our source?"

"Claire, just wait. Let me show you how it works. This is"—he held it up and squinted—"the belt. It makes it run." He poked the well of the motor where the brush turned. "Well, I can't remember everything. It has wheels to push it, and, I believe, there is a pushing away and a snapping back. I remember that clearly." He stood up and handed my mama the cord. "Plug it in, Annie."

"No, sir. No sir."

"Oh, it's not going to bite you." He looked around. "Socrates, you come plug it in." I took it from him and stretched the cord out to insert the head in the hallway charger. "Plug it in, Socrates. We're all waiting."

I pushed it in and stayed in the hall. I didn't want to watch. Mr. Ashby twisted the switch on. A high-pitched sucking sound made me hold my hands over my ears. I peeked into the room. The vacuum cleaner grabbed the carpet and began pulling it into the motor like it had teeth. It whined and bucked, and Mama tried to yank the carpet out of the motor. It ripped out of her hands making a gaping hole where the wooden floor showed through.

"My carpet," Mrs. Ashby cried.

"Unplug it, Socrates," Daddy said.

A burning smell filled the room, and smoke wheezed from the motor. Afraid it was on fire, Daddy got water from the kitchen and doused the vacuum cleaner. We looked around, and Mr. Ashby was gone. Mama and Mrs. Ashby rotated the carpet so the hole was hidden under the settee. Mama stashed the newest discovery in the hall closet, and we all drifted away thinking about how it could be used in its next life.

I should have exited through the kitchen, because as soon as I stepped out the front door, Mr. Ashby called my name from the driveway next to the barn. "Socrates, don't forget. We're having guests tonight, and I want Walker to pitch. You'll have to catch for him." He walked around the car bending over to check the wheels like a farmer inspects his horses' hooves.

"Yes, sir." I looked out at the fields. Trask was walking between the rows of the small green cotton bushes. He was wearing his long dark coat and large hat, but his boots were missing. "Mr. Ashby?" He had opened the boot of his car and disappeared under its cavernous lid. I tried again. "Do you know what is Trask doing? He doesn't have any boots on." I hesitated. "He's barefoot."

Mr. Ashby raised his head quickly and bumped it on the underside of the lid. "God damn it, Socrates Bravo, what did you say?" He tossed his head to the side and the flap of unruly black, hair that grew on the top pitch of his forehead flopped forward. He pushed it back over the top of his head and turned to watch the man—the proxy sent from the Federal Farm Board—mincing his way through the rows tossing dirt over his shoulder every ten yards.

I am sure Trask did not know we were watching him. He used his toes to burrow into the hills of dirt and paused every few bushes to pick up a handful of dirt. He smelled it and then let it drift out in a cloud of dust behind him.

"Socrates"—Mr. Ashby pulled away from me driving his car—"don't pay attention to Trask. He's nothing but mountain trash. He'll leave soon enough as soon the crop comes in." I was dismissed.

Chapter Three

I did not go home. Instead, I laid in the tall grass on the side of the barn, a length of alfalfa straw between my lips, and watched Trask's odd dance through the rows of cotton bushes. He had appeared one day, dropped off at the end of our farm road, carrying a decrepit carpet bag only lightly packed. In a few words, he informed Mr. Ashby he had been assigned to our farm by the Federal Farm Bureau to oversee the cotton season of 1928. Mr. Ashby, in a bluster of anger and indignation, set off for town to talk to the people at Gideon Bank. When he returned, Trask had committed the greatest of sins on the farm. He was pushing himself on Mr. Ashby's porch swing. He had refused to say more than a few words to Mama and Mrs. Ashby, so while they waited for hell and damnation to descend on him when Mr. Ashby returned home, the two women were in a quandary.

Was he an educated guest equal in social stature to the Ashbys, meaning they should prepare him a room in the house? He was alone with worn clothes and few belongings. He had a permanent slump to him as if life had not always been kind, and his words betrayed a vocabulary rooted in the hills of Georgia, but he had been professionally trained somewhere to perform a vocation. Finally, Mama and Mrs. Ashby improved the summer kitchen for him as a waiting place for him to stay until it was time for him to walk back down to the end of our farm road. We were after all, living in the decade in which women raised their skirts, daredevils flew airplanes upside down, and a literary renaissance had started in a place called Harlem; perhaps Trask was part of a new social class that did not yet have a name.

———

EDWIN TRASK HAD BEEN CALLED A RASCAL, RUBBISH, A squatter, a cracker, a lubber, swamp bottom, a mudsucker, a scalawag, a hillbilly, a degenerate, a lint head, and a redneck. He didn't mind. He'd been called worse—by his own mother.

After Celia Trask's stray goat of a husband left her and their son, Edwin, she had to find a way to make a living that kept her out of prison and allowed the boy to hide from others.

Edwin helped her fill a wagon with supplies, and they made their way to a camp in the hills where tumbling spring water reflected the clear sky and the bitter chill of its pools lay ready to cool the whiskey kegs. She knew her whiskey would have to be the best to bring runners from Atlanta speakeasies, underlings from the state legislature, and purveyors from King Cotton conventions to her.

Customers stumbled up the narrow, rocky paths of the Georgian Appalachian hills to buy her whiskey. Her recipe included the same wheat, rye, corn, sugar, and yeast the other moonshiners used. Her secret ingredient? Sweetness. Whatever fruit she could locate growing in the orchards in the area—overripe peaches and apricots laying in the grass, dried prunes and desiccated raisins— went into the fermenting barrel, their essence bringing as a mysterious fleeting taste on the tongue and a lingering scent in the nose.

Celia wondered what Edwin's gift to the world would be. He was excruciatingly thin, mute as a swan, and appeared ashamed on one half his face. They lived without a mirror, so he did not have to look at himself.

With the success of Celia's whiskey, they had to move the operation frequently to evade jealous neighbors and the reach of the law. The usual practice took a year to age whiskey in a twenty-gallon burned oak keg, but Edwin discovered a way to hurry along the whiskey when he pulled a pelt of moss from a disintegrating log and a puff of warm air curled between his fingers.

Edwin and Celia filled some kegs, scattered them around the property, wrapped them in burlap, lowered them into the ground, and stuffed horse manure down the sides of the hole and over the top. They planted grass to cover the kegs. They experimented with the number of days necessary for aging and decided that after just a month, the flavor was as good or better than their year-aged whiskey.

Edwin discovered his gift when the kegs had to be relocated and dug up. He had an ability to use his feet to locate the random locations of the kegs. Somehow, the soles of his feet and the delicate searching of his toes could find the ridges and ravines of his footsteps from when they'd first planted the kegs. He counted his footfalls between barrels and estimated the circumference of the planted pasture. When he had plotted out all the locations, Edwin and Celia dug up the barrels and rolled them to the creek, where they created an eruption of roiling steam when they plunged the barrels into the frigid water.

On the day his mother left, Edwin climbed to the top of the dirt pile made by the earth tossed to the surface when they anchored the kegs in the holes. He stood high at the top and slid to the bottom. He repeated it and repeated it. His skin was a uniform brown, and you could not tell which half of his face was marked. He sat at the top of the mound, supremely happy, and took a handful of dirt to his mouth and tasted it. Once he got past the mud-like texture, he separated the elements from one another and rolled the dirt in his mouth, coating the insides of his cheeks, filling the cracks between his teeth, and letting it slide, a bit at a time, down his throat.

"Dirt-eating trash," Celia Trask screamed when she saw her son cramming a handful of dirt into his mouth. She climbed the dirt hill and grabbed him by his shirt. "You squatter, tucking into mud holes like rubbish!" She struck him on the face and clawed at his mouth. The two of them tumbled down the dirt hill and fell at the feet of the sheriff who had been looking for a moonshiner but instead found a child abuser.

Edwin Trask was taken from his mother that day. When the headmaster of the Benevolent Home for Georgia Boys asked why he ate the dirt, the boy looked confused. "I need earth in me. My feet know it. There's parts of the taste that stays in my head and holds me to the ground, so I don't fly away."

Chapter Four

"Carry it careful, Socrates," Mama instructed, putting three glasses on the silver company tray. "I don't want them thinking we don't have enough of that's devil's juice. Bees Knees for a drink, who thought of that? Silly name, if you asked me."

She sniffed the sweet drinks and held the back door open for me. "I suppose those men will come around if they want something," she snorted. "Likely, they'll find it in the barn."

I stepped off the stairs, carrying the tray. I tightened my fingers and used my thumbs to grip the bottom. It was still early spring. Usually, it was the first part of April when the dirt was finally warm enough for the plants to grow knee high, but we were still only two weeks into March. Daddy had shaken his head that morning. "How many picks?" I heard him ask himself.

My head was down and focused on the tray of drinks, so when the smell came over me in an unbearable wave, it was too late. As Trask marched toward me, the putrid smell grew like a foul gas haze. Quietly, Daddy had examined the privy Trask used, and when the man was not present, there was no lingering odor. The mystery continued.

We did not know why the stink had a thickness to it that felt like scum on our teeth. I was too embarrassed to state my suspicions to Mrs. Ashby that it was excess hydrogen sulfide. I could not figure out how a person could constantly break wind without sound, and when I played out the entire conversation in my head, I realized I had best leave it alone.

Trask stopped. "Did a package come for me? It was supposed to come by delivery." He took one of the glasses from the tray and drained it in three swallows.

"Please don't," I implored. "I'm going to get in trouble. Mama's afraid we don't have enough of the devil's juice."

He laughed and tightened his grip on the glass. "Tell Mrs. Ashby that was mine since she didn't invite me to her party. Do you know why I wasn't invited?" He drained the second glass.

"Hey," I protested.

"Why," he persisted. He reached for the last glass.

"I don't know." I raised my voice in frustration. "Ask her yourself."

"Better be careful talking to me like that," he whispered and leaned in so my face dipped under his hat brim. I pulled back in fear, and the tray slid to the ground. The contents of the last glass drained into the dry earth, and the glass rolled to a stop in the dead, yellow grass.

The left side of his face was a sallow white color, peppered with several days' growth of grizzled whiskers. On the right side of his face, a dark-red-wine-colored mark shaped like the continent of Africa started out fat and wide above his eyebrow, covered his eye and slid down his cheek, and landed at the corner of his thin, chapped lips. It was a port-wine stain, *nevus flammeus*, a birthmark caused by a capillary anomaly. When the baby emerges from the birth canal, a ruby-red mark glows from the baby's skin usually on the face or trunk. It persists for life.

When his right eye flicked open wide for a second, it was yellow where it was supposed to be white and exhausted where there should have been life.

"You know Ashby will send you to the field so he can stay on his porch swing, don't you?"

"No, the Jeffersons have never picked. We grew up here with the Ashbys."

He looked amused. "You have a lot to learn. Better get back to your mama. She might paddle you for this mistake."

"No, I won't." So intent on our exchange, we didn't see Mama standing on the stairs of the back stoop. She pushed me behind her and motioned for me to go back into the house. She stood close enough to Trask that he took a step back and his hat pushed up on his head. She handed him a small, square package wrapped in brown paper. I watched her, and she didn't flinch when she saw his wrecked face in the streaming sunlight.

"Here's your package. You go about your business, and we'll do ours." She turned to climb the stairs and stopped. She didn't look back at him, but her voice was clear. "You stay away from my family. You don't want to mess with the Jeffersons. Do you hear me?" I saw her hand tighten on the latch. It shook just a bit as she pulled open the door.

"Do you want to suffer because of Ashby's mistakes, Annie?"

"Don't you 'Annie' me. There's more to the Ashbys and

Jeffersons than you'll ever know." Mama slammed the kitchen door. On the counter were three fresh Bees Knees. "Socrates, this time you go out the front door to the porch. I don't care how it looks to those visiting ladies. Don't stop for nothing. Do you hear me?"

"Yes, Mama." I squeezed the handles of the tray and walked down the hallway toward the front door. I nudged it open with my knee and strode rapidly around the house.

"Mrs. Belknap." I held the tray steady and handed her the tall glass filled with lemon juice, sugar water, honey, and the devil's juice. The ice was melting rapidly in the heat, and beads of water ran down the side of the glass. "Mrs. Chastain, here is yours." I handed it to her, and the tray tipped as she bumped it.

"So this one is mine." Mrs. Ashby caught the third glass sliding down the surface as my fingers quit on me and unfurled. "Thank you, Socrates. Hmm. As always, your mama makes a perfect cocktail."

"I love the way gin smells, don't you? Mr. Ashby must be like his father—able to find liquor in a dry state, hmm?" Mrs. Belknap slurped her drink and waved her handkerchief at her throat. She was wearing the new style of dress that showed her knees above her white, nylon stockings. As she was puffy, plump, and as red as a crab, her knees didn't impress me much.

"Socrates." Mrs. Chastain waved her hand at a bee swooning over the scent of the honey in her drink. "You're Claire's pet, am I right?" I felt my face burn. "Let me look at your head." She leaned forward to examine the scar on my head, and I saw her naked breasts swaying loose in the gaping neckline in her dress. I didn't know where to look. Mrs. Chastain smiled at me with her lips part way open as I searched for a place to put my eyes that didn't make my body do things I couldn't control. Mr. Ashby called her not original, meaning that she was the second and much younger Mrs. Chastain. She took a long drink of her Bees Knees keeping her eyes trained on mine. "You're going to be a handsome man someday. Women will find your scar quite dashing. Tell me the background of your name."

"It's Socrates Bravo."

"What does it mean?" Mrs. Chastain pushed.

I took a deep breath, pushed my glasses up to the ridge of my nose and prepared my usual answer. "Socrates was an ancient Greek philosopher who liked to ask people questions. His style is used in universities and called the Socratic method." I paused and Mrs. Ashby laid her hand in the middle of my back. It said, *More, Socrates. Teach them more.* I continued. "He desired to expose contradictions in thinking and encouraged the pursuit of validity and truth."

Mrs. Chastain and Mrs. Belknap drank their Bees Knees rapidly.

Mrs. Ashby put her arm on my shoulder. "It means he will have a strong voice in his future. He will be leaving us in the fall. He's going to Parson University Preparatory School."

Mrs. Belknap choked. "How? He's a child."

Mrs. Ashby grew tall next to me. "Socrates has already studied more mathematics, science, history, and literature than most college graduates. He will take the exams in four months, and the school will accept him." Mrs. Belknap fluttered her handkerchief. "Once they see his promise as a scholar, his age will not be a problem. There are exceptions to every rule." She laughed the polite way

ladies do when they want to change topics. "The first
Socrates would have agreed with us, wouldn't he?"

I nodded my head and edged toward the stairs.

"What about the picker children? Any of them bound
for college?" Mrs. Chastain's voice taunted Mrs. Ashby.
She pulled her dress fabric up and crossed one leg over
the other. She swung her sockless, creamy-white leg in a
slow circle. I could tolerate Mrs. Belknap's ignorance
because she was fat and overheated, but Mrs. Chastain
used her words like the strike of a snake.

"Every year I find a competent older girl who teaches
the children, and I pay her salary to teach in the country
school." Mrs. Ashby wiped the perspiration from her forehead with the pale underside of her wrist.

I had not thought of it before, but Mrs. Chastain's
question had an uncomfortable ring of truth in it. Mrs.
Ashby didn't forget the picker children living in the shacks
next to the lowest field, but she also didn't look for any
potential college-bound students. She once tried teaching
a winter session of school as a young bride with noble
intentions, but when she discovered one page of her trea-
sured world maps—Asia Minor—torn and used for
kindling for the potbellied stove, and her beloved books
left on the porch in a dust storm each ruffled red-dirt page
too dirty to read, she removed both of us from the school
and began my education in the classroom, not in the
school next to the fields.

Her requirement for every picker child to graduate
from country school was to be able to read a story from
the newspaper, recite the Pledge of Allegiance with their
hands over their hearts, and make change for fifty cents.
Each student got to keep the money if they passed. Mrs.
Ashby felt it was my responsibility to participate in the

testing of the children at the end of the year, but it made me uncomfortable to watch them hold the shiny, heavy coins in delight. I knew, even from a young age, that it was just a matter of time before someone would pry their fingers open and take the coins. I believe the children felt only a passing regret, however, because there was nowhere to use their skills learned in school. As the young pickers grew to adulthood, they didn't see many newspapers, the heft of the solid coins they'd once held in their hands soon became one of the unreadable numbers in the owed column of the commissary book, and the Pledge of Allegiance, well, that memory was so far in their past, I bet their hands would sometimes wander over their hearts without knowing why.

Mrs. Chastain drained her glass, wiped her mouth, and let a small ladylike burp escape her lips. "Socrates, get me another Bees Knees, would you?"

The radio was playing dance music from a station in Mobile while the Ashbys and their guests dined. I sat under the window ledge and watched the action in the dining room, including my mama setting the plates in front of the couples who didn't bother with a thank-you. A fog of smoke hung over the table, and Mrs. Belknap and Mrs. Chastain smoked long, thin cigarettes. Mama was right: the men had found drinks in the barn. They'd brought their canning jars full of liquid that smelled like paint into the dining room.

"So, Ashby, have you been to New York City lately?" Chastain released smoke from his nostrils.

"No, not lately." Mr. Ashby had never been to New York City.

"What's in New York City?" Mr. Belknap must not have worn his hat during the ferocious spring weather. Long curls of dead skin flaked off his bald, sunburned head. He and Mrs. Belknap were a matched set of well-worn salt-and-pepper shakers on the verge of running dry. The couple was necessary to carry some of the conversation at the dinner table, but what they contributed lacked flair and substance.

"Courtlandt Street. It's called Radio Row. Every store sells radios—"

"No, it's more than that." Mrs. Ashby's cheeks bloomed into pink circles as she leaned forward. "Crowds of people stand outside stores and listen to the news, music, and shows. They dance on the sidewalk. When I was there, I heard Puccini, one of his operas. It made me cry, it was so beautiful." I could tell she was remembering the day as she tilted her head to one side and patted the nest of hair on her head. "Excuse me, I interrupted you. Go on."

She looked down the table to Mr. Ashby who stared at her through the smoke. She was the mistress of the farm, but she didn't understand the rules. When Mr. Ashby brought her home to be his Southern wife, he failed to explain what her job entailed: act like the grand South still existed and talk of nothing of importance. "Talk of the weather," her mother-in-law had advised before she died. "Everyone likes the weather."

"Oh no, Claire, you didn't interrupt at all. I'm surprised you have been to Radio Row." Mr. Chastain held out his hand to his wife who took it and caressed it in front of the others. Mr. Ashby and Mr. Belknap stole looks at their originals. "Just recommending a trip up north. You could pick up a new radio." Mr. Chastain tipped his head toward the large box in the corner of the living room. It was old, one of the first ones built. Mr. Ashby purchased it in 1920, and it did look a bit worn with its exaggerated dials and wires going nowhere. Daddy worked on it constantly. He and Mrs. Ashby ordered new parts when the signal became unintelligible. They did it for us, for all of us, so we could listen to baseball games and Sunday shows.

On those Sunday nights, Mama covered the grass with sheets outside the living room window to protect us from chigger bites, and we ate our Sunday supper from a picnic basket while the Ashbys sat inside their living room with china plates on their laps. Daddy would lay his head in Mama's lap and stretch out his tired legs until the crackle of the radio drowned out the sound of the game, and Mr. Ashby would yell, "Get in there, William, before we miss the last out." Daddy would jump up to jiggle the wires and inch the dials a bit at a time until the signal became clear again. Walker would be up and hollering, especially if the Birmingham Barons were playing, but Mrs. Ashby would be in her own little world laying on the porch swing. She'd call to me and point out the constellations. "Venus is the brightest when following the moon," she'd say, but she loved the northern sky, especially Cassiopeia, a bright cluster of stars in the northern hemisphere. Laughing while twirling her hair, she'd sigh and say, "Cassiopeia, the mother of Andromeda, declared they were the most beautiful of women," but then Mrs. Ashby'd grow quiet and say that their true beauty was the faith they showed following the North Star on its path. Baseball, stars, and my mama's cooking. Those were the nights I knew we were a family.

"Why don't we go on out to the porch and watch my boy, Walker, throw the ball?" Mr. Ashby rose out of his chair and scraped it backward. He tossed his linen napkin on his plate. Mrs. Ashby went around the table picking up the napkins, and Mr. Ashby stopped her. "Let the woman do that." Mrs. Ashby squeezed them and laid them down.

"We are so proud of William and Annie's boys. Socrates, my student, is studying for his exams presently." She held the screen door open for Mr. Chastain. "Please go ahead. I'll hold the door."

The sun dropped toward the horizon, and the rays of weary sunlight slanted into the fields. The cotton bushes cast shadows on either side of the empty farm road. The lowest field swept to the left as it followed the creek. The bushes became dots in the distance, and finally, they were smudges on the barely visible hill.

"Beautiful land, Ashby," Chastain commented. "Your grandfather broke ground here?"

"Oh yes, my grandparents came from North Carolina over a hundred years ago." Mr. Ashby cleared his throat and lowered himself to sit on the old wagon seat mostly hidden in the tall grass. "They left their families and the plantations. On principle," Mr. Ashby said. "They didn't like the selling of Negroes. They brought a free Negro couple with them for help and settled here in this corner of Jackson County."

"Interesting story," Chastain reflected, blowing smoke rings from his cigar. "Did the Negroes stay free? People might have seen them as agitators. Especially during the War between the States."

Mr. Ashby bent his knee and held his kneecap in his laced fingers. "Jeffersons grandfather was the one that came. Three generations of Ashbys right here." He pointed to the fields with his soggy cigar. "What was your grandaddy's name, William?

"Elijah," Daddy said over his shoulder. He had heard this story many times.

"Good man, I hear," Mr. Ashby said. He stood up. "I'll have to walk around a bit. I'm having a little trouble getting around on this knee. It seizes up on me sometimes. You know it's why I didn't go to the war." He limped down to Daddy who had gone to the war in his place when the county board said a man had to go from the Ashby farm. "He going to be ready soon?" Mr. Ashby whispered.

"Yes, Mr. Ashby."

"Good, I'll be in the barn for a moment. Don't start until I get back." His limp was exaggerated until he turned halfway to the barn and shouted, "Belknap, Chastain? Refill?" When they rose to follow him, he scurried to open the door on two perfectly capable legs. The corner of Daddy's mouth twitched.

Unlike our home plate at the Patch, we measured out the official sixty feet between the pitcher's mound and home plate and anchored the equipment in the driveway at the big house.

"You're wearing this to protect your scar," Mrs. Ashby insisted as she handed me a mask made of leather she'd had Daddy fashion in the barn.

"I can't wear my glasses then. Walker throws awful hard," I muttered.

Mrs. Ashby turned midstep. "I can get you more glasses, but I can't conjure up another brain, Socrates." I would have preferred a thick piece of leather to stuff inside my glove since each practice pitch was faster and harder than the one before it, and every time it burst into my glove, the burn started in the center of my palm and radiated through my fingers.

"You ready now, Walker?" Mr. Ashby emerged from the barn. Walker shook his arms loose and turned his head on his neck. He pulled his arm across his body to stretch it out. Last of all, he did a series of sprints to the edge of the cotton field and back.

"Well, we're in for a show," Mr. Belknap commented, swirling the new amount of clear liquid in his glass jar. "Where should we stand in case there's a wild pitch?"

"There won't be," Walker and Mr. Ashby said in unison.

"Watch this," Mr. Ashby said. "William, you call the pitches."

Standing next to the plate with a bat on his shoulder, Daddy called, "Fastball, inside." A white streak skimmed the inside corner of the plate. "Splitter, top to bottom." I tensed up on my toes. Walker's splitters were tricky to catch; they were fast and broke so close to home plate. Without my glasses, I had to focus particularly on Walker's release of the ball. If it spun crazily sideways, I was in for a curveball, and hell-bent straight on was his fastball.

"William, call them louder. We can't hear you." Mr. Ashby puffed hard on his cigar. I stood up and walked to the mound to talk to Walker. We put our mouths inside our gloves so they wouldn't see what we were saying.

"Walker, take some of the speed off," I urged. "I think my hand is going to break. It's not a game. Save your arm, please. You are killing me."

He pushed my shoulder. "Socrates, you never know when someone is watching who can change your future. One of those men could know someone in the Negro League. I have to throw my hardest every chance I get. Do you hear me?" His lips jutted out over his chin. They were filled with a gummy, brown substance.

"Walker"—my eyes got wide—"you're chewing tobacco." Thank goodness Mama couldn't see his swollen lips.

Daddy knew, I'm sure, but his job was to make the night happen without incident.

"Shut up, Soc. It gives me more energy. I'll spit it out before Mama can see." He turned me around and patted my back. "Go, Soc. Go catch for me, please."

"William, what are the boys doing? You get back there, Socrates. Claire"—he turned, looking for his wife—"tell Socrates to quit talking and get back behind the plate."

"Mr. Ashby, he's there now." Her voice was light but strained.

"You know, I might try a swing or two." Mr. Chastain took the bat from Daddy and motioned for him to move away. A decaying syrupy smell, not unlike the prickly ash in the spring, poured from his skin. "I used to be quite the baseball player in my time." He took a few swings and put his hand above his eyes, pretending to watch the ball sail. "Boy, I am waiting for you. Throw it in."

Mr. Belknap staggered off the porch. "Chastain, I'll take a swing too." He hustled down the hill and stood next to Mr. Ashby.

Mr. Ashby's face glowed with sweat, and his teeth shone white except for the dark hole where a tooth used to be. He was usually self-conscious of the hole and careful to keep his lips over his teeth, but he was so excited by Chastain's and Belknap's interest that air whistled through the gap. My scar was swollen under the pressure of the face mask, and my stomach twisted like Mama's taffy, only tighter. The Jeffersons didn't need the Ashbys' guests to look like fools when they couldn't put the bat on the ball.

"I don't know, Chastain. I don't think you've hit talent like this before." Mr. Ashby grinned, his imagined knee pain forgotten as he perched his foot on the wagon seat.

Daddy stood to the side, watching Walker throw his leg high in the air as he came down and released the ball. I saw his finger tremble. Fear. His toe tap was for lying. His finger trembling showed fear. The cheek twitch was frustration. There were other shakes, tremors, and spasms too. I didn't see it often, but my daddy was afraid. The men's eyes, shiny from the oily smelling liquid sloshing in the clear jars, were crisscrossed with red streaks like roads snaking across the state of Alabama. It was the dead-end roads Daddy feared most.

"Mr. Ashby, it's going to be dark in a half an hour," Mrs. Ashby called from the porch. She stood on the steps above Mama, who had removed her apron and was biting her thumbnail, tearing it off a bit at a time.

Mrs. Chastain slipped her arms into the sleeves of her husband's coat and twirled in circles, her bare feet crushing the damp grass.

"Walker," Daddy warned.

"Daddy," Walker resisted.

Walker threw a half-speed pitch. Chastain swung the bat violently and barely stayed upright. I stood up to grab him, but Daddy eased him out of the way.

"Here you go, Mr. Chastain. That ball was way outside, off the plate." Chastain shook his head and stepped away. Looking up, I watched him cock his head and study Walker. Mr. Belknap appeared to wisely decide it was not his night to swing the bat. He slowly backed up until he ran into his wife standing behind him. She laid her hand on his arm and pressed her fingers into his flesh until white marks appeared. Mr. Ashby tilted back and forth on his doll-like feet and peeled the paper off a fresh cigar and chuckled to himself.

"Walker hasn't even started, Chastain. You don't know

his power and control." A match flared, and he pointed the red-tipped cigar at my brother. "Walker," Mr. Ashby commanded, "throw to your potential."

"Walker." Daddy's word sounded like the reverberations of a slammed door. He turned and stared at Mr. Ashby as if a curtain had been pulled back between them. Mama and Mrs. Ashby heard their exchange and hurried toward us. The pink-and-orange clouds of the sunset reflected in the glass windows of the big house, and in the indistinct light, I saw what the house might have looked like when it was grand. I stood up with the ball held fast in my glove. I was not returning it to Walker until a détente was reached. He was pacing around the pitcher's mound, slapping his hand against his mitt. A dribble of spit exited the corner of his mouth.

Lights began to flicker in the high branches of the oak trees circling the house. Fireflies popped to life, sputtering in batches, and blinking in a swath of dim stars. The sun was almost gone, and a low line of purple clouds on the horizon was all that was left.

"Soc, throw me the ball." Walker held his mitt up high. I ignored him and looked to Daddy. The ball's searing whiteness and potential for hurt was far more substantial than the fanciful fireflies.

"Well then." Mr. Ashby's shoulders dropped just a fraction. Daddy had won the unspoken battle between them, and its reason was unknown to me. "Walker, throw one of those pitches you've been telling me about. The tricky one. Tell Chastain and Belknap the secret. Men, he's the only pitcher in Jackson County can throw this one. He learned it from a broadcaster on the radio."

The electricity between Mr. Ashby and Daddy stopped as fast as a lost radio signal. I felt my heart lift. I tossed the ball to Walker as he came in from the mound. He gave Daddy an angry look as he ran by. He had wanted to throw hard, and he was tired of Daddy holding him back.

He walked to the circle of people. "It's called a knuck-leball." He showed them how he put his thumb and two outside fingers on the side of the ball and then gripped the top seams with the knuckles of his first and middle fingers. "The knuckles don't grip like fingers, so it flies different. Watch."

He waved me back to catch and took his place on the mound. He threw it, and the ball appeared to float without a spin. I squinted, leaning toward the incoming ball, and stuck my glove out as far as I could reach. We watched it glide, almost able to count the stitches on the leather, until it snapped into my glove. I sank back onto my heels relieved. Walker grinned like a pumpkin cut for Halloween. "I learnt it from Satchel Paige, the best base-ball player ever."

"Who's that?" Mr. Chastain said, not looking at his wife but holding his hand out to her for his jar of liquid.

"Plays in the Negro League. Over twenty wins his first year. Made up a lot of pitches. Famous pitches no one else can throw." He waited a beat. "Except me." I jumped to a crouch as he let a pitch go that veered toward the group but tacked back to the glove and hit it square on. His slow curve.

"What is he saying?" Mr. Belknap said. "Where would you get a name like Satchel? Sounds like a suitcase."

Walker muttered under his breath, "The boy got the name carrying bags at the train station making money for his mama—that's where." Mama ripped a large piece of skin off her thumb, and Mrs. Ashby reached out and wrapped Mama's thumb in one of the linen napkins. Mama drew her eyebrows together. Now she'd have to get that blood out.

"Kid, I'm talking about real baseball. Who do you like?"

Walker didn't hesitate. "LeRoy Satchel Paige didn't throw dirt on an umpire because he was too fat to stretch a single into a double." His sinker seared into my glove.

The ball fell out of the leather pocket and rolled into the twilight.

Walker had just insulted Babe Ruth.

"Boy, I can't think the Ashbys let you carry on like this. It's disrespectful." Mr. Chastain rolled up his shirt sleeves and stepped toward Walker. Walker watched him come, standing like a king on his hill.

I stood up, my legs stiff from crouching in the catcher's position for so long and pushed between the Belknaps and Mrs. Chastain. I opened my arms wide like I was standing on a stage, and I blocked the track Chastain had to pass through to get to my brother. I raised my voice and prayed I could summon the courage to be just as fascinating as a knuckleball. I kept my eyes averted from Mrs. Chastain's chest where two little bumps on her dress looked like bees searching for honey. I threw back my shoulders. Mrs. Ashby said that presentation is everything.

"I went to the woods because I wished to live deliberately, to front only the essential facts of life, and see if I could not learn what it had to teach, and not, when I came to die, discover that I had not lived. I did not wish to live what was not life, living is so dear; nor did I wish to practice resignation, unless it was quite necessary. I wanted to live deep and suck out all the marrow of life, to live so sturdily and Spartan-like as to put to rout all that was not life, to cut a broad swath and shave close, to drive life into a corner, and reduce it to its lowest terms, and, if it proved to be mean, why then to get the whole and genuine meanness of it, and publish its meanness to the world; or if it were sublime, to know it by experience, and be able to give a true account of it in my next excursion."

Mama handed me my glasses and thumped me on the back twice with a proud hand. My sight came into focus, and I could see everyone clearly. Blood pounded through my scar like the ticks of clock that won't stop. I sucked deep breaths in and blew them out in small, deliberate puffs, hoping I wouldn't bust out in those sobs that made people turn away in embarrassment. Chastain swayed on unsteady feet, baffled as to the purpose of my oration. Mrs. Ashby made small little claps with her fingertips, a large smile spread across her satisfied face.

Recitation was important to Mrs. Ashby. She said it made you think about the words and keep them as your own. She was right. I felt the edges and the smoothness of the letters and saw them stark against the white page behind my closed eyes. The words fell from my lips without a break or a moment of forgetting. I wondered, how broad could you cut your swath without coming too close to someone? How deep was the marrow in the bones, and what could be reason enough to suck the fragile sweetness?

"Ashby, do you have any control here?" Chastain pulled on his coat and emptied his jar in a final swallow. "My family's been here as long as yours, and your daddy was a legend. He'd be disappointed; that's all I can say." He pushed his wife toward the house. "Get your things." "We're leaving."

Mrs. Chastain picked up her shoes and clutched them to her chest. She walked fast to the porch not looking at anyone, most of all my mama, as she went inside. Her husband sat in the idling car.

"Thank you, Timothy and Claire, for an enlightening evening. We'll return the favor soon." Mr. Belknap and his wife strolled to their car. Mr. Belknap paused and motioned to me to come to him. "Where'd those words come from?"

"Henry David Thoreau, a transcendentalist." Mrs. Belknap reached out and patted my cheek.

"Keep up the work. That was remarkable." I felt shame burn my face when I thought of the mental insults I'd made about her weight and intellect.

"That was a nice evening for the most part," Mrs. Ashby said cheerfully. "Nice roast, Annie."

"Thank you, Mrs. Ashby."

"Pitching was strong, Walker." I was startled to hear impudence in Mr. Ashby's voice that I knew could only be directed toward Daddy.

"I know." Walker leaned over and let a long stream of tobacco and spit slide out of his mouth.

The only sound was the lone stamp of a horse's foot and shake of his mane in the pasture.

"Go wash your face, Walker." Daddy was furious. Walker was not going to get the paddle or the walk and talk. I didn't know what was in Walker's future that night, but my daddy did.

The cicada bugs burst into sound in the prickly ash copse for the first time in the season. They lived underground for seventeen years, and some generations were hardier than others. This year's brood must have emerged during a full moon. I had to put my hands over my ears to think when I stood too close to the trees where they hid.

"Hey." The cicadas stopped midsentence when the gruff voice pierced their frenzied sound. "Throw me one." Trask stood in the grass striped by the moonlight. "One throw." He picked up the new, white baseball and tossed it at Walker's feet.

"It's dead dark, Trask. I don't want my sons to get injured," Daddy said flatly.

"No, I'll do it." Walker picked up the ball and headed back toward the mound.

"Socrates, you are not catching for him." I stayed back with Mama. I had never heard Daddy or Mama speak to a white man, even one like Trask, with disdain.

"I don't need a catcher. Throw it to me. Like the others." Worried gnats filled the air. Trask swatted them away. The cicadas burst into their teeth-grinding whine. "Throw it," Trask yelled over the din and awkwardly hunched in the general direction of home plate. His fingers were intertwined halfway up the bat. I relaxed. There was no way he was going to make contact.

I didn't know if Walker would lob it in to save Trask's vanity and perhaps give our family room to breathe, or would he, in Mr. Ashby's words, throw to his potential? I knew Walker. He paid up if he lost a bet, took on the heavy end of the chores and didn't complain when he was punished. He was a simple person with an unbearably big spirit.

Walker let go of the ball, and it streaked toward Trask. It was an honest and hard pitch. A fastball doesn't pretend to be anything it's not. Trask swung. and the crack of the wood against the leather startled me as if a clap of thunder exploded overhead. He hit the ball square on in the fattest part of the bat. It traveled so far we didn't even hear the plop when it landed in the field.

Trask tossed the bat at Walker's feet and walked away toward his room in the old summer kitchen. As he passed the prickly ash copse, the fireflies went out. and the cicadas stopped their cries.

"Boys, go get my ball. I want it on the table tomorrow next to my breakfast." The hall light flicked on as Mr. Ashby slammed the front door.

"It was just one pitch, Walker. Mr. Chastain didn't even get a piece of his," I proffered. We ran next to one another, our gloves tucked high under our arms. We slid down the bank into the field dark as a grave. Daddy joined us, and we each took a row kicking at the dirt under the small cotton bushes. We bent over, feeling between the branches to see if the ball got lodged somewhere. When we reached the end of our rows, we each took another row going the opposite direction back toward the house. It was hard work, the thorny casings tore at my skin, and my back ached after thirty minutes of looking.

"Socrates and I are going for some sleep, Walker. Come with us. We'll get up before sunrise and find it then," Daddy said.

"Nope," Walker said. methodically working every bush. He found it at sunrise, and Mama put it alongside Mr. Ashby's grits and eggs. Trask was right. Mr. Ashby could send the Jeffersons to the field anytime he liked, and we were helpless to do anything about it.

The Curse of the Bambino flitted across our little world that night. I'm not a superstitious person, but Walker's disparagement of the most famous white baseball player ever to have a candy bar named after him felt a lot like the day in 1920 when the Red Sox announced they had sold Babe Ruth for $125,000 to the New York Yankees. Some moments you can't get back. The Red Sox can't find a pennant much less the World Series these days, and although he slipped into bed next to me when the weary cicadas went mute at first sunlight, Walker was gone when I awoke, leaving only his sweet smell tangled up in the sheets.

Chapter Five

Not much was said about Satchel Paige or Henry David Thoreau in the days following the Ashbys' party. One afternoon after my lessons, I wandered down the hill toward the commissary and the cotton fields. I rarely had a need or inclination to go to that part of the farm. My life was centered around the big house which was on the highest point of a hill looking out over the fields and the land beyond it. Tall oak trees were scattered around the yard like pickup sticks, and the barn, horse paddock, pasture, summer kitchen, and pond all curved around the big house like a crescent moon. The Jeffersons' house a few yards away was more than a cabin but not quite a house. It had inside walls of wallpaper-covered lathing and two tiny bedrooms plus the kitchen for heating and eating. We had a single privy for our family and a water pump, while Mr. Ashby's father had an indoor water closet and piped water from the well brought to the house before he died. The Jeffersons always had a vigorous garden and an ample number of chickens behind their house, while the Ashbys had either bare dirt rectangle waiting for dahlia tuber planting or a thirty-foot-by-twenty-foot jungle of dahlia flowers growing over one another like squabbling children.

It took decades for the families to carve out the areas for the fields, commissary, and picker shacks. To create fields where crops would receive the best and longest sunlight, the two families turned over ribbons of dirt in long sections down the hillside. As fields were added, the rolling ribbons began to look like alternating stripes of a flag. There was High Field, close enough to the big house and the commissary you could call to someone and be heard; Middle Field, where the rows stretched so far sometimes you didn't hear the whistle indicating the end of the day; and Low Field, too close to the creek to be trusted with more than a bag full of cotton seed but too much land to waste on nothing. The Patch and the picker shacks also occupied Low Field. As Low Field was developed last, not much thought was put into the construction and placement of the picker shacks. Thus, most of them were built on stilts to protect the people from the overflowing creek bed, halt the water snakes that reveled in the marshy ground, and stem the amount of refuse flung out the back window in the general direction of the inadequate number of privies. There was no calling from Low Field to the big house. The pickers were on their own. The flag created on the Ashbys' land flew at the level they wanted to see.

There was one last piece of land on the farm: the one-hundred-acre longleaf pine forest in the far east corner of the Ashby land adjacent to a former plantation called Jubal Ridge. The trees grew close to one another, and the brush was waist high. The trees were difficult to cut down due to their tough bark, and the sap that spilled from them left a sluggish swamp of sticky tar that would catch an unknowing boot and pull it under. Mr. Ashby's father had eyed the forest before his death and told his son to cut it down and make more fields. It was useless and worth more dead than alive. When the senior Mr. Ashby died, the forest was still intact, and our Mr. Ashby visited its edges and threw his father's boots in and said, "Take them under for me."

The Ashbys' farm was coveted for its rich yield of cotton, its presence on a hill, and its house built with excellent materials, but the long line of Ashbys were proudest of the view beyond their farm. "Look beyond the cotton fields," they said, "and you can see as far as Georgia to the east, Tennessee to the north, and Alabama, our birthplace, under our feet, to the south, and even behind us to the west." The guests agreed the view was inspiring.

Brown hats and white scarves bobbed up and down in the rows as the pickers picked the early cotton from the plants. Some pickers wore gloves to avoid the razor-sharp edges of the casings, but the ones who picked the fastest used their bare fingers to choose the best cotton on the bush and leave the immature bolls for a later pick. A great picker was one with red hands streaked with white scars healed over from years of picking. The hands were not useful for much else.

It was May 1, and it looked like a good first pick six weeks into the season. If Daddy had been in the fields, he'd have been striding through the rows reminding them to leave enough for the next pick and the next after that. Discipline was when you had to train your eye on the future to keep your share in black pen in the ledger book. With bushes so heavy to start, however, there were many pickers at the end of the rows emptying their bags onto sheets tacked into the dirt with a stake. Once the fifteen-foot bag was empty, the picker would ask for help to pull the other side of the sheet over to secure it. It was Daddy's practice to weigh it right then in front of the picker. A good number meant the scarred hands knew where to pick; a low number and Daddy suggested they leave the gloves off and maybe even pick the low cotton close to the ground. He'd fashioned some knee cushions for that kind of picking. By the time the field trailer took the Ashby cotton to the gin, pickers were no longer interested in the cotton they worked so hard to pick. There was always another row.

"Daddy, where are you?" I put my heavy geometry book on the steps and climbed the three stairs to look through the window. I saw a blur below me grab my thick, new geometry book and scamper off the stairs to the top of the hill.

"Why your daddy charge so much for an apple?" A scrawny boy with dirt encrusted in his neck folds held my book aloft mocking me.

"He doesn't. Someone else sets the price." The book's spine cracked as he let it swing open in his filthy hand. My breath caught in my throat. Mrs. Ashby demanded that each book be respected for the knowledge it contained.

"No. that's a lie. My pa says he changes the price to make Mr. Ashby rich. Traitor." He kicked dust onto my pants. "You's one of them. You ain't like the rest of us. Why you so important? Why don't you have to go to country school? Even your brother went to country school before he quit." He jutted his chin in the air, and I realized who he was: Joseph Sutter. We'd been thrown together at Sunday School a couple of times until the church informed Joseph's father that the offerings went to poor widows with children not to fully capable men who tried to work less and steal more. Mama said the Sutter family made picking look like a dirty business.

Daddy came up the hill from Middle Field and picked up his pace when he saw the dangling book. Sweat drenched his shirt, and he smelled clean, like rich dirt, new grass, and horses. He went to the commissary and emerged with an apple. "Here. No charge. Give Socrates the book, please." The boy dropped the book and ate the apple in two bites. He wiped his sleeve to catch the juice running out of his mouth. He even swallowed the seeds.

"My granny said maybe an apple tree grow in my stomach. I'm smart. Just as smart as you."

I picked up the book and shook the dust from its pages.

"That'll be a dime on your account, William." Trask appeared. "You gotta pay like everyone else." The red stain on his face throbbed like a heartbeat.

"Of course," Daddy said. "That boy was hungry. I'll pay for an apple."

I looked away from Trask and wondered if I would have given Walker a target if Trask would have fanned the ball.

"Mr. Trask, what can I do to help you?" my daddy asked.

"Mister?" I sputtered. My daddy silenced me with his eyebrows in an angry line.

"I need to see the furnish and settle ledgers for as far back as you have them for these pickers."

"I thought you didn't do pickers," I blurted out.

"Socrates Bravo Jefferson." Daddy moved swiftly to grab me by the elbow. "Get to the house now." I marched up the hill, watching Trask over my shoulder. Daddy went into the commissary and came out with a stack of leather-bound, long ledgers used to capture the best and worst moments in a picker's life. Daddy handed them to Trask, who tucked the pile under his arm and left.

There are two times a year a picker meets with the farmer or an overseer. Furnish day happens in the spring, when pickers buy clothes, tools, seed, and staple goods from the commissary on credit. No money exchanges hands. If a picker happens to have credit in the book from the last harvest, they can do well, their numbers staying in the black ink or maybe just dipping their toe in the red ink where they are sure they can make it up. It's the pickers who are in red row already that Daddy had to tell they weren't getting a furnish that year. No sugar for pies, shoes for the little ones, or a new hoe for the father. "It's not the owing of the money that's the worst," Daddy said, "it's the feeling in that moment that others witness."

The other day of the year where a picker finds out where he stands in the world is the settle day. Sometime after the last pick, a whole season's worth of picking boils down to a single number. He is paid for the number of pounds of cotton he picked and then whatever he has left on furnish is subtracted from the settle number. If the final number is black, the picker goes home with pepper-mint sticks in his pocket for the babies. If the number is red, the picker must look at his purchase list and cross off what he and his family can live without. The families who never climb out of the red must rely on their neighbors or families to help them. Many of their children go hungry. A single line of black deposits and red debits was the history of a family. And now Trask carried the lives of over one hundred pickers and their families under his arm as he sauntered up the hill, his baggy trousers flapping on his butt.

Chapter Six

"What's going on, Mama?" I entered the big house from the kitchen and heard a commotion going on in the classroom. I opened the door and saw Trask grab a large stack of Mrs. Ashby's books off a bookcase and thump them next to the wall by the door. Mama was fussing behind him, asking him to stop.

"Please, Mr. Trask, don't touch Mrs. Ashby's things. They are from her father's study up north. It all came down on a train when he died. They are precious to her, please." Mama didn't say please very often.

"I'll be taking this room. Bring a bed down from upstairs. Do not touch my things in the outdoor room. I will bring them in myself. Tell William I want a lock installed on the door." Trask grabbed a stack of books and tucked them under his chin.

"What are you doing?" Mrs. Ashby pushed open the door and bent down to pick up a pile of books. She clutched them to her chest.

"I've told her I want a bed from upstairs, not the one from outside." Trask walked swiftly across the room. "I need a desk and space for my things." As he turned, his shirttail hooked onto a coffee can full of pencils, and they spilled all over the floor. Mrs. Ashby rushed to pick them up by handfuls, the sharp ends interchanged with the soft pink erasers. She stuffed them back into the can in the silence that had overtaken the room.

Mama blinked quickly.

"Wait." Mrs. Ashby dropped the books she cradled in her arms and lunged forward. Trask picked up the globe and grunted under its weight.

"Give it to me." Mrs. Ashby grabbed the old heirloom that had belonged in her family for generations. "Let go."

Trask let go of the globe. It bounced once and rolled across the floor in a crazy fashion. The side was crushed from the fall, and Mrs. Ashby stared at it and bit her lip. She carefully picked it up and put it outside the room.

"Mr. Trask," she said., "Annie and I can make up this bedroom for you so it will be well-appointed. Let us, please?" Her back was to him as she spoke. She gazed at a spot on the wall where a picture of Notre Dame had once hung. Now the picture was crumpled in the broken glass.

"Fine." He turned to go as Mama picked up another stack of books. "Claire, the bank papers say the house is not separate from the farm, so I need to know the house-hold costs for the records."

"Her name is Mrs. Ashby," Mama muttered.

Trask attempted to ignore Mama, but I saw his hand clench in his glove. "I also need the job description and the salary for the help—the house and the barn." He spit the word *help*, and there was no doubt who he meant.

"Help? Who are you calling the help? I'll show you help. I've run this household since I was twenty years old, and my mama ran it before me and my grandma before her. You're not—"

"Annie, that's enough." Mrs. Ashby took my mama's shoulders and turned her away from Trask. "You go in the kitchen, and I will be there in a moment." She snapped her fingers at me standing in the doorway. "Socrates, go with your mother. Now."

Maneuvering Mama out of the room took brute force. "Stop talking, Mama." I held my fingers to my lips. "I'll go listen." She nodded tearfully.

I cracked the door open and watched Trask as he wove between the piles of books and the furniture scattered in the room. "This needs to go. It's no good. I want a better desk." He pushed our classroom table, and the left leg, always weak, cracked, and the table listed to the side. It looked like it had fallen to its knees.

"Mr. Trask, why all this?" I saw Mrs. Ashby raise her hands and gesture at the mess strewn around her.

"A snake. A black snake came onto my bed, and I felt it sliding against my leg." Trask narrowed his eyes as he piled the books into higher stacks. It made me nervous to watch him. He paced around the room, cracking each of the knuckles on his fingers. His mouth looked like he was chewing, but there was nothing there. "I am not a servant, and I want to be here, to take my meals here, and to live in the house." He cleared his throat. "That's all."

"Oh, Mr. Trask, I am sorry about the snake. Very sorry," Mrs. Ashby said over her shoulder unstacking the books and making shorter piles against the wall. "Yes, we can make this room up for you, but Mr. Ashby said you would only be here another couple of days."

"I'll be here more than that, but I don't know the exact time. While I am here, I'm writing reports and sending them back to the government office. When I have finished determining the full value of the farm is when I make my recommendation to the bank and to the Federal Farm Bureau."

I saw him try to meet Mrs. Ashby's gaze with only the good side of his face looking toward her. It didn't work. He turned to look at her full on. I watched her reaction; she didn't blanche at the sight of the half of his face stained ruby red like port wine. In fact, I saw her face soften.

"Oh, my goodness," Mrs. Ashby said slowly, searching her hair with her fingers. "Mr. Ashby must be confused. He said that the loan would be paid back as soon as there was enough cotton sold."

"There has to be a completed harvest before the split can be determined and the pickers' debt can be calculated. He knows that. Most of the farm's worth is determined by the amount of money it brings in when the season is over."

Mrs. Ashby was quiet for longer than I expected. "Tell me about this government loan we took out. When was it?"

"1916. By Mr. Ashby's father. It was from a Federal Farm Act approved that year. Farmers could borrow money to improve their farms. I do not know what the money was used for here." Trask leaned against the wall and rested his boot against it. It made a black scuff mark that would make my mama seethe when she saw it.

"Well, there. Don't you see, Mr. Ashby's father died in 1916? We didn't know about the loan. I'd only been here on the farm for a little over two years then." Mrs. Ashby smiled as if everything was now neatly tied up like a package.

Trask pushed away from the wall and looked out the

window. I had stood in his place every day of my school life. In early summer, the bright blue skies, cotton bushes dotted with white bolls, and the long green rows leading on forever made the farm look prosperous. He turned away and faced Mrs. Ashby.

"Initially, Timothy made enough payments to warrant just a warning from the Federal Farm Bureau, but in 1920, he only paid interest on the loan and requested a forbearance due to the boll weevil. It was granted. Then in 1926, when the bureau agent came to talk to him about the delinquency of the loan, he took out a second mortgage on the farm with Gideon Bank and paid three thousand dollars toward the principal of the Federal Farm Bureau loan. But he stopped after that. The terms of the loan are up, and unless the debt can be paid, the government will foreclose on the farm at the end of the year."

"How much?"

"You owe the United States government eleven thousand dollars with penalties."

I thought of my childhood and the possessions that had been purchased over my lifetime: cars, horses, the radio, the icebox, other "discoveries" and trips that Mr. Ashby made by himself where he disappeared for days and we were all relieved he was gone. Eleven thousand dollars could have fixed the sloping roof on the back stoop where a brood of termites slumbered or bought a tractor so the rows could have been worked by more than hand-held hoes, the picker shacks had never seen paint, and the country school, I blew air out from between my lips, could have had new books. I certainly had them.

"Oh Lord." Frustrated, Mrs. Ashby tried to pull our table upright. It collapsed again.

Trask stood over her as she jiggled the leg. "You are

supposed to be an educated woman. How could you not know?"

Giving up on the table leg, Mrs. Ashby plopped into a chair and searched her head all over, feeling for the pencil usually stuck in her loose bun. Her cheeks were flushed with anger, and as she tried to compose herself, strands of hair began drifting onto her shoulders and sinking to the floor. "Oh dear, this will be the death of me. Where is my dratted pencil?" Her searching fingers dislodged it, and as she bent to pick it up, she bumped heads with Mr. Trask, who had reached for the rolling pencil too. They both stood up holding their foreheads and mumbling sorry.

Smoothing her hair back and tucking it behind her ears, Mrs. Ashby said, "I have a degree from Amherst College, so yes, I suppose you could say I am an educated woman. What about you? Did you go to college?"

Trask shook his head and wiped his face with his gloved hand. He peered at his palm as if something might have rubbed off. He tried to lean against the table. It leaned dangerously, and he had to pull himself back quickly. "I came out of the Georgia hills and went straight into an orphanage. I did not grow up in a house or had a life like those Jefferson brats. I went to industrial school, and the government trained me to be their bill collector. I count everything—every stick of furniture, piece of equipment, horse, car, and even jewelry in your box upstairs—and decide how much the whole farm is worth." He bent to the table and pulled the leg straight. It scraped on the floor but caught hold.

"So after you have determined the value of the farm, what happens then?"

I took a deep breath on the other side of the door. Mrs. Ashby was standing now, and the two of them looked oddly alike, with his shabby clothing badly repaired with white thread and her faded dress with limp lace at her wrists. They were a pair of misfits. I felt my stomach flop.

"I have to go meet John Carr. We can finish this discussion later." Trask moved to the door, and I scuttled down the hallway so he wouldn't see me.

"Bottom line, tell me, please." Mrs. Ashby raised her voice to Trask as he stood in the doorway. "What's it going to take to pay the government back?"

Trask wrapped his hand around the door frame and leaned back into the room. "Gideon Bank has a vested interest as well. If the government takes possession of the farm, the bank will have to petition to get any money. They want to make a deal."

"What kind of a deal?"

"I don't know."

"Mr. Trask. From now on, communicate with me. Mr. Ashby will be relieved not to have to deal with all the details."

Trask stepped back into the room. "What kind of a husband is that?"

"Mine," she said, hefting a tall pile of books into her arms. "Don't be late for your meeting. Annie and Socrates and I will be right down. And, Mr. Trask, if you know what is good for you, don't refer to Annie and William as the help. They are the backbone of this farm, and I won't allow you to hurt them."

Trask snickered. "Fine by me. You can call them what you want, but it doesn't change the truth." He went out the front door, and I saw down the length of the hall Mr. Ashby's going-to-town hat fall off the hat rack. Mrs. Ashby dug her heel into it causing a hole on the top. Grimly, she picked it up and smashed it back on the rack.

"Mrs. Ashby, he called me the helppp," Mama hiccupped.

"Enough!" Mrs. Ashby said, grabbing a dishtowel and tossing it to Mama. "Pull yourself together. We need to know what is happening at the commissary. John Carr from Gideon Bank is here." She grabbed Mama and me by the arms and yanked us outside.

The picker families stood in a half circle with their bags spooled in bunches at their feet. They wondered what a meeting was. At ninety degrees on the first of May, the temperature didn't bother them yet. Word was Jefferson was going to try to beat his record of seven picks in a season. Steady would be the rule.

We stood off to the side as Trask joined a stranger on the steps of the commissary. Daddy stood in the doorway watching the two men. I looked around for Mr. Ashby and saw a curl of smoke escape from under the shadowed porch. The swing glided back and forth.

The pickers slouched and stole looks back at the cotton. The meeting was cutting into their picking time, which was the equivalent of their dinner one day in the future.

Trask counted the pickers and nodded to the man confirming everyone was present. The visitor's arms hung down his sides in a gray woolen coat, and a black hat with a curled rim sat on his head. He held a sheaf of papers in his hands and sniffed his nose.

"My name is John Carr. I work for Gideon Bank in town. Mr. Trask and I are assisting the Ashbys in restructuring the payment system for the pickers here on the Ashby farm. At the end of the season, Mr. Ashby will receive one half of the proceeds because he owns the farm. You will receive the other half of the money, and it will be split between all of you according to the amount of cotton you picked."

The pickers began talking in loud and excited voices to one another. In the past, pickers had been paid by the pound, and there was concern Ashby was going to drop the price again two years in a row. Watching them celebrate, I shriveled inside. The idea that their take would equal that of the farmer made their hearts beat faster, and they envisioned not just credit but money in their palms after the settle. Many, feeling they had heard enough, tried to return to the fields.

"Wait!" Daddy shouted. "Come back. He's not done." He was the one who would have to explain that each of them would not receive half the money. In 1928, when a white man says a Negro man will get equal pay, someone is not telling the truth.

John Carr continued. "It is not difficult to understand. Each of you get part of the half. Some of you who pick a larger portion of the cotton will get a bigger part. If you pick a smaller amount, you will get less. No matter how much you get, though, as a picker on the Ashby farm, you are required to purchase all of your supplies, food, tools, and more at the commissary. You will also pay rent based on who lives in your house and who works in the fields. Keep in mind, as far as the commissary and the rent goes, you would have to pay that on any farm where you picked cotton." Mr. Carr shuffled the papers and glanced at Trask.

"Mr. Ashby charges us ten dollars a month rent no matter who lives in our house. You're changing that?" A young couple with three little children walked to stand in front of the man from the bank who was ridiculous enough to wear a winter coat to a cotton field in spring.

"The rule is being modified so it is fair to everyone." Sweat rolled down his neck and into the collar of his coat. "Here are the conditions."

"If all adults and children who live in the dwelling work in the fields, the rent will be ten dollars a month for the family." He stopped and looked around for signs of comprehension. "That was the old rule, and it still abides as long as everyone in the house works in the fields." Trask shifted on his feet and yawned.

"It has been discussed that there are people living in the residences who do not work on the farm. Each of them must pay rent to live here. Ten dollars per person each a month."

"Wait." An elderly woman cleared her throat. "I'm old. My family can't pay for me."

"You have a choice—pick or pay." Trask's words were laced with disinterest. I saw him flick a glance at Mrs. Ashby to see if she heard him.

Men looked at the ground, and women reached for their handkerchiefs. Fear was palpable. Young children played in the dirt, letting it slide between their fingers like money that would never be theirs. The joyful mood of a few minutes ago was gone. The couple with the three children threaded their way to the back of the group. They set the youngest, a baby who had just learned to sit up, in the lap of the oldest girl. I judged her to be about five years old.

"There will be exceptions," Mrs. Ashby called, stepping forward. "I promise we will take care of the children. They will go to school and learn other trades. You will not be charged rent while they are school age."

Mr. Carr glanced at Mrs. Ashby. "Claire, I have to correct you. If the children pick during the season, there is no additional rent. Timothy has agreed to waive the rent requirement while they go to school between the settle and the furnish which is about three months. School ends for children on their thirteenth birthday. After that there will be no exceptions. Timothy signed a contract with the bank, so Mr. Trask here can finish the evaluation of the farm. Timothy understands the conditions. It is too late to make any changes."

"Mr. Ashby," she called, her shoulders bunched up in anger. She walked a few steps up the hill to see if he was there.

"We want to make sure you understand the commissary and rent rules." Mr. Carr went on as Mr. Ashby failed to appear. "Your purchases and your rent will be billed to your account. If you owe the Ashbys after the settle, you are required to stay on the farm and pick cotton next season. If by chance you do not owe any money, you may choose to stay at the Ashby farm or leave for another location. Is that clear?" The group was mute. *Pick like hell*, they were thinking.

"Gideon Bank and the authorities are working together to make sure all debts are paid before anyone leaves town. The roads and the train will be patrolled. Arrests will be made." He waited again. "Of course, we hope that doesn't happen. Jobs are hard to come by. I encourage you to think carefully about your...responsibilities." The gap between the words felt like a threat.

"What about the Jeffersons?" a man called from the back of the group. He stood with his hands on the shoulders of a small, dirty boy. It was Joseph Sutter—the child who believed an apple tree might grow in his stomach. I rolled my eyes. Suddenly, I was pinched hard. It made my eyes burn. I looked up, expecting my mama, but Mrs.

Ashby was the one with her fingers squeezing the skin on my arm.

"Socrates Bravo, you are better than that."

"I'm sorry, Mrs. Ashby, ma'am." I tried to make myself shrink.

"No person or family on this farm is any more important than anyone else." Mr. Carr coughed and raised his voice. "Everyone must meet the same rules to stay on the farm. Mr. Trask and I have read the commissary ledgers where your accounts are kept. With few exceptions, almost everyone who works here owes a balance."

"Listen to me. The more you pick, the more Mr. Ashby makes, but you still have to pay the commissary and the extra rent. That means he could get more of the share." Daddy stepped down out of the shadow of the commissary's porch. "Why don't you come down here?" he shouted up to the porch. "You own the land. Why are you letting the bank make the decisions?" The swing stopped moving at the end of Daddy's shout as if it was deciding what to do.

"There are real costs to the commissary goods and routine maintenance to the residences, Jefferson. You know that." Mr. Carr wiped his neck with his hand and shook the sweat off it. Daddy turned to the step where Trask and Mr. Carr were standing.

"The prices here at the commissary are twice that of the store in town. Let them at least buy their goods there. There is no maintenance on the shacks. Some of the roofs are fifty years old. The rent—" Daddy stopped. "The rent...why take it out on the old and the sick. They are only going to get older and sicker when they have to go back to the fields. Children—" Daddy shook his fist in the air. "Children won't go to school. Why should they?

They're just going to end up in the fields so their granny can die in peace." He paced in front of the commissary. I had never seen my father fall apart. He was the most sober man I knew. Walker wouldn't believe it when I recounted the story later. I squeezed my eyes quickly to stop the stinging tears.

"Mrs. Ashby, we have to knock some sense into my husband." Mama marched through the crowd of pickers and turned her head away when she passed Mr. Carr and Trask.

"William," Mrs. Ashby called, following Mama through the group of pickers. "I've thought about this, and we have some options. Wait for us, please."

The three of us forced our way to the commissary steps. The pickers stood in wonder. They had never seen a Negro man go plumb crazy in front of powerful white men. My daddy had lost it. They knew what it felt like, but for them, the feeling was blunted, hazy, and had only pierced their consciousness a few times in their lives.

The pickers pressed in on us, closing the gap between themselves, Daddy, us, Mr. Carr, Trask, and the silent swing. The men in overalls with their skin like dark satin in the sunlight dragged their bags out of the way of the crowd. The long bags were expensive to purchase and more often were inherited, inspected, and repaired carefully when needed. But they knew if they filled them hundreds of times in a single season it meant extras like cigarettes, candy, women's stockings, maybe even a store-bought smoked ham—all could be paid for out of the black row of numbers in the ledger. They cradled their bags and stood at the edge of the crowd.

The women pushed past the men and gathered in a group of flour-bag blouses and long skirts. Their feet were bare and stirred up the dust. In the field, as fast as their hands moved and their bags hummed along behind them, they also watched for the shaking leaves at the bottom of the cotton bushes, indicating the slithering of snakes working their way toward their wandering toddlers, or worst of all, they listened to the wretched cries of new babies that awoke before the end of the row.

School-age children wound their way around their mother's and father's legs, holding onto their hands and then letting go. They learned that the more cotton they put in their parents' bags meant a bigger spoonful of sugar on their hoe cakes or even a lingering hand on the top of their heads that passed as love. To earn the sugar and the love, their hands had to survive their first year of a serious pick. The little webs between their fingers would be torn by the shards of the casings. If they survived the cuts—some startling red with infection, some already white and healed over—they knew to pick until someone told them to stop.

The old women, after decades of picking, tending to men and children, birthing babies, and pretending that a little food could feed many, were bent in half with humps on the tops of their backs. The elderly men had white eyes that could no longer see after years of squinting in the sun and searching for the sunset to come and bring the breeze that had held back all day. The elders snoozed in rocking chairs on the porches, with drool dribbling on their clothes and wetting them through.

A picker's life was lived each year between the furnish and the settle, starting and ending somewhere in the row of black or red numbers. If they were lucky, a picker experienced love, joy, and hope in the rightness of time from a grandparent, parent, lover, and child. They, with luck, were either the giver or receiver of a kiss in the sweet crease of their skin; with luck, they were the recipient of kind words; with luck, they rose each morning to a breakfast that held them through until they sat down to a supper of greens, salt pork, and pie on the porch steps. Lucky or not, though, pickers experienced a tiredness that was never overcome. They slept like the dead at night and walked it during the day. The rows never ended.

Daddy's hands were clenched into fists, and he pushed past Mr. Carr to storm up the hill to the big house. He stood on the ground that held his sweat and tears as much as it held Mr. Ashby's inheritance and debts.

"My family has lived here for three generations. I know this farm better than anyone," he shouted at Mr. Ashby. "I run this farm." Mama sagged. Daddy had broken the unspoken rule in the South just like Walker— never tell a white man you know better or can do better.

"But you don't have to pay the bills, do you, William?" Mr. Ashby stood up and rushed down to the last step to glare up at Daddy.

"What about the boys?"

"We all have to do more with a little less, William."

"My sons will not go to the fields."

"You'll be picking cotton, then." Mr. Ashby turned to climb the porch stairs. Daddy grabbed his arm.

"Sell the horses, Timothy. The money will go a long way toward paying the debts. They were your daddy's idea. Not yours."

Mr. Ashby turned around and wound himself up, so he was on his toes. He slapped my daddy hard across the face, leaving a white mark that turned ugly red in seconds. "This is my land and my horses. Your family has been treated too good for too long. You and Annie and the boys are pickers just as much as the rest of them. Get out of my way."

The pickers fell away from us, gliding back into the fields, brown hats and white handkerchiefs bent to the green bushes. Little ones ran through rows, the white cotton catching on their curly hair until they looked like small ghosts, and the babies, the precious babies, slept under the protection of the sharp casings and dirty bolls of raw cotton.

Chapter Seven

It had been two weeks since the moment no one had forgotten—the meeting where Mr. Ashby slapped my daddy in front of God, Mr. Carr, Trask, Mrs. Ashby, Mama, me, and the pickers. Although my lifetime was just a scant thirteen years and three months, I had never heard silence so deep that one could hear the longleaf pine needles rub against one another.

Everyone was quiet except for Mr. Ashby. He talked to everyone, asking about their days, commenting on the weather, encouraging the picker children to work to their potential, and complimenting my mama on her cooking. The only one Mr. Ashby didn't speak to was my daddy.

Mr. Ashby accompanied Trask on his methodical trip around the farm, where he searched the picker shacks, barns, and outbuildings for items of worth. He counted the machines, the livestock, and, Mama harrumphed, the fish in the pond. Trask counted the pickers' plates in the cupboard and number of shits in the privy to ensure his numbers were correct.

"Trask, I've never known so much about my farm since

you've done all this work for me. I must say I'll have to thank the government for once. What do you say about that?" Mr. Ashby's hands were clasped behind his back, and he waddled from shack to shack, struggling up the steep stairs that stood between the pickers and the creek.

"I'd say you were an asshole if you thanked the government. They're going to take everything you got," Trask said and took two stairs at once, leaving Mr. Ashby teetering on the lowest step.

I wonder if I would have known who was driving up the lane to our house if it hadn't been so quiet, but when I heard the purring hum of the well-cared for truck, I took in a breath. I had to find my mother quickly. I could only guess how she would greet Mr. Grindall. I don't think she'd offer him water on the porch, no, sir.

"I'm looking for Ashby. He home today?" Grindall parked the car close to the porch stairs, violating the grass rule around Southern homes, farms, and plantations. Just because it wasn't green didn't make it any less of a front yard. Grindall climbed out of the truck and slammed the door. He walked to look at the view and whistled a sharp acknowledgment of its grand vista. "Beautiful."

"Our family's always been here." I clasped my sweaty palms together and tried to see out of my glasses that had a film of dust obscuring the lenses.

"Your family," Grindall said, the right side of his lips sneaking upward in a twisted smirk. "Socrates, correct?"

"Yes, sir," I mumbled. "Socrates Bravo."

"Tell me something the famous Socrates wrote, and I'll see if I remember it from school. I hear you like giving speeches." The leg muscles in his clean, ironed pants flexed, and he crossed his arms across his chest. "Come on, Socrates."

I started to speak, but my voice cracked. I cleared my throat and began again. "He wasn't a writer. People think he was, but he wasn't. His friend Plato wrote about Socrates when he talked with people in Athens. He wanted people to arrive at ethical truths on their own." I blushed. Even without Mrs. Ashby there, I still felt a responsibility to explain the character of my namesake to people when they asked. Mr. Grindall, I realized, asked for another reason. He asked so he could belittle me.

"Well, bravo then. That's what I was supposed to say, right?" His unlined face allowed for a careful blank expression, but I could see his eyes. They were cruel. Their icy-blue glint meant to hurt.

"I'll go find Mr. Ashby," I mumbled.

Mr. Grindall walked to the pasture fence and nickered for the horses. All five trotted to him tossing their manes and tapping their hooves against the ground in high steps that sounded like the thumps of my mama's hands as she kneaded bread dough.

"What does he want?" Mr. Ashby stood at the side of the big house where our garden was growing over the fence and curling toward the path.

"I don't know." I tried to scoot by him.

"Go ask him." Mr. Ashby put his hand on my back and pushed me so I stumbled. "Go find out. If he asks, tell him the horses are not for sale."

"Mr. Ashby, my stomach is hurting terribly. I'm afraid I am going to get sick." I gurgled in my throat.

He hesitated and then muttered, "Fine. Go. I'll talk to him." As he strolled toward the fine-looking man with tall, shined black boots, I heard him say under his breath, "I wouldn't walk across the street to piss on him if he was on fire, but the Ashbys aren't nothing if not polite."

Mr. Ashby pushed his hair back over his forehead and pulled down his shirt that strained at the buttons. My mama had been feeding him too well lately. Daddy said she couldn't make a heart attack happen. They just do. "Oh, I can have a hand in it, William. New kind of pie every day will fatten him up even more now."

"Yes, but how's that going to help?"

"It might hurt a bit until the doctor gets here," she reflected. "Not a bad one, just a little painful."

I walked backward watching Mr. Ashby's rotund little figure approach Grindall. The horses saw him coming and threw their heads up and cantered away.

I was so intent on watching Mr. Grindall and Mr. Ashby that I backed into something solid behind me and fell.

"Walker," I breathed. "Where have you been?"

He offered me a hand and pulled me up.

"Town, sawmill, baseball."

"I've been doing your chores."

"I know. Thank you. I'll do yours for a while."

"If you could clean out the stalls, that'd be the best help." His fist shot out and punched me on the arm. "Ow," I complained.

"Too much, little brother, too much." He beamed. He looked like my brother of a few months ago. Too full of piss and vinegar for his own good, as Mama would say. "Come here," he said, grabbing my shirt. We bent over and scooted around to the opposite side of the house where Mrs. Ashby had recently moved the Victrola to the window that overlooked the dahlia bed. The plants were lengthening and reaching for the sky, but the flowers were still tight in small, green buds. "What is Grindall doing here?"

"Not sure. Mr. Ashby wanted me to talk to him, but I told him was feeling sick." Walker raised his eyebrows. I was known to have a sensitive stomach, and I couldn't control its potential for creating general mayhem when it erupted. Unfortunately, it usually impacted someone else's clothes or something else that could not be cleaned.

"Walker, Socrates, come here." It was Daddy's voice, and he didn't sound happy.

"Damn, we should have made a run for it," Walker whispered as we rounded the house into the dead brown grass in front.

"They'd always catch us you know," I mumbled in return.

"Not always, Soc. Not always," Walker said. He pushed me to the side and said, "Race."

"Like it is even a damn contest," I huffed.

He took off and sprinted for the pasture fence. He did a wide circle around Mr. Grindall to come up on Daddy's side and stand a little behind his shoulder. As I chugged along, dragging my feet, I heard Mr. Grindall say, "Have you had a chance to think about my job offer to work the trees, Walker?"

"Well, that's ridiculous," Mr. Ashby said.

"Walker?" Mr. Grindall ignored Mr. Ashby and leaned around him to look at my brother.

"Daddy." Walker looked at him for help. I could see Daddy's unrevealing look. Clear as day, his face said, *You call yourself a man. Use your own words.*

"I'm doing pretty well at baseball, thanks, Mr. Grindall. Twelve wins and the season is only half over. I'm hoping to beat Satchel Paige's record even though he's in the Negro League and I'm not...yet." Walker went through the motion of delivering a slow pitch. It looked kind of outlandish when no one said anything.

"Walker, would you like to pitch for Mr. Grindall? He's here to visit the farm. He's not been here since he moved to Gideon," Mr. Ashby queried.

"I'm not interested in his pitching," Mr. Grindall said, rubbing the nose of Lean, our blond-caramel-colored horse. Lean tossed his head abruptly, and Mr. Grindall pulled back in time to save himself a bloody nose. "Whoa." He raised his hand and stepped back from Lean. Walker drew himself up and stuck his chest out. I sidled over and flicked his hand with my thumb and finger. *Not now, not with him,* I silently communicated like I was Mama.

"There's five of us. Why don't we ride over to your pine forest, Ashby. What do you say?"

"Oh, Socrates and I have had a stomach illness lately. That's not a good idea. How about I walk you to—"

"I'd like to see the forest," Grindall interrupted. "Jefferson, get your boys to help with the gear."

Mr. Grindall was keen to ride Lean. He put the saddle on him, pushed the bridle into his mouth, and pulled himself up on to Lean's back. Daddy betrayed no interest in Grindall's curiosity in Lean. If he wanted to know more about the horse, he'd find out soon enough.

Lean had come to us as an obstinate horse with a perfect pedigree. He liked to lean on things, hence our name for him. At over five feet high at the shoulder, he had a lot of power and creativity. He leaned against the other horses. They would have dismissed him, but he learned to push on their full body length, pinning them against the pasture fence. When the fence gave, he scampered away while the victim struggled to get up from its side. He pressed against Daddy's powerful frame while he was being brushed, and more than one time, Daddy had to jump back to get out of the way. The horse forced his stall door to strain at the hinges until they broke and the door flew open with force. He labored against the tired, old barn wall until he felt the weakest point and cracked several boards. Mr. Ashby said to take the whip to him, but Daddy resisted. So Lean ran the pasture but allowed Daddy to hold sway over the barn. Someone had to feed him, and the horse was smart enough to know he couldn't force his way into the hayloft. There was nowhere to lean.

"Are you ready?" Daddy said to Mr. Ashby. Everyone knew he hated to ride.

"Yes, Jefferson, are you?" He tapped his little heels on the back of his horse's flanks. There was a coldness between them, and Daddy avoided conversing with him unless he had to. Daddy had cinched up the stirrups to their highest clasp and shortened the reins on Blaze, our oldest black horse, who did anything but move fast. We all started off walking, but soon, Grindall went out in front and pressed Lean to run. I snuck a glance at Walker, and we both urged our horses forward. We wanted to be there when Lean arrived. We had neglected to tell Mr. Grindall that sometimes Lean took his time responding to instructions. It usually happened when there was something in front of him—a fence, a tree, a wall—and he waited until the last minute to comply.

"Whoa, horse, whoa," Grindall yelled. He stood up in the saddle and yanked hard on the reins. He brought Lean's front feet off the ground, and when he dropped down, Grindall was bent over under the lowest swinging branch on a tree on the edge of the pine forest path. The thicket was high and scratchy as the path grew narrower and darker into the forest. Walker and I swung off our horses, and we waited without speaking while Daddy and Mr. Ashby ambled up.

"Boys, get over here and help me off this beast." Mr. Ashby grabbed Walker around the neck as he tried to jump off Blaze. As he shook his foot loose of the stirrup, he landed on the pine-needle-covered forest floor with strands of Blaze's wavy black mane hair clutched between his fingers. When Blaze felt Mr. Ashby's weight gone, he threw his head and bolted before Daddy could grab him.

It was the time of day when the sun was lengthening its shadows and the pickers knew there was about two hours left in the workday. They moved slowly through the field, and there were a few who even paused to talk over the top of the bushes. A whisper of a breeze stirred the longleaf pine needle bunches that graced the branches' tips like fancy cuffs at the end of men's sleeved shirts.

Grindall waited until we had all tied off our horses. He carried a stiff leather bag over his shoulder and slung across his body, and when he took his hat off to wipe the sweat off, I noticed his straight hair was thinning, with a large circle of bare skin on the top of his head.

He pulled the bag off his shoulder, unwound the lash, and pulled out a hatchet with a gleaming silver blade. There were bees hanging high over our heads, and we swatted at them while we watched Grindall walk around a few trees, laying his hand on the trunks and putting his ear against the rough bark of each of them. A humming sound grew louder, and I looked up to see bees flying in a lazy circle high in the branches. Whack! Grindall slammed the hatchet with the shiny blade into a tree. Whack! Whack! In seconds, Grindall had split the bark of the tree into three short horizontal drives about two feet apart.

"Oh Lord," Mr. Ashby sputtered.

"It's just one tree, Ashby. Wait until you see liquid gold spill all over this forest floor."

Mr. Ashby leaned forward to inspect the hash marks. "Look, that poor thing. How vicious." He put his diminutive finger in the gap and tilted his head as if deciding curiosity or protection should win over. He offered the tree to Grindall. "Proceed, Grindall. Liquid gold. Show me."

Grindall reached into his bag and brought out a long, flat piece of steel that looked like Mama's digging tool for rooting out weeds. He took the tool and rammed it forcefully under the slashes in the bark while tapping the back of the hatchet head to wedge the steel farther up under the bark. The tree made a groaning sound as Grindall shoved and winched the tool up farther under the bark. Pencil-yellow tree flesh began peeking from under the bark as the rough outer bark fell away in chunks. Grindall examined his slash marks carefully judging where the weakest bark remained. The final strip of thin interior skin was all that was left, and Grindall reached up and tore it from the tree like a scab removed from a cut that wasn't quite ready. I felt sick.

The bees drifted toward the noise and the open wound of the tree. They began to swarm the uppermost cut and bunch on the line between the healthy bark and the slick, naked wood. I glanced at Walker. Keeping our actions unobtrusive, we shuffled backward a few feet.

"Oh my God, what have you done?" Mr. Ashby, stricken, made his way through the thicket to the tree. He tried to grab Grindall's arm, and he shook him off.

"I'm showing you money right here on your land. You are wasting it while you are going broke, Ashby." Grindall squatted down at the base of the tree and chopped a rough box in the intersection between the tree and the roots. It fit into the cup of the earth, and when he had driven the last blow, he stood up and spat into the dark hole. He was proficient with the hatchet accomplishing in a few, short blows what would take another man a longer time. Grindall stared at the tree for a minute like an artist at a canvas.

"Listen. You can hear it." He looked at us with savage eyes, his pupils so large I couldn't see the blue of his iris. He tossed the hatchet by its swell knob at the base, and the head of the hatchet spun wickedly in the air. He caught it by the throat in the middle of the spin in a dead, cold stop.

"Hear what?" Daddy said.

"Crying." Unexpectedly, Grindall slammed the hatchet into the tree's tender yellow belly in alternating notches as high into the tree as he could reach. He struck the tree with angled shots, going right and going left, until there was a row of cuts that looked like cat whiskers where they met in the middle. The tree began to weep, and a flood of shiny, clean, amber-colored syrup oozed from each of the cuts. The pine tar slid down the slippery trunk and began filling the box at the bottom of the tree.

Pickers, their shadows now as long as the rows they worked on, turned to smell the fresh pine scent that, at one time, reminded me of beautiful fall mornings when the first pinewood fires were to lit to warm the fields.

"You know my place, Jubal Ridge, is on the other side of these woods. I'll buy your pine forest. You won't have to bother with tapping the trees; my crew will do it."

Mr. Ashby was staring at the box overflowing with pine tar. "What is it used for?"

"Goes into a copper still and gets boiled down into turpentine. Nasty stuff. This amount? Boiled down will make a few dips of a cup. But it is pure," Grindall said. "My turpentine is fine because I use virgin pine, first tap. The turpentine gets added to paint, varnish, and wax." He patted the tree trunk like it was the withers of a tightly tied prize horse.

"The best part of turpentine is that it can help anything look brand new, or cover mistakes, or color something just slightly so it looks richer than it is. The South likes its turpentine, but to be fair, so does everyone else."

The bees were three and four layers on top of each other up at the top of the first cut. Their buzzing was getting louder. They dashed at one another, greedily sucking the pine tar. The run of the pine tar changed from an oozing slide down the tree's flesh to a hurrying stream of clear, shiny snot. Realizing their error, the bees struggled to escape, but the glowing liquid covered them and froze them in place. I looked down at our feet, and the pine tar had silently climbed to the laces of our shoes.

I tried to speak. "Hmm." I grabbed Walker's arm and pointed to our feet.

"Turpentine"—Grindall interrupted me—"even cleans what you started. No one knows who started this cut. Except for you all." Grindall laughed and took a bottle of a smelly liquid out of his bag and poured it onto a rag. He rubbed it all over the hatchet, so it looked new and unused. "What do you say, Ashby? Eleven thousand dollars? Ten for the forest and a thousand for the horse?" He looked at Lean with interest. "That's a hundred an acre. No one is getting that for forest land around here."

My heart started thudding and banging in my chest. Mama had told Daddy what we owed the government. Here it was, the money could be stretched out in a hand, ready to be sealed with a handshake. Eleven thousand dollars would send Trask packing, buy more time from Gideon Bank, give the pickers something more than the thinnest of lines to hold onto, and allow me to sleep at night so I wouldn't worry about Mama and Daddy when I went to school in a few months' time.

"No," Mr. Ashby said. "No, I won't sell my land or my horses to you or anybody else."

Daddy stepped forward and put his back against a tree next to the one Grindall massacred. He leaned back into the bark. A branch up high bounced against Grindall's tree. Ignoring Daddy and us, Grindall edged around the pine tar pooling in the pine needles and pointed to three trees sheltering Mr. Ashby's head.

"Here, those trees alone would take a day and three men to tap. There is a fortune here in this forest," Grindall snapped. "Are you an idiot? Why won't you sell?"

Daddy leaned back and reached his hands behind his head. He bent his knees and pushed hard against the tree trunk. A fresh group of bees floated down toward us in lazy circles.

"No Ashby would ever split a family property. My grandparents chose this land, and they must have had a plan for the forest. I need to meet with someone and decide its worth. I'll talk to Trask. He might have some ideas."

"Trask is not your friend, Ashby, and you're a fool to think he wants to help you," Grindall said. "He's got a personal interest, you know." He stepped back to his bag. "I'll pack up here. You are going to lose all of it, and I'll buy it from the next owner." Grindall's hat fell off when he bent to the ground, and his angel halo of bald skin turned up to the sky. He kneeled in the sticky pine tar to marvel at the sheen and liquidity of the overflowing tree blood in the box at the base of the tree.

I strained my neck to look up to the top of the tree. Inside a hole in the trunk, a flaking gray ball of paper was teetering on the edge, rolling with the momentum of Daddy's actions and the tree branch bouncing against Grindall's tree. Daddy glanced up at the hive and motioned to Walker, Mr. Ashby, and me to move back. Walker and I dragged Mr. Ashby backward, Walker holding his finger to his lips to silence him. Daddy reached up one more time and leaned against the tree pushing it while watching to ensure Grindall wasn't paying attention.

The beehive fell, bouncing from branch to branch, chunks of it breaking each time it hit the rough bark. It dropped onto the top of Grindall's tender pink bald spot.

"Grindall, move. Bees. They were shook loose when the tree was cut," Daddy shouted.

The hive exploded into pieces. Hundreds of bees swarmed from the hive with murder in their genetic code. The pine tar held our shoes fast, so we left them behind and ran from the forest. The bees swarmed us diving and stinging without mercy. Daddy grabbed Mr. Ashby and carried him into the pasture. Grindall was still behind. He didn't emerge from the woods.

"Walker, go see if that man is dead from a torrent of bee bites," Mr. Ashby groaned, laying on his stomach.

"Stings," Walker and I said together.

"Go, boys, both of you." Daddy picked dead bees off
Mr. Ashby's back.

Grindall had taken his bag and left through the forest
toward Jubal Ridge. He would return later that night to
retrieve his truck. What he couldn't retrieve was the
hatchet buried in the box he had cut in the base of the
tree to catch the liquid gold. It was entombed.

Walker and I stumbled out of the forest, running from
the last of the angry bees. My brother wordlessly pulled
up his shirt to show me a half dozen or more bees alive
and stabbing his skin. I smacked his belly with the palm
of my hand, and the breath whooshed out of him like
Lean when he was pleased. Before he fell to the ground,
Walker gave me a smile of profound satisfaction.

"Why'd you do that, William? Why'd you knock those
bees down?" Mr. Ashby's face was swollen with reddish
purple lumps dotted with white centers where the
stingers had pierced his skin.

"It is my pine forest too." Daddy got to his feet and
walked toward the big house. "Damned if Grindall gets a
piece of this farm. Come on. We have to get to Annie
before the poison makes us sick."

We all dragged ourselves through the pasture toward
the house where Mama would layer all of us, even Mr.
Ashby, with pasty crusts of baking soda and water until we
completely healed days later.

Chapter Eight

"Mama? Where are you?" I stood in the big house's kitchen, looking at my mama's starched tablecloth with cross-stitched daises draped over a little table in the corner where a blackberry pie sat cooling. I picked those blackberries just yesterday, and my arms and legs were now a hazy lilac color that combined the juice of the berries, the weeping wounds from the bee stings, and the itchy paste of baking soda and water.

I asked her that morning, "Mama, don't you think this misery I've endured cancels out the need for punishment for my accident at the Patch?"

"No, Socrates Bravo, I sure don't. Since you're feeling so bad, Daddy and I decided the pain of the paddle isn't right for your punishment." I smiled then, and she caught my look. "Oh no, son, you will not receive the paddle for your punishment. Instead, you will spend all day with me doing what I tell you to do. Understand?" Mama had patted me on the head with a gleam in her eye. "See you at the big house in a few minutes." That was ten minutes ago. Where was she?

I hoped she was gone. I sat on the chair and picked tiny bits of the pie crust off and squished them into a ball in my hand. I wondered if she was gone on some errand that would take her hours to accomplish. Something that would delay her return. Indefinitely.

"Socrates?" She emerged in the doorway from the dark staircase leading to the Ashbys' basement. "What are you doing to my pie crust. Stop that." She slapped my hand as I put the dough ball on my tongue. "Spit it out now. It's not for you. Now spin it around so nobody can see it from the front. It's for Trask," she whispered. "Don't eat it."

I tilted my head sideways. Mama looked nervous. I slid the pie around so the broken crust faced away from the chair.

"We're going to the basement?" Dirty, damp, and dark, it was a child's nightmare. My nightmare. "Why?" I growled.

"I have to clean out a corner to put all of the classroom furniture in. We can't leave it in the hallway forever. Trask, ooh"—she caught her breath—"his knickers are in a knot today, and I don't know why. It's time to move it all, and I think your head is all healed up, don't you?"

I dipped my head in resignation. A thick rag hit me full force in the face.

"Put it on, Socrates. Spiders down there. You don't want them in your hair. Tie it tight. There's going to be cobwebs too."

Mrs. Ashby entered the room. "Oh, my goodness. Socrates, how are you? Working on your studies? Ready for our next lesson?" I nodded. Since Trask had moved into the house, we'd taken to meeting on the front porch. "I'll see you then." She turned, her hand on her belly as if her stomach was upset, and asked, "Annie, have you checked the dahlias today? Have the boys put the stakes in yet?"

"I think they got them out of the barn, ma'am." I looked at my mama, whose fingers were crossed behind her back. The stakes and wire were most definitely not out of the barn yet, and we all kept forgetting to do it. Mrs. Ashby left the room without responding to Mama, but her retreating stiff back said volumes.

"Mama, what was that about? Is she sick?" I tied the dreaded rag back on and tightened it in the front.

"Hmm. Not sure. Most of the time I know. She's put distance between us right now. She had a big hissy fit with Mr. Ashby after he hit Daddy."

"Is she still mad at him even after the bees? Daddy only leaned on the tree because Grindall made him mad too. He was standing up for us all of us."

"Socrates—" She stopped midsentence, as if she decided to swallow what she really wanted to say. "We are all going to get up early to stake those flowers. Do you hear me? If one blooms, they all bloom. Those buds are all swollen like they're about to give birth. You get on that as soon as we are done here. Now come on."

"Furniture goes down there." She pointed to the yawning darkness of the basement. "I'd like you to fix that table leg if you can. That hurt her when it happened. The books shouldn't go down here, should they, Socrates?"

"No, the damp would make the pages curl up and stick together within weeks."

"I know where they can go, but you have to keep quiet about it." She pointed as we passed Trask's room. "Nap-time. He doesn't feel well either." Mama pulled her gauzy green sleeves down. "Sometimes pie doesn't sit well with him."

I heaved a load of thick bound books into my arms and followed Mama up the stairs. She led me down a dim hallway until we reached the end. She motioned for me to get another load. I brought load after load of books to my mother, who had climbed halfway through a little door built into the wall. She was on her hands and knees in the hot crawl space and placing books in stacks through the small opening. A faint smell of cigar smoke hung in the air.

"Is this over the porch?"

Mama nodded. "Look inside." I crawled over to her and stuck my head into the opening.

"Whose are those?" I opened a small bag of marbles, balls, and a handful of jacks. Mama picked them up and put them in her apron.

"Later."

We finished with the books and then carried the furniture down the stairs to the basement. The hallway looked barren until Trask jerked open his door. "Annie, get me some lunch." Mama turned and walked back into the kitchen.

He sneered. "Nice hat."

His unique smell wafted out of his room and hit me full on. Stepping out of his filthy room with clothes thrown on the floor, empty bottles stashed on the windowsill, and the everlasting dead-egg smell permeating the walls, Trask leaned in to touch the knot of my rag covering tied on my forehead. A whiskey smell swirled out of his pores, and his eyes shone red. Small wisps of chest hair crawled between the top buttons of his shirt, and a lump in his throat, as red as his face, was large and straining at his skin.

"Do you even think about how your father and mother are going to meet their debts every month?"

Mrs. Ashby had signed a note guaranteeing that she would cover my portion of my parents' rent so I would continue my studies. She wanted to do more, but Mr. Ashby said no. He said the Jeffersons were to be treated like everyone else. Mama stayed in her position as the manager of the house, but the burden fell to Daddy to take care of the horses and pickers and pick his own portion of cotton. Walker was supposed to pay his rent, but we were thinking he was playing more baseball than working at the sawmill as only a few dollar bills drifted into Mama and Daddy occasionally; he'd yet to make a full month.

"Annie, it may be time for him to make his own way," Daddy said last night as they sat on the porch together. I watched them from my bed where the fluttering curtains allowed a rare night breeze into our house. The moon was high and bright, and my eyes had to squint against its glare.

"Not, yet, William. He's still my baby." My mama laid her head on his shoulder, which I had seen her do only once before when my granny passed. My parents' hands were loosely joined, and they leaned their shoulders into one another. Something stirred in my belly. Sadness. When I left for school, I would be without them.

The swoop of Trask's smooth red blemish on his face moved like waves in water when he smiled with his crooked, brown teeth and thin lips. "Socrates, you could be working in the fields when you're not studying. I told Mrs. Ashby so, but she was against it. You sure are special around here. Like everyone's baby." His breath was a stench. He had been drinking whiskey.

"I have your lunch ready, Mr. Trask." Mama stood behind us. "Sweet tea too, made just you like it." She pushed through both of us carrying the pie. "I'll put it on the porch for you." I reached over and tried to break the crust again for spite, but she held it high out of my way. Once back inside, she grabbed me and opened the door to the basement. "Get down there, Socrates. You have work to do, and it's not going to be picking." She pulled the door shut behind her and sat on the top step. She started to cry. When she pulled a hand-kerchief out of her pocket to wipe her eyes, the small toys fell out of her apron, bounced, and rolled onto the dark, dirt floor below us. "No," she cried. "No."

I crawled around on the dirt floor, muffling my shrieks while I looked for the marbles and the balls. The jacks had fallen and stayed put, but the marbles shot off in all directions. I could hear the balls still bouncing into the corners. Mama cried with great heaving shoulders, and I was at a loss. What do you do when your mama cries harder than you ever did as a child?

"There's twelve marbles, Socrates. Three each for us."

"Who? Who are you talking about?" I reached my hand under a cupboard that held canning jars filled with long forgotten beets. The jars wobbled when I pulled my hand out. I shivered. "Don't even think about it," I whispered straightaway.

"Your daddy, me, Timothy, and Maddie," she said, hiccupping. "They called us the Four."

I climbed the stairs and handed the marbles to my mama. "Here are the marbles. I lost the balls; they are still bouncing. I'll get the jacks too, but I need a moment."

She pulled my head to her and kissed my scar. "Such a boy. I should have known the night you were born you would turn everything upside down. It was bound to happen. Sit, my sweet Socrates. We'll talk. Don't think I didn't know you weren't listening last night when we were on the porch." She looked at me in the hazy light coming in from a small window built into the house foundation. "I'd suggest we'd move, but I can guarantee no one will come looking for us here. I wanted to name you Elijah. Did I ever tell you that?"

"No, Mama, you didn't." Something drifted across my forehead. I swatted at it, and I tipped dangerously close to falling backward down the stairs. Mama looked faraway and didn't notice. I plopped down on the step below her. No taking chances.

"Our life is a picket fence. We know what ours is, but it's sure on display to the world." She rubbed a sky-blue marble against her cheek. "This was Timothy's favorite. It matched the eye he liked the best." She rolled it between her palms like cookie dough at Christmas.

"I want to know why Daddy let Mr. Ashby treat him that way."

"I have to start at the beginning."

"If you think it will help," I mumbled. "Fine."

"You've heard Mr. Ashby talk about his grandparents coming here to Jackson County, but a slave couple named Elijah and Sybil Jefferson came with them. They were your daddy's grandparents."

I grunted.

"Thomas Ashby did something no white man in Alabama would think to do. He handed Elijah and Sybil their free papers. He told them they could go. He didn't own them." I scooted over to my mama to look at her to make sure she wasn't pulling my leg.

"And they stayed?" I asked in shock. "Our family could be anywhere now."

"Elijah and Sybil had a new baby, Louie. They wondered what to do. Thomas and Constance invited them to remain on the farm. They offered to pay them, provide them with a house, and allow them to leave anytime they liked. Even though they were former slaves living in a state that needed slaves to survive, they decided to stay with the Ashbys."

I shook my head in disgust.

"Socrates"—she flicked me on the back of the head —"you have to see it from their perspective. Thomas and Constance gave them their freedom. They were equals except the Ashbys owned the land. Elijah and Sybil stayed, Socrates, because they owned nothing, had nowhere to go, and didn't know how to do anything other than what they learned on the plantation back home."

"Socrates, are you paying attention? Did you hear that part?"

"Yes. So, Mama, you are telling me our family has always been free, and we didn't leave."

"Yes, I guess you could see it that way."

"Why are we here then?"

"The next generation changed things. The War between the States was over, but some people didn't know what their place was in the world. Thomas was the first Mr. Ashby, and the second boy was Timothy's daddy. By the time I was old enough to know his name, we called him Mr. Sir. I never learned the name God gave him. My mama and daddy were careful not to talk about him and his wife. They were closed people, if you know what I mean." She shook the whole handful of marbles in her closed fist. They tinkled against one another.

"Mr. Sir didn't marry for a long time, but he finally came home for good and picked a girl from Gideon. Mrs. Sir was quiet and real young. She was sweet and beautiful but took longer than a month of Sundays to read a book, if you know what I mean." Mama tapped the side of her head. I smiled in the damp basement air. Breathing in the dampness was uncomfortable, but the dust was pretty suspended in the low light of the window. "Her parents were keen on her marrying Mr. Sir. This farm was the biggest and most successful in the county back then."

"You really called them Mr. Sir and Mrs. Sir?"

"Yes, we did. You do what you must do to keep the peace on the farm. White and Negro had their own rules to live by."

"Were they rich?"

"Yes," Mama said. "Yes, they were. They were until the boll weevil came."

"As children, we were all friends, and seeing how Timothy's father was Mr. Sir, we allowed Timothy to think he was the head of us because he didn't have much else to him. If that boy had possessed an idea in those days, it would have died of loneliness." The glass marbles rubbed together with a faint squeaking sound. Mama snorted. "Come to think of it, now too." She pushed her back against the step to get more comfortable. "You know his given name is Timothy. That's what he was called. Not Timmy when he was a baby or Tim when he grew up. Timothy. It never changed, just like he's never changed."

"You called him Timothy?"

"We were little when we started playing together. No one ever said we could start or stop calling him by his

name. Things changed only when life forced them to."
Mama wiped her face, and her smile caused her dimples
to show in her cheeks. "Don't think he was in charge.
Maddie was. She was in charge from when we were all
littles."

"Who was Maddie?"

"She came to the farm as a baby. Both Mr. and Mrs. Sir
liked her as they had a boy already and she was a girl. She
lived in the big house with them but was as sassy as a girl
can be, and she got away with it. Maddie was tiny; some
people thought she was too little to play with us. That is
until you heard her boss us. She'd make your blood run
cold when she didn't like what was happening. I..." Mama
faltered. "I miss her. We were the Four. There was your
daddy, me, Timothy, and Maddie."

"Where is Maddie? I asked. "I've never heard you talk
about her until today."

"Maddie grew up independent and successful. She
still lives around here. She owns a restaurant outside of
town on the highway the other side of Gideon. She's..."
Mama struggled to find words. "Her hair was long. She
wore it in braids. She hated it, but Mr. Sir wouldn't let
nobody cut it."

"What did Mr. Sir have to do with her?"

"He liked her spirit."

"Why hasn't she been back to visit? Mama?" I felt like
a child finding out about a secret kept out of my knowing
my whole life.

Mama shook her head, and the subject of Maddie was
done. Done enough even I knew it was a door slammed
shut. "William started working with Mr. Sir's horses the
year he turned thirteen. His daddy, your granddaddy
Louie, taught him how to run a horse barn. William didn't

learn horses by books—he just knew it. Granddaddy Louie ran the barn, but Mr. Sir preferred your daddy. He watched him with horses. Even though his son, Timothy, was the same age, he acted like it was just your daddy was on the road to being a man, not Timothy." Mama was quiet, but I leaned in to hear her words. "It wasn't fair; William wasn't much more than a boy."

"So, Mr. Ashby was jealous because Mr. Sir liked Daddy better?" Mama ignored me.

"Is that why Mr. Ashby called us pickers?" Bitter-tasting spit flooded my mouth.

My mama didn't slap my head even though I know she wanted to. Instead, she rubbed my back. "My mama was in the house, William's daddy was in the barn, and Maddie was just Maddie, underfoot or out of sight, but never when you wanted her to stay put."

"Wait, Socrates. Just wait. Patience." As if my mama was the most patient person in the world. "We loved being together. We'd beg for sandwiches from my mama and then use the crust to try our hand at fishing at the creek. At night, we'd sneak out of our houses and lay in the sweet grass with the cotton bolls making soft popping sounds as they opened. The four of us didn't talk. We watched God's parade of stars pass by."

I was touched by the poetry in my mother's words. Keats and Wordsworth and Shelley had their privileged upbringing, but my mama, in her simple uneducated way, exceeded their knowledge of nature. She could see the way a slant of light showed a fading season even though the new one had not yet arrived. Somehow, she used the knowledge of the going and the coming of seasons to be prepared—to pick tomatoes before the first frost, to plant the hollyhocks facing north so their colors didn't fade, to call in her children and take cover when the sky turned green—she did it all as if she alone wound God's clock and kept it moving on its steady way.

"We had a problem, though," Mama continued, unaware of my pride in her. "Timothy was more scared of horses than he is now. The rest of us were good riders, but the horses could sense Timothy's fear, and they would stamp their feet and throw their heads. William wanted to help him, so he would hold the tamest one and whisper in its ear and stroke its neck. Those were good times for the Four," she reflected. "Maybe not so much for Timothy, though."

"Like how he won't sell the horses now?" I shook my head. "Mama, I'm having a hard time believing this all. If Daddy and Mr. Ashby were such good friends, why does he hate Daddy now?"

"Oh, Socrates, Mr. Ashby doesn't hate your daddy. Not at all." Mama exhaled. "I know it is hard to understand, but he actually loves him like a brother. You know when the wind blows sideways in a bad storm and all the cotton turns brown and it can't be ginned? Some evil people are like that. They ruin people, and they don't care. They set a storm in motion and walk away kicking the dust up behind them just for spite. That was Mr. Sir, and in some ways, Timothy learned the worst from his daddy." She slid the marbles back into her apron pocket where they lay hidden and muffled.

"Mr. Sir was one mean man. He wore tall black boots that he didn't take off at the back door. Dust, mud, rain, all of it, he tracked through my mama's kitchen. It was her kitchen. She took care of it. Like it is mine now. She'd get out her broom or mop and start fresh. She took pride in her job. She never said a word to him." Mama was restless and shifted her weight on the hard step, and it creaked.

"Mr. Sir's wife didn't come downstairs much. She mostly stayed up in her room with the shutters closed on her windows. My mama would go up there and bring Mrs. Sir a sandwich. The two of them would sit together and listen to Mr. Sir yell. When Mr. Sir yelled at his son to get him something, Mrs. Sir would go to the window and open the shutter just a bit. Mrs. Sir would watch Timothy, who was scared of his own shadow. She always closed the shutter after that."

"Well, then he should have worked harder like the rest of you did," I objected.

"Yes, but if your head is held down in fear and the man shouting at you is your daddy, it doesn't matter what color you are."

"Oh." I didn't know what that was like. Even a walk and talk left you feeling loved.

"We were sitting in the hayloft trying to stay quiet and out of sight. We were hiding from my mama who wanted us to beat the carpets hanging on the clothesline. That was not a fun job." She stopped talking, and I saw her considering it. My shoulders drooped. It might become a job for me or Walker. "Keep going, Mama."

"Mr. Sir and Louie were talking below, and so, we listened."

"Mr. Sir said, 'There's a stud coming, Louie. Name's Midnight. After we break him, we'll rent him out to other farms. All the farms will want the colts that come from him.'

"'How much are you going to break him, Mr. Sir?'

"'We'll have to see how bad he wants his freedom.'

"At those words, the four of us looked at each other. It made us want to keep our freedom."

"Did it, Mama? Did the horse stay free?"

"For a while, Socrates. Sooner or later every living thing had to bend their will to Mr. Sir."

I started to get up. Mama pulled me back down. "Midnight arrived at the farm in the middle of the day. The four of us stood back and we peeked out from the side of the barn. Your granddaddy called for William to come help. Maddie, Timothy, and I stayed in our hiding place. We were nervous. Spending too time around Mr. Sir made him notice you. You didn't want that."

"The driver backed the trailer up to the paddock gate. Mr. Sir and Louie opened the trailer door. I'll never forget the sight of that horse." Mama took a deep breath. "Your daddy went forward when all the others took a step back. He wasn't afraid."

I didn't say it, because sure I would get the paddle, or worse, a hurt look, but I wanted to ask, what is the difference between not being afraid and not fighting back?

"He had to be thirteen hands easy," Mama said her voice distant. It was like she was back there, a little girl, watching the spectacle. "Maddie came out from behind the barn and made me sit on the top rail and watch with her. She wasn't afraid of nothing. She'd toss her braids over her shoulder and stretch her feet so they could reach the lower rail. She was different in another way; she wasn't afraid of Mr. Sir. Ever."

"What about Mr. Ashby? Did he sit with you and Maddie?"

"No. He stayed on the side of the barn. He was shaking he was so scared." Mama made that sound in her throat when she sees the farm dogs surround a fawn.

"Midnight kept running in circles around Mr. Sir. No one could stop him, so they just watched, waiting for him to tire himself out. It was hard. It took him a long time. He just kept running." My mama's hands were agitated, twisted and folded on top of each other.

"Then Mr. Sir called to your daddy, 'William, get my whip.' Your daddy didn't hesitate. When we were young, our trust was wide and shallow. Trust should be narrow and deep, Socrates. You need to know that."

"Yes, Mama." My stomach was doing flip-flops.

"Mr. Sir had a whip made especially for him. The handle was thick and twisted. It kept curving and curving so it could never be laid flat. The braid became thinner and thinner until, finally, it became reed thin at the end. When Mr. Sir raised his fist into the air, a long hissing sound flew out. Then the whip came down, and whatever it hit sizzled. It sounded like it burned what it touched. Wherever that whip made a mark, it is still there."

"I didn't want to see Midnight get hit with the whip. I told Maddie we should leave, and that's when Mr. Sir saw us. 'Timothy, you get out from behind the barn. Be a man. Come watch this horse.'"

Mama shook her head. From the look on her face, I guessed she was remembering Mr. Ashby as a boy. "His face was bone white, and his hair was wet with sweat like he had gone swimming. He was unsteady on the fence. It was dangerous. On Midnight's next pass around the paddock, he swerved toward Timothy. I don't think he meant to hurt him. He just wanted to show the boy who was boss. Midnight came inches from hitting him, and his hoof just barely touched Timothy's face. But it was enough. That's how he lost his tooth. We all tried to go to him, but Mr. Sir raised the whip in his hand and cracked it hard. But he wasn't aiming it toward Midnight." Mama dropped her head. "He cracked it near Timothy. He shouted at him, 'Get in the house. Seeing fear will ruin him.' So Timothy ran to the house and left the rest of us. We didn't know it, but our friendship was broken when that whip whistled through the air."

"Finally, Midnight stopped running. Mr. Sir tossed the whip to your daddy and told him to hang it on the ring. I think it was part of Mr. Sir's plan. Bringing someone or something to exhaustion and walking away as if it didn't matter was more shameful than a fair fight, as far as I was concerned. Being around him made me think on who I wanted to be, Socrates. I'm grateful for that, even if it was painful when it happened."

Mama stood up. She stretched and opened the door. She looked around the kitchen. She pulled her hat off and stuffed it into her apron. "Let's go for a walk, Socrates." We left the house out the back door, and I noticed the dahlias were beginning to bend over from the top. They did need stalking. Their time was coming.

Mama and I started down the road I hadn't been on since my accident. The green was unbroken except where a wave of white peaked out from the bushes. The bolls were popping.

Mama kept striding down the road. "So, at dinnertime, my mama was at the big house, serving. Mr. Sir and Mrs. Sir and Maddie were all at the table. Timothy was missing. My mama got us. The sun was going down, and it worried us. We called to him and checked all our places—the creek, the pasture, the barn. That's when we noticed that Midnight wasn't in his stall. Oh, Lord, I can still feel how terrified I was." Mama walked faster. She was barefoot. She must have forgotten her shoes or else left them off on purpose. Maybe she was living in her thirteen-year-old world. I could tell from the length of her strides that having her two worlds clash together dulled the painful impact of the sharp rocks hidden in the road.

"William saddled up Daisy and Trot, and we set out together. I rode behind William, and Maddie was alone on Daisy. That's how it usually was. Maddie..." Shaking her head, Mama's lips were crooked somewhere between a smile and a grimace. "Maddie, she learned from Mr. Sir too. When she was upset, she got hard. She could say a whole lot of words when she was angry, and each one felt like a fist hitting you in the stomach. We didn't like her then." Mama paused. "If I'd been older, I might have known it was her way to stop the sadness."

"Mama, tell me more about Maddie."

"Not this time, Socrates." Her face was set and distant for the rest of the story. "William's plan was to get Midnight back in the barn before Louie or Mr. Sir noticed he was gone. We rode looking down in the dust for Midnight's prints. We saw the hoof prints leave the road here." She pointed across the field to the circle of short oak trees and stones that blocked the entry to the Patch.

Mama laid her hand on my shoulder keeping a gentle pressure so I wouldn't leave. "It was our secret place too. But it changed after what happened the night." Mama sat down in the dust and wrapped her arms around her knees. Looking at the side of her face, I saw her as a thirteen-year-old girl. She must have been tall, gangly, and yet had a grace that still lined her face.

"The tall oak trees inside the Patch blocked all the sunshine. It always felt cool even when it was blazing hot in the field. The branches reached across the top, and the leaves touched each other. They weaved in and out like a quilt. Nothing could grow under the branches, so there was cleared earth. We mostly played in the branches of the oak trees."

"It still feels like that, Mama." In fact, someday, I'd tell her those were my words too and my thoughts about the clearing.

"Remember how I said that was the night our friendship ended? Before that day, none of us had a place we belonged yet. William was the first. We knew he was leaving us for the barn. Our lives were about to change. We just didn't know how."

Kind of like Walker, I thought. Her hand drifted over the top of my head, and with one finger, she traced the wide scar that split me in two. "Our time together was almost done."

I felt something start up in my body. A jolt, a crackle, a coming to life. It wasn't all that pleasant, but without saying anything, I knew its arrival was necessary.

"We tied Daisy and Trot up. We walked in each other's footsteps on the path. William said, 'Timothy, where are you? Is Midnight here? Mr. Sir is going to be angry. We have to take him back.'

"Inside the clearing, we saw Midnight drinking from the waterhole. His bridle was out, dropped to the ground with the reins. Timothy was sitting on one of the low branches swinging his legs. He was happy. He said, 'I did it, William. I got him to follow me. He let me take out his bridle. I pulled it real slow just like you and your daddy do.' His lips were all puffed up and bruised, and he talked just like he does now."

"I cannot believe Mr. Ashby would go near a horse that big."

Mama let a chuckle escape, but it soon became a

choke. "You sound just like Maddie. She was so mad at him. She reached up and grabbed his foot and yanked him out of the tree. He fell off the branch and landed on his bottom. She said real mean-like, 'You are the stupidest boy I have ever met. You'll be nothing when you grow up. Nothing. You'll never learn to be a man. Mr. Sir hates you.'

"William and I started to talk back to her, but she turned on us and said, 'You know I am right. Let's get that horse back.'"

"It's too bad she was right, Mama," I said quietly.

"I know, Socrates. You should have seen Timothy's face. It was like he was looking down a real straight road where you couldn't see the end of it, and he kept looking hoping he'd see one of us waiting to walk along with him so he wouldn't be lonely. Your daddy picked up the bridle and put it back in Midnight's mouth. Maddie and I stood there in front of Timothy and we acted like grown women, our hands all on our hips. I asked him, 'Why'd you do it?'

"'I didn't want Mr. Sir to beat him,' he said. "I loved Timothy and hated him at the same time, because I knew Mr. Sir was only capable of hate, and we were going to pay the price. We weren't even out of the trees when Mr. Sir found us. Mr. Sir looked at Timothy and said, 'Who stole this horse?'"

Mama waited for me to put it all together. To see where it all fell apart. Because, as she said, it was a mistake to have trust that was wide and shallow.

"Mr. Ashby lied and said Daddy stole him, didn't he?"

Mama nodded. She raised my hand and slid the marbles into my palm in one uncompromising stream that didn't end until it was finished.

"Yes, and Mr. Sir beat your daddy with his whip."

"And the marks are still there," I finished.

"Later that night, Timothy came to your daddy's bedroom window where your granny was trying to put salve on the lash marks. He said, 'William? You're still my friend, aren't you? Please be my friend.'"

"Daddy said yes, didn't he?" Mama didn't shake her head or flinch. "Why did you tell me this story?" I could feel a red wall of anger building in me.

"Because the marks will never go away, but they remind us what we want for you. We are like Sybil and Elijah, but you aren't. You're going to leave like they should have. You're going to school." She held out her hand and motioned for me to pull her up. "Your daddy is picking cotton now for you and Walker just like he took that slap on the face. Don't be angry at him. You boys are going to have to make your own lives happen. Daddy will pick cotton, and I will work in the big house, and you and Walker will find a way to leave the farm."

"What did Maddie do when Mr. Sir whipped Daddy?" The words felt like spoiled food as they left my mouth.

"She left. We haven't seen her since." That was the end of it. The story was done.

"Mama, watch this." One by one, I threw the marbles into the field. They dropped into the cotton without a sound. With each throw, my rage grew. I shouted, "Damn you, damn you, damn you!" The words echoed against the hills.

"Where are the jacks? Give me the jacks!" I faced her. "I want to throw those too. I want it all gone. Everything you and Daddy do for them. Where are they?" Mama's face was scared at the sight of her son's unhinging over an old, dead story. I wanted to be Midnight. I wanted to run in circles without stopping so my daddy would never have felt the crack of the whip. She clutched the jacks, looking at me.

She settled her shoulders back and set her feet like she was Walker, king of the pitching mound. I could not tell if her transformation was about my behavior or the retelling of the beating all those years ago. She set her feet, took the jacks from her apron, and started throwing them into the field. At first, they didn't go far, but her arm grew stronger. They flew, making whistling sounds as they cartwheeled across the green leaves. One bounced and stuck in the bursting cotton boll that was mature ahead of the others. We could see the jack's orange spindling pieces hanging on by the little bumps at the end of its legs. I longed to go to it, to drive it into the ground, to smash it flat so we would no longer see it.

Mama held me back. "Wait." While we watched, it slipped off the bush and fell and disappeared into the plowed earth. It was gone. "It did it to itself, Soc." We turned and walked back to the house. I allowed my mama to hold my hand. I let our palms join like the curving parts of a shell held tenuously together by the last thread.

Then, she jerked my arm so I fell into the dirt in the road. "Socrates, what's this whole swearing thing about? You have a whole bunch of fancy words in your head and all you can come up with is 'damn'? You have to use that brain of yours to come up with a plan to change things around here. You and Walker have to leave. I'll miss you something awful, you know?"

A spark inside me broke out into a full-on crashing lightning storm where you don't know where to look because it is all around you. I broke loose from my mama's grasp and danced backwards, facing her.

"We need to make things a holy mess around here.

Out of chaos comes order." My voice came out confident
and deep like a man determined to fix his world.

"Who said that?" Mama was suspicious.

"A philosopher, kind of like a philosopher. Don't
worry. He doesn't live around here."

"Good thing," she said, shaking her head. "I'd have to
talk some sense into him." Mama stopped, and her forehead frowned in the wrinkles that were getting deeper by
the day. "Wait, you're named after a philosopher. You're
not going to sit around, not as long as I am alive. You're
doing more than that, I promise you, young man."

"His name was Nietzsche. He's not from Alabama,
Mama." We kept walking. "What is the most disruptive
influence on the farm right now?" I asked.

I could see my mother rolling the words *disruptive* and
influence around in her head, turning them syllable by
syllable until the meanings matched our struggles on the
farm. Her eyes gleamed. "Trask and Mr. Ashby," she whispered. "They could do with a little chaos, don't you
think?"

"And let's hope it is the first step toward order," I said.
We picked up our pace and headed home. It was time to
act. What Mama didn't recognize, and I didn't voice, was it
wasn't just Trask and Mr. Ashby who needed to be run
over, hair tousled, and breath taken away—it was all of us.
We'd all contributed to the problems on the farm. It had
started from the very first Ashbys and Jeffersons, but it
was the Four who let it all go to hell. To get the farm back,
we'd all have to bring order out of chaos that started a
long time back.

Chapter Nine

"I've got a plan." My family sat in a row at the table, looking at me, and Walker tipped back on the chair, balancing on the thin legs. Since he'd come home to find Grindall petting our horses at the pasture fence, no matter how much I tried to reach him, his eyes drifted out the window and he cared little about the goings on of the farm. My brother was slipping away. I had decided not to tell him the story of the Four. People are different in the types of burdens they can bear. For Walker, the knowledge that our daddy was beaten because of Mr. Ashby's cowardice would have hung on him like a tick sucking the life blood out of him until he was wasted and done. Instead, we needed him to embrace Mr. Ashby and build him up.

I cleared my throat. "We're going to create chaos so we can find order."

As I stood before my brother's indifference, my daddy's exhaustion, and my mama's nervousness, I was petrified. It was hot already, even though the sun had only been up a few minutes. It was time to work on the dahlias, and we were all going to help to make it go faster. This meeting was using the time it took to pinch the side leaves, snip off the runty flower buds, sink the stakes, and water them all. It was all about helping the full, flush ones stretch toward the sun. Every minute we stayed in the hot kitchen allowed the sun to grow hotter and rise higher in the sky. I hurried.

I wasn't head of the house; Mama and Daddy were. But each of us would play a role in the drama that was about to begin. I would be the director telling the players when to enter and exit the stage, what to say, and who to influence. It was a big job—future scholar or not. I looked at each of them knowing they were going to have to live a life of lies, treachery, and dishonesty all with the goal of keeping the farm. I scratched my chin. Was I doing the right thing? I knew what Mrs. Ashby would say: "Go to your books, Socrates, and search who might have untangled this mess long before you."

I started by swallowing the big lump in my throat. "I stayed up late last night thinking, and there are two problems: one, we owe the government eleven thousand dollars; and two, the pickers are going to lose most of their settle because of Gideon Bank's contract with Mr. Ashby."

"We all know Mr. Ashby doesn't pay much attention to the farm, but after watching him turn Grindall's offer down, I think he is seeing more than we thought." They were silent. "I think he's decided to take as much of the pickers' settle as he can get. So, to stop him and help the pickers, Walker, you'll have to take him." I turned to my brother. "Mr. Ashby is disappointed when you don't see his inventions—or discoveries, as he calls them—when he brings them home. So if you could tell him there was this new invention where everyone would listen to him, I think he would put all of his attention into it and wouldn't bother with the farm."

"What is it?"

"Here." I unfolded an article I tore out of the newspaper Mr. Ashby had left on the porch swing. In the picture, there was a man standing his pajamas with his mouth speaking into a pipe sticking out of the wall. A floor below him, a woman ironing clothes held her ear to a pipe listening to the man talk. "It's called a voice pipe. You cut holes in the walls of your house and then install pipes from the bedroom to the kitchen, or the living room out to the porch, wherever you want. When someone hears Mr. Ashby talking, they would have to yell back to him through a pipe. Think about it. It is so simple, and yet, it will make him feel powerful. People will finally listen to him."

Mama's face was thoughtful. "Who is he going to talk to mostly?" I studied a fly on the wall; Daddy checked the bottom of his shoes.

Walker started to laugh. "Mama, who do you think he is going to talk to?"

"Oh, Lord. No, you're not saying that, are you, Socrates? This is just too much." Sweat dripped down my neck and splashed on the tabletop. I knew they could only stay a bit longer before chores, people, and problems would call them away.

"The other problem—Trask. I know we don't like him, but we need to keep him on the farm as long as possible. We must make Trask feel he is valued for more than just his job." My hand trembled and I wiped the sweat off on my pants. "We have to make him feel like he is important. He needs to care about the farm. The more he cares, the higher value he will put on it. He will recommend the bank keep the mortgage and not sell it to someone else."

"Oh shit," Walker groaned.

Daddy dropped his head in his hands. "Socrates, you're damn well killing me."

Mama jumped to her feet, and the kitchen curtains swayed. "Walker, don't you swear. You either, William." She turned to me. "Socrates, there is no way in hell we are doing that. My mama would roll over in her grave. Much less Maddie." Daddy jerked.

The back door opened on its creaky hinges. "Well, I'll tell you what. All of us better get off our asses and do something." Mrs. Ashby stepped into the kitchen from the back stoop. "Don't even shush me, any of you." She came to the table. "I am not going to stand around and watch everything fall to pieces." She was wearing her large gardening hat and carried a basket with clippers and gloves. "This is my home as well." She turned to me. "I heard all of it, Socrates. I got up early to help you all, and I got tired of waiting. I've been standing on your stoop for twenty minutes."

"Mrs. Ashby, there is more to the plan, and I don't think you should know..." I scrambled, my words stumbling out of my mouth.

"I'll do it," Walker interrupted. "I'll take Mr. Ashby, but I'm still going to find a scout. I'll put holes in the wall with him, but I have to play ball. You all have to know that."

We were silent, waiting for Mama. She surprised us. "Fine, Walker," she said, rubbing her hands together. "But if you want a home to come back to when you ain't playing baseball anymore, you better use your muscles to put a lot of holes in the wall before you go to the sawmill. In fact, Mr. Ashby can drive you to town on his way to the hardware store." She had her chin up at Walker, but his was even higher.

"Okay, you two, enough," Daddy said loudly. "We have to work on Mr. Ashby and Mr. Trask. I understand, but we have to protect the pickers. They are the ones who are going to save the farm—not any of us." He dipped his head to Mrs. Ashby to acknowledge her. "They have to pick until October to bring in enough to stay in the black in the ledger, and then there has to be enough for Mr. Ashby to pay off the government loan."

Walker raised his hand. I sighed. "Yes, Walker."

"What do we care about the pickers? We just need them to make the money." Mama reached over swiftly and pushed the chair forcefully to the floor. "I don't ever want to hear you speak those words again. They are hard-working folk, and you'd be out there picking alongside them, but your daddy is picking your share. Walker, I am ashamed of you."

Walker dropped his eyes. "Sorry, Mama. I guess I just don't understand what Socrates is yapping about." I watched the legs of his chair rise slowly off the floor again.

"If the pickers buy everything from the commissary and pay the rent Mr. Carr set, they are going to lose their percentage of the settle," I said. "Mr. Ashby knows that, and that's why he's not worried. What he doesn't understand is that there is no incentive for the pickers to harvest more cotton if they are so far in debt they can't see a way out." My family all tilted their heads to the side as I explained the problem. "There is a solution, but..."

"Spit it out, Socrates. This is our home. Whatever we have to do, we'll do it." Daddy wiped the sweat off his forehead.

"Yes, Soc, we'll do it," Mama thumped her fist on the tabletop.

"You think we should keep the commissary low on supplies on purpose, so the pickers don't have to pay the inflated prices." Daddy's voice was blunt. "What if they don't have any food?"

"Well...it's not really cheating, but if you can buy supplies in town and turn around and sell the supplies to the pickers for what the prices are in town, they'd spend less at the commissary." Mama and Daddy looked at one another. "We'd just need some money to get started," I said meaningfully.

Mrs. Ashby clucked at me with irritation. "That's enough, Socrates. Don't act like a willy-nilly. The end justifies the means this time. You are right. The pickers should not have to pay for the sins of others. Yes, I will figure out how to get the money for the first delivery of supplies. Then, it will support itself. I'll just tell Mr. Ashby that William will occasionally drive me to town to pick up some necessities."

Daddy tipped his head back to look at the ceiling. He dropped his eyes to look at me with a hard stare. "The rent. What's your plan to overcome the extra rent they are asking for?"

"Okay, so listen. Mr. Carr didn't say how much cotton a person had to pick to count as a picker in the field, so let's just say you go for a walk with Miss Cora and Brutus, for example, and pick a row together. They'll be in the ledger book then as pickers, and their rent will drop to ten dollars a month."

"How's your daddy supposed to hold the hands of the old folks, carry the babies on his back, and pick his own lot?" Mama asked, her words like a hot knife slicing through butter.

"I'll do it. I'll do it all." Daddy stood up. "Wait, Son, are we telling them about it?" I struggled to overcome my shame. "You want me to trick them, don't you?"

I looked somewhere over the top of his ear instead of meeting his eye. "Not trick them exactly, but if they know what we're doing is intentional, it might get back to Mr. Carr."

"Socrates, you're asking all of us to do things we know aren't right." Daddy's voice was very low, and it stung.

"And we're going to do it, William." Mama stood up and smoothed her hands down her gardening apron. "Let's go. If we're going to dance with the devil, the least we can do is get out there and root out some weeds in this blasted heat."

"The devil is in the details, Annie." Mrs. Ashby reached up and patted her snarled hair. "I am going one step further. I can distract Trask and Mr. Ashby. I will make both men fall in love with me." She smiled. "Or at least one of them fall in love with me again and one for the first time."

My family stood like statues in the sweltering kitchen.

"Now, y'all, that hurts my feelings," Mrs. Ashby said in her best imitation of the way Southerners talk. "I've lived in this godforsaken corner of the South for years. I've learned a thing or two about wooing men. I'm not a young thing anymore, but I am smarter than all of those empty-headed girls sashaying in town looking for husbands. Annie, we'll have to start with my hair, don't you think?" My mama's head bounced up and down as she tried to speak, and nothing came out but puffs of desperate air.

"Mrs. Ashby, what's the point of making them fall in

love with you?" I asked. My family sank down to their
seats and waited for her answer.

"There are two ways to change an evil man." Mrs.
Ashby traced the outline of a heart in the sweating damp
on the top of the table. "Teach him how to love or break
his heart."

"Who is the evil one?" Walker said, confused.

"We'll see," she said, her tone light. "Socrates Bravo,
which Shakespeare play am I talking about?"

I refused to say it out loud. I knew how the play ended.
Sweat dotted Mrs. Ashby's chin, and she wiped it away
with a starched handkerchief. She arched her eyebrows at
me. She was not going to move until I spoke. My heart
aching, I mumbled, "Lady Macbeth."

"Very good, Socrates Bravo." She cleared her throat.
"Would you leave us alone please?"

Mama, Daddy, and Walker left the kitchen, my mama
despairing over the dirty dishes in the sink.

"Sit down." Mrs. Ashby returned from the stoop with a
large stack of books. She handed me an envelope "Read
it." She pointed to the letter and pulled Walker's chair up
to the table.

I held it in my hands. I had never seen my name
written in anyone else's handwriting, apart from Mrs.
Ashby's *Socrates Bravo Jefferson*. The ink flowed across the
thick, linen envelope. Her name and address were near
the bottom of the crease, but my name marched boldly
across the center. I turned it over and ran my fingers over
the wax seal of Parson University Preparatory School.

I slid the letter out.

Dear Mr. Jefferson:

Mrs. Claire Ashby wrote to us about your desire to matric-
ulate at Parson University Preparatory School in the fall of

1928. She submitted examples of your essays and tests in English literature, mathematics, science, and history. The skills and knowledge demonstrated in these examples, in our opinion, exceed those of most first-year students at the university.

Hence, upon discussion with my colleagues, we agree with Mrs. Ashby's assessment of your abilities. We are willing to offer you provisional entry to Parson University Preparatory School upon the condition that you complete the requirements listed on the following page. When we receive notification of your completed courses of independent study, you will be admitted to the school without reservation.

It is not often we have the opportunity to teach a promising young scholar such as yourself. We look forward to meeting you in October.

Sincerely,

Robert Smiley, PhD

Academic Dean

Parson University Preparatory School

"THANK YOU, MRS. ASHBY." I TOOK MY GLASSES OFF AND pinched my nose. I focused my on the tabletop where the heart she had drawn had disappeared. I trained my eyes on white patches of softened wood where hot dishes had left their mark. I hope she understood that a man, even a young one, needed time to process all the letter represented. My chest constricted; it was my education sitting on my very breastbone. What I had wanted and been told I wanted was now within reach, and my hand shook with indecision.

"The list is here," she said, pulling it from the envelope. "You will need to write four essays, one each in literature, history, science, and math. We'll work on them together. The school wants to know you can explore one topic on a deep level in each area. The topics will be your choice, and I have something for you."

She opened the screen door and held it with her foot while she lifted something heavy. She jostled it a bit to wrap her arms around it. She came back through the door, carrying a black typewriter with a white box tipping precariously on top of it. I put my hands underneath the shiny, black typewriter and took it from her carefully. The arm slid downward, and I quickly righted it, so it was even. I clutched it to my chest where its solid mass felt like a part of me. I peeked inside the box, and a thick pile of onionskin paper and a wound ribbon of ink sat inside. They were new and fresh.

"Thank you. I'll have to start now. It's June already."

Mrs. Ashby stood up from the table and cupped her hand under my chin. She raised my head to meet her merry eyes. "I'll accept your thanks when I climb back on the train in Macon County and head home to Gideon with an empty seat next to me. Yes?" She looked down at her wrinkled dress. "I better have Annie iron a few dresses too, don't you think?" She stopped next to me and put her hand on top of mine. "I am so proud of you."

"Mrs. Ashby, your plan? I don't want you to do it." I put my hand on the typewriter to keep it safe and scrambled around the table to reach the door before she stepped out. "Lady Macbeth didn't survive. It ate her up inside. You don't have to be her. We can do this without that happening."

Again, she pressed her small hand to my face. The space I used to try so hard to keep between us shrank to nothing. Her holding me as a baby on the night I was born slammed into me. "Yes, but we know this will work.

Why wonder? Why wait?" She smiled over her shoulder. "Besides, I think it will be fun. If only my mother knew." She waved her hand over her head. "Those dahlias need watering, and they must be staked today. Bye, Socrates. See you in a few minutes."

No one asked me what I was going to do to save the farm, but after listening to Mama's story about the Four, I knew what I needed to do.

Chapter Ten

I started out in the dark the next morning. I didn't know how long it would take me to walk, and I wanted to get there before sunrise. I walked several miles along the dirt roads where all I could make out were the dark cotton fields on both sides. I kept going through Gideon, where the storefronts were still shuttered from the night before. I was frightened some of the store doors would open and the white store owners would look at me with staring eyes, trying to figure out why a Negro boy was alone and in town before the sun was up. I began to think my idea was a mistake as I left the streets and trudged along the lean edge of the highway. The few cars out that morning roared fast next to me, and my heart jumped in my throat. I knew only two vehicles—the farm truck and Mr. Ashby's going-to-town car—and I had never seen either of them go faster than me running alongside them. The large, heavy cars and the trucks with their formidable grills shook me as they whooshed past. I finally saw the long white building ahead and stopped. I smoothed the collar of my shirt and reached down to brush the dirt off my Sunday shoes.

Part of the sign was obscured with tall, dense bushes, but I could make out the faded words "Home of the Best Biscuit in Jackson County." I ran across the highway and passed the sign with a thudding heart. I bent over and scooted around to the back of the restaurant and flopped to the ground. This had better be the right place. I was dizzy and breathing hard. I now knew what it felt like to be a heavy rock dropped down a well to see how deep it would go. As far as I was concerned, I was still falling. While I wasn't a boy anymore, I wasn't something else yet either. I crept to the edge of the pine trees ringing the back of the restaurant and sat on my bottom. The scraggly weeds sticking up around me were wet with moisture. A garden formed a hedge around the back of the house. Fat tomatoes hung down heavy, slim okra rattled, peppers of all colors pulsed, and victorious beans, peas, and greens climbed up strings tied to branches in the trees.

I chewed my fingernails and cuticles, ripping them with my teeth and spitting the bits into the grass. When blood welled up and spilled across the pale half-moons, I finally stopped. It wouldn't be appropriate to shake hands smeared with blood.

The dew soaked into my pants, and the front of me looked like I had wet myself. Time crept like warming molasses at Thanksgiving when the pumpkins sat next to the stove waiting to cook. Just as the sky began to turn from the gray dawn to the sunrise, the light on the back porch went on, and one by one, more windows lit up with a lemon-yellow glow. Negros, including my family, didn't have electricity at the Ashby farm, and only the icebox and a few lights in the big house had power. Watching the windows glow reminded me that thousands of years ago someone like me felt the same awe when fire erupted into heat and light. It was a comfort, I decided, that something made by man could push aside the darkness.

Shadows began passing across the windows. Doors slammed in the front of the building, and the smell of frying pork and fresh biscuits wafted out the door. My nose quivered, and my stomach turned in tight circles, begging for food. I didn't notice the slow opening of the screen door until I heard its squeaking hinges. A slip of a woman in a simple house dress emerged out of the darkness and into the light. She went to a small shed and opened a door low to the ground.

"Come here piggy, piggy, piggies," she crooned. "Come to Mama Maddie. Breakfast for you all," she said, shaking greens with bacon grease mixed in with broken edges of white, creamy biscuits. Buttery, shiny grits hugged the plate, slid down, and plopped into the pen. My stomach roiled in hunger. Maddie twisted her head in both directions. "Who out here?" Her voice was husky and deep like a preacher at a church wearing down his parishioners to his way of thinking. The pigs snuffled the remains with tiny, happy pig groans. Maddie stood on the porch, her hand on the door. Turning to go inside, she stepped across the threshold, and her arm eased the door shut behind her.

"Wait." I tried to rise from my crouched position. "Wait, Miss Maddie." My legs, asleep so long, gave out from under me and I dropped into a heap at the bottom of the stairs. She peered through the screen and stared at me. I struggled to stand up again, and this time, I stamped my feet against the ground, trying to get the blood moving. Dust clouds from the dirt under the last stair blew up from my footsteps, and Maddie waved them away irritably.

"Who are you? Why you in my yard hiding near my pigs? You gonna steal one? What do you want?"

"A job," I said, "please." I brushed my hands down my arms and shook my legs out. My limbs were on fire. "I'm Annie and William's son, Socrates. Mr. Ashby owes the government money. We need help." I clasped my hands in front of my pants. They were still wet, and I was no longer sure it was from the dew. I was a mess.

"Well, if that isn't the be all," Maddie said. She went back into the restaurant, letting the door slam behind her. "Well, come on now. Get in here," she called from inside.

I scrambled up the steps using my hands and feet, relieved she hadn't thrown me off her property. I tripped on the top step and lunged toward the door. My face smashed against the screen just as she stepped into the light. Only inches apart, our faces appraised one another. Boring into me without blinking was a blue eye and a brown eye exactly like Mr. Ashby's. Maddie's eyes, though, were more terrifying embedded in her face than I had ever seen in his jowly, wrinkled face. She titled her chin up daring me to sputter the words she knew were on my tongue. How do you ask a scary, strong Negro woman if a puny, lackluster white man was her kin?

"Are you the older boy or the younger one?" I tried to answer. "Definitely the younger one. You are coming into your arms and legs but not there yet." I opened the door and stepped inside She pointed to a chair pulled up to small kitchen table just the size for a person to have a cup of coffee and a bite between shifts.

"You need food. You all pale and scared looking. Come on now. Here, sit yourself. You need your stomach filled. I think you might faint." Maddie placed a plate stacked with bacon and eggs in front of me. "Eat," she commanded. "We'll talk afterward."

The kitchen was clean but worn. It looked like it had received too many vigorous scrubbings. All kinds of bowls and platters were stacked neatly on the countertops. The wooden floor buckled in front of the sink like bent slats on a porch swing. I ate, bite after bite, and stared at everything. There was an electric icebox and a giant gas stove pouring heat into the room. I couldn't imagine what the heat must be like at noon.

I studied Maddie. What Mama had said was true. She was small but strong. She grunted when she dragged heavy pots of grits onto the stove and stood on her tiptoes to bring down weightier pans for oatmeal. I almost offered help, but when I saw her determined face reflected in the shiny metal, I stayed silent. Maddie's black hair was lined with silver. She wore it as Mama said she had as a child, woven into braids. Now, all grown up, she wound the braids around her head and held them in place with some queer-looking combs that held her hair tight. Some of them had wiggled loose, and her hair bounced like tiny springs. Mamma had left one part out: Maddie was the lightest Negro I had ever met.

Unlike my mama, who'd been experimenting with Mrs. Ashby's rogue and eyeshadow, Maddie's face was clean-scrubbed and free from womanly additions. Her skin was a tawny brown like the color of frozen winter wheat that grew in the pasture as a cover crop. Her steps were determined and followed a path worn into the floorboards for a long time. Maddie's most prominent feature were her eyes. They were large, and shaped like ovals in her small face, and when she turned to address me, I got

lost in their color and the story they held. She was a beautiful woman, but she was missing what my mother had
amply—life. Maddie was brittle, and that made me sad.

Maddie's white-aproned employees entered the
kitchen one at a time and flipped pancakes, turned
bacon and pork chops on the stove, took steaming plates
out the swinging doors, and washed dishes in clouds of
soap. Young men entered the back door, carrying bags of
flour from the shed. They dropped the bags on the floor
next to a workbench tucked in a small area under a staircase. When the dishes were brought back from the
tables, piles of scraps were taken out to the pigs and
dumped into the pen. Old dish water was tossed on the
closest greens by the back door, and young girls filled
buckets of hot water and a bit of ammonia and scrubbed
the tables in the dining room. Although the mixture
made my eyes water, all the windows were open to the
dusty parking lot, and a cool breeze streamed across the
tables.

"Where is Ned?" Maddie threw open the door to the
dining room and looked in the corners. "Where is that
boy? There ain't any biscuits. Maddie's Restaurant is not
going to run out of biscuits." Maddie jerked the broom
closet open and shouted, "Ned, you better give your heart
to Jesus, 'cause your butt is mine." I saw a tall boy about
Walker's age try to sneak behind her to go out the door.
Backing up, Maddie pinned him to the wall and pointed a
floured finger between his eyes. "Where were you?" she
uttered in a death whisper.

"I ain't doing it no more, lady. You're a dragon lady,
always yelling, always pinching. Too tough, too tough," he
mimicked. "Don't want to work for you no more." He
looked like a ghost; he was covered in flour, and his hands

were webbed like frog feet with biscuit dough wedged in tight and sticky.

He pulled away from her grip, tore his apron off, and careened out the back door. "Biscuits. Biscuits. Always about biscuits." His shouts faded as he strode away down the dirt road. Maddie and her crew stood on the porch their aprons, making a white wall that fluttered in the slight wind. They watched as Ned bent over and shook his floured head, working his fingers through his hair.

"Dummy," Maddie said. The group around Maddie almost dwarfed her small frame from view. They giggled. Ned had forgotten the sticky biscuit dough in his fingers. Even at a distance, he looked like a bristling old porcupine that'd lost half its quills. "Well, that's done," Maddie said with satisfaction. She pulled me from behind the table. "This here is Socrates. He's our new biscuit boy." The group looked at me and returned to their jobs. "Get all back to work you people, or you're next." Maddie started to laugh, a big earthquake laugh that rumbled up from her stomach and erupted from her lips.

"Socrates, get up. It's time to work." She turned on the water in the big sink. "Come here." Impatient, she grabbed my arm. "Annie and William's boy. I never thought I'd see this." A smile darted across her face, and she stole a look at me. The blue eye flashed with excitement, and the brown eye sparkled with pleasure.

"Here got to be clean. Put this on," she instructed, dropping a bleached white apron over my head. "To you and everyone, I'm Maddie. Nothing else, just Maddie." She tested the streaming hot water. "You're gonna make biscuits. My place is famous for its biscuits. I only want one boy working the flour. Girls want to make changes. Boys follow the rules after they be trained up right. Girls think they can outdo the boys with jobs." Maddie pursed her lips together. "It's true. Girls pretty much can," she acknowledged. "But I always want a biscuit boy."

"Yes, Maddie." I shrunk into my apron when I saw my reflection in the giant soup pots. Even with knowing Maddie was one of the four children who had played together on the Ashby farm, I was afraid I would not meet her expectations. I didn't want to show up back at the farm with biscuit dough stuck in my hair.

Maddie tapped my cheek with her calloused hand. "Yeah, you may live at the Ashbys' place, but you work here now. Understand?"

"Yes, ma'am," I said, awed.

"Yes, Maddie," she corrected. "I'll pay you a dollar a day, and you work from five a.m. to one p.m., and another crew takes up for lunch. That's it boy, right?" I nodded. "All right, stick your hands in that sink and scrub your arms in hot water and soap. Don't take them out until they are burning. Git going, now."

I scrubbed and scrubbed, wincing as she turned up the hot water. My skin was on fire, and I had tears in my eyes by the time she turned the water off and handed me towel.

"See how soft your hands are now? Got rid of all that old, dead skin. Every day, you wash like that, understand?"

"Yes...Maddie."

She turned and stared down the others who were snickering at my bright-red, angry arms. "Get to work. I don't want anyone even guessing that Maddie not making all their food. I be done with this boy in a few minutes." She turned her attention back to me.

"Look straight ahead. What do those signs say?"

"Flour eight cups, baking soda one teaspoon..." The tin canisters were lined up on the shelf in front of me.

"Hurry up." Her hands were on her skinny hips, and her hip bones jutted out painfully from between her fingers.

"Baking powder sixteen teaspoons, salt three teaspoons," I finished.

"What about the sign next to the salt?"

"Butter half cup, lard half cup, and four cups butter-milk cold." I stopped looking for more signs.

"You're done. Good." She put her hands on each side of my face. Her fingers felt race horse strong. "Socrates, you are going to make biscuits now. No other food matters as much as biscuits, got it?" When she said my name, a shiver of pleasure flew up my back.

"Yes, Maddie."

She went to work talking all the time, her arms and hands moving without stopping. "There's always two bowls, Socrates. Dirty and cold. You finish with a dirty bowl, clean it, and put it in the icebox. When you done, you pull out the cold bowl and start again." She turned behind her to open up the icebox and I pulled back to stay out of her way. "This be the cold bowl. This be a sifter. It goes on top of the cold bowl. Now, these you use." She held up a battered cup, teaspoon, and half-cup measurer.

"Yes."

"These the only ones you ever use to measure biscuit mixings. Do you understand? Her eyes challenged me.

"Yes, Maddie." I swallowed hard.

"They part of every biscuit ever made at Maddie's." She guided my hands. I stood on my tiptoes and scooped my first cup of flour. It was cool and light on my skin. "Count." Silently, I counted eight cups and shook the flour through the sifter. "What's next?" I sifted the baking soda, baking powder, and the salt. I stirred the dry ingredients gently with the teaspoon.

Maddie nodded her head pleased. "Make a hole now," she instructed. I looked at her confused. "Right in the middle of the flour. That's called your well, now." She showed me how to measure out the lard and the butter. "Now, you have to work fast. Use your fingers. Tickle the flour and the butter and the lard together."

She looked down at me fiercely. I turned red with a dusting of white. I looked down and tickled my fingers as fast as I could go. Within minutes, the bowl looked like it was full of tiny new peas just shucked from the garden. I went to rub my hands on my apron, and Maddie said, "Not yet, Socrates. You're only half there." She poured the buttermilk for me, and tipped her head, saying, "It's all you now. Show me you're the biscuit boy."

I looked at the bowl. I remembered one day years back when I couldn't have been more than four or five. Mrs. Ashby must have been on a visit up north. I found myself at the creek and slid my fingers into the mud on the bank. Thinking of that blissful day, I put my hands into the dough and closed my eyes. I let it slide though my fingers. I made small little balls that I pushed together. My hand continued skimming the sides of the bowl feeling for any last liquid. When I opened my eyes, I held a ball of dough. The sides flaked just a bit. It was a solid mass, but it had some give to it, some air, some life.

Maddie held it up inspecting it from all sides. "Hmm," she sniffed. "Look like you been taught well."

I spent the rest of the day making dough. Maddie didn't believe in rolling pins, so I laid the dough out turning it in endless circles, moving my fingertips from the center to the edge. I cut the biscuits and put them in a hot oven. By the end of the day, I had made twenty dozen biscuits. I was dog tired. My legs hurt from standing, and my arms stung from the hot water, but I felt like a man. It only lasted for a moment.

"Hey, hey," I heard the voice that made my shoulders bunch up around my ears. Trask was standing at the doorway to the kitchen. Maddie took one look at me and took a giant step to stand between me and him. With the half door open between the kitchen and the dining room but the bottom door shut tight, there was nothing he could do but hiss. "Who do you think you are? That boy is from the Ashby farm." Trask tried to grab me. "What are you doing here? Why aren't you studying? This isn't right. It's cheating on Carr's contract with Ashby."

"I don't know you, but I know this boy's name is Socrates, and he works for me. He's my biscuit boy." Her head began to shake alarmingly as she talked, and the rows of black braids tucked in with combs on her head wobbled like a trembling dog crouched over a patch of nettles.

"No, we agreed he would study, and Claire—I mean Mrs. Ashby—would pay his rent." He came close enough to pinch the skin on my elbow. "Mr. Ashby's not paying Walker's rent, and your daddy's having to pick to make up for him. You are taking advantage of her." Trask made to grab me around the side of Maddie, but she moved smoothly to pin his bony arm against the doorway.

"Does Timothy know William is working as a picker?" Maddie's voice had changed. It was both soft and hard at the same time.

"Oh, dammit. You skinny old horse, get out of my way. I'm taking him back to the farm, and we're going to sort this out." Trask lunged for me again, and there was a sudden scraping of chairs and shuffling of feet. I peeped around Maddie's tiny waist to see a restaurant full of Negro folks standing at their tables and booths. They were men and women wearing that worn look of working for white people nicer than Trask, but still difficult all the same. No one held a fork or a spoon, but there were some tough-looking stares streaming straight for my nemesis. The big front door slid open with a creak.

"Mr. Trask?" I squeezed my eyes shut when I heard Mr. Ashby calling the name of the Federal Farm Bureau agent currently living in my classroom. "I send you in here for some biscuits, and you are arguing again? We have an appointment at the bank. Get the biscuits…"

His words failed as he saw me standing next to Maddie. She seemed to shrink inside herself, and suddenly, there was room for me next to her, curved to her hip. I was covered in flour, but even so, I saw the man whose face was as familiar to me as my own daddy's.

"Hey, Mr. Ashby," I mumbled.

"Socrates." He pulled his wet cigar out of his mouth so it wouldn't fall out. "What are you doing here?"

"He's my biscuit boy." Maddie's voice was low but rumbled like a train from far off but still knows where it is going. I looked at Maddie, who had stepped forward to stand directly in front of Mr. Ashby.

"Timothy," she said with a tone that said, *I'm warning you*. They stood face-to-face, and as I looked from one to the other, I felt a scary beat from my stomach kick up and rattle my insides. Mr. Ashby put his cigar back in his mouth. They knew each other. They knew each other like people who'd known each other for a long time.

"Well, Maddie, congratulations. You've got yourself a

good one there. He's a nice boy." Mr. Ashby pulled his hat low over his eyebrows so his eyes, a match for Maddie's, were hidden under the shadow of the brim. "William and Annie?" It was a question that had words missing in some places.

"Not now, Timothy. Not time."

"See you for biscuits later this week then. Biscuits better be good." He gave me a pat on the shoulder with his limp gray hand. Then he walked out of the restaurant, waving at the standing Negros whose lunches had long gone cold.

Trask reached over one more time to grab me. As he lunged, the sound of ripping fabric pierced the air. He froze as the breeze from the windows fanned the fabric that should have been covering his backside flap forward. He reached back and tried to pull the sides together, but the seam continued to slide open down his legs like a zipper coming free on its own volition.

Mama, I thought. She knew Trask did not wear underwear.

Trask backed slowly out the door, trying to cover his dirty legs and bare butt with the fabric disintegrating with every step. As the door slammed behind him, a thunder of laughter came over the restaurant patrons. They laughed until tears ran from their eyes and salted the biscuits on their plates.

"Go hang up your apron for the day, Socrates. You've worked long enough." Maddie handed me a bulging bag of biscuits as I tripped down the back stairs. "You know, Socrates, your folks don't know Timothy and I are on speaking terms. Maybe it should stay that way for a while? I don't know where we all stand. Keep your mouth shut, would you?"

I nodded. She turned and put the cold bowl in the refrigerator while she reached for the flour to start the next dozen biscuits.

By the time I moved on several months later, I made enough biscuits, one after another, to crisscross all of Alabama's old dirt roads. I had a lot of time to think as I stared at those signs. Flour must be what God gave us to make a life. Soda and powder seem to give us the start, the reason to live. Lard, or as Maddie called it, the ends of all the ends, hold us together while butter makes it sweet. But it's nothing without salt. Love isn't love, happiness isn't happiness, nothing is nothing without salt. We can't really taste until we are ready for it to come to us.

Chapter Eleven

The plan was working. Over a month had passed since we had all taken up our roles in the drama to save the Ashby farm. The pickers were on their third pick of the season, and each one seemed larger than the one before it, which was impossible, Daddy said, but if God was lending a hand, he wasn't going to argue. The trailer was always in motion as huge bags of cotton stood on the side of the field ready to be loaded. One night early on, Daddy came in a changed man. There was a lift to his step that'd been gone a long time.

"It's a good crop, Annie. They're listening."

"Who?"

"The pickers. I think the settle will be in their favor. Trask, the debt, I'm not sure."

Mama poured him a glass of water. "What happened today?"

Walker and I exchanged looks.

"Well, Trask asked me why they weren't buying their staples at the commissary, and I told him the pickers didn't eat as much in the summer because their blood runs too thick from picking. He didn't believe me at first, but then he grabbed my bag and started down the row. He ruined the bushes for another pick because he was yanking so hard on the bolls, but he talked all the way to the end. He kept saying it wasn't that hard to pick cotton until his hand was all cut up and bloody."

"Ahh!" Mama crowed. "He didn't tell me how it happened, but don't worry. I took care of it."

"Mama, what did you do to him?" I despaired.

"Socrates?" She looked at me as if I had injured her. "I just told him to keep pouring that medicine bleach Mrs. Ashby brought from her doctor on the wound and make sure it didn't foam up. Foam was a sure sign of blood poisoning, you know, I told him. He came back to me six times until I finally told him the foam wasn't all that bad. I bandaged it and told him to pull on the wound every now to make sure the blood brought the poison out."

I closed my eyes and tipped my head back.

"No, no, no," I said, pointing at each one of them in turn. "This has to go bit by bit. Remember: we want to Trask to stay here with us. We want him thinking we care about him."

Walker and Mama looked glumly at one another, but I could see it in their eyes. They could smell blood. I'd have to keep my thumb on them to hold them back.

"What about Mr. Ashby?" I asked.

Daddy ran his hand over his face. "I'm thinking Walker needs to put more pressure on him."

"I did." Walker balanced on the back legs of his chair. Mama whacked the back of his head, and the front legs crashed down. "Ouch, Mama." He frowned, drawing his eyebrows together till they looked like a fat, furry caterpillar crossing his face. "We've already put ten holes in his bedroom walls trying to find the kitchen, which, by the way, I have been smart enough not to tell him it is right underneath the floor no matter how many walls he hammers holes into."

"Walker," Mama cried. "That's where the mess is coming from. I'd like to think the ceiling is coming down."

My brother closed his eyes and tried not to bust out yelling. "Then we drive to town, and he has to look at every pipe. He buys one of all of them. He put some in the back seat today and almost took out a car's window by backing up, so now he's having them delivered tomorrow. I don't know how much more I can take. He talks all the time, and his cigar drips everywhere. It makes me want to puke."

"Sorry, Daddy, but he says you'll be helping him install them." Walker grabbed for a biscuit I brought home.

"Son, I won't be alone. You'll be helping too." Daddy moved to stand next to Walker's chair. Walker was forced to look up at him.

"No, I won't. I've got a game."

"Where's your rent money, Walker?" Mamma interrupted.

"I'll have it for you later." Walker stuffed another biscuit in his mouth and shut up.

"That's not a good enough answer. Your mama and I are working extra jobs to pay your rent. You will pay us ten dollars next Friday. No arguing." I heard a door creaking shut in my daddy's thinking.

"I'm getting Mr. Ashby to help me with a scout. I told him there was no one else in the county smart enough to find a scout. I told him he had connections." Walker tipped back on his chair again and then dropped to the floor when he saw Mama's look. "I suggested going to

Birmingham. Those Barons are a good team." An unhurried grin spread over Walker's face. "Besides, between punching holes in the wall and Mrs. Ashby leaving the light on for him, he is as happy as a pig in a poke. A scout coming to see me would just top it all off."

Mrs. Ashby is pulling her weight—yes, sir, she is," Mama said. "You know that. She does keep the porch light on for him. She's waiting up." Mama scratched her head with her fingernails wondering why a woman needed to light a path to the house where her husband had lived almost forty years already.

"She's working hard. She's a fine-looking woman now," Daddy commented. Mama jumped out of her reverie. A plate flew across the kitchen and missed Daddy's head by inches. Walker and I dashed out the door before it even opened fully. I didn't look back. Mama meant business. It was one thing for all of us to be joking about Mrs. Ashby's allure, but Daddy not only crossed the line—he vaulted it. Toe tapping, finger trembling, cheek twitching, poor Daddy, he'd have to put up with a bit of finger pointing until Mama ran out of words or breath, whatever came first.

After our family meeting, Mrs. Ashby set to work on her latest project: herself. She had Mama wash and cut her hair. I dropped my book when I saw her shiny hair swing in the sunlight like I remembered from my childhood. It was cut short in the fashion of the day and lay flat on the sides of her cheeks, and her bangs were cut in a straight line across her forehead. I was uncomfortable with the dresses she wore that exposed a bosom that appeared larger than I would have thought, her little girl chest suddenly blooming into breasts that made me turn pink. She was cheerful in her new role, and when she turned to wave at me, her blood-red lipstick slashed unevenly across her lips. I made a mental note to tell Mama a tutorial was in order as she too had taken to experimenting with Mrs. Ashby's cosmetics.

I watched Mrs. Ashby that first day, and every day since, sidle up to Trask and pop open a shade parasol over her head. She'd lay a gloved hand on his wrist and ask for a tour of the farm, a visit to the horses, or a walk down to the slow-moving creek that encouraged soft talk. Trask, blushing and tripping over his new too-long pants, walked her around the farm, giving her the numbers he had counted in the barn, the commissary, the fields, and the picker shacks. While Mrs. Ashby kept him busy, Daddy managed the pickers, picking a row at time with a new mama, or an elderly, bent over man. He weighed and loaded bags for the cotton gin, tightened the tarp down, and drove the trailer down the road to the cotton gin. He was busier than a one-armed paper hanger.

My family was having the time of their lives tugging the strings of their puppets, but I was worried. Moths too thought they were invincible until they were entranced by the flame. I worried most about Mrs. Ashby. She was burning the candle at both ends, and the wear was showing on her. When Mr. Ashby set out to town in the morning, looking for the lost supplies that he swore were piled up on the side of the house, he was unaware that Mrs. Ashby and Daddy returned them once a week to get credit to buy the groceries. Old Timothy Ashby did not know he was putting food on the table of every picker on the farm. On the days he disappeared, looking for a scout from the Negro Baseball League, Mrs. Ashby set her sights on Trask. When Trask left for town after supper, she turned to Mr. Ashby and gave him the kind of attention he had never received in years of marriage. She sat next to him on the swing and put her feet in his lap and asked him to read to her. She told him she loved the sound of his voice.

For myself, I walked in my sleep in the morning and dragged my tired body home in the afternoon. The five-mile journey and six hours of standing on my feet using my fingers to make tiny little white balls of biscuit dough was only part of my day. After the first couple of days of grilling me about my whereabouts each morning, they stopped asking. I wondered if my flour-covered clothes gave them an idea, but maybe it wasn't just Maddie who wasn't ready to ready to heal the rift between them. I kept my promise to come home each afternoon to read my school books and work on my essays, but as soon as I stepped away from my writing table on our porch, Mrs. Ashby was knocking on our back door, carrying brown-paper-wrapped, narrow packages full of tightly packed colorful parasols. It was a blazing, hot summer, and she worried her dahlias were struggling in the cruel sun. The blooms were late coming, so, after walking one day with Trask, she realized that the relief her parasol gave her from the sun could be used for her flowers as well. She selected the parasols from a mail-order catalogue, and when they arrived, she instructed me to string them above the dahlias by looping the wire through the ribs so the fanciful shades would hang above the flowers. The line of simpering colors, polka dots, swirls, and stripes grew each day until there were forty parasols snapped open and swinging around the wires shading the flowers below.

One day in the high heat of the late afternoon, I snuck away. It was the dog days of summer where no self-respecting dog would be working. I strode past the nodding dahlias, the dancing parasols, the pickers in the field, and Mrs. Ashby napping on the wooden swing without acknowledging any of them.

I needed to walk off my worries, so I decided to go to the Patch. I had not been inside its sanctuary since my accident, and I yearned for its quiet, aloneness, and cool water. I crawled on my hands and knees through the tunnel Walker and I had made. It was mostly grown over again, and my hands and arms grew bloody and burned from insect bites. Once I exited the brush, though, the Patch waited for me. I sat on the edge of the watering hole and dropped my legs into the water. I waited until my heart slowed.

My mama and daddy were the swaying-on-their-feet, hands-held-palms-up, eyes-closed-believing kind of worshippers. I took a bigger view. I knew that it took science more than seven days to make the world, but I also believed some powerful fingers had set it in motion. I respected my parents' principles, and to some degree, made them my own as well. Our pastor, despite his strong beliefs, was more pragmatic than most. If he knew a widow needed help, he'd look in the offering basket and announce no one was leaving until three more dimes made their way forward. He'd walk to each picker shack to shout a hello if the family had been gone more than two weeks. He had ten farms to cover, so he had a lot of night walking. It was his pragmatism and principles that made its way to our back stoop one evening.

"I'm not saying what you're doing is wrong, but the others who've noticed it are the ones talking." He waved away a sweating glass of tea from Mama. "Joseph Sutter Senior and a few others are saying that you helping pick a row or two is taking away from the final settle where real pickers are depending on the result. All I can say, William, is do what's on your heart. It'll tell you what's right from wrong." He'd slipped away in the darkness, and I saw my mama and daddy on their knees on the side of their bed praying on what to do.

I prayed for forgiveness and help. Our plan had grown beyond its primary intent and become a monster feeding off its triumphs. We originally agreed to create chaos for the sole purpose of bringing back an order that would save the farm. We, mainly me, had chosen to shove God's hand away. What we did not realize was it made us believe we were gods ourselves.

Walker was lying to Mr. Ashby. He knew, with each day that passed, the man who believed in him more than anyone was making a fool of himself knocking holes in the walls all over the house and installing pipes to talk to people who didn't want to listen to him.

Daddy, my daddy, was lying to trusting people who did not know when they were being used. Mama? I swallowed hard. My mama was slowly killing Trask by doctoring his food, altering his clothing, and expressing care and concern for him. Truth be told, he was more alone now than he had been when he arrived. He thought we cared.

Mrs. Ashby? I splashed some water on my face and thought about letting myself sink as far as the water would let me. She had become something I never would have thought she could be. Her smile was wrong, she spoke like a Southern woman with untoward intentions, and she held her body in a way that made me wonder where her head and heart had gone.

The worst of it, until the pastor's nighttime talk, was that we had forgotten the ones who were innocent and helpless, the pickers. All it would take was an unexpected downpour to cause the cotton bolls to swell up and fall off the bushes, or a dust windstorm that left the cotton on the plant brown and useless, or a drove of wild pigs that turned the field into a wallow. If any of those acts of God happened, the pickers were done. They would owe Mr. Ashby for life.

The Patch had owned me since the day of my decision to jump headfirst into a pile of rocks hidden by treacherous, dark water. Much of the unraveling of our lives had happened because of, and since, my accident. It was like we were blind, naked moles who'd never seen the shine of light into our nighttime existence until now. Clearly, the light was false; I did not know if I agreed with Mrs. Ashby that the end will justify the means.

A rasping squawk came from the bushes and caused me to jerk and come close to falling in. It sounded like a bird scolding me. It squawked again three times. I stood up and hopped on my tender feet to the bushes. I rattled the branches, trying to scare it away. A thundering squawk burst from the branches above my head. I grabbed a thorny stick and hit the general area of the bird's accusing voice. I heard a ruffle of feathers that settled back into place. It was a pleased sound, as if he owned the perch and I was the intruder.

"Mockingbird," I growled seeing him through the leaves. He stood with his legs curved around the branch and didn't sidle away. He was gray with a creamy-white chest, and one thing was for sure: he did not like me.

He thrust his narrow head and long yellow beak at me. "Squawk," he screamed.

"Mockingbird, who are you now?" I backed away and put my clothes on. The sound of his squawks continued accusing me. I thought about all the birds the mocking-bird could imitate. I couldn't place this one. It took a minute. I couldn't place it because he was singing his own song. I made for home. Even a mockingbird tells the truth when forced to. Sunset was coming, and the song I was singing was not my own.

"SOCRATES," DADDY SAID AS I LAY IN MY BED.

"Yes, sir." My dry eyes bored holes in the ceiling above my head.

"I won't be picking with Miss Cora and Brutus and the likes anymore. Just wanted you to know. Night now."

"Night, Daddy."

I cried, thinking that I was the one who caused Mama and Daddy to search their consciences, but it wasn't until I smelled Trask passing by our house, all alone, looking up at the Ashby's window that blinked off, that I realized the worst of it—I had set in motion a world where a man had likely come undone and could not bind himself back together.

Chapter Twelve

"You look like a specter, all glowing white, in that sun going down." Mama used her fingers to brush some lingering flour from the hair over my ears. "Socrates, don't argue now." I cocked my head at her as she patted my shoulder and gripped me in her large hand. "I found him, Mrs. Ashby. He was out back," she called.

"Socrates, come here, please." I heard Ashby clear her throat around the corner of the big house as Mama marched me down the steps and gave me a little push toward the calla lilies. Mrs. Ashby stood with her garden clippers in her hand. The long, bloodred petals of the stiff tubers were sagging all along the tall stalks. They were about to meet their maker.

"Speak of the devil and he shall appear," my old granny used to say. I waited for the scent of Trask to ooze from his pores in a new and eye-watering version, my nostrils beginning to tremble like those of a rabbit. But he stood there, silent and scentless.

I dug my toe into the dead grass. "Socrates, stand up straight," Mrs. Ashby ordered. My eyes widened at the impatience in her voice. "I realize the sun will set soon, but I'd like you to take Mr. Trask to Miss Cora and Brutus's house. It's a little hard to find, and I want you to help him. Do we understand each other?"

"Yes, ma'am. I'll take him there." I hoped the long shadows from the house hid my lips all pursed up like I was sucking on a lemon.

Mrs. Ashby and Trask had a serious going around after he revealed to her that I was making biscuits for Maddie in the morning and, in his thinking, was taking advantage of her offer to pay my rent so I could commit all my time to studying for my exams and preparing for school.

"Is that true, Socrates?" she asked, tossing her bangs out of her eyes. We stood in the household garden together. She watched me search for green beans for dinner.

"Yes, Mrs. Ashby, but it's not for the money. I was not trying to deceive you. I'm trying to help my parents with their expenses."

"And? What else?"

"I can't tell you. You would be disappointed in someone," I said, thinking of Mr. Ashby.

"Well, I am disappointed in you." She yanked a vine instead of a bean, and the whole plant came out of the ground. "Darn it," she said, stepping carefully out of the bed. She was wearing a long, loose-fitting house dress that must have been heavy in the stifling heat of late afternoon. Her statement stung. She had never spoken anything but encouraging words to me my whole childhood. "You have no idea how hard I had to work to secure the opportunity for you to submit the essays."

So she agreed with Trask and rescinded the arrangement to pay for my rent. I now paid my parents ten dollars on the second Friday of the month. Walker was still late on his payments, and I quietly wondered if spending so much time with Mr. Ashby impacted his indifference toward money. Walker was the only one in our family who knew how to select a cola from the automatic machine in town, and Mama and Daddy flat out said it wasn't a talent to be proud of.

Ironically, there was an agreeable outcome to Mrs. Ashby agreeing with Trask. He felt heard and vindicated. It was as if now that Mrs. Ashby recognized I could exist outside the parameters of the farm, I had earned some measure of respect from him for having a job. He and Mama still had their go arounds with him stamping around ordering my mama to make him lunch and wash his clothes, but he had ceased threatening me bodily harm. We had reached a truce of sorts, you'd call it.

We started off walking down the farm road toward Middle Field. I shuffled my feet in the dust, and it drifted toward him coating his pants.

"Knock it off."

"Sorry," I muttered. "Why aren't you going to their house during the day?"

"Quicker at night. Old people talk too much in the day. They worry."

"They should worry, shouldn't they?" I protested. "You can take their things, can't you?"

"No, I don't take their things. A picker is not going to have anything of value like Mr. Ashby's horses or his car." Trask took his hat off and fanned his face. "Who are Cora and Brutus?"

"They are the oldest people on the farm. Brutus was a

picker, but he has the shakes now and can't get around. Miss Cora is a baby catcher," I said.

"What the hell is a baby catcher?"

"A birther. Helps the labor, pulls the babies out, stitches the women up." I walked ahead of him tilting my head on my neck to match my light footsteps.

"How old are they?"

"They remember the first generation of Ashbys, so probably in their eighties. Their kin came right with my mama's family, so they were a step up from regular pickers. They had status."

"They're a liability."

"What do you mean?" I turned and walked backward, facing Trask.

"Help light this, would you?" We'd passed Middle Field and were on a spur road leading toward the pine forest. Trask held the lamp up high while I struck the match and adjusted the flame. "They don't bring any value to the farm," Trask said. The light from the lamp kept ahead of our footsteps pushing the shadows out of our way. "If they aren't working, they're staying in a shack another picker family could be using."

I countered. "Some women still want Cora there at their time even though she's old. She uses herbs instead of medicine. She says giving women gas while they are in labor puts them in danger." Trask nodded, head down, listening. "She's not a liability, Trask." I caught myself. "I'm sorry. *Mr. Trask*. You can't put a price on a skill. She caught all of us when we were born, even Mr. Ashby."

"So what do I tell someone at the bureau is the monetary value she brings to the farm?" Trask's voice toward me had changed. It was cautious, without motive. We were having a conversation.

"She wouldn't dream of asking for money," I shuddered. "She's like Mama that way, except Mama's most known for her opinions, of course." Trask made a strangled sound in his throat. "I mean, you know Mama believes God handpicked her to run our corner of Alabama, but Miss Cora is different. Being a baby catcher is a calling, a gift. People thank her with bags of potatoes, or chickens they've already plucked, or a load of firewood." I paused. "They do things for her too. Work in her garden, get her house ready for winter. On a farm, you need people like Miss Cora and Brutus. Taking care of them makes us better people." We walked side by side. I offered my hand to carry the lamp.

"No, I got it. You're still a kid." Trask shook his head in frustration. "Socrates, you talk sometimes more than book talk. I don't know the right words to call it, but it's like idea talk. You...you...you..." He struggled. "You say something like 'makes us better people,' and it gives words to what people do but don't know they do it for a reason."

"Thank you, I think."

Embarrassed, Trask swung the lamp in larger circles. "Don't think too much about it."

I pointed ahead of us at a small cabin tucked into the edge of the pine forest. It was dusk, the sun had dropped below the horizon, and I could see the coming light of the moon in the east. Miss Cora was sitting on the porch smoking a pipe that sent tendrils of smoke into the navy-colored sky.

"Who's there?" she called out. Miss Cora struggled to see since the blue clouds had taken over her eyes, a fact I had neglected to inform Trask about. My omission had been intentional in the beginning, but now a cold hand crept over my chest, and I felt young and stupid, the same place I was in just a half hour before when Mrs. Ashby had spoken sharply to me.

Miss Cora leaned forward into a pattern of light and dark from an oil lamp shining from between the weathered boards of her home. I could see the outline of Brutus lying in a chair in the flickering glow.

"It's Socrates, Miss Cora. I'm here with Mr. Trask, the bank man." I cleared my throat, and it dipped a bit like a man's voice. I slowed to a reluctant creep and stopped.

"Why does everyone call me the bank man?" Trask growled. "I'm with the government."

"Pickers don't know what the government is, but they know the bank is where their cotton money stops before it comes to the farm," I whispered.

"Don't make an old woman wait, Socrates. Bring that man here." She stood up in the shadows and turned her head a little to the side to try to see us. She told Mama there was just a little sliver of sight left. Trask coughed into his hand a few times, trying to clear his voice.

"Good evening, Miss Cora, I am..."

"I know who you are. Get on up here. Brutus will be in the house with you. I'll stay in the yard with the boy. I need work done."

"Yes, I won't be but a few minutes." Trask was as nervous as a long-tailed cat in a roomful of rocking chairs.

"Come here, Socrates Bravo." Miss Cora summoned me. Her hair was sparse and furry- looking in patches. Her arthritic fingers crossed one another, frozen in place after years of stretching beyond reason to discover small skulls that needed help finding the light.

Trask opened the screen door and ducked his head as he entered. "I'll just need to see the house; I'll show myself around." The light bounced with Brutus's nod.

"How's your mama? I haven't talked to her in a while."

"She's fine, Miss Cora. Mrs. Ashby's needed extra care these days."

"That's what I've heard." Miss Cora said. "Socrates, come closer. Here, help me with my plants." She reached for my hands. Pulling them toward her, I blinked my eyes shut and felt her skinny, hard fingers squeeze mine. "Feel the ribs of the cabbage leaves." I rooted around until I felt a string of hard, round bugs underneath the stiff, fleshy leaves. I slid them into my palm and brought them out into the dim light from the lantern in the house. The moon was taking its time. "Drop them in the jar." She held out a canning jar of clear kerosene that sloshed in the glass. The bugs sizzled and shrank when I dropped them in. "Hold the jar, son. There will be more."

Miss Cora and I walked through the paths of her garden. The edges were surrounded by pink, yellow, and orange zinnias planted to bring the pollinating bees to help the squash and vine fruits. The corners were planted with sunflowers to bring the songbirds in to eat the hurtful bugs. Miss Cora knew where she was in her garden in two ways: the touch of her fingers on the tops of the plants and the scents they gave off with the rising breeze.

"Pull up some oregano from over here and plant it back by the cabbage. It will need water, Socrates," she instructed. "Hurry, now." I checked the health of herbs, pulled some, moved some, let others go. I was sweating and breathing hard and wondering what was taking Trask so long. The cicadas started in the mimosa trees, and their racket made my head hurt.

"I know you heard your birth story." Miss Cora's eyes glittered like a light blue sky in winter. She held out a tomato hornworm larvae as long and thick as her pinkie finger, and I dropped it into the kerosene jar. The larvae convulsed and went still. "Come work these hornworms with me," she demanded. "They're choking my tomatoes. None of them bugs gone to moths yet." I went to her side and reached past the fat globes of the ruby tomatoes to search for the thick larvae. The tendrils on their feet grabbed my fingers, and I shook them into the jar.

"I don't know how much your mama told you, but I was right upset Mrs. Ashby was there that night. It's not right for a barren woman to stand between a baby catcher and a woman giving birth. It's bad luck. Bad feelings float in the room." She spit on the ground. "A birthing room is a godly place." The moon had finally climbed over the horizon, and I saw Miss Cora clearly. The leathery skin on her lined face was like the rings in the trees' middle.

The cicadas stopped in mid-hum, and a sudden rush of wind blew through our clothes. Miss Cora's apron flew up, and the handful of hornworm larvae she'd nestled in the pocket scattered. Bending, she groaned as she searched the dirt for them, feeling with her fingers and cocking her head sideways as she attempted to see. She picked them up one by one.

"Let me help, Miss Cora." I bent down to her feet and put the jar on the ground. My glasses fell off in the jostling, and I came face-to-face with the full jar of dead bugs and larvae. In the light of the full moon, their lifeless faces stared back at me. I carefully picked the jar up. "Why don't you sit on the porch," I advised. Even though my sight was not as bad as Cora's, it didn't take glasses to see an uncomfortable conversation coming down the road straight at me like a train careening out of control.

"Fine, Socrates. Help me then." I settled her down on

the rocker on the porch. I started to sit next to her, and she grabbed my wrist and pointed back to the garden. More work, Socrates."

"Yes, ma'am." Where the hell was Trask?

"Did you know Mrs. Ashby had lost a baby of her own on that day?"

"No." The air sucked out of me.

"Well, it's not my place..." Cora demurred.

"Please, Miss Cora. Mama didn't tell me that." I yanked a whole tomato plant up and the fruit rained all over the ground. I stuffed the plant, covered with hornworm larvae, into the jar. A slosh of kerosene spilled over the ground, and the vapors filled my nose like a helium balloon. Immediately, I felt dizzy.

"Did you spill the jar, Socrates?"

"No, ma'am." I lied. "The hornworms filled it up. I guess I'll have to stop."

"Well then, sit for a while, and when the bank man is finished, he can help us with the white flies. If they aren't killed early, they take all the juice until the plants fall apart in my hands. Breaks my heart then." She lit up her pipe and started rocking in the silence. The cicadas went silent too.

"That night was bad, I have to tell you, Socrates. Mrs. Ashby stood there and watched. She held a rag under her nose like someone was cleaning out a chicken coop. Mrs. Ashby didn't know about birthing. She never made it past the second or third month. She put her hand on my shoulder, not thinking about the struggle you and your mama were going through."

"What happened?" I understood Miss Cora's irritation. Mrs. Ashby had the bad habit of standing too close to people. She didn't know it made you feel suffocated even though she thought she was showing interest.

"She cried," Miss Cora said. "It was the most pitiful sound I have ever heard. She gave you back to your mama, and she was a broke woman. I've only heard sorrow that deep one other time I my life, and it was from a man."

"Do you think she cried because she lost her baby?"

"She lost something. I don't think even your mama knows."

The screen door creaked open, and I realized Trask had heard Mrs. Ashby's part in my birth story. "What needs to be done to prevent the white flies?" he asked.

I watched the emotion on Miss Cora's face as she listened to the tenor and cadence of Trask's voice and saw the shadow of his leanness in the moonlight. "Never mind, bank man. Take Socrates home. Now that I put my mind to it, those plants are too far gone to save."

Chapter Thirteen

The War between the States was still close enough in the memories of the older generation that they approached the Fourth of July with wariness. Life hadn't changed all that much to believe independence was anything beyond a word. On the nation's birthday, the pickers on the Ashby farm folded their bags on the porches and weighed them down with rocks so they wouldn't blow away. The hoes leaned against the porches of their shacks, and even the working horses snoozed in the pasture.

Negro children and adults stood in a line that snaked around to the back stoop of the big house like characters in a Dickens novel. The pickers held their hands in from of them and accepted their quarters if they were adults or their dimes if they were a child. Babies received kisses on their foreheads and a whispered blessing in their ears. Some curtsied to Mrs. Ashby, but she was so delighted at the attendance of the pickers who lived on their farm, she didn't realize that the line of shuffling pickers were putting on an act of subservience until the quarter was in their hands. They walked out of the farm road then, lit cigarettes, and shoved each other as they imitated Mrs. Ashby.

After I received a quarter—yes, she deemed me an adult due to my entrance to Parson University Preparatory School—a group of young children clutching their dimes followed behind me as I walked with my parents into Gideon. Walker had gone ahead, and my mama sighed. "He's gone already. Not much of him left here."

When I turned and faced the youngsters trailing on my heels, they scattered and then came together once my back was turned again. We stopped when the Ashby car approached us.

Mr. and Mrs. Ashby's car spilled over with red, white, and blue ribbons draped off the doors and the boot. The back seat was crammed full of massive bouquets of dahlias—orange, red, yellow, bronze, and purple flowers that waved out of their stacked milk jars. Mrs. Ashby called my name and waved her arm at me as she passed. She turned to watch me, half standing up in her seat. Against my better judgment, I waved back. She had forgiven me for my decision to work at Maddie's, and she still saw us as co-conspirators striving to save the farm, but the farther she walked out on the tight rope without a net, the more afraid I became. Despite her insinuations as to her intentions to Trask and Mr. Ashby, I refused to see her as Lady Macbeth. Shakespeare's character was ambitious, strong, and willful, but Mrs. Ashby was not cruel or duplicitous. Duplicity, I then realized with a feeling like a cold hand squeezing my heart, was more successful the more impossible it seemed to be.

"Are you going on a train?" I turned and saw Joseph Sutter. He seemed to find me when I felt most far away from myself.

"Yeah, I'll be going to Parson University Preparatory School. I'll go there for two years before I go to college."

"Why?" A little girl about eight years old walked up to me and tried to hold my hand. Flies circled her tightly braided head. Her mother had tightened her hair like knots, and the smell of the young, sweet scalp entwined in the braids brought the insects to the edge of madness.

I shook her hand off. "Where's your parents?" Two other girls joined steps with me. I was now surrounded by the children. I tried walking faster, and they scampered in the dust to keep pace. If I slowed down, they pulled on my arms and touched my clothes. My parents were far ahead, and Mama turned and waved to me with a beaming smile on her face.

"Who told you I was going to boarding school?" They squeezed into the space around me, and one of the boys leaned forward to smell my shirt. His nostrils flared. I stopped in the dust and cleared a space around me with my hands. "Why do you care about my going away to school?"

"Miss Cora told us," one of them piped up. "She says you's special."

"What is boarding school anyway?" Joseph asked. He was chewing on a plug of cork, passing it from cheek to cheek. Biting his lip and leaning forward, he spit it out of his mouth, and it hit me in the middle of my chest. It left a wet mark in the shape of a circle.

I was about to smack him, but I stopped and took a deep breath. He was barefoot, and it was clear there was nothing on under his overalls. There were round, red marks on his arms, some of them scabbed over and others freshly burned into his skin.

"Boarding school is a big school for boys who are

studying to become a teacher or a scientist, or a doctor," I said. "You live there and study all the time. And you like it. You like it a lot."

"Do you have to pick?" one of the girls asked swinging my hand in hers.

"No." I pulled my hand loose and started walking again.

"Are your parents there?"

"No."

"Do you have your own bed?"

"Yes."

"Can you eat?" I stopped and stared at Joseph. His eyes looked hungry like he was a dog chained to a fence post.

"Yes., you can eat. You eat with other people."

"Do they take your food?" He threw his hair sideways to see me.

"No, Joseph. Come here." He didn't move. "Come here. I'm not going to eat you." The others twittered and ran ahead of us. "Hey, Joseph, come on." I motioned to him with my hand. Reluctantly, he caught up with me and we walked side by side. "I work for a restaurant in town. How about I bring you some food sometimes?"

"What kind of food?"

"Biscuits mainly," I conceded. "but maybe some meat. How would that be?"

"Don't come to my house. I'll meet you at your privy. I'll be under that bush there, the one where you can hide, and it smells like flowers mixed with manure?" He reached out a red-spotted arm and touched the buttons running up the front of my shirt. "Sorry about your shirt."

"It's all right."

"Really, you'll give me food?" I nodded my head yes. "I

ain't going to boarding school, though." His eyes were defiant.

"It's up to you. But if you wanted to go to college, you probably could. You just have to study a lot."

"I'm a picker. I'll have my own bag next year. I won't let my daddy take my cotton and put it in his bag anymore. I'll be a picker on my own." He ran ahead, hollering for his friends to wait for him. I slowed my steps, choosing not to catch up to my parents. I wanted to think about Joseph's contention that yearning for your own picking bag, where at the end of the day you can measure your worth to be the person you believe yourself to be, is a road to dignity every bit as important as taking the train to boarding school.

Chapter Fourteen

Firecrackers bounced across the road as I entered town. Packs of Negro children and white children played on both sides of the street, but when the firecrackers jumped the sidewalks and sent smoke near the doorways of the shops, all the children ran to stamp them out. They waited in the street watching for their turn when the little pops of fire exploded in the street.

I tilted my head in a silent hello to a few people I knew from the restaurant's kitchen. Gideon was the original county seat of Jackson County, and that distinction awarded our small community a two-story redbrick courthouse with luminous Greek columns and a soaring turret protected by overlapping copper plates on the roof. Granite steps led to shadowed doors that, at five a.m. when I was running to Maddie's, were always closed. A square in front of courthouse was covered in thick green grass. There were park benches facing the courthouse and, during holidays, Negros in the back and whites in the front, spread blankets on the grass and laid out a picnic.

The courthouse seemed to belong to all of us as long as the unwritten rules were followed.

The realization made me stop. I pulled my shoulders back and raised my head. I looked up and met strangers' eyes and tried to calm my fluttering stomach. I was no longer a child who rarely left the farm. I passed through Gideon every day in the morning dusk and returned in the brisk afternoons. When asked, I directed a man to Gideon's hardware store, which was on the same block as the blacksmith, sawmill, and feed store. He thanked me. I counted off the barbershop, bank, funeral home, church, post office, and general store as I passed them. At some point in the last six weeks, I had changed. Although I made sure to walk on the sidewalk closest to the street in case I had to veer off, I knew the little town. As a young Negro boy, I did not intimidate the townspeople with a deep voice asking for groceries at the general store or possess a tall frame with broad shoulders developed through hard work, but I kept my eyes focused on my steps following the length of the sidewalk.

Back when I was little and frightened of the picker children's cruelty about my name, Walker had warned me, "If you can't run with the big dogs, Socrates, you'll have to stay under the porch, and that is no way to live." I smiled and settled my cap on my head. I may be the runty afterthought, but I was running in the sun along with the others.

A man exited the barber shop, and he looked familiar. There was something about his gait and the way he hitched his pants up.

"Trask. What the hell?" I said under my breath.

I was trying my best to learn how to swear under the

right circumstances. Close to being a man, I was determined to throw a few colorful terms into my speech to
make me seem taller in other's eyes. Walker, seeing my
ineptitude, decided to help me. He called it "swearing for
effect." We talked about it when we were shoveling the
dirty straw out of the horse stalls.

"Did you say effect?" I asked.

"You are not the only one who knows big words, Soc."
He pushed the heap of straw into a pile.

"Okay. What else should I try?" I was using the handle
of the broom to get into the corners.

"'What the hell' is probably best. It makes you sound
grown up, but even women say it, so they can't get mad at
you if you say it." He grunted and shoveled the stinking
hay into the wheelbarrow.

"Okay."

"Soc, take my advice. If you are going to say it, do it for
effect." Walker pushed the wheelbarrow to me and
dropped it so the huge pile of straw and shit steamed next
to my chest. "I gave the advice. You take it out."

"What the hell?" I ducked behind a group of women
fanning themselves in the heat. He looked almost human.
The barber had trimmed his hair, and the scruffy mess on
his neck and under his chin was gone. His port-wine stain
was vivid against the smooth whiteness of the other side
of his face, but with a haircut and a shave, it seemed
contained. He wore a belt to hold his pants up, a long-
sleeved shirt, and shoes that had laces. He walked through
the crowd and politely waited for a gap to cross the street.
He tipped his hat to women and sidestepped children
wrestling in front of him. I could see him scanning the
crowd looking for someone, so I followed him. When he

reached the decorated car contest with all the cars lined up outside the general store, he made his way, sliding sideways through the groups of people clustered around the vehicles festooned with ribbons and hand-lettered signs celebrating the holiday. He scanned the crowd and stepped off the sidewalk to walk in the street to the passenger side of the Ashbys' car where Mrs. Ashby sat fanning herself and blowing her wet bangs off her forehead.

"Oh no," I muttered. "This is a hell of a mess."

I knew without asking that Mrs. Ashby had tried to decorate their car, but the ribbons were falling off in the heat, and the few bouquets of leftover dahlias were losing their petals. Mrs. Ashby rested in the passenger seat with a pale-pink parasol laying on her shoulder, and Mr. Ashby stood with his foot on the running board talking to a small group of men. Trask removed his hat, and a smile crossed his whole face as he reached the side of the car. His curving lips caused the smooth red skin of his blemish to turn upward. Opposed to the last time I saw him up close at Miss Cora's, his teeth looked clean inside his smile.

Mr. Ashby stood in the cluster of Gideon's wealthiest men gesturing with the new cigar he had lit for the special day. White smoke streamed out of his nostrils and floated straight to Mrs. Ashby. She waved her hand in annoyance.

"Mr. Ashby, would you please point that cigar smoke somewhere else?" she asked irritated. Then she added in a sweet voice, "Please, darling?"

When Trask heard her call Mr. Ashby "darling," he bloomed in anger so his whole visage looked like a blood-red full moon. He leaned over to whisper to Mrs. Ashby, and he laid hand on hers.

I watched Mrs. Ashby shake it off and heard her say, "Don't."

A motley group of young boys jumped away from a firecracker at their feet and knocked me off the sidewalk and straight into Trask. He stood up and whirled around.

"What are you doing here?" The cleanup hadn't changed the man underneath, which meant the conversation I shared with the man on the way to Miss Cora's had been an aberration. The old Trask was back. He reached to squeeze my shoulder with his clawlike grip.

"Mr. Trask, don't treat him that way." She motioned to me. "Socrates Bravo, help me out of the car, please." I cut in front of Trask and opened the car door. As I pulled the heavy door open, the fabric of Mrs. Ashby's dress caught on the door handle. The pink shirred lace with the low bosom pulled against her stomach, and I almost lost my balance. I stared at the perfect, small roundness of her belly that looked just like a plump baby melon that had moved recently from flower to fruit. My teacher, my mother's charge, and Mr. Ashby's wife was pregnant. Undeniably pregnant. This one had stuck.

"Socrates, Trask, I'll help my wife. You are done here." Mr. Ashby tamped his cigar out and put it in his pocket. "Darling, would you like to hear the fiddler? He is here today." He offered her his hand to hold in the crowd. He tossed the pink parasol into the back seat.

"Oh, Mr. Ashby, that's not who he is. He's the Violin man." She smoothed her dress and sidestepped both men, ignoring Mr. Ashby's outstretched hand and Trask's silent figure. She pulled me through the crush of people, her hand gripping mine tightly. She stretched back and whispered in my ear, "Only a few people know, Socrates, and I want to keep it that way as long as I can."

"Yes, ma'am." I felt sick. I didn't want to share it with anyone either. *How did I not realize it?* I wondered. It came back to me. There were signs. The stomachaches. The ripening breasts. The loose nightgown in the garden.

Mr. Ashby and Trask pressed against my back trying to reach Mrs. Ashby. I stopped and turned around blocking both from catching up with her. I think she was searching for my mother. Mr. Ashby looked at me thoughtfully, a blatant look of sudden interest, as if I had just then become a real person, someone who just might have some weight to him. Pulling his cigar from his pocket, he strolled away, waving at two men talking together. He glanced back at me. I felt a flutter in my stomach. Mama was right: it was best Mr. Sir didn't see you. Maybe that interest was inherited.

"Scram, kid. Get out of here," Trask snarled in my ear.

I looked at him full on without fear. "Your haircut does wonders for you, but Mrs. Ashby will not acknowledge you in town. You're different from her." It was a cruel thing for me to say. He studied me, and I saw a flicker of doubt in his flat, chestnut-brown eyes.

The throng of Jackson County residents surged toward the courthouse square. Blankets were snapped and settled on the ground. White women and their Negro maids unpacked picnic baskets and laid out fried chicken, vegetables from their gardens, hardboiled eggs from their chickens, and pickles. As soon as everything was laid out, the Negro women faded to the back of the grassy lawn to join their own families. In many cases, their daughters had already laid out picnics identical to the ones of the white families.

I saw my parents and cut across the grass to join them. Mama was fretting. "Why didn't Mr. Ashby get out their picnic? She needs to eat. I better go tell him." She struggled to stand and snapped at us with her fingers to help her up. Daddy and I looked off into the far distance, hoping to dissuade her from stomping through everyone's lunches looking for Mrs. Ashby's picnic basket.

"Mama, I see them. If they look like they want the picnic, I'll go get it for them." I looked up at her trying to catch her eye. I needed her to know that I knew, so she didn't carry the full burden alone. She gave me a brief glance and, seeing my face, turned to look at me full on.

"You know?" I nodded yes. "I am worried about her, Socrates, but we cannot talk about it." She sat back down with a sigh. "William, where is our picnic anyhow?"

From the rubbing of his hands together, I think the Violin man knew the crowd was growing in front of him. Pale white skin gave him a ghostly look, and his thin clothes revealed his stark build. He leaned his back against a mimosa tree. His brown jacket and black pants were patched and worn but clean and showed no sign of wilt despite the heat. His hands hung down past the cuffs, and his wrist bones were skinny and crisscrossed with large tendons honed from his work. His eyes were beautiful. They were the blue of spring lupines blooming all along the roads before the summer dust settles over them. Everyone swore he looked right at them at one time or another as his chin settled into the curve of his instrument, but we were all tricked. The Violin man was totally blind. When he came into town and when he left, he swung a long stick back and forth in front of him, and his little dog, a young mutt with a tongue going sideways, raced next to his feet.

I don't know how he managed to make a living walking the old roads of the South playing for people he couldn't see. Maybe he was ageless, an apparition, and his playing opened the eyes of a Southern town for a single day once a year. Add all those days together and maybe it would be enough to pry open the heart of the South. Maybe we could all see with more than our eyes when he came to town.

"Did I hear the Violin man when I was younger?" I asked Mama while leaning over the picnic cloth and pulling chicken off the bone with my teeth. She flicked her hands vigorously motioning me to sit back and quit hovering over the food.

"You was in my belly the last time I heard him. I was wearing a coat. It was like you pushed it aside. You changed your mind, of course, just like a man, and stopped moving the whole time he played. I thought you were either dead, asleep, or listening real hard." She slapped my arm. "Like to have scared me just like your brother too, but as soon as the Violin man stopped, you got real restless. You kicked against my belly so hard for a moment I held your heel in my hand. Scared me. It was like meeting you before you came out." She met my gaze and her eyes crinkled. "Eat," she ordered.

From the moment he started playing, I remembered. Maybe it wasn't the actual music from over thirteen years ago, but hearing it made me feel different, better, like I could see a long distance without crowded hills blocking my view. There wasn't a place—his arm or neck or fingers —where he and his violin were apart. He couldn't have put it down if he had wanted to. The songs ended and began without a break. The Violin man didn't play the scratchy songs from the Victrola records we sometimes heard from outside the big house's window. He played his own music.

In the morning, his music was lively. The slight man dipped low and pulled up tall with the music soaring high and bright. The notes would fly from the bow as it bounced against the strings. The music leaped and jumped, and I felt pulled forward like I was commanded to stand. Shocked, I watched women pickers I thought were worn down by life rise to their feet and sway back and forth, the hems of their dresses brushing the grass. The picker husbands began to wiggle in their dusty shoes and boots. Finally, they gave in and jumped to the feet and began to dance. The white people in the front of the square also danced, some looking behind them to see if their Negro families were dancing too. My mama didn't dance. She struggled to her feet without our help and turned her face up to the beating sun, letting it shine on her face, and raised her hands out from her side with her palms facing up.

Somehow, the Violin man knew what had happened, and he played faster. By the time the songs came to an end, everyone, Negro and white, was smiling at one another. There was forgetting both ways about what was proper. People laughed, gasped for breath, and leaned against one another as they dropped to their blankets.

The crowd buzzed with conversation during the lunch break. Quarters, dimes, and nickels tinkled into the Violin man's instrument case lined with fraying red velvet. Mama watched Mrs. Ashby with squinted eyes, and finally, she threw her hand up in the air. "William and Socrates, you come and help me up." Daddy and I hefted her to her feet.

"I need to get over there. Socrates, you clear ahead."

I walked in front of Mama, mumbling, "Excuse us. Excuse me. Please, we need a path." People moved out of the way, leaning in over their blankets as Mama and I made our way to the Ashbys.

"Mrs. Ashby, honey, I think you should get out of the sun. It's not good for...you. Where is your umbrella?" My mama hated the word *parasol*. She said it sounded dainty, and a woman can't be dainty if she needs to be strong. She stood over them, blocking the sun and creating a slice of shade for Mrs. Ashby. Her face was fierce. People around us stopped talking and watched my mama do what she does best: win.

"I'll go get it," I volunteered. "It's in the backseat of car."

"What a good idea, Socrates. You run along, boy." Mr. Ashby waved his hand, dismissing me.

My mama turned to look at him as he called me boy. Her face wrinkled with questions, and I saw her put distance between her and Mr. Ashby. He nodded his thanks as he lounged on his side, his elbow propped up to hold his head in his palm. His hand was close to Mrs. Ashby's belly, and he reached for moment to squeeze it through her dress. Mrs. Ashby looked down and blew him a kiss as she moved his hand away.

I jogged through the squares of blankets spread on the grass and made my way to the closed off street where flowers from gardens all over Jackson County sat gratefully under the shade of the awnings. The vases of fancy flowers paraded in a row past three storefronts. I looked carefully as I passed each bouquet on the tables. Mrs. Ashby's gay bouquet of dahlias that looked like a kaleidoscope of colors spilling out of a jar, did not have a ribbon. I searched for the blue-ribbon winner. I found it attached to a large vase of plain red roses. I turned my back to the flowers and reached around behind me and pushed the vase off the table. I lifted the blue ribbon free and wandered back to Mrs. Ashby's display and pushed the ribbon onto the jar. I had done my best; now her flowers must hold it tight.

Deed done, I returned to the Ashby's car and reached in to grab the pink parasol. I felt dizzy after dashing about in the heat, so I put my hand on the hot metal of the car and lowered myself to rest on my heels. I heard voices, and my stomach climbed into my throat. Mr. Ashby had put the top up on the car, but the windows were rolled down. I heard three men talking on the other side of the car.

"It's true," Trask insisted. "She's pregnant."

"Trask, I'll run you out of town before I let you talk that way about one of Gideon's finest ladies. You?" Carr asked distastefully as if Trask was rancid meat. "If the Bureau hadn't put you on that farm, there wouldn't be a time in your life, you'd get close to a woman like that."

"Are you saying she is too good for him?" Grindall's words were clipped.

"Grindall, you are not from these parts. I can't imagine Northerners talk about polite society with people like him either."

I cringed and ducked closer to the tire so they couldn't see my feet.

Trask slammed Mr. Carr against the side of the car, and it rocked against my shoulder.

"Okay, enough," Grindall commanded. "Stick to the plan. Understand? Trask, value low. Carr, you're going to sell the whole farm to me. You'll both get a payment after I bring in the first pull of the pinesap. Let's get out of here. We shouldn't be seen together." It went silent on the other side of the car, and I heard footsteps walk in different directions.

It all hit me. Our plan was pointless. We all changed ourselves for the worse and hurt innocent people, and we had been outsmarted before we even attempted to rein in the chaos. Without warning, a hot mess broke out of my stomach and spewed in an arc that splattered on the side of the Ashby's car like bird shit hitting the side of a house. The hubcap and door were littered with partially digested friend chicken, biscuits, fried okra, and chocolate cake. The storm in my body continued until my stomach was hollow. I pulled my glasses off my face and held them tightly in my hand. I pressed my back against the searing metal of the car and put my head between my knees. The parasol laid on the ground next to me. It was covered with vomit. It was ruined. I couldn't take it to her.

Feet shuffled to a stop and stood before me. I looked up at Maddie, who studied the side of the Ashby's car. I busted out crying. Looking at her face, I knew there was no way I could not tell her the truth. Plus, I had to at least let a little of the pain inside me come out, or I was going to break apart, my arms and legs snapping off one at a time, my head popping and floating away like a balloon, and last of all, my slick, throbbing heart left alone on the pavement afraid to beat any longer.

"Do you think he's the father?" Her chin jutted out, and her eyes glittered.

"No, Maddie. Don't even think of it." My mama spoke up. She had come to get the parasol. Picking it up by the handle, she dropped it in the trash bin, holding her nose with her other hand.

My mama and Maddie stood face-to-face, their hands on their hips, tapping their shoes. My tall-drink-of-water mama, thickened by childbirth and tasting the Ashby's food before she could eat her own, towered over Maddie. Maddie looked like the child she had been once with her bones jutting out of her skin and her nose turned up as she gazed at Mama. There was distrust between them, and I couldn't tolerate it.

"Enough. You two have let enough time go by. You make up now," I commanded and then shrank inside thinking of what the two of them could do to me if they wanted to. Their skin color, shape of their faces, and heft of their limbs were different. Yet best friends sometimes grow to look like one another without even knowing. They were two peas in a pod gone in different directions, but, if need be, they would pull that pod around them and do whatever the other asked. They just didn't know it.

"It's been a long time, Annie," Maddie accused.

"Twenty-five years." Mama reached out and squeezed Maddie's arm. "Long ones."

"You had William, not that it helped all that much. A man's not a friend, you know," Maddie sniffed. "You don't know how long twenty-five years is when all you're known for is biscuit making."

"No, Maddie, that's not true," Mama scolded. "You help all the young people who come to you. Everyone knows that. Thank you for helping Socrates." She looked at me with a scowl. "You think I didn't know?"

Maddie gave me a sideways glance. "He's good enough, I suppose. Good biscuits, though, even if he is William's son." Maddie fanned her face with a lace handkerchief and held out a big red umbrella. "Here Annie. Take this. That silly woman won't even notice it's not hers." Mama grabbed it and scrambled across the street.

She held up her hand at a coming car and made her way determined to get to the Ashbys.

After she was gone, it was just Maddie and me. Even though I was still hiccupping and wiping my eyes, I kept stealing looks at her. She wasn't wearing an apron—that was for sure. Clad in a bright-pink dress with mounds of lace spilling out of her chest, Maddie strutted like a peacock back and forth on the sidewalk. Long, arching ostrich feathers dyed brilliant blue spouted out of the top of her hat, and her crazy blue-and-brown eyes darted back and forth under the hat's brim. She shifted her legs, trying to get some air, and a glimpse of a lacy slip flashed by my eyes. I got to my feet.

"I'm going home. I'm going the hell home."

"No, you are not." Maddie blocked the path between the show cars and set her lips in angry line. "You are going to go back and sit with your mama and daddy and smile big. That's what you do when you is hurt like you are right now. You do it for that woman. Even if she is crazy as a loon for naming you after someone who's not a relation. She done right by you, and you will not make her question where you went to. Now you get over there, and I will see you tomorrow morning."

She took her gloved hand and swept chunks of puke off my shirt. She folded my collar back so it looked respectable again and laid her hand on my rising and falling chest. "You are a brave boy, Socrates. What we don't know doesn't kill us, and this time, what we do know ain't going to either."

My legs ached as I wandered back to my parents. I stretched my body out and laid face down on the blanket. I handed my glasses to my daddy and mumbled, "I just don't need to see right now." He took them without asking any questions. I didn't care if people thought I was an odd duck. I felt scooped out and light like cotton. I didn't have any seeds in me either. Those were scraped out too. I closed my eyes and listened. I'd like to think that even if I was deaf, I could still hear the Violin man's music.

Trask, Mrs. Ashby, the farm, Midnight's story, I thought I could not take any more pain, but the Violin man softened it and soothed me. He seemed to make the bow flow to the end of the violin for an impossibly long time. He pulled me on a journey where I saw the world rush by in colors and feelings that I knew were out there, but I had never dreamed I might see or feel. It was a sadness I couldn't explain, a longing for something I couldn't name, and a meaning to something that I did not yet know. The music healed me and, at the same time, made my pain all the greater.

I observed there wasn't a person moving, just like I didn't move in my mama's belly. Time had slowed, and a breeze replaced the heat. Dogs dropped into exhausted circles, and babies lay slack in their mothers' arms. Men took off their jackets and folded them in their laps, and women undid the pins in their hair and laid their hats aside. Children lay on their stomachs with their cheeks burrowed in the grass. I scanned the crowd, looking for Mrs. Ashby, but she and Mr. Ashby were gone. With the last note, the Violin man dropped his head, exhausted, his quivering arms shaking like the leaves of a mimosa tree whose flowers release their scent only in that moment between sundown and twilight.

And, that's when I heard it. "Bravo" was whispered from different pockets of the courthouse square. There was no shouting it aloud as I envisioned back when Mama told me the origin of my middle name. It was breathed instead of spoken like the music had meant something different to everyone. Daddy handed me back my glasses so I could see.

Everyone wandered away then. Few coins dropped into the case in the afternoon, but the Violin man didn't seem disappointed. In the morning, he played for his livelihood and to soften us for what was to come. In the afternoon, he played for us and what was possible.

He sat under the tree while people shyly walked past him. Some folks forgot he was blind and held out a hand to him. When he did not shake it in return, they pulled back embarrassed. When most people were gone, I watched the Violin man empty his case and gather up the coins. He rubbed his fingers on the edges of the coins. The thin small pennies he put in his left pocket with the thick, chunky nickels. The slim, almost weightless dimes went in his outside right hand pocket. The quarters, he picked up carefully. He felt the ridges and the heft. He put them in an inside pocket sewn small and just big enough for the quarters not to jingle.

I grabbed a peach, a handful of pecans, a bag of biscuits, and a jar of water from Mama's basket. When I lowered myself to the ground next to the Violin man, I cleared my throat and said, "Excuse me, sir. I have some food and water for you." Heat radiated from his coat, and it reminded me of Walker and the clean smell of his sweat after a baseball game. The Violin man, too, had a satisfied smell to him.

I touched his hand lightly and placed a peach in his open palm. He skimmed his fingertips across the fruit, and the fuzz on the orange orb rose to meet his calloused fingertips like it was greeting him. He cradled the fruit in his hand and put his nose to it. He sniffed it deeply.

"Thank you, young man. This feeds more than my belly." He sniffed it again. "Would you like a bite?" he asked.

I shook my head no. He still held out the peach. I remembered he could not see me.

"No, thank you," I whispered. "I have biscuits and pecans too."

"The nuts, I'll take. Keep the biscuits. They don't last." He sunk his teeth deep into the peach, and the juice drizzled down his face. He used his threadbare sleeve to mop his mouth. His voice was young, and when he smiled, his teeth were white and even. He leaned his head against the tree and pulled his hat off. His pale forehead was slick with sweat, and I was surprised to see his head was full of thick, brown hair free of any gray streaks. The Violin man was young. It was just his music that was old.

He turned to me, and his unseeing eyes stared into my own. "I meet cheaters and angels every day. You're one of the angels. You are not afraid to sit with a blind man. Why?"

I sat still. He ate his peach and the nuts while he waited for my silence to pass. "Someone important to me...might be making a mistake."

"Are you talking about a woman?

"Yes, sir."

"Young man, don't 'yes, sir' me. It makes me old before my time. If she is important to you, this mistake, as you say, is for a reason. It may be for the very best reason." He pulled out a handkerchief and poured some water onto it. He scrubbed his face and hands.

"When somebody helps me, like you, I remember it. I can't see you, but I know what help feels like. It is solid. I can take it out and hold it, and I can turn it in my hands; it is different every time." He pulled the rope tied to his violin case over his head so it slung across his body.

"What does hurt feel like?" My words hit the matted grass with a skid.

"It can't be held. It turns to ash. It streams away when you let go. It falls apart, and nothing wants to stay with it."

"Would you like to come home with me?" I asked, hesitant. "My Mama's an awful mean cook. Biscuits, gravy, greens, pork..." My voice trailed off into silence. I watched his blue eyes consider the offer.

"Not this time. But maybe next time. I got a friend in the next town expecting me. I got to get there to see him." He tossed the pecans in his mouth. "What's your name?"

"Socrates Bravo Jefferson."

He tipped his head sideways considering all the possible responses. "I won't forget you, Socrates Bravo Jefferson." He held out his hand for me to shake. I took it and gripped it. His skin was as soft as butter and the calluses on his fingertips felt like hard little coins. His fingers drifted out of mine, and he turned to leave Gideon, Alabama, on Independence Day in 1928. In time, I learned to do as he suggested and help others with acts that felt solid, ones that you could see. Ones that, thanks to Maddie, were like biscuit dough that came together with ease. The other memory, the hurt, when it comes, I drop it to the ground and grind it like a wet cigar under my foot. I make sure there are no embers still burning.

On the long walk back to the farm from Gideon, each time I thought about Trask speaking about Mrs. Ashby with disrespect, wretched bile flew up my throat and strangled me. He brought shame on her, and I struggled to let it go like the ashes of the Violin man's words.

I couldn't help my small self that night. I wanted only

revenge. Before he returned to the farm, I snuck into his room and selected a whiskey bottle that was close to empty. I removed the plug and slid the bottle down to the floor. Carefully, with my best aim, I relieved myself into the bottle without missing, dripping, or spilling.

I returned later when I heard Trask shut off the engine of the little truck. While the truck went through its series of clicks, groans, and a final sigh before the engine stopped, I waited a few minutes before stepping out my bedroom window. I had learned to become a phantom at night, roaming the farm and pressing myself against the clapboards of the big house to listen to words that were not meant to be heard by anyone other than the inhabitants of the four walls.

I crouched under the windowsill of my former classroom and waited to hear a strangled cry brought on by a slug of whiskey that smelled and tasted of a long and painful day. Instead, I heard the voice of the one I thought I could trust without ceasing, without doubting.

"Edwin, I must go. He is my husband. If he wakes up, I must be there. That is what a wife must do. I cannot be in two places at once. I will see you in the morning."

The bedsprings creaked as she rolled to the edge of the bed. I rose to look over the edge of the window. I watched her gather a silk robe and pull it up around her shoulders. Trask, his knobby chest flushed, kissed her right shoulder and pushed her hair off her neck. She pulled away and knotted the thin belt about her waist above her swelling bump. She tiptoed across the floor, her hair tousled and curling all over her head.

I swallowed fast like I was trying to down the green beans I hated, and I blinked so hard I could feel my eyelashes brush against each other. She turned to say good night to her lover. A shard of moonlight cut across the room and revealed my eyes peering in from the window. I looked at Mrs. Ashby, my true north, and melted away into the darkness, leaving her with lips open in a perfect circle of shock.

Chapter Fifteen

I kept silent during the frequent discussions my mama and daddy had regarding when Mrs. Ashby's baby would be born. Mama thought it might be more than a month out, maybe more. She wanted it to come sooner. "If she is more than seven months along, it is not Trask's." I heard her whisper to my daddy on the porch one night. "I still don't see how she could have allowed it to happen. She is as disgusted by him as the rest of us."

"Annie, keep your opinion to yourself. No one knows what happens behind closed doors. You don't want her angry at you."

"Well, William Jefferson, you're not a woman. There's parts to a woman that require willingness if not love." She slammed the door on her way into the house.

I lay in bed, my hands behind my head, and contemplated the darkness until my eyes burned. Several weeks had passed since the night my childhood hitched a one-way ride out of town. Each day, I woke up hoping it had been a nightmare, but when Mrs. Ashby looked away from me when we crossed paths, I knew that no matter how unfathomable it was, and whether it was willingness or love, Mrs. Ashby had yielded.

I struggled for days with my conscience until I told Daddy about overhearing Grindall's plan. It could have been so easy to just act surprise when the ending came, but I finally spilled the beans. We discussed going to Mr. Ashby, but we ultimately decided we'd let it all play out. None of them—Trask, Grindall, or Carr—would admit to their role in the scheme to take the farm, and we didn't want to admit that we had a plan just as ruthless as theirs. Trask would be the deciding factor—him and the pickers' yield.

Two of the essays were finished—math and history. I started the science section, and I was saving literature for last. I chose to write on the process of cross-pollinating plants for the purpose of creating intentional hybrids. The problem? The plant I chose—the dahlia—had more chromosomes than other flowers and that affected its process of hybridization. Another problem? I didn't want to ask for help. As my mother would say, "There's the rub."

"Annie, what are we to do? Poor Mr. Trask is so ill I am concerned for him." Trask now suffered from bouts of spewing diarrhea, violent vomiting, and crushing headaches that caused him to whimper as he lay in his darkened room. My head knew it was wrong, but I felt a satisfaction in his misery that matched my mama's.

Mrs. Ashby swept the broom out the door, covering me with dust. Mama said she'd been nesting for a week and that baby better be born before she was out of a job. I looked through the doorway to see Mrs. Ashby smooth her hands over the baby under her dress. Her belly was too large to hide the pregnancy now. All that remained was the due date, and she was not sharing that with anyone. Mr. Ashby was strutting around the farm, handing out peppermint sticks to the picker children and informing them that the Ashby lineage would continue. The poor children with rotted front teeth chased him in his going-to-town car that he had taken to driving on the farm roads. Trask was watchful. Each time he saw the car leave the drive, he searched for Mrs. Ashby until he found her lying on the settee in the living room or walking the creek path through the woods. The one place neither man was allowed was the dahlia bed. It was hers alone—unless she wanted my help.

"Annie, do you need Socrates right now? We are going to the dahlia bed. Keep working on Mr. Trask. He must get better soon." Locking eyes with me, Mrs. Ashby strode out the kitchen door, stamped down the stairs, and gripped my arm. "You come with me, young man."

"Wait, Mrs. Ashby," Mama called. "Socrates, come back for a minute. I need to speak to you." I walked back to my mama. She yanked my ear to her mouth and whispered, "When she is done with you, go to Miss Cora. Tell her I want some of that Red Rocket flower. Grind it good. Enough sugar in his sweet tea, and he'll never know it. Wicked headache he'll have later."

I saw her flap her apron in the air. Bits of lobelia flowers drifted to the ground. Mama sprinkled the little blue flowers across Trask's food and informed him it was a fancy garnish from France. I checked the description of the flowers in my botany book. The herb induced debilitating diarrhea. The book cautioned against use. Mama realized she couldn't berate Trask for daring to dabble in the Ashby's marriage, so she came up with a different plan: she would kill him just a little at a time. Mama and Miss Cora had a plan, and poor Trask was suffering.

"Don't you worry, Mrs. Ashby, honey. I'm fixing him every soothing dish I can think of. Bye now. Socrates, you be a good boy."

Mrs. Ashby raised her voice over the sound of Mama's whistling. "He's a man now, Annie, remember? Going to boarding school soon."

We entered the flower bed with the tall dahlias looming over us. Once we passed under the filtered light of the parasols, the grass between the rows was cool. I laid my botany book down and reached out to help Mrs. Ashby. She struggled to sit down and shrugged off my help. She finally sat on her hip with her legs tucked under her like a little girl. She pointed a finger at my face and began to speak. Her lips trembled with the words I knew were difficult to utter.

"First of all, looking in someone's window is illegal, wrong, and unkind. You invaded our privacy, and I am very hurt. Do you understand me, Socrates Bravo? Let's settle this between us so we can be friends again. What do you want to know?" I watched her belly moving in waves. I wondered what it sounded like inside a woman's womb.

"Do you love him?"

"No."

"Do you love Mr. Ashby?"

"No."

"If you feel that way, why..." I labored to find a way to ask a delicate question. "Why be with them?"

"I don't expect you to understand, Socrates. It's complicated. I must make something right. It is from my past."

"All right. I don't think I want to know anything else." She patted my arm. "Well, I do have a question," I interrupted myself. "The baby. Who?"

"That I will not answer or even acknowledge. It is inappropriate. Are we clear now?" Her hands fluttered over her belly. I stared at them. They were swollen like sausages, and there wasn't any room between her fingers.

"Mrs. Ashby, I don't know anything about being pregnant, but I don't think your fingers are supposed to look like that." I pointed to them.

"I don't know, Socrates. I don't know anything about being pregnant either." We smiled at each other. "I want just Miss Cora and your mama with me during the birth, but Timothy insists on bringing the doctor."

"You call him Timothy now?"

"It's about time. Don't you think?"

"Yes, I think so too."

"So, Soc, you can let it go? What you saw?"

"I want to. I don't want to think about it."

"It's up to you to decide if I am wicked or not, but you know you are the most important person in my life, yes?"

"I do." I willed the quaver in my voice to stop. "You're not wicked. Not at all."

"I'm not asking for forgiveness, Socrates. I'll answer for that myself."

"Yes, ma'am."

"Come. Let's check the flowers." She let me help her up and walked slowly past the glowing, riotous-colored faces of the flowers. I followed behind her carrying a toolbox with twine, stakes, and clippers in one hand and a bucket of sloshing water in the other. My botany book was tucked under my arm.

"I'll carry the book. Hand it here," she said, holding out her hand. "More twine on that one." She pointed to a slumping plant. I pulled a length of twine off, clipped it, and tied the thick stem to the stake.

"Water," she said without glancing behind her. I sloshed water on the plant. "Next one," she said like a doctor tending to a patient. She stopped when we reached the next tall stem. "Jane Cowl," she said to a flower with pink, peach, and cream petals. "You Hollywood beauty." She walked faster, and I hurried behind her operating on each of the plants as she called out the instructions. She slowed her steps and touched a group I knew she liked best.

"Look at that." She laughed as they brushed against her large belly. "They seem to know it's there. How unusual," she exclaimed. "Bishop, golden scepter, Wisconsin red, and floorinor, you, my dear, are my one of my favorites." Mrs. Ashby sank down and leaned back on her elbows. "I'm feeling a bit faint. I better sit in the grass for a moment."

"I'll get more water, and you can have a drink." She was flushed and having trouble catching her breath. She used the book to fan her face.

"Don't worry, Socrates. I feel fine, just huge. I'll point, and you work for a while. Plant hybridization. Why did you choose that topic?"

"I thought it would be straightforward. No one ever told me creating dahlia hybrids was so much more involved that other plants. Four chromosomes together? Why the extra two?" I went to the barrel where we kept the water. I filled a wooden bucket and struggled with both hands to haul it back to the place where she rested.

"I hope I am around to see you a grown man. I want to see you manhandle things like they are easy." She wiped her forehead. Her chest was rising and falling rapidly as I handed her a cup of water.

"Mrs. Ashby, I am not Walker. Daddy says I likely won't even be as tall as him."

"What does your mama say?"

"About how big I will get?" I grunted as I raised the heavy bucket. "She says my heart will more than make up for it." I sloshed the water under the leaves.

"Not too much. Remember to stop while it is still drinking. That makes it work for it all the way to the roots." It was quiet between us with just the sound of grateful flowers seeping up the water. "I love the parasols," she commented, watching them twirl on the wires above us. "They are a lovely touch. I'll have to get them down before winter comes."

"You will be busy with the baby, Mrs. Ashby. I'll take them down." The bucket was almost empty.

"You'll be at school, Socrates. Making a name for yourself."

I looked at her shocked. She was right. I would finally know what it would be like to enter a library with so many shelves of books I might not be able to read them all. "I've missed studying in the classroom. I wish it would all go back to the way it was."

"Really? With all that's happened? Doesn't it make you feel more alive even if it hurts?" she asked. I stayed quiet and went to get another bucket of water.

"Socrates, you've never heard me talk about my past. Sit." I collapsed on the ground and set the bucket aside. I looked up in time to see the polka-dot parasol twirl in the breeze. It looked like it would fly away if given the chance.

"I didn't have a mother like yours who cares about so much about her family she would do anything for them. I was an only child, and I had a governess who tutored me." She laughed. "It never occurred to me, but it was very much like the arrangement you and I have had. That's funny."

"I grew up in in a big place on the shore. Our house was bigger than anything you could imagine. Here we have plantations. In the north, they are estates. The estate my parents had gardens as big as our house, barn, garden, and dahlia bed combined. They were arranged like rooms with hedges between them. My mother loved gardens but didn't like gardening." She leaned back on her hands, and her fingers turned white. "I'm glad I'm different from her."

"There were forty men who worked year-round on the gardens. Half of them were assigned the hedges—making sure they were uniform and straight—while the other half worked in the flower gardens, making sure the flowers my mother liked were free from weeds. I'll bet you can guess which flower she didn't like?"

"Dahlias."

"She felt they were showy and too varied. She wanted her flowers to look all the same." She reached over and squeezed my hand. Her fingers felt tight, like they couldn't bend.

"The summer I was sixteen, something happened in my parent's marriage. They each went a different way. My mother took a ship to Europe, and my father moved to a hotel in New York. Neither wanted to bring me with them, so they hired a companion for me. Her name was Ellie Ely. Isn't that a funny name? I'd like one of those, Socrates, please." She pointed to the huge Thomas Edison near us. I clipped a large one and handed it to her. Thomas Edison, a dahlia the size of a dinner plate, had one true color: deep purple. It didn't mind the heat, and the stems and flowers grew beyond the top of their stakes. We always lashed another stake to the top of the first one. She brushed its petals across her face and over her closed eyelids.

"I was quite the wild thing. I don't know if I was angry at my mother and father, but I liked to disappear for hours and wander where I wanted."

"It was Ellie's job to help me with my studies, prepare me for marriage, and show me how to curb my wild impulses. If anything, she taught me how to be alive." She laid the Thomas Edison down next to her.

"Drink more water, Mrs. Ashby," I urged. "Even though we're not in the sun, it's still hot out." Like a child, she obediently dipped the cup in the water bucket and drained it in one swallow.

"Thank you for taking care of me, Socrates."

"I think I would like Ellie Ely. If she would have liked a Negro boy, that is."

"Of course, she would. She wouldn't have cared. You would have gone on adventures with us." Mrs. Ashby blew out a long slow exhale trying to slow down her breathing.

"Maybe we should go talk to Mama. You don't want to be sick."

"Let me finish the story, and then, we will go. I haven't forgotten your essay either." She held up a finger. "So Ellie came for the summer with a dozen potted plants she kept on the patio. She was in the middle of a big project. She was in the process of cross-pollinating different species of dahlias and waiting to see what they looked like when the flowers opened. She was obsessed with creating a hybrid that had whorls of color. It was attempting the impossible: a dahlia composed of a new combination of flower shape, petal arrangement, and color."

"How could you modify all of those elements at the same time?" I asked, intrigued.

"They become each other," she said, her eyes sparkling. She grabbed the pencil from behind her ear. She opened my book to the empty pages in the back. She started to draw. "People are diploid in chromosomes. The twenty-three chromosomes join in twos. Dahlias are octoploid in chromosomes. They have sixty-four chromosomes organized in eights. Remember: each chromosome has a different purpose. Think of all the DNA swirling around in a helix."

"Before she came to me that summer, Ellie had been working for two years at cross-pollinating plants until she weeded out the characteristics she didn't want and identified the ones she did want."

"So they all impact each other?"

"They become each other, Socrates. That is a true hybrid."

"How?" I felt like we were back in our classroom where we debated topics and Mrs. Ashby pushed me to think beyond my limits.

"This is where the dahlia hybrid becomes a mystery. Think about isolating a color. Choose pink. The chromosomes contain different shades of the same color or different colors altogether. You don't know which color will emerge, so you keep trying. If you want pink, it may take you several tries to cross-pollinate plants with pink flowers to finally get rid of the other colors and even the different shades of pink you don't want. Each time, though, your chances of success increases."

"So she had to do it with color." I paused. I couldn't remember the other two elements.

"Petal arrangement and shape," Mrs. Ashby finished. "Yes, all three."

"Socrates," she began.

"Yes?"

"Socrates, what would you think if I told you there was a different cross-pollination that summer that created a perfect hybrid on the first try?" Her nose was peppered with tiny freckles she had gained from the summer days spent in the dahlia bed.

"From what you told me, I'd say it was unattainable."

Mrs. Ashby poured a cup of water and drizzled it down her neck and shoulders. "Oh, that feels good." She shifted in the grass and grimaced.

"It happened. It was perfect from the beginning. We became each other. I loved her, Socrates. We had secret silly names for each other. We used parts of our last names so no one would know. I called her Fly and she called me Net. One way or another, we always caught one another, or so we said."

Mrs. Ashby waited for me to process her secret. I imagined two young women gazing at each other with love on their faces, stolen kisses in garden corners, and intimate scenes such as the one I had witnessed between Mrs. Ashby and Trask.

"Oh," I said slowly. The weight of it hit me then. In our small community on the farm, I was the only person who knew Mrs. Ashby's most important lover was a woman. I couldn't breathe for a moment. I struggled to put it all together like the pieces of a puzzle I sometimes envisioned as my own life, and then I realized how hard it must be to put the pieces in the right place for Mrs. Ashby.

"I'm sorry."

"Why? There is nothing wrong with loving another woman," she said, hurt.

"No, I'm sorry that the one person you want most isn't here."

"Sweet Socrates, thank you for understanding. Here, feel him move." Mrs. Ashby took my hand and laid it on her belly. I tried to pull away, but the little being hovered under my hand and turned a somersault.

"Oh," The feeling of something being alive and independent yet contained and held fast was thrilling.

"It was like that. Our time together was something new every day. Like a baby growing inside a woman." Mrs. Ashby stood again. It looked like it was getting harder for her to stand every time. "Let me water for a while. You can fill the bucket for me. I need to see these flowers grow."

I kept pace with her, holding the back of the bucket while she carefully dribbled it down the row. She paused often, turning leaves over to for look for shiny snail tracks. If a plant was showing signs of stress due to aphids or red spider, she pulled it out of the ground and tossed it in the burn pile. "No sense in letting anything suffer," she commented and moved on to the next one.

"Fly wore a tweed skirt and a safari hat while she gardened. She'd talk to the flowers and I think they heard her. Let me try and see what happens." She reached on her tiptoes and pulled a flower down to her face. "Hey, blended beauty, smile for me." The flower wobbled, and all the petals fell away from the face and twirled to the ground. She looked wistful. "How Fly would have laughed over that one."

"She taught me everything I know about dahlias. Plant the tubers in March two feet apart. Don't water then until the stalks and leaves appear, fertilize on the top of the soil, and dead head the flowers. Always dead head so there is room for more." She looked steadily at me. "I think we need more water, Socrates." She held out the empty bucket. I ran to fill it and hurried back with water bouncing over the edge.

"How did you know you loved her?" I asked.

"Socrates, it knocked me over, and the air left me. I felt like I was flying and falling at the same time. She was six years older than me, but she saw it in my eyes, and I saw it in hers. Social norms dictated that women could not love one another like a man and a woman do, so Fly grabbed my hand. We stood there in the garden, squeezing one another's hands until they were white from lack of blood. We knew."

"Were your parents angry?" We had reached the white aster, which wasn't an aster at all. The tuber was cultivated in Europe, and it arrived in the United States in 1879. It was an ivory globe with a drop of honey in the center.

Mrs. Ashby gathered a handful of the delicate flowers. "They never knew," she said, letting the flowers go. "My love affair with Fly was mine. I have not shared it with anyone. Until you." Her swollen hand lingered on my arm. "Dahlias are simple flowers, really. Plant the tuber. The flower grows. The flower dies. Pull up the tuber. It is amazing to me how people can ruin a life that's meant to be simple."

She sat down. "This baby has about done me in. No"—she shook her head—"I've done it to myself."

"Fly's hybrid worked. The flowers opened, and they looked like a Monet painting of a sunset on water." Mrs. Ashby stopped and pulled the scissors from the toolbox and snipped a length of twine. While she finished the rest of her story, she used the scissors to cut the twine into tiny pieces. She made her cuts with deliberation, and when she finished, our laps were covered with bits of useless string.

"Fly took the dahlia to the Dahlia Society of America in New York to have it authenticated and entered into the society as an approved hybrid that could be replicated and grown in gardens all over the world." Clip, clip, clip went the cutting shears. "The men who were in charge did not allow her to enter it in the competition. Fly was devastated. She followed every rule. She kept a diary documenting every part of the hybridization process. She brought examples of all the parent flowers and the generations they created. The final hybrid, perfect in every way, would be ready to propagate from seeds and cuttings at the end of the season, but it would be several years before tubers became part of the plant. She brought the only plant that existed."

"The judges turned the pot upside down and shook the dirt from the roots looking for the tubers to prove it was not a new hybrid. There were lengths of roots that would become tubers in time, but it was too soon. The flowers all died from the trauma, and Fly was never the same."

With an energy that shocked me, Mrs. Ashby stood up and walked to the middle of the last row of dahlias, the ones that backed up to the fence. The dahlias were the most protected from the wind. We reached the flowers that, in all my childhood, did not have a name. Mrs. Ashby had always brushed it off claiming it was a wild one.

"So," Mrs. Ashby said as she laid her lips gently on the cactus-shaped blossom with swirling colors of red, yellow, orange, and a deep pink easing into one another, "she named it Fly's love." She clipped a flower and tucked it behind her ear. "It's gorgeous, Socrates, isn't it?" Carefully, she cut every bloom off the plant and made a bouquet.

I poured water in a vigilant circle around the feet of Fly's love, making sure all the roots had a chance to drink.

"I buried the handful of roots in the back garden where my mother would not find them. They came up the next spring and the spring after. In two years, there was a set of tubers all strung together like a ring of keys. Every year, I overwintered the tubers in a box in my bedroom. When I married Mr. Ashby, I brought them all with me. I don't think the tubers exist anywhere else. When the judges at the competition denied its entrance into the society, they wrote in their notes, 'It showed the natural genetic tendency in instability in color and would likely evolve into something else someday.'" She shrugged her shoulders. "Like Fly and Net. A genetic tendency in instability."

"What happened to Ellie?" The heavy bucket I had just filled sloshed all over the ground. "Damn it," I whispered.

Mrs. Ashby laughed and took her shoes off. She wiggled her toes in the muddy water. They looked as fat and white as her hands. "You are growing up. Swearing like a man. Or"—she smiled—"more like your mama, hmm?" She sat up and wiped her toes clean with her see-through socks. "Ellie's spirit was broken by the way the judges treated her and Fly's love. Her parents sent her away. They said she suffered from a fever caused by too much time in the sun. I believe she went to a hospital for people who have a sickness in their brain, an eternal sadness."

"She wrote a book while she was there. It was called *A Woman's Garden*. She painted pictures of all the dahlias.

She must have painted them from memory. I heard the hospital was out west in the desert." She turned away from the rows of dahlias. "I never saw her again."

"Remember when I told you there are two ways to change an evil man?"

"Teach him how to love or break his heart," I said in a heavy, cracking voice. "Which one is Trask?" I asked. "Did you break his heart?"

"No," she said, shaking her head with an impatient motion. "Edwin has learned to love, and that is a punishment from which I am scared he may not recover. It was only meant to open his heart."

"So, Mrs. Ashby, that means…" I was confused.

"Yes, I will break Timothy's heart. In the worst of ways. He could become the nastiest version of himself that would rival Mr. Sir. I don't know if I can live with myself if that happens. The charade was to make him whole." She turned around to face me. "What are the words between Macbeth and his lady, Socrates? You know the ones I am thinking of."

I stared at her for as long as I could not without breaking our locked eyes until I knew I could not outlast her. I whispered, "If we should fail? We fail! But screw your courage to the sticking place, and we'll not fail."

"Very good, Socrates. As you can see, I have more to do until I have this baby." She dropped the bunch of Fly's love flowers into a jumbled heap onto the grass. "I believe you are right. I don't feel well. We best go back to the house."

Chapter Sixteen

Mrs. Ashby's story of her love for Miss Ellie Ely stayed with me for the month following our talk in the dahlia garden. I dragged myself to Maddie's restaurant at dawn and struggled home in the afternoon to the porch to sit for my studies. I finished my hybridization essay, and all I had left was the literature section. Each day, though, the typewriter was quiet, and the words didn't come. I had chosen Shakespeare's plays for their universality in theme and beautiful language but watching Mrs. Ashby play out the role as Lady Macbeth intent on the destruction of a man's world exhausted me. My heart felt freshly bruised and sore, and I had no idea what it must feel like to be Mrs. Ashby with a heart left untouched for decades around the most tender, emerging feelings a person can have, falling in love.

One night, I battled to keep my eyes open when Daddy asked me to check the arithmetic in the furnish and settle ledger against the cotton gin's numbers. I blinked my tired eyes.

"They look accurate, Daddy. If the pickers keep

picking at the same rate, a lot of them will be out of debt or might even have money by October. You are reminding them not to buy anything at the commissary, right?" Daddy nodded.

"Has Mr. Ashby seen the ledger?"

"Do you think I am going to tell him? He'll be forced to use the ledger to settle the debts and the picker's take at the last of the season." Daddy stopped. "Socrates."

I looked at him across the table. My daddy looked old. Gray hair had crept into his sideburns, and his cheeks were hollow.

"I think about money every day, and that's not the way I want to live, but we are part of a farm where someone has to think about it because Mr. Ashby can't. I'm afraid he would see all the money and go buy a horse or a new car. Even if the plan works and the Farm Bureau is paid and the bank doesn't call the mortgage, I am afraid we'll be back in this position in a few more years. And, Soc, there's nothing I can do about it. Try living that life."

All my childhood, it was not a surprise to see a team of horses hauling a horse trailer up our long road spitting dust in its wake. The driver waited to take the horse out of the trailer until someone who knew what he was doing was there to help. Usually, it was my daddy. Mr. Ashby would come out of the house with a check in his hand and dismiss the driver. Mr. Ashby would stand outside the fence watching my daddy soothe the horse and put the bridle in its mouth. When the horse allowed it, Mr. Ashby would turn, clasp his hands behind his back, and walk back to the house, pretending he was talking to someone who was not there.

As I handed the books back to Daddy, a line of red numbers jumped out at me. "Wait, let me see it again." I pulled the ledger back. "Why does it say the Jeffersons owe money?" I leaned over the book to study the name next to ours with clean black numbers in every box. "It says Miss Cora and Brutus are even. How can that be? They are too sick to leave the farm or pick cotton."

Daddy reached for the large book. "Nothing for you to worry about, Soc."

"It says you owe eighty dollars. Even with all your other work, you are still picking more cotton than anyone else." I pointed to the picker ledger where it said Daddy had picked five hundred pounds of cotton in the last week. "With Mama, Walker, and me all contributing, we shouldn't have any debt and have some in savings. What's going on?"

Daddy grabbed the book away from me. "Socrates, I don't have to explain anything to you. If you live in this house, you are still a child. Mr. Trask may make the decisions outside these walls, but inside, I am in charge!"

"You don't have to call him mister in this house," I said under my breath.

I didn't see it coming. The blow from my daddy was swift, and I felt my face grow hot before the pain took hold. I held my hand against my cheek and tried not to weep.

"Socrates, you are not a man. I don't care what Mrs. Ashby calls you. A man helps others in need. Miss Cora, Brutus, and others would go hungry if your mama and I didn't care for them and pay their rent. Get out of here now before I get the paddle out too."

Chapter Seventeen

"Can Socrates come out here?" I heard Walker's voice in the rear yard as Maddie threw out the dirty dishwater.

"I suppose he can come out, but I won't let him until you ask right proper for him," Maddie snapped.

"Please, may my brother, Socrates Bravo Jefferson, come outside for a minute, ma'am? I'd be appreciative," Walker said.

"Fine. Socrates, y'all come out here," she bellowed. "There's someone here's to see you." Maddie slipped into the kitchen. "Be quick. We have lots of hungry people expecting hot, fresh biscuits." She rattled bowls and turned the water on so it thundered into the sink. "I guess it be all right if you give him a piece of apple pie. I'd just have to throw it out if it doesn't get eat. And you know I hate throwing out good food—even if it does make those pigs nice and round." She turned back to the sink and clattered pots and pans together.

"Hey, Walker," I said balancing the piece of pie on a plate while I fanned the flies to get them away. "What's happening?" I sat on the sloping step next to Walker as he held the pie up to his eyes to appreciate it. The apple pieces slid in the juice, and the cinnamon dotted the flaky crust. Crusty pieces surrounded Walker's mouth. His eyes were closed, and he looked like he was praying.

"Look." He handed me a newspaper article. "Read it to me to make sure I'm not seeing things," he mumbled through a huge mouthful of pie.

"Brick O'Malley, the former catcher for the Chicago Cubs, will be attending tonight's Negro country league game to scout for the first Negro player for the major leagues. He has been traveling the United States, looking for a pitcher who can provide a unique pitching style unfamiliar to the top contending teams in the nation. Locating a new pitcher for the Chicago Cubs late in the season would give the team an advantage going into the playoffs."

"They're talking about me, Soc. You know it."

"Maybe he's here to check out the other pitcher too," I proposed.

He paused and gulped another bite. "Why? You know I am the best."

"You'd be better off putting that pie on top of your head and letting your tongue beat your brains out trying to get to it. At least, we wouldn't have to see all the way to your stomach every time you take a bite," I commented in disgust. "Do Mama and Daddy know yet?"

Walker licked all the way around his lips. Walker grinned at me and rubbed his hands together to clean them. "I'm going to tell them when I get back. I have something to do first." He handed me the plate and jumped up. "It's going to happen, Soc. I wanted you to know." He stopped and looked at my bruised face. "What happened?"

"It's okay," I said, my eyes cast down. "I deserved it."

"Was it a picker? Did you get in a fight?" Walker stood flexing his hands into fists.

"No."

Walker leaned forward and took my head in his hand. He inspected the bruise carefully. "Was it Daddy?" I nodded my head, tears oozing from the sides of my eyes. "It's okay, Soc. He is going to feel bad later."

"Daddy has been lying to us. Instead of keeping us in the black, he's been paying Miss Cora's rent and buying their food and helping others with rent. Daddy's paying down their debt. He owes the farm eighty dollars," I whispered. "Mama and Daddy are going to end up just like them."

"No, they won't. I'll be able to help with their debt after tonight's game. I'll make sure it's all paid up. Mine too." Walker stood up. "Trust me, Socrates: I'll take care of them." He took off trotting down the road. When he was just a stick figure on the horizon, he turned the way that led up to some farms in the hills. I watched him go. He had a plan that didn't include me. Home was the other direction.

"So he's a baseball player?" Maddie's hands were on her hips. Large damp streaks ran down her apron and soaked through to her plain white dress.

"Yes, Maddie. A scout from the Chicago Cubs is coming to see him play." I washed my hands in hot water at the sink.

"Don't they have white players? Who brought this man from Chicago down here to see a Negro kid from Gideon pitch the baseball?"

"Maddie, Walker is really good. Mr. Ashby must have brought him down. He's been looking for a scout for

months. It took longer because he and Walker have been
making holes in the wall for the voice pipe." I turned the
water off and wiped my hands on my apron. I dusted the
board with flour and got out the cold bowl. Over my
shoulder, I kept talking while I measured everything. I
could do it in my sleep now. In fact, I did make biscuits in
my sleep. I woke up with my hands kneading the sheets.
"Mr. Ashby bought Walker gloves and balls. Ever since he
was little," I said, mixing the lard, butter and flour. The
dough peas were forming.

"Why would Timothy do that?" she asked suspi-
ciously. "And what's a voice pipe?"

I shrugged. "I don't know why he brought him all the
baseball equipment." I reflected for a moment. "Maybe
because he didn't have his own kid until now, and the
voice pipe, well, he's put holes in the wall all over the
house upstairs, looking for the best place to put a pipe so
he can talk through it to Mama downstairs while she's
ironing."

"Well, if that man doesn't think the sun comes up just
to hear him crow," Maddie said, shaking her head. "And
your Mama? What does she do?"

"She sets the new vacuum cleaner in the corner and
turns it on so she doesn't have to listen to him."

"And William?"

"He thinks Mama could win an argument even if she
was in an empty house, so he just goes and charges the
battery for a while longer."

"That'd be William for sure. Making it work for those
two. Where's the game?"

"Walker said Livingston."

"Are you going?"

I looked away. "No, Daddy can't drive the truck off the

farm. Mr. Ashby doesn't want him getting in trouble out on the roads. You know. The patrols look for pickers trying to leave," I added.

"I'll take you." She pulled her apron off. "I'll take you and your parents. It's about time William and I had a heart to heart. I got something to say to him." Maddie untied her apron and pulled it over her head. "I got to pick out something to wear. Tell your folks I'll be by after supper time."

"Ah, Maddie, thank you. Can I go now? I want to tell Mama and Daddy."

As I thundered home, my legs and arms going in wildly different directions, I said the name Lefty Grove again and again like it was a mantra. He was a big-league pitcher Walker admired because he had thrown a perfect inning. Nine pitches, three strikeouts. I kept saying it to myself, "Lefty Grove, Lefty Grove, Lefty Grove." When I said it nine times in a row without having to catch my breath, I counted it as an inning. I know it was impossible for a pitcher to throw that many strikes in a row in more than one inning, but Walker would be the one to do it if he knew a scout, especially a big-league scout, was there to see it.

Chapter Eighteen

Maddie's truck turned off the road and bumped slowly through the ruts toward the big house. The little truck, black with rust lining its running boards, stopped, and the horn beeped twice.

"Load 'em up," Maddie growled like she was driving a train of people. I vaulted over the wheel well. Maddie held out her arm to stop Daddy while Mama climbed into the truck. Maddie looked Daddy straight in the eye while grasping both his arms in her scrawny hands. "William. It's been too long. It was my fault for not back coming back. You are the only family I got." She took a deep breath and waited. Daddy kissed her on the cheek.

"Welcome home, Maddie." He looked inside the truck to see if there was room, and then, I believe he reconsidered that idea. "I'll ride in the back with Socrates."

The truck hurtled down the road as Maddie shifted the gears and went around curves without using the brakes. The tires whined as rocks flew out behind us. Livingston was about thirteen miles away. It was going to be a long ride with a silent daddy. I ventured, "I suppose I could have sat on the side over the wheel well, but only Walker's brave enough to do that. He wouldn't mind if he got bumped off."

"Walker would think twice if he rode with Maddie, I think." Daddy patted his leg with his hand and reached over and tapped mine as well. "Socrates, what I did was wrong. There's a difference between paddling your boy and hitting him. I feel ashamed." We bounced as Maddie hit a rut. "I'm sorry, son."

"It's okay, Daddy. I needed to be brought up short. Part of being a man is knowing when to stop and when to keep going. I should have not spoken up to you about the money. Do Miss Cora and Brutus know?"

"Yes."

"And Trask," I said. "He checks the ledger every day."

"He and I have an agreement." Daddy shifted his legs and brought his knee up to rest his hand on.

"What's the agreement?"

"He allows that Miss Cora's worth as a baby catcher can't be put into dollar and cents. He lets me put down just ten dollars a month in rent. He isn't letting them pay nothing, though. Your mama and I are paying their rent. I agreed it was only fair to the others who were working for their rent by picking."

"Trask is changed," I admitted.

"More than, you know, Soc. The farm has changed him."

Livingston was a bigger town than Gideon. Downtown streets fanned out in all directions, and men held doors open for women as they entered hotels and restaurants. The sunlight was slanting, which meant it was coming on toward sunset, and the metal of cars, trucks, and horse wagons shone as they lined up next to each other in front of the stores. I heard music coming from a place where window shades blocked the commotion going on inside. A honied smell wafted out the door and a second odor that smelled like flowers drifted in the air too. It made me want to sneeze. It was later that I realized that when homemade whiskey and women's dusting powder joined together, it smelled just like Trask's room.

Negro men drove as many trucks as white men, and their arms dangled out the windows in a lazy way that showed they weren't afraid. I could see the reflection of Maddie's old truck in the store windows as we drove by. For sure, it wasn't a perfect town, but it did make Gideon look tired and in need a fresh coat of paint.

The ball field was on the edge of town. It sat between the white school and the Negro school, and the Negro boys waited outside the fence until the pimply-faced white boys were done. The Negro school was an old creamery building that had been left behind when the milk factory moved to York a few miles away. It was long and low with small windows up near the roof line. The siding was like a patchwork quilt; new boards were slid in next to the old ones still hanging on. The ground was bare of weeds, and someone was keeping the grass mowed. It looked respectable enough, but I still smelled the stench of ancient spilled milk we drove by.

We had to buy tickets, fifty cents apiece, and I saw Daddy look at Mama as he unwound the coins from his handkerchief. He looked over at Maddie. "Maddie, we'd like to buy your way tonight since you brought us." Daddy's voice was full of pride. I bought my own ticket from my wages. I gave most of my money to Mama, but I kept some for myself to save up for school expenses.

"That's fine. I'd appreciate it, William. But I am going

to buy us all popcorn. No one should watch baseball without popcorn." Daddy nodded his head okay. I thought of that thirteen-year-old boy he'd been. Likely they'd henpecked him to death then too. Mama grabbed Maddie's arm and squeezed it.

We could barely see the teams in the growing darkness. Walker said that throwing in the last of the sunset helped you feel where the ball was even more than seeing it. He started off with practice pitches to warm up his arm. They started throwing close together, and then the catcher kept backing up and throwing long to Walker. My brother threw the ball fast and on a straight line. I could hear the catcher complain to "save it for the game"—his glove hand hurt already. Walker's throws to the catcher's mitt sounded just like the infielders who threw the ball hard to one another. It sounded brisk, like a smack of flesh on flesh. Daddy and I didn't look at one another as everyone flinched around us—except for Mama and Maddie, who were twittering and laughing.

The stands were packed, and I was surprised to see many white people at a Negro baseball game. The news of Brick O'Malley's scouting visit must have made it beyond the newspaper. We found some of the last seats. The stands were ten feet high with ten rows in each section. When Maddie and Mama hefted their way onto one of the top rows, Daddy and I looked at each other and tried sneaking into seats a few rows below them, but we were motioned up to follow Mama and Maddie. We were stared at by the folks already there, so we took deep breaths and lowered ourselves onto the gray, worn boards. I prayed it would hold all of us. Just as I wiggled into my seat next to Maddie, she handed me a quarter and told me to go buy popcorn. I climbed down the stands, searching for the next foothold, and reached the ground. I couldn't see a popcorn stand anywhere, so I started following my nose. I saw a burner glowing bright with red logs and headed straight for it. I stood in line and tried not to bump into anyone in the twilight. The bags smoked in my hands, and I handed them up to my daddy.

"Butter," Maddie said with closed eyes. She and Mama reached into the bag at the same time and broke it open. Whooping, they gathered it all and held it in their cupped hands on their knees. Daddy and I put our hands in our pockets and edged as close to the other people sitting next to us as possible.

When the last bubble of sunlight slipped behind the edge of town, car headlights burst on, and I heard the chug, chug of trucks turn on all around the field. I shaded my eyes with my hand and scanned the other stands. It was harder to see in the bright light than in the twilight. I couldn't make out any colors, and everyone's faces were white instead of black. It was unnerving—that was for sure. I counted ten trucks circling the field, and people sat on the tops of the truck cabs. The collective headlights were so blinding I could see through women's dresses to their slips and easily pick out who had gray hair lining their heads.

I searched the crowd for people I knew and sucked in my breath when I saw Grindall and a man wearing a Chicago Cubs baseball hat, sitting in the front row near home plate. Mr. Chastain and Mr. Belknap were sitting behind them and talking in Grindall's ear. Our team, the Gideon Bulldogs, were lined up in the visitor's dugout, pulling their suspender straps tight and stuffing newspaper and cotton in the front of their stirrup socks.

Although it was just a country league, spiking was against the rules but rarely enforced.

Walker left the dugout and walked to the stands where he held out his hand to shake Brick O'Malley's hand and then Grindall's hand. Grindall stood up and clapped for Walker. He motioned the rest of the crowd to clap too. The crowd whistled, shouted, and booed. Walker, already in deep concentration, ran back to the dugout.

"What the hell is going on?" Daddy whipped around to look at Mama. "Grindall is with the scout. We have to get Walker out of there."

"You think so?" Maddie interrupted. "Is he as good as he says he is?" Mama and Daddy nodded their heads yes. "Let him do it. If you pull him out now, it will eat him up, and he will blame you. I know a little something about that."

Maddie looked straight on at Daddy. To me, they looked like they were reliving the night of Midnight's escape when everyone's life changed with Mr. Sir's beating of my daddy. They carried the story in them every day. I wondered if it fluttered around their rib cages and struck them when they weren't ready for its blow. That's what it did to me. I felt bruised when I thought of the Four and their last night together.

"Maddie, you don't know this man," Daddy started.

"Maddie's right. Walker would never forgive us if we pulled him off the field." Mama poked Daddy. "You know so too."

Daddy's back was rigid, and I looked for moving toes, twitching muscles, or shaking fingers, but he was as cold and still as stone. There was nothing he could do but watch.

I tuned out Mama and Maddie's excited talk so I could

think about Walker. I knew he would never shake Grindall's hand under normal circumstances. What made him do it in front of a hundred people he didn't know? Then it dawned on me. Brick O'Malley played for the Chicago Cubs, and Grindall had moved to Gideon from Chicago. How did they know each other? The day of the longleaf pine tree massacre, Grindall said he had no interest in seeing Walker pitch, but how did he know a famous baseball player like Brick O'Malley then?

Brick O'Malley sat a couple feet apart from Grindall directly behind home plate in the second row. He held a stopwatch in his hands and had a clipboard on his knee. He was a big man with a curly bar mustache and a large coat that was tight across his shoulders. The interested fans in the stands stood up to look at him, and the players on the field stole nervous glances at his impassive face. They slapped their gloves against their legs with a clapping sound. After watching Walker shake hands with him, the Livingston and Gideon fans were curious. It seemed more like an interview than a scout's visit.

Inside myself, I was so proud it was like a huge balloon kept filling up with more and more air. He wasn't there to see any of the rest of them. He was there to see Walker William Jefferson play baseball or, more specifically, to throw the ball. That is what he was looking for, the article said, a unique pitcher who could baffle unsuspecting hitters. That was Walker all right. I watched Brick O'Malley pull his watch out of his pocket and flick it open. The gold flashed in the light and the creamy face of the watch said seven o'clock straight up. The umpire motioned to the teams to line up, and they poured out of the dugouts and faced each other along the first and third baselines. After the Pledge of Allegiance, the Lord's

Prayer, and the Star-Spangled Banner, it was time for the game to begin.

I watched the Livingston pitcher start his warm-up pitches. He was a meatball pitcher. He threw across the plate to get the other team to hit the ball. He left it up to his team to turn the hits into outs. Most country teams had meatball pitchers, except for Gideon. Walker Jefferson believed his pitches were not just tosses across home plate. When someone called from the stands, "Put it in play," he broke his rule about not looking to the stands, and he'd glare right back at them. To just put it in play meant that a pitcher didn't care. In baseball, caring is what it is all about. It's about caring how your foot sweeps across second base with the right scraping sound for a double play so there'd be no doubt on the call or believing your sprint into the deep outfield with your hands held in a basket in front of your chest would result in an over-the-shoulder catch, and for Walker, it meant that he knew how to hit the corners of the plate so his pitches would fade off the plate or crowd up against the batter.

The fame-hungry batters chased low and outside pitches all day long, and the belligerent hitters needed to fan high and tight pitches to teach them a lesson in front of their girlfriends sitting next to their mothers. For the few hitters who took their time to match their practice swings to the speed of the pitch, Walker tipped his head to them in appreciation. They cared. The battle between a great pitcher and a great batter was a thing of glory, Walker said.

We had first ups since we were the visiting team. Our first three batters got out, two ground outs to the shortstop and one fly ball to center field. As the teams streamed past one another after the final out, Walker walked slowly and deliberately to the mound. He stood for a few moments adjusting his hat, tying his shoes, and swinging his arms in circles. It was for effect, and I must be honest: I was disappointed in Walker. He was a good pitcher, good enough for the major leagues, and he didn't have to fall back on showboating to capture fans' attention. By the time he was ready to throw his warm-up pitches, the other players were done warming up. Everyone—the Livingston team, the Gideon team, the fans, and the scout, Brick O'Malley—had nothing left to do but watch Walker warm up.

Walker's windup was slow and easy. It started with his hands dropping behind his head while his leg rose off the ground and kicked forward toward home plate. When he planted his foot, his elbow almost brushed his ear as his throwing hand came forward and his wrist snapped at the last second to drive the ball toward the batter. Last of all, his back leg, the full energy behind every pitch, kicked up behind him like a matador with his cape, judging with skill, daring and grace, how close he could paint the black lines, or in other words, streak the ball on each side of home plate.

I sat up straight in my seat. All the games Walker and I had listened to while lying in the grass outside the Ashbys' living room window had prepared me for this game. I had seen it in my mind, and now everyone was coming to life. The umpire crouched over and put his hand just a bit on the catcher's shoulder. The catcher shifted on his feet, his knees rose slightly and the ball soared out of Walker's hand. The batter, tipped forward on his toes with his hands gripped half up the bat, swung, and the umpire called a strike. Mr. Brick O'Malley rose to his feet and tapped his thumb on the stopwatch. He put his clipboard under his arm and slowly clapped his hands together. I watched the retired catcher of the Chicago Cubs stand up and applaud Walker's fastball. He shook head in disbelief.

"Oh, Lord," Daddy said and gripped the shuddering seat underneath him. Maddie and Mama stood up and jumped up and down on the boards. They hollered Walker's name. People sitting below us turned around to stare at them.

I took a deep breath from the bottom of my lungs. Walker was going to pitch the game of his life. He was going to become the first Negro player to cross the color line and play in the big leagues. I knew it deep down in the place where faith comes from. Faith is believing and knowing. Hope? Hope only goes halfway. Hope leaves room to wiggle out and backtrack while faith goes full in even if it means you run on a fly ball without tagging up. There's a chance you're going to get called out, but with faith, you're certain the ball is going to drop in the gap out in the outfield.

Walker struck all three batters out, and he even left the mound and trotted back to the dugout before the umpire called the third strike on the last batter, who never lifted the bat off his shoulder. Gideon had the chance to bat three times in twenty minutes as Walker dismissed nine Livingston batters in three innings with his special mix of fastballs, sliders, curveballs, and a few changeups. He held back on the knuckle ball, and I guessed he was saving it for near the end of the game.

Brick O'Malley was scrawling in a notebook spread across his lap. I watched as Mr. Chastain and Mr. Belknap took sips out of a silver flask and passed it to Grindall. The former Chicago resident took a long slug and tried to hand it to Brick O'Malley, who shook his head no and continued to write notes.

Then disaster arrived from the back of the crowd. Sliding sideways and ducking his head under people's arms, Mr. Ashby, the only one missing of the Four at the game, his bald head crowned with a few wisps of cobweb gray hair, threaded his way through the crowd shouting shrilly for people to get out of his way. I prayed he didn't see Mama and Maddie sitting together in the stands. Last I heard, the reunion was still on hold.

"Who are you?" Brick O'Malley lifted his head and tipped his head down at Mr. Ashby. His lips turned up in revulsion at Mr. Ashby's round, childlike body straining on its tiptoes, trying to catch his attention. I watched Brick O'Malley stare at Mr. Ashby twice in a row at his different-colored eyes. I wondered if they were saying the same message or if they were fighting against one another.

"Timothy, you are right!" Mr. Belknap shouted down to him. "That young man of yours is putting on a show tonight. He's got a big leaguer interested in him." Mr. Belknap pointed to Brick O'Malley.

"What are you doing?" Mr. Ashby hung on Brick O'Malley's arm. "He's a Negro. He can't play in the big leagues. They aren't allowed."

Brick O'Malley shook off Mr. Ashby's arm. "Listen, man, this kid is good. I think I can get him a tryout with the Cubs. I'm taking him back to Chicago with me."

"Brick's a friend of mine. I guess I'll be the one helping Walker leave Jackson County now. What do you say, Ashby?" Grindall leaned over and flashed a grin at him as if they had a special relationship.

"Walker is not leaving my property without my

permission. His family owes me money, and he has to stay until it is paid."

"How did he find that out?" Daddy pushed past me and jumped to the ground, wading through the fans to join the group of white men creating a scene next to the field.

"Socrates Bravo, put your lips together. You're going to catch a big old june bug in there if you don't button up. People keep saying how smart you are. Better look it too." Maddie waved a hand in front of my face.

"Are you the kid's father?" Brick O'Malley asked Daddy.

"Yes, Walker is my son." Daddy's face was like granite. As he spoke, Gideon hit into a double play and left the field to get their gloves. Walker walked out of the dugout, stretched his arm, and stood on the mound waiting for the catcher to get his gear on. I felt fear slice through me then. Walker's thumb was tapping against his leg just like Daddy's.

"He's a Negro. He will play in the Negro League," Mr. Ashby insisted.

"He's good enough to play anywhere. You know that, Timothy. Why would you hold him back?" Daddy's angry voice didn't hold back and some of the fans shifted in their seats uncomfortably.

"He's a Negro, William," Mr. Ashby turned away. He pointed at Grindall. "How are you involved in all this?"

"Just an interested party, that's all."

The umpire came over to the knot of men. "Enough now. You are disrupting the game. Settle down or you will have to leave."

"Look, I'll pay the kid's debts. He could be the one. We've been looking for a Negro player to come up to the big leagues," Brick O'Malley tapped his fingers on his closed notebook.

"Will you take care of him?" Daddy asked. "He's just a boy."

"He'll have to take care of himself," Brick O'Malley replied. "The first Negro to play in the big leagues will have to keep his cool, keep his focus. From what I see of this kid, he could be the one. It's all about temperament."

"No, no, no!" Mr. Ashby stamped his little foot, his tiny hands tight in small fists. "No, he can't do it. I won't allow it. I decide where he plays baseball."

"Who are you anyway?" Brick O'Malley asked, irritated. "Get out of here. You don't understand. Baseball may look like it's about luck, but without talent, you won't last long." Brick O'Malley studied Mr. Ashby's little body. I believed he wondered how such a small man—physically petite and mentally small in intellect—could limit a potential bust-out star because of the color of his skin. I bet Brick O'Malley didn't have his own Mr. Sir.

All the while, Walker was pitching to the Livingston batters. One of them knocked off a single, and a Livingston runner was aboard for the first time all night. He was bunted around the bases, and the Gideon team fumbled several times to throw him out. He finally scored on a sacrifice fly. The score was tied. Walker stopped and called time. The umpire's hands flew into the air. The catcher ran out to the mound and patted Walker on the shoulder. I knew what was coming.

The catcher conferred with Walker and settled back down behind the plate. There was two strikes and two balls on the batter. Walker squared up and started his windup. I watched his hand, and sure enough, the seams of the ball were held in place by his knuckles. The ball floated toward the batter and then smack! It hit the glove. Brick O'Malley jumped to his feet. "Was that a knuckleball?"

"Yes, sir," Daddy said proudly. "It sure was."

"That's it," Brick O'Malley. "Let's get this game over. I gotta get that kid on a train going north."

I watched Grindall listen to Brick O'Malley's words. "Three outs yet?" he asked, standing up. He gave Daddy a look who returned it with his own. Brick O'Malley held them even on the scale that weighed Walker's talent. Daddy's stiff neck told me he knew Grindall hadn't changed. Something was wrong. He was still the man who destroyed a tree for show and took off through the woods rather than allow us to see his bee-stung swollen face. Grindall reached his hand for Mr. Chastain's flask. He drained it and shoved it back at him.

"Grindall, you're a pig," Mr. Chastain protested. Grindall turned to him and shoved him hard so he teetered on his seat.

"Shut up." Grindall spat and put a toothpick in his mouth. "I'll be back."

"Let me down," I said. "I gotta go bad." The people parted, and I jumped to the ground. I followed Grindall as he walked down the first base line to join the umpire who had lit up a cigarette in the shadows outside of the truck lights. I couldn't hear them talking, but when I saw Grindall hand the man a thick roll of dollars, I wanted to barrel him to the ground and punch his lights out.

"Fine," I growled. "if Walker has to make it all about temperament, I'll do it too."

I turned and ran back to the stands where the Livingston fans were roaring for their team. "Mr. O'Malley!" I shoved myself in front of Mr. Ashby pushing him out of the way. "I'm Socrates Jefferson, Walker's brother. Does he have to finish the game, or could he go with you right now?"

"That's quite a name for a lad like you," he said, leaning over. "Gumption. I've seen enough. I'll take him now if he wants to go." I watched Grindall tense up and pick a piece of tobacco off the tip of his tongue.

"Thanks, I'll go tell him."

"Walker." I banged on the dugout wall. "Brick O'Malley says he'll take you right now to the train station to Chicago. He says he wants the Cubs to give you a tryout. Don't finish the game. Come on."

"Oh my God, Socrates. Are you kidding me? I'm finishing the game. Get out of here." The crowd thundered when they saw Walker stand up from the bench and head out to the mound for the final inning.

I knew then I had one last card to play, and I'd have to do what my brother and my daddy had both done with impunity—tell a white man he was wrong. I tugged on Brick O'Malley's sleeve. "I'm sorry to interrupt," I said, feigning unctuousness, "but Mr. Grindall gave the umpire money. I saw it out in the field. I think it was to stop Walker from getting a tryout."

"You little pissant, Socrates. I owed the man some money. I was just paying him back. How dare you say that about my character?" Grindall turned to Mr. Ashby. "Have someone whip him tonight for speaking about a man's character like that."

"I will if you keep Walker in Gideon. I don't want him going to Chicago. I won't let him go. I made him." He repeated it. "I made him." He turned to Daddy. "You will whip Socrates, or paddle him, whatever you call it, when you get home tonight, William. Do you hear me?"

"What is all this talking about beating the young boy with the odd name? What has he done? He said his piece, and Grindall cleared it up. Now everyone stop talking, and let's get this game over." Brick O'Malley shook his head in annoyance.

"Walker is his own man, Timothy." I heard Daddy say forcefully into Mr. Ashby's ear. "You talk of beating either of my boys, and I'll take you out to the Patch once and for all—do you hear me?"

"I'm leaving, William. As far as I am concerned, you didn't say that. If you did, I'd have to do something about it." Mr. Ashby struggled into his coat and begged people to get out of his way. He watched Daddy over his shoulder as he scurried to his car like a frightened mouse. This was a William he didn't know.

There was a change in the air, a heaviness, a coolness. Things were starting to unravel, and I pushed the thoughts away, but they kept creeping back. It was the end of August. The heat of the day disappeared by night, and in the final moments of the game, the fans leaned into each other seeking warmth from a cold wind that was picking up in the valley and making its way toward us.

I turned to watch Walker, and I realized he was on batter number two of a Lefty Grove. He had dispatched the first hitter, who swung three times in a row, chasing a slider and a curveball before a fastball blew past him. Three strikes down. The second batter kept stepping out of the batter's box to try to distract the pitcher from his rhythm, but Walker bore down and struck him out with three called pitches. I felt my heart lighten, and I hoped Walker would be leaving town tonight with Brick O'Malley. It didn't register it at the moment, but my thinking had changed from faith to hope, and that is where I failed my brother.

The third batter came up. He fanned on his first two pitches. Walker only needed one last pitch to end the inning with a Lefty Grove—a baseball moment of triumph no one would ever forget.

"Lefty Grove," I yelled. Walker couldn't hide his smile. He threw a hard fastball straight down the middle, directly over the plate, and past the batter's belt buckle. It was a strike any day, anywhere, for anyone. Except tonight. The umpire didn't move. He stepped back and waited for Walker to get in position to pitch again. His silence meant it was a ball.

"Are you kidding me?" Walker shouted. "Are you kidding me? You did that just to take it away from me. 'Cause you're a lousy ball player who never made it and you don't want anyone else to either. You..."

Walker let loose a string of swear words I didn't know he knew, and some I didn't know what they meant. Daddy dropped his head in his hands and the catcher ran out to Walker and held him back. Walker kept screaming obscenities at the umpire, who finally raised his thumb in the air and ejected him from the game. Inside the dugout, Walker kicked bats, threw his glove, and ran his hands through his hair screaming.

"Temperament," Brick O'Malley said tersely and packed his notebook and stopwatch in his bag. "Too bad. What wasted talent. That young man might have made it past the tryouts. He's certainly good enough. Talent's one thing, but it is nothing compared to temperament. You can't teach that. Either you have it, or you don't. Grindall, take me to the train station, would you? I don't want to hang around this town any longer."

I looked at Grindall, and I realized he had told the umpire to pick the perfect moment to prick Walker's pride so, like a balloon, it would pop in his face. It took only one bad call to unleash Walker's fury. My brother had lost his chance at the big leagues because he couldn't stomach one bad call, one lost chance at a Lefty Grove. He had faith in himself to perform to the level necessary for the big leagues, but what he didn't factor in was that some-times life—in the form of someone evil like Grindall—can destroy that faith for no real reason at all other than spite.

I searched for Maddie and my parents. I didn't even know how the game ended; all I know was that Livingston won, and the Gideon team wasn't speaking to Walker. Trucks and cars were cutting across the corn field to avoid the line leaving the ball field. There were laughter and shouts, and the Livingston team taunted the Gideon boys, who climbed into their few trucks in silence.

Mama, Daddy, and Maddie stood, holding blankets and talking in low voices. They were waiting for Walker. Walker came to us. He handed his gear bag to Daddy and stood in place, his eyes far away and flinty. He cracked each of his knuckles while Mama fussed over him.

"Ready to go, Jefferson?" Grindall said, grinding his cigarette out under his toe. "I'll take O'Malley to the train station and come back by your place."

"What the hell are you talking about?" Maddie demanded.

"Who are you?" Grindall looked down with displea-sure at the small, loud Negro woman who stood with her hands on her hips her eyes looking at him without waver-ing. He backed up a step. "Walker and I arranged a bet today. If O'Malley offered him a tryout with the Cubs, I'd give him a hundred dollars. Right, Walker?"

Walker stared off into the distance. "Yes, sir."

"I'd like to hear you say it out loud."

"I'm chopping wood for you until I pay off a hundred dollars from our bet." Walker looked at us with dead eyes.

"Well, this little family drama is interesting to watch, but with the drive back to Gideon, the trip to Ashby's, and then back to my place, we're looking at a couple of hours. Hurry up, Jefferson."

Daddy moved forward to get into Grindall's truck, but Walker held him back. "He means me now, Daddy."

"How long will it take to pay off his debt? I will come work for you too." Daddy turned to Grindall.

"Old man, you couldn't do what this boy is going to do. He's going to swing an ax all day. You don't have the strength to do that." Grindall laughed in a way that made my skin crawl. "Besides, Ashby's been too soft on you all these years. I'll make a man out of your son. It's not just a hundred dollars. It will be more than that. He'll buy his equipment and pay for his meals. But it's good enough work. He can pay it off, but it will probably take a few years. We'll see." Grindall shrugged his jacket on. "Didn't think it got cold here in the South." He pulled his collar up around his ears. "Don't worry. Walker will have his own shack just like the pickers. It's a little smaller than the ones on Ashby's place. But it's just his size."

"Thank you, Walker." Grindall looked me up and down. "Socrates, you are fortunate you are still a child." He stuck his face close to mine. "I'll let your rudeness go this one time, but if you do it again, there will be hell to pay." He walked off toward his truck and broke into a jog. "Hurry up. Get him back to Ashby's."

"Why, Walker? Why would you take a chance on ruining your future like that?" Daddy's face was contorted into a featureless mask.

"Because I knew I would win. It's that simple. You know it too."

Maddie snorted. "Son, I only know you from the messy way you eat apple pie, but nothing's sure in life. Just ask your mama, daddy, and me. We let twenty-five years go by because of something just like what happened to you."

Daddy, Walker, and I climbed into the bed of Maddie's truck. Walker sat between us. Instead of the warm body I expected, he was ice-cold. I looked over my shoulder into the cab of the truck. Maddie and Mama were no longer laughing together. They rode in silence. Mama was crying. Maddie stared ahead into the darkness. They knew what was coming.

When we got home, Maddie's truck sat idling for a minute. "You want me to stay?" she asked. Sadness rippled through her voice.

"No, thank you, Maddie. You sure did us a favor driving us tonight. We'll be fine. Bye now." My daddy's voice was formal and distant. It was as if the kiss on her cheek had never happened. He didn't want any outsiders knowing what the inside of our life looked like. But Maddie wasn't an outsider, I wanted to yell. She was family.

Then lights flashed across the barn and the pasture. Grindall pulled into the drive and turned his truck around so it was ready to leave. He yawned as if he was tired of us always being in his way. He said to Mama and Daddy, "I offered him fifty cents a load of wood. I'll stand by my word on that." Walker stepped up to the truck and heaved his bag in the back.

"Leave it here. There's nothing you need. I'll sell you your supplies." Walker handed me his bag and looked around for our parents. "Say your goodbyes, Walker." Grindall put the truck into gear as Mama ran out with my grandmother's quilt and a pillow and tossed them to Walker. Grindall chuckled, his arm resting on the open window. He revved the motor. "He's not a child. A quilt's not going to help much, but fine, he can bring it." Daddy came out of the barn carrying a large, heavy ax. "No, that won't do." Grindall called as he let the clutch out. "Not with the trees he'll pull down." My parents, their arms empty, hugged Walker and stood back so I could say goodbye.

Walker embraced them and held out his hand to me. I took it trying to be a man, but instead, I slammed into his arms and hugged him with all the fierceness shared between brothers whose shared childhood was gone. He pulled my arms from him and climbed into the back of the truck. As Grindall drove out of the road, he beeped his horn at some pickers standing on the side of the yard road.

Rain began to fall as the truck lights disappeared. Daddy put out his hand and waited until the water slicked into his palm. He rubbed the drops between his fingers. "This isn't blowing over. It's going to stay awhile." Daddy kicked the dirt and rubbed his wet palm on the side of his pants. "Annie?"

"Yes, William?"

"Tenant farmer from York told me wild hogs took a field near them." His back was to us.

"How long will they be in Jackson County, Daddy?" I asked.

"Until they're done, Socrates. Then they move on." He looked at the rows of cotton that disappeared into the darkness.

Chapter Nineteen

The rain did not stop. It was unrelenting and seemed to hover intentionally over the Ashby farm. The final bolls in Middle Field and High Field had not popped out of the seed casings, so my daddy walked the rows, squeezing the water from the pods, hoping to save the last couple of picks. The pickers worried and watched. They were so close to freedom, to being even. I even spoke to Joseph, who wanted one more pick of the season so he could buy his own bag. His arms were blistered again, and I imagine his father dozed through the rain, smoking one cigarette after another, blowing clouds of bitter smoke through their house. Although it was not my life, I imagined if his father fell asleep with a cigarette held between two fingers, Joseph learned to tap the ash in the tray before his father awoke. He determined how to stay safe, and I was angry because the consequences of Walker's pride did not understand that simple necessity.

We talked about it until we could talk no more. Walker made an impossible bet with Grindall and was now paying the price. I wished I could go to him and tell him how much Brick O'Malley thought of Walker's abilities as a pitcher, but after my accusation of Grindall's motives for giving the umpire money, I didn't want to get caught on his land. I struggled to process all that happened at the game. I had accused a white man of cheating; Mr. Ashby had refused to see Walker as a person outside of his race or as a pitcher good enough for the big leagues. My daddy spoke up directly to Brick O'Malley, a powerful white man, and whispered a threat into Mr. Ashby's ears that had hung between them their whole lives, but most of all, Brick O'Malley treated us all the same whether we were white or Negro. It made me wonder: if the North could create one man who didn't see color when he looked at those around him, how could it also create Grindall, another man, who saw nothing but opportunities to impose his cruel will on others?

Chapter Twenty

Trask asked about Walker when he noticed he was missing, and he came to Mama in the kitchen the night she was canning the last of the vegetables she had saved from the rain. My job was to pinch the jars with the clasp and pull them out of the water when they had boiled long enough. The windows were dense with dripping water and the humidity was unbearable. I slipped my glasses to the end of my nose so I could try to see the jars in the steam.

"Annie, I heard about Walker. I'm very sorry. I could try to talk to Grindall if you think that would help."

"Mr. Trask, I've told you before: the Jeffersons can take care of their own." Her back was to him as she stood at the counter lining up the jars.

"Fine then." He left the kitchen without looking at me.

"Annie, I don't understand you," Mrs. Ashby had been standing in the hall and heard my mother's angry comment. "Trask has done his best to become part of the farm, and you won't let him in. Why is that?"

Mama couldn't help herself. She stole a look at Mrs.

Ashby's enormous belly. "I just want our life back the way it was when no one told us how to live." She wiped her hands across her eyes.

"Annie, someone told you how to live your life every day back then. You just didn't see it. Good night, you two." Mrs. Ashby walked back into the hall and climbed the stairs holding the handrail to keep her steady.

"Mrs. Ashby?" Mama said, her hands tight on the edge of the sink.

"Yes, Annie?"

"Next time the eye doctor comes, can I get glasses? I have always needed them. I can't see the letters on a page."

There was silence on the stairs. "Of course, Annie. Of course. I'm sorry I didn't ask earlier." Mrs. Ashby's footsteps faded when she reached the door to her bedroom.

"Socrates, all my life I did for others and they didn't know what I needed. Now maybe you'll think about that. Go home. I still have the dishes to do."

———

THE RAIN CHANGED THE LANDSCAPE OF THE FARM. Thankfully, the pickers finished the lower field of bolls before the rain started, so it was the two upper fields that still held enough bolls to harvest if the rain stopped and the sun came out. The creek's bank gave way in places, and the lower field became a shallow lake where migrating mallards, green-winged teals, and common loons filled the waters calling to one another looking for food. Hundreds of silent golden-winged warblers and blue-headed vireos filled the trees, but it took only a chattering chickadee or titmouse to cause them to take flight, bending the small branches as they moved on in their journey.

Mrs. Ashby was edgy during the worst of the rains. She was tired of her body and the wait it forced her to endure. She wanted to stretch her legs and walk to the point of exhaustion, but my mama and Miss Cora convinced her to save her strength. Mr. Ashby? He did anything he darned well wanted to do, like always.

Daddy spent most of his time walking the edges of the Ashby's acres. His boots sunk into mud over his ankles, but the stick he carried helped him loosen his trapped boots. The rain was a concern, but more importantly, if the wandering pigs came upon the fields, the harvest was over.

Wild hogs were unpredictable and difficult to find. The hogs terrorized the countryside for weeks. They rooted the ground with their snouts and created pockets of earth and muck. They tore up crops, destroyed fences, killed chickens and farm pigs by trampling and eating them as they marched. They destroyed ponds where livestock drank, fouling it with feces as they turned it into a wallow to cool their prickly, insect-bitten skin.

We didn't see them often, not more than once or twice a year. A farmer in North Carolina had imported hogs from Europe with curving, sharp tucks to make a game reserve for city men who wanted the experience of hunting. He thought a circular pen would hold them because they wouldn't be able to take hold of a corner. He did not realize, however, that his pigs would reproduce at such a rapid rate that the walls would buckle under the pressure of the ever-increasing population. The pen broke. Not only did the marauders stampede through the wood shards left of their prison, but a boar and a few others stopped and devoured the man. Once in the wild, the drove of wild hogs spread across the south and split off into new groups growing more savage. They roamed fields, forests, and swamps. Once the roots, ground crops, and small animals were decimated, they moved on. They came like lustful coyotes slaughtering sheep in an otherwise safe field or like a single red wolf that lingers on the edges of a forest for a few days until it drags a colt full of promise from a string of horses. There was one difference though: hogs would eat their own.

"Daddy, Mr. Ashby wants to see you in the barn. He said he had a few questions about the horses." I stood on the road next to High Field. Daddy kneeled in the dirt, checking to see how far the water had penetrated.

"Man's almost forty years old, and he wants to learn about horses. God almighty." Daddy stood in the mud and struggled for breath as he used his stick to pull himself up. "Help me up, Socrates." I pulled him out of the mud, and we walked in silence to the barn.

There was nothing to say. Walker was gone.

"So, William, how much do the horses eat?" Mr. Ashby stood primly on the straw-covered floor of the barn. He was wearing new boots that must have been made for children. His feet fit in the boots, but they only came up to his midcalf, which made him look like a duck ready to paddle in the pond. The horses' breath warmed the air and crowded out the cold of the rain. Lean stamped his feet in his stall. I saw him turn his eyes to watch Daddy.

"Enough. Depends. Not always hay, alfalfa too." Daddy grunted.

"Alfalfa? Never heard of it. Is it a grain? A flower? Maybe Mrs. Ashby is familiar with it."

"It's grass."

"Well, that will help the budget, won't it? It's easy enough to come by, isn't it? We'll just have some pickers pull it, and it can come straight to the barn."

"Timothy, leave me alone. This is nonsense. You've never cared about the horses," Daddy barked. "What are you going to do about Walker?"

"I'm not going anywhere, and I'm not doing anything about Walker, William. Walker made his choice. The fact that Walker made a bet with Grindall is not my concern. My job with him is done. His life as an adult is just beginning. It's the way of life." Mr. Ashby reached a tentative hand out to stroke Lean who dipped his nose and almost laid it on the top of Mr. Ashby's head. "I'll teach my son about life just as you have with Walker and Socrates, won't I?"

"Here you go." Daddy abruptly tossed the currying brush to Mr. Ashby, who fumbled to catch it. "Your son will need to learn about horses, just like you did from Mr. Sir. Go on in there and brush that horse." Mr. Ashby looked uncertain as he pushed the lock up to open the stall.

"Mr. Ashby, why don't you go on in and check on Mrs. Ashby," I recommended. I grabbed the brush from him and pushed back on the door to Lean's stall. The boards of the gate strained against the horse's weight.

"Yes, Socrates. That is a good idea. You take good care of that horse now, you hear?" He walked out of the barn and scurried to the porch, pulling his coat over his head to avoid the rain.

"Daddy, why'd you do that?"

"I'm done, Socrates. As soon as Brick O'Malley left, I knew Timothy would never help us." Daddy grabbed the brush and pushed back on Lean. "You get back, now.

Now," he ordered the horse. Lean turned his head toward Daddy and flicked his mane. Daddy growled low. Lean backed up. Daddy dropped the brush and walked out into the pelting rain leaving me behind without looking back. He called, "I'll brush him later. He and I aren't going anywhere."

Chapter Twenty-One

I hurried into Maddie's yard. Her rusty truck was parked next to the sloping porch that covered the front door. The windows were closed, and paper shades were taped to the glass. There was a note on the worn front door: "I need a break. See you later."

I stepped back off the porch and squinted at the second floor. Maddie's bedroom windows were sealed tight with the paper too. I climbed the gray steps and pounded on the door with my fist.

"Maddie, where you at?" I found myself dropping into her way of speaking.

The restaurant felt lonely. There were no cars or trucks snuggled up in front, breezes sweeping through the windows, or packed tables of people lifting biscuits dripping with butter. There was no smell. That's what was missing the most. There was no smell of biscuits coming from the kitchen.

"Maddie, can you hear me? Mama wants to know how you are." I waited. There was no big, gruff voice hollering for me to come on back. I pounded on the door again. Still nothing.

I followed a muddy path around the side of the house. The grass was dug up like she'd had a delivery to the back door.

"Socrates, I'm here." Maddie was sitting on her porch with eyes so puffy and red I didn't know how she could see.

The yard was destroyed. The pole beans we'd tamped down into hills of dirt were jagged holes so deep I couldn't see the bottom. Half-eaten melons were tossed around the yard trailing stems and wilted blossoms that would never become fruit. The pea vines we wrapped around the low-hanging branches were yanked so hard that the leaves were stripped bare. Red and green tomatoes were smashed like they had been stamped into the ground, and the wild tangle of collards, creasy, mustard, and turnip greens were torn out of the ground and used to line a big hole in the center of the yard. Its smell was primeval as it filled the entire yard as if it was solid. I pulled my shirt up to cover my nose and tried not to gag.

"Wild hogs. They were here last night. Even made a wallow for themselves. Used my greens that are loved all over the county to make their bath soft." She pulled her hair scarf off and rolled the cuffs of her overalls to her knees. She wiped her face and shoved the handkerchief into the top of her overalls between her bosoms. It was an intimate action usually reserved for family who knew she'd haul it out later and wipe her face again. She'd do it as many times as she needed to in a day. Only those who live inside her circle know that. My face flushed with both embarrassment and empathy. "Want to help?"

"Yes."

"That smell will go home with you. All of Jackson County will know the smell soon enough." She handed me a rag and motioned for me to take my shoes off. "I've got some boots you can wear. Don't want to ruin your shoes. Here's a hat too. Keeps the rain off a bit." Maddie's voice was flat, and her shoulders turned into her chest like it would be too difficult for her to stand up straight. "Here's a basket. Let's find anything they missed. Maybe if we wash some of it off, we might still eat it."

"Maddie, Mama will give you anything out our garden. We just finished some canning. We even have beets." I looked around at the disaster, tied the rag around my neck, and pulled the hat down tight. "Oh no." I sloshed my way over to pigpen. The posts were yanked from the ground, and the fencing was peeled back like the rings of an onion. "Oh, Maddie." I couldn't look at her.

A mound of a partially eaten pig was pushed up against the wire fence. Ropes of intestines spilled out of its gut, and its snout was gone leaving a hole that tunneled into its brain. The chest was wrenched open, and the dark heart meat was separated from the body and punctured with holes.

"Those were from the tusks," Maddie said. "Listening to that pig die was awful. I came out on the porch with my shotgun, and the boar made a turn at me. It was spite. I asked him what did I do to him? He stamped his foot and jumped. I went back into the house then. Who wants to be known as the woman stabbed by pig tusks? Not me." She sank a shovel deep into the earth under the pig's body. She grunted under its weight and slid the remains into the bed of her truck. "I have to take it far out of here. They'll come back for the body. People say they love dead meat. I think they are just mean." She leaned the shovel against the pigpen and spit. "They let the other one go with them. I always hated that pig. He was going to be bacon soon. Wasn't fair to my baby though. He didn't do nothing to die that way."

I stepped into the muck. Just putting my foot into the mess made the smell rush through my nose. I looked at my hands and wondered how long it would take to get the smell out. I was sure my professors at Parson University Preparatory School would not tolerate wild hog smell in the classrooms. "Maddie, do you have gloves?"

"Don't worry, Socrates. I'll wash your hands and arms with real hot water like the day you showed up in my backyard. It will be fine." She stepped into the wallow. "Stay out of this. It's slippery because of the greens. I like you, Socrates, but not enough to give you a boiling hot bath with you all naked. Oh look," she said, holding a slightly bruised tomato. "There will be more."

The rain slowed, which helped us keep our balance as we looked under piles of smashed vegetables. When we found a cache of untouched green tomatoes, we grabbed each other's arms in victory. Then we realized the muck was now covering our arms up to our shoulders.

"Maddie. I am just going to ask, and you don't have to answer. Why do you and Mr. Ashby have the same eyes?"

Maddie didn't turn or speak. I thought maybe she didn't hear me. She held up her hand to shush me. She handed me a rake.

"Pull it through real gentle. Maybe we find food just a little covered with pig slop. Wild pig slop," she corrected herself. "We have the same daddy. Mr. Sir was my daddy too."

I leaned over and put my hands on my knees. Of course. It made sense with her being on the farm and treated special by Mr. Sir, but I didn't know who Maddie's mother was.

"Don't go falling, Socrates. You be sleeping outside if you go home smelling like this. Your mama won't like you for a while."

"Do you know about it, Maddie? I mean how it happened?"

"I've known as long as I can remember. Somebody must have whispered it in my ear without my hearing it." She pulled deeply with her rake. "Plus, Mr. Sir would call for me a lot. He took an interest in me you might say." She pointed. "How's that raking going?"

"I'm looking, Maddie. I'm looking."

"I gotta start with my mama. She went to college," Maddie began. "Don't get yourself all too proud, Socrates Bravo. You aren't the first I knew who's going to college. She was living in Nashville, Tennessee, and going to a place called Fisk University. It was one of the first colleges for Negro people."

"She was twenty-three years old, and she was a looker. Her hair was long and black with no curl to it. She had light skin, and that is where I got mine. That and from Mr. Sir. Every now and then, God made some Negro people almost as light as white people. Don't matter what anyone say; they don't fit in anywhere. Whites don't think they're white enough, and Negros think they are too white. No one remembers there's no difference in the color on the inside—that's the problem." Maddie took out her hand-kerchief and blew her nose.

"Peola Porter in the world thought pretty high of herself and acted like she was something different. Imagine that Socrates," Maddie said with a grin, "my mother thinking she was pretty special."

"That college she was going to ran into money problems, and it was going to have to close if the teachers and the students didn't think quick. So the college chose nine students and made a singing group called the Jubilee Singers. The name came from the Bible, and it meant the year of being happy when the Jews were let out from being slaves. All but two of those nine people had been slaves themselves, so it was a right proper name. Don't you think?"

I nodded yes.

"Peola was one of the nine. The Jubilee Singers needed to be different so people would come hear their concerts. Peola suggested they sing the Negro spiritual songs that were sung in secret during slavery. They used to carry messages, and Peola thought they still did. The other singers hated her for thinking of it—it felt like betraying the old grannies and granddaddies whose singing gave them hope for freedom—but they went along because they knew it was true. Somehow, Peola knew that the spirituals would loosen up that ache inside white folks and help them let it out." Maddie shook her head and mused. "Funny, though, if twenty years before those same white people would have just opened their windows, or walked their fields, or sat outside the slave churches, they would have heard the same songs. Only then, they didn't think there was nothing to be guilty about."

"So Peola was a bit high and mighty, but she was the best singer too," Maddie said by way of apology. "I've always thought it was unfair of God to leave me without a mother so young and no singing abilities, but He's the mystery, and I am only Maddie," she concluded.

"Everywhere on the streets of Nashville, people

thought she was beautiful. Being so light skinned, a lot of white men stared at her, not knowing that she had a Negro mama and daddy. I think life was hard for her, Socrates."

"So, along about this time, she met Mr. Sir." I shivered with shock. Maddie sighed. "I know, Socrates, but he is my daddy, and I can't never forget that. So just let me tell this story and you keep your feelings to yourself, all right?" Her face was stern.

"One day, Peola was coming out of a dress shop, and Mr. Sir was walking along the street, not watching where he was going. Well, he ran right over my mama. She dropped her package, and he stepped into the box with one of his big muddy boot prints. Lord, Peola was so angry she let loose a stream of words that said Mr. Sir was stupid, clumsy, blind, and had the backside of a horse. The funny part was she did it in her highfalutin college language that Mr. Sir—an old country boy—couldn't understand. So when Peola had to stop and take a breath before she blasted him any further, he put his hand over her mouth and let her know that she was fine-looking."

"Well, I suppose my mama was a little vain and full of herself. So she walked away and left Mr. Sir standing there with that dirty dress in the broken box. But he was pretty stubborn too, so he went right into the dress shop and ordered them to clean the dress. 'Then,' he said, 'I want another one the same size but in a different color with more lace on it. Then when you are all done with that, I want to know who that girl is and where she lives. Deliver both of those dresses,' he boomed. He pulled a wad of dollars out of his pocket and threw them down.

"The dress ladies did as he said. Mr. Sir was in town for a meeting of the plantation owners. It was an important meeting, with lots of drinking and voting, and men standing up and bragging on their land when they didn't even say that it was the Negro people who was working it. Mr. Sir sat in the meetings and smoked cigars until the room was blue and foggy with smoke. He was talking cotton but thinking Peola.

"The next morning, a note was delivered to Mr. Sir's hotel room. The note said she didn't want the dresses Mr. Sir had sent, but she'd pick up her own. She signed it Peola Porter. Well, Mr. Sir forgot all about his meetings, drinking, and bragging. He wanted to find the girl who wouldn't take a gift when it was offered to her. He went back to the dress store, and they told him she was probably in the library—she read a lot of books.

"Now, Soc, here's where the story gets interesting. Mr. Sir goes storming into the college library where all around him Negro men and women were studying. He announces in his foghorn voice, 'Where's Peola Porter? I have to talk to that girl.' So when Peola rises from a table nearby, he doesn't even recognize her as a Negro in a room full of Negros. He saw her as a beautiful woman who knew how to jerk his reins. They went together to have tea and argue about the dresses even further. But by nighttime"—Maddie paused uncomfortably—"I guess you could say, Socrates, they knew each other like people who make babies know each other. I've always thought they whispered to each other in the darkness so others wouldn't hear them. Mr. Sir was forgetful that night too. Just a day's ride away on the train he had a pregnant wife waiting for him at home."

"Maddie?"

"Yep?"

"Do you think they were in love?"

"Yep, Socrates, I do. And if you be quiet, I'll tell you why," Maddie said sober and soft.

"Mr. Sir stayed in Nashville, and Peola saw him every day and night. One night, she said she couldn't come to see because she had a concert with her college group. Mr. Sir still hadn't lifted that veil over his eyes and realized that Peola was a Negro. He bought himself a ticket and went to the concert." Sadness passed across her face. "Fool. He was pretty surprised when eight Negros and Peola walked onto the stage. He was going to leave, but when he heard her singing, he couldn't get out of the chair. He stayed and listened to the whole concert. When he left, he didn't go back to the hotel. Instead, he walked the streets of Nashville until the sun came up. And then he had made up his mind. He was going to stay with Peola even knowing the truth."

"How do you know that part, Maddie?" I interrupted. She glared down her nose at me, and I imagined her blue eye shooting lightning bolts at me and her brown eye trying to boil me in mud.

"Because Mr. Sir told me so, that's how. Can I go on?"

"He told you this whole story?"

"It's the story of how my parents came together. Don't you think he wanted me to know? When he got back to the hotel, there was a note waiting for him from the train station. Mrs. Sir had the baby, and it was a boy. A white boy. A white boy who would inherit his land and carry his name. Poor Peola didn't have a chance. Mr. Sir left Peola an envelope full of money at the hotel desk and a note that said he was sorry he had to go back home. But what Mr. Sir didn't know was Peola was carrying her own Mr. Sir's child, me, Maddie Porter. A Negro woman with no family and no daddy's name." Maddie shrugged her shoulders.

"Keep going Maddie," I said.

"Peola hid my bump for as long as she could. But soon her secret was out, and she was asked to leave the university and the Jubilee Singers. Word is she didn't sing again after that. She went to a home in the city where girls who weren't married had their babies. My mama was pleased I was light like her. She thought maybe it help Mr. Sir to love me."

"Did she try to find him?"

"Yes, she did what she thought was right. She took the train to Gideon, Alabama, and carried me from the station to Mr. Sir's fine place. Peola looked around and imagined if she were the madam of the farm how would she feel and what it would be like to have a daughter with her belonging to this world. Well, she walked up to the porch, knocked on the door, and asked for Mrs. Sir. Socrates, when your grandma told Mrs. Sir that a fine-looking lady with a baby was waiting for her at the door, Mrs. Sir was curious. She came down to see us.

"My mama handed a sleeping me to Mrs. Sir and said, 'Tell your husband that this here is Maddie Porter, and she needs looking after.' And then Peola left me in Mrs. Sir's arms. I woke right after she left, and my blue eye and my brown eye stared right in Mrs. Sir's face. She was looking at her husband's evil deed and her son's kin, but she didn't know it. She sat in her rocker and fed me. She sang to me when I fussed, and I stopped right away. She was still holding me when Mr. Sir came in into the house for dinner wearing his dusty old boots. He wasn't inter-ested in me at first, but when he heard my name, he rushed out the door and jumped on the back of one of his fastest horses. He was almost to town when he pulled up. There was a group of people all standing outside the train station. 'What happened?' he asked. 'Oh,' a man said, 'a woman stepped out in front of the train when it was going past. Better not look. It's a mess.' Mr. Sir sat on that horse a long time. He turned it and headed home."

Maddie was quiet and dragged her rake gently throw the top of the mud.

"Miss Cora told me once she happened upon him crying. She said it was the queerest sound to hear a man keen over a dead woman no one else knew. Mrs. Sir, you may have heard, was a lamp that couldn't stay lit, so she never thought I was a Negro. As long as I lived there, she never questioned where I came from. I lived in the big house with them, and Mr. Sir didn't say anything to his wife. I was one of the Four." She stopped. "But you know all about that."

"So, did Mr. Ashby know about Mr. Sir being your daddy?"

"I think it came to him later when someone told him the eyes we have come down through your parents, but he thought I was his white sister. Do you think he would have believed it if he knew I was a Negro? Would you believe it?" She wiped her hand across her lips and let a small burp exit her lips as she raked near the steps. "Mr. Sir started talking to me when I was a little older than a baby. He didn't talk much to Timothy. Called him a mama's boy since he was so lumpy and afraid of everything. Mr. Sir and I, we'd ride out into the pasture on one of his horses, me sitting in front of him, and he'd tell me a story about Peola and how she went to a Negro college and read books every time she could. He told me the dress story about a hundred times. We'd get back to the barn, and he'd swing me off the saddle to grab onto the paddock fence. Timothy, William, and Annie'd be waiting for me. Back then, we were all the same, and it didn't matter our skin color or whose daddy belonged to who. It was the only time in my life when I was treated equal and acted equal."

We raked through the muck and finally Maddie started smoothing it over like it was a grave. "Imagine being a child and in one night you see what an adult sees, only you weren't ready," she said. "As long as it took for Mr. Sir to whip William, I learned there was no such thing as equal. I tried to stop Mr. Sir, but he raised his hand to me and told me he could whip me too." Her voice trembled.

"When he told me that, I knew I was a Negro in his eyes, not his white daughter. That night, I learned being a Negro put a big old sign on your back that said, 'Whip me,' even if you don't deserve it. I learned that one of my best friends—my brother—could make another person take his punishment just because his white skin said he could. I learned you could start the morning a happy girl and end the day an angry Negro woman."

We stopped dragging our rakes through the mud and sat down on the steps of the porch.

"So, Socrates, it was small of me, but I got even with Mr. Sir. Until the day he died, he was afraid of who I was. I learned a word that says what I did to Mr. Sir. It's called retribution."

"What was your retribution?"

Maddie laughed. "I told Mr. Sir I was going to tell Mrs. Sir that he loved my Negro mama more than her. He got fear in his eyes. I had him. He whipped William, but I made him pay."

"So the Four fell apart because..." I was confused.

"Because I ended it," Maddie said. "William thought he should have been responsible for Timothy taking Midnight, and I said that was hog shit. Annie sided with William. Timothy was a coward and asked your daddy to forgive him. William did. I couldn't stomach it. I wanted out."

"Mr. Sir had options, if you know what I mean. He had money, and he knew people. He took me off the farm and away from my family. I left that night. I packed up my things, and Mr. Sir drove me here. He ordered them to give me a job and a bed to sleep in. When the owners died, I found out Mr. Sir bought this place to give to me. So, it's been the Best Biscuits in the Jackson County for twenty-five years. I hadn't talked to your mama and daddy since the night I left. Until you came and opened it all up again. It's been like pulling a bandage off and being afraid to see what was underneath it."

"Why didn't you see each other?"

"Because it wouldn't have been the same. Your parents worked for Timothy. The Four was gone. That hurt the most." Maddie pushed the muck over to cover a cantaloupe slashed into pieces.

"Your folks are just like me except they don't own property. I'd like to think Mr. Sir knew I'd be successful in owning a restaurant. I hope he didn't know Timothy would lose the farm." She clucked her tongue.

"How come you and Mr. Ashby made up?"

"When Mr. Sir died, I didn't go inside the church when they were praying on him and singing hymns. I stayed out in my truck and thought about him. I closed my eyes, and I made myself think of our horse rides and talks about my mama. When I opened my eyes, there was

Timothy standing there in that queer way of his with his toes pointing out each direction."

I smiled.

"He said, 'Hey, Maddie. Got any biscuits?' Then he drove that wife of his home and came back to the restaurant. I made him biscuits the way he likes them—a little soft in the middle—and we sat down and drank our coffee and talked about Mr. Sir. We agreed not to let him split us up."

"What about my mama and daddy?" My eyes brimmed with tears, and it was not because Mr. Sir died.

"Well, Socrates," Maddie said, sighing, "it just wouldn't have been the same. We kept it just us."

"Maddie, why didn't you come back after he died?" I sank my head down into my neck and covered my ears with my shoulders. I was ready for more retribution if it came.

"The Four wouldn't have lasted anyway, Socrates." She gulped. "I would have had to leave the farm one way or another. Your folks could stay because the farm was theirs like it was Timothy's. But if we all had stayed together and gotten older, sooner or later, somebody would have asked where I belonged. I could have married, Socrates. Trust me: there were lots of men who asked, but they've all gone, and I am happiest alone. There is a brokenness in this world, and it is about what you have and what you don't and why it matters and why it doesn't, and I was tired of my mind spinning all the time with questions. It's not hard to make biscuits. That's what I chose."

I let her answer sink all around me, and the stink pulsed in there as if the wild hogs had returned. I didn't say anything. I was quiet for so long I saw her lean forward and check to see if I was asleep. I finally spoke up in a low voice just like my daddy's when he is trying to make a point.

"You're dead gone wrong, Maddie. You belong with your family, and if you can't see that, then I shouldn't be your biscuit boy anymore." I got up from the stoop and leaned my hoe against the railing. I walked out of the stinking mess and started to run as soon I was out of her sight. I was done with the Four feeling sorry for themselves. I pushed my long legs to stretch further and cover more ground. Mr. Sir had done his best to ruin as many lives as he could. I wondered how many more marbles were covered with dust and lost in the corners.

Chapter Twenty-Two

The next morning, I spied Mama backing out of the baking closet as I opened the back door. Her hair, face and neck were covered with white flour. Beads of sweat mixed with the flour, and a ring of little white drops lined her skin like a fine pearl necklace. There was a look to my mama's eyes that I knew was more than a teapot blowing its steam. She was about to blow the top off and spew boiling water on whoever came near her.

"What's your problem, Socrates? Do you think we're going to have a baby born in a dirty house? I'm nesting for both of us." She hefted a twenty-pound bag of flour to her shoulder. "My baby, Walker, ain't living in a clean house, I'll tell you. I know that. There's no Mrs. Grindall to make sure people are treated well. My Walker." Water spilled out of her eyes, and it was hard to tell where the sweat left off and the tears started.

"I thought I'd go check on Maddie again," I said, using my mama's trick of crossing my fingers behind my back.

"Oh no, you aren't going anywhere until I say you can. Are your papers done?"

"Yes, Mama. I finished my last section. Literature." I had completed the essay on Macbeth after my final conversation with Mrs. Ashby at the dahlia bed. I steeled myself to write about Lady Macbeth, pretending that I had not sat witness to a story so like the one written by Shakespeare.

"Well, that's good. I hadn't heard the clack, clack, clack sound for a while. You're weren't going anywhere unless you finished it." She slammed the bag on the wooden floor of the pantry and the air filled with flour.

"You were just there yesterday. I need help around here." She shrugged her shoulders. "Oh, it's all such a mess. Go ahead then. Mrs. Ashby might have the baby today. She's showing the signs, and since you is a man, you couldn't deal with it anyhow."

I didn't think much about Mama's words as I left the house. When I returned, the day would be with me for life, seared into me as if the date were tattooed on my body so I'd never forget. Maybe it's lucky for people not to know when tragedy had arrived on the doorstep.

My feet followed my worn path to Maddie's until I veered off to the left onto a narrow dirt track with grass growing between the marks made by some tires. I bent over and studied them. Someone drove on it daily, but there were other tracks, large ones, like a trailer attached to a truck. I was on the lost road to Jubal Ridge.

No one knew how Grindall had come to settle in Jackson County. His property, Jubal Ridge, named for one of the first families to settle northeastern Alabama, sat on a bluff overlooking a river. Although Jubal Ridge was large enough to be considered a plantation with a drive lined with oak trees leading to the main house, the buildings had begun to cave in, slumping in the middle with broken roof ridges. There were no kin to inherit the house and land, and the bank decided it was a lost property due to "crop mismanagement"—too many years of dead dirt. There wasn't anything left to it. It wasn't worth a nickel. The bank was more than happy to practically give it to Grindall.

When I saw the dark row of Southern live oak marching toward the house, I stepped off the road and began walking parallel to it listening for the sound of voices or axes. The rain had slowed to a mist, so mosquitos buzzed around my head landing on the delicate skin atop my ears. I lifted my feet high and selected the bramble canes to stamp down to clear a path ahead of me through a thicket. I was getting more confident until I stepped forward too fast and came face-to-face with a spider lounging in the middle of her web. Dead flies lay tangled in the delicate rings, and they looked shrunk like all the blood was sucked from their bodies. When I blew air out slowly to calm my pounding heart, the web shook, and the spider lifted her head. I army-crawled under the web, pinching my lips together holding back a scream.

I could see the thicket thinning ahead, so I bent down and watched my moving feet to keep from stepping on twigs that would crack. When I could see the opening, I lowered myself to the ground. I heard horse moving impatiently, stamping their feet as they stood next to the trees. The air was hazy with flies, and the horses' tails were flicking, and they shook their manes, making the metal bridles rattle.

Two guards swung off their horses and tied the reins to the tree branches. They stood under the branches smoked cigarettes and watched the workers. Dropping their cigarettes and grinding them in the brush, they climbed back into the saddles and ambled away. One of the cigarette's embers was burning, but just as a puff of smoke poked out of the bushes, it went black.

I heard the shout, "Break!" so I left the thicket and dashed to a group of trees that were tall and close together anchored in thick brush. When I slid my hand along their trunks to help steady myself, the bark felt like sandpaper. I could stand up if I wanted, and the first branch would still be over my head.

There were seven men. My eyes jerked along the line until I saw Walker. He was standing off to the side, drinking out of a metal cup. The others sat on a log, fanning themselves with their hats. He stood with his hands on his hips his back to the group. His back was drenched with sweat that turned into steam when it hit the cold air. His skin was covered with red welts. Horse flies. The bites were deep without remorse. Walker's mouth was clenched together, and he didn't speak to the other men. They didn't speak to him either. A deep sadness dropped from my head to my belly as I thought of my brother who had never met a stranger in his life. Now there were six strangers, eight if you counted the men and their guns, and it didn't look like any of them were going to become friends.

After the break was over, Walker took his place at the end of the line. He patted a stunned and dying tree that had lost all of its life blood just a few minutes before and laid his hand on the trunk for a moment. I believed he blessed it before it fell. His face hardened, and he slammed the ax into the base with a few sharp and merciful blows. When the trunk broke from the stump, sap oozed one more time and flooded the ground.

Walker dismembered the tree into rounds and then

into quarters. He stacked it on a trailer higher than his head and jumped down. He did this over and over until there was no evidence a tree had ever stood in that place.

Without speaking to anyone, Walker grabbed the rope at the front and leaned forward to get his footing. The trailer, piled high with wood, slowly began to move. His feet slipped as he hauled the trailer with the rope over his shoulder.

He was walking the gum path. Daddy said it broke men, even if they did get paid more than pickers. They shook their heads when they talked about it. Walker's boots were thick with pine tar, and with every step, the needles of the pine trees stuck to the sticky bottoms. I watched him fall several times. The moving trailer almost rolled over the top of him when he was on his knees. One of the guards on horseback trailed behind him, and with a punch to my gut, I realized he was following Walker to make sure he didn't run.

I turned and crawled back through the tunnel I had made through the thicket. I couldn't watch any longer.

Chapter Twenty-Three

I lost my way several times in the dark as I put distance between myself and Jubal Ridge. I skidded through the mud and strained to see ahead of me in the pounding rain. Water was starting to spill over the top of the ditches. The puddles were to my knees in places, and then I stumbled into a pit of cold, brown water that engulfed me to my waist. I almost fell, and my feet found the wooden slats of the bridge close to our farm road. The bridge was built by the county thirty years ago, connecting Gideon to towns in northern Jackson County. It sat at the confluence of several farms where flooded fields and swollen creeks drained into a slough that served as an overflow for the Tombigbee River.

I felt the bridge shudder and groan under my feet, and I used my hands as paddles to push through the water. I gulped a deep breath of air each time I felt my body sucked downward into the lung-crushing, runaway current. When I reached the other side of the bridge and climbed up higher, I fell flat on my face. I pulled my dangling legs out of the way just as an old toolshed from the Ashby's farm swept down the creek and smashed against the side of the bridge. I heard the bridge begin to groan under the pressure of the stuck toolshed. With a whining cry, the underpinnings of the bridge gave way, and the wooden planks popped free from their nails. In a few seconds, the bridge pulled free from its pilings and broke into three large pieces. Slamming against the bank on each side, I lost it in the darkness. With the pressure of the water carrying it, anything in its path would be destroyed.

"Daddy, the bridge is out," I called out of breath. The commissary, our house, and the big house were on high ground, and water would not reach them. "Mama," I shouted. "Where are you?" The farm was silent. The picker shacks were dark, and there was only a single lamp burning in a window in the second story of the big house. I wrenched open the door to my childhood home and looked in the rooms. The house was empty.

"She needed you. Where were you?" Trask stood at the back door. Dirt was smeared around his mouth, and it slipped from between his lips in muddy streaks. His eyes were bloodshot and swollen, and the smell of sweet whiskey and anxious sweat reached me from ten feet away. His hand shook, making the light from the lamp he held bounce on the walls. "She wanted you. Why? Why not me? You are a kid." I looked at his other hand where my typewriter dangled by its arm.

"Please, let me have it. Please, Mr. Trask. She loved you," I lied.

"Don't insult me." He raised his arm and hurled the typewriter out the screen door. "She's gone." He kicked the door as he left, ripping it off its hinges. Outside, I heard a torrent of weeping that gradually faded, eclipsed by the sound of the rain striking the roof.

I heard his words, but they didn't register immediately. I sat on the back stoop and looked at the mangled mess of the typewriter stuck in the mud. My brain struggled, trying to put the pieces together. *He said she's gone. Who? Where did she go?* I wondered. Then, like the clack, clack, clack of the typewriter, when my words and thoughts married on the page, I realized he meant Mrs. Ashby. She was gone.

Chapter Twenty-Four

"Socrates, come here." I saw the glowing tip of Mr. Ashby's cigar as I ran toward the big house. He was sitting on the porch swing in the dark. "Come here, boy." His voice was rough. I stood on the edge of the porch where the rain showered on me. "Come closer. Get out of the rain."

"Mr. Ashby, the bridge is out. There's no way to Gideon. At least, not that way," I pointed. "It's really bad. I saw a—"

"I don't care," he interrupted. "Do you have any knowledge of my wife having relations with that man Trask?"

"Mr. Ashby, I'm a kid. I don't know what you mean." I backed up into the sheets of water. I wanted the water to rise and swallow the prickly ash copse behind me. The afternoon I hid under its branches, ignored Mrs. Ashby's calls, and suffered my accident caused all the events to happen. Mr. Ashby lunged for me, leaving the chains of the porch swing rattling against each other in alarm. He grabbed me and yanked me to stand before him, and I could see his teeth up close, minus the missing one, stained a chestnut brown. His mouth curled up cruelly. Mr. Sir was alive and well in his son.

"Answer me. Did they have relations?"

"They became friends, I know." I tried to pull away, but his spongy fingers gripped my arm, and he started to twist it.

"That's enough, Timothy. Leave my son alone." Daddy stood in the yard, watching us. "Don't take this out on him. He didn't do anything." Mr. Ashby stood up and pushed me away. All four chains crashed together, and the swing smashed against the house. Mr. Ashby stomped to the barn, his clothes drenched by the time he reached the door. Inside, Lean neighed loudly, and I heard him kick the stable wall hard.

"Daddy, what happened? Trask said she's gone. What does that mean?" I started to cry, and every bit of my thirteen-year-old man self peeled away, and I became a little boy who couldn't control his sobs. I heard myself begin to wail, and in my hysteria, I knew it was true.

Mama opened the door, holding towels for me. She wrapped my body in them and rubbed me all over with brisk hands. "William, go get him some more clothes. We're all staying here tonight. If the floods get us, at least, we're all together." Her voice shook. "Almost all together." Walker wasn't with us.

She wrapped me like a mummy, and I couldn't see as she guided me through the house toward the kitchen. "Sit, child. Sit," Mama soothed and kissed my head. "You need to hear it all. Your tears will stop when you know. There's sweet with sorrow. Look at Claire's baby girl."

I pulled the towel off my head and saw a baby laying in a basket next to the woodstove. She was tiny with hands the size of little seashells and lips that pursed into a flower

bud still tightly closed. She shifted in her sleep, and the blanket fell away. Across her naked shoulder was a red birthmark the shape of a cactus dahlia. The mark was a perfect circle with red-wine petals fanning out around the edges. I would tell no one, but it was the same shoulder Trask kissed with wonder while I watched. I leaned down to touch her, and my glasses slid off my face. As I settled them back over my eyes, the baby came into focus, and she looked exactly like Mrs. Ashby did when she sat across the table from me smiling and twisting her hair. I caught my breath, and my pounding heart slowed.

"The doctor said she died from a stroke. Miss Cora and I were with her, and she struggled so. She shook so hard she bit her tongue,"

"A *clonic seizure*," I whispered.

"The doctor said she died then. He reached in with big spoons and pulled her out," Mama said, nodding to the baby.

"They are called forceps."

"She's gone, Socrates. It doesn't matter what those metal things are called." She scowled at me. "She wanted you. Where did you go?"

"I went to see Walker."

"And?"

"Bad, Mama. It's bad."

"I can't know right now. This all is too much." Mama cried giant, fat tears matching the streaks of rain on the windows. "Let me pull myself together."

"Mama, the baby?"

"Her mama never held her." Mama paced the floor, her slippers flapping against the floor with every step. I looked around. Daddy's shirts were hanging next to Mr. Ashby's in front of the stove.

"We're living here?"

"Who do you think is going to take care of the baby?" She looked at me as if I was an idiot.

"Timothy doesn't know how to fix roof leaks or broken shutters; do you think he knows how to care for a baby?" She took a step toward me like she might slap the nonsense out of me. She sat down heavily in a kitchen chair. "He needs your daddy here too."

"They are not getting along too good right now," I said, pulling the blanket back over the baby's shoulder.

"Mama, Trask...I'm worried about him. He had dirt in his mouth, and he looked like he wanted to hurt someone or himself."

Mama's swollen manlike feet, broken all over with spiderweb veins, stopped tapping the floor. "I haven't seen him since we told him."

"He was down at our house. He wrecked my typewriter. He threw it in the mud and kicked our back door. It's broken." I spoke in careful sentences, capturing the events without emotion. She didn't give me a glance but looked at the baby with a softened face.

"He's not here," she said, tapping her head. "He is lost."

Trask had a crossed a wide sea while I was gone. His fury and rudeness had transformed into grief and despair, and my mama was the one who saw it up close.

"It's terrible, Socrates. Trask says the baby is his because of the red mark, and Timothy refuses to think his wife would ever be with Trask."

"Trask can't take the baby, can he?"

"He wants to bring the doctor back from town, but he can't get through because of the bridge being gone."

"Mr. Ashby tried to get me to tell him, but Daddy told

him to leave me alone. He turned mean, Mama. He hurt my arm. It was like he was Mr. Sir."

"He's lost too, Socrates. His brain isn't working right either. None of us...Walker?" she finally asked.

I considered my words. "He's working hard. I didn't talk to him, though. He was too busy." Mama looked at me with eyes both tender and harsh at the same time.

"Are you telling me all of it?"

I thought about crossing my fingers, but that game was over. "No, that's not all of it. I'll tell you and Daddy when we are together." The baby started to cry then, and Mama handed her to me.

"Hold her." When Mama placed her in my arms, she felt as light as a single book I used to balance on my fingertip and spin in a circle.

"What's her name?"

"We don't know. You do."

Mama handed me a note. I could barely make out the letters in Mrs. Ashby's usual perfect handwriting. It was hurried, and I could tell from the jerkiness she was in pain when she wrote it. It said: "Socrates will name the baby. He knows what I want."

"Mm. I'll think on it." I knew already. Fly and Net would live.

Chapter Twenty-Five

A wind began to blow the night of Mrs. Ashby's death. It whistled through the gaps in the loose clapboards and lifted the edge of the tired roof to enter the house and swirl down the stairs. I believe what was left of her sailed out of the house on a gust of air. Mama washed Mrs. Ashby's body gently, wiping away the ravages of childbirth, trying to erase any evidence of the suffering she bore. My mama dressed her in the softest night gown and braided her hair so it curled around her head and lay on her chest like she was a little girl.

All of us except for Mr. Ashby took turns sitting in the room with her so she would not be alone. It was more for us than her, but she looked as though she was only asleep, and we wanted to be there in the case it was all a mistake, and she would come back to us. Trask took his turn, staying until one of us put a hand on his bony shoulder and helped him to his feet. Mama's last act against Trask was patting his sheets over the bed of poison oak behind the barn. He scratched his skin without comment. I wondered what had happened to make the poison oak take hold in such awkward places. The skin was raw between his fingers and lines of bright red trailed from underneath his hairline to below his collar and out of sight. His shirt, front and back, was wet with random circles. The red patches oozed a clear fluid that caused a piercing pain so intense it could make a sane man crazy. But all that Trask could manage when he left Mrs. Ashby's side was to pick at the food my mother prepared for him. The meal was simple, chicken broth soup and biscuits. Trask ate it and mumbled, "Thank you." I found my mother in the pantry, crying, choking on the lump of regret in her throat. Trask was real to her, and she no longer saw his birthmark, his pasty white skin, or his troubled eyes. She saw Mrs. Ashby's lost one, the one she had tried so hard to save.

Mr. Ashby used the telephone in the front room to call his wife's mother, Mrs. Gannett, to tell her the news of her daughter's death. Ten other listeners on the party line learned of the tragedy at the same time. The lost bridge kept the women, their plates of cookies, and their curiosity from descending on the farm. It took but a day for the whole town of Gideon to learn that Mrs. Ashby had died and her small girl lived.

Mrs. Gannett informed Mr. Ashby that her daughter must return to her childhood home to be buried in the family plot that held important people vital to the North's success. She did not have any interest in the baby born in the South with all its failures. Mr. Ashby did not try to change her mind, and arrangements were made to put the body in a casket and return it to the estate in New Jersey. Mama hid in the hall and listened to Mr. Ashby's side of the phone call. She came back into the kitchen, expressing disapproval about Mr. Ashby's cowardice toward Mrs. Gannett. Mrs. Ashby may have been born in the North, but her wee one was born in the South, and she should have her mother near her for comfort. I knew what Mama really meant. She didn't want Mrs. Ashby so far from her.

Our odd group—Mr. Ashby, Mama, Daddy, Miss Cora, and even Trask—pressured me about Mrs. Ashby's wishes for the baby's name. I clamped my lips shut and gave them all a silencing stare. The baby, so diminutive you could hold her head in your palm and steady her feet with your elbow, was seven or eight months, Miss Cora believed. According to Mama, either Trask or Mr. Ashby could be the father. Watching her chew on her lip thoughtfully, I wondered if my mama was beginning to see the scales of the baby's future tip in another direction. I decided the baby would stay nameless until I decided how much of Mrs. Ashby's story to tell and what parts should depart in the casket with her.

The northern wind swept across the whole Tennessee Valley. The swollen creeks and rivers continued to rage, but the banks alongside the moving water stabilized and invited the water to slow and flow into the fields. It wasn't the first time so much of the farm was swept away, but the ground needed the freshly deposited minerals to burrow back into the earth so the cotton would flourish next spring.

The pickers began to emerge from their shacks to inspect the condition of the cotton in Middle Field and High Field. They wandered in loose groups, lingering by the pond and petting the horses, who were only recently let free as well. Several of the pickers, including Joseph Sutter, brought gifts of simple food, knitted baby caps, and bouquets of forest leaves newly red and yellow and laid them on the front steps while Mr. Ashby watched from a chair on the porch. When he had grabbed my arm and the swing had crashed against the house, the swing had split in two halves. Mr. Ashby asked Daddy if the swing could be repaired, and Daddy shook his head no and walked away. It now sat on the burn pile behind the barn, and the next clear, dry day, my daddy planned to let even the chains be consumed by the fire.

The wind was temperate, cool and dry, and it encouraged Jackson County to get back up on its feet and find its grit. Much was lost in the floods and powerful storm, but there was a chance, a new chance, for the people to examine the earth beneath them to see what was possible. Now that the old, malnourished clay in the fields was swept away and the new dirt filled in the fissures created in the fire-hot early spring, there was faith another good cotton season would come next year.

With the rain, my journey to see Walker and Mrs. Ashby's death, I had not checked on the dahlia patch. I prepared for the worst, thinking that the flowers would be lying on the ground waiting for me to stake them again for a renewed fall bloom. The putrid smell reached me before I saw the carnage. Wild hogs had discovered the crunchy, knobby brown tubers. The muddy ground had deep grooves that looked like the hogs delighted in running their snouts from one end of the patch to the other, flipping the tubers out of the ground in their wake. The stakes were broken and twisted, and the stems that held the flowers aloft had been chewed and discarded. There were no flowers. I could not see any wayward petal or flower face that survived. I do not think they were eaten; I think they were ground into the dirt by uncaring hooves, turning and twisting as the animals fought one another for the sweet tubers. The sunlight was strong and hurt my eyes. There was no shade, no sound of delicate fabric flapping in the wind. I looked up. The parasols were gone.

I stepped into the steaming muck, and it rose above my ankles. Ignoring the malodorous smell and the visceral feeling that the solid, heartless bodies still occupied the space, I waded through the middle of the patch, toward the location where Fly's love had last stood. My belief in God had always been skeptical at most, but any stock I had in him, much less the universe, would be lost for good if the only evidence of Mrs. Ashby's and Ellie's love for one another disappeared as if it had never been.

The pigs had not trampled the grass by the fence, instead focusing on the richness of the tubers in the middle. I'm sure the tubers from the tall, gracious Thomas Edison flowers distracted them because, on the other side of the fence, there was a single bunch of dahlia tubers attached to one another by wispy roots. It appeared they had been shoved away, too slight and narrow to bother with. The bundle lay in the same general location where Fly's love was planted, but I couldn't be sure. They looked like the ones Mrs. Ashby had described to me. There was no way to know if they were the right ones until they were planted. When the faces emerged and the petals unfurled, we would know. A year from now, Mrs. Ashby's baby could grasp a flower in her hand. My fingers wrapped around the muddy, tortured tubers and shoved them in the pocket of my shirt. Fly and Net feared the Dahlia Society judges destroyed the only dahlia, but the roots they planted enabled the plant to survive. I stood amid the destruction, and I realized the judges' overturning of the plant and rooting through the dirt searching for the tuber was not all that different than destruction of the patch by the wild hogs.

I climbed out of the patch and made for the creek. There was no way Mama would let me near the house while I carried the hog smell on my skin. I passed the picker shacks and glanced back to see the amount of damage they incurred. Expecting torn roofs and mud-covered porches, instead, I saw joy. The ragged picker children were playing with the dahlia parasols. They must have flown from their wires and landed around the pickers' shacks like gifts from the sky. The delight Mrs. Ashby would have found in the sea of undulating color and movement broke me. My chest constricted, and I cried like Mama did in the pantry. She cried with remorse for the unkind things she did to Trask, but I cried for the final gift Mrs. Ashby gave to the picker children: beauty.

Picker children, some as young as babies and others old enough to pretend they were fancy ladies, were playing with the parasols. The children tossed them in the air, jumping in circles before they floated to the ground. The little ones struggled to lift the parasols over their shoulders, and their siblings helped put them in place. The boys held them in the wind until a gust blew the parasols and their scrawny bodies shooting across the wet fields. It looked like a circus with dancing ladies skipping up the road with polka dots and stripes swirling behind them, tightrope walkers putting one foot in front of another on a pasture fence, trusting the parasol would support their balance, and clowns tossing parasols in a blur as if they were juggling bright balls for the crowd.

Daddy walked with me to the creek keeping his distance from the stench. "I talked to Trask this morning. The Farm Bureau didn't accept his evaluation of the worth of the farm without the final numbers of the settle. He tried to convince them, and they fired him. He's looking to leave, but the baby is holding him here. He's real broken up about Claire, and he feels like he let us down." Daddy put his hand on my shoulder. "He says he is sorry about the typewriter, and he'll scrape up the money to get a new one sent down to your school when you get there."

"How can I go to school when everything has fallen apart here? You and Mama? Walker? I can't go."

"Oh, you are going young man. Claire made the arrangements, and you did all the studying, didn't you?"

"Yes."

"What are you going to do, Daddy?"

Daddy kicked some rocks into the creek while I washed my feet and legs. "I don't know Socrates. Mr. Carr called, and the farm is selling as soon as they can get the bridge fixed and can get a truck in here to load the horses to take to auction. Mr. Carr wants to get the money first before the Federal Farm Bureau calls the loan. If Gideon Bank takes possession of the farm first, the bureau will have to fight with the bank for the money instead of fighting with Timothy."

"Won't the bank have to pay the Farm Bureau too?"

"Yes, but they can set the terms then instead of the other way around."

"Do you think this is Grindall's plan come true?"

"Trask's not part of it, Socrates. Poor man is ruined. I don't know if he will recover."

"Mrs. Ashby used those same words."

"I'll bet she had regrets herself." He clapped his hand around my neck kindly. "I have to go talk to the pickers and explain what happens when the sale goes through."

Daddy walked off toward the group of pickers waiting for word of their futures.

We were close to the center of the picker shacks. Men were coming out and leaning against the porch. Women were standing up from the rocking chairs, bouncing babies against their shoulders. Children flew toward us in a rush of color and motion, twirling their parasols so the colors blurred.

I walked backward up the road, watching Daddy talk to a group of men who gathered around him. When he finished, each of them came forward and shook Daddy's hand. Knowing Daddy, he had given them options. He might have suggested that since the bridge was out, they could leave Jackson County if they decided quickly. He might also have told them he didn't know, but they could possibly still have places on the farm to pick cotton. So much unknown bothers people without a vision, but Daddy's words likely went a long way toward comfort.

The farm truck was pulled up to the back stoop of the big house when I arrived. A closed wooden coffin sat in the back. It stuck out beyond the end even with the lift down. Rope was tied across the end of the coffin to the sides of the truck to keep it in place. It made me sick. She was leaving.

I walked into the kitchen and was smacked in the face with shouting voices and scuffling feet. Above it all was the shrieking cries of a newborn that made my stomach constrict painfully.

"Here," Mama said and pushed the baby into my arms. "Socrates, you are a part of this. Take this baby girl out of here." I hurried out into the hall and slipped into Trask's room. I peered inside the door, and it was empty. All the clothes were out of the closet, the dresser was cleared, and the whiskey bottles were gone.

A clear bottle with a picture of a beautiful woman with flawless skin sat pushed to the back of one of the bookshelves. I picked it up and pulled the stopper out of the top. Immediately, the rotten egg smell filled the room, and the baby girl began to shriek.

"Socrates, you better be caring for that baby. You hold her. Don't you put her down, or I will paddle you," Mama yelled.

I put the baby on my shoulder and squinted at the tiny writing on the bottle:

MME. A. RUPPERT'S WORLD-RENOWNED FACE BLEACH—No matter how blemished the skin, Face Bleach will make it perfect. The marvelous improvement after a few applications is most apparent, for the skin becomes as nature intended it should be, smooth, clear, and white. It cannot fail; this is the only thorough and permanent way to achieve whiteness.

POOR TRASK. I WONDERED IF IT EVER OCCURRED TO HIM that he wished for his birthmark to whiten to feel accepted, respected, and ultimately loved. I realized that he had ceased stinking at some point in the summer, and it must have been around the time Mrs. Ashby embraced his whole kit and kaboodle, in a manner of speaking.

The baby nuzzled against my chest, and I stuck my pinkie finger between her small lips. Using her tongue and the top of her mouth, she sucked my finger with force and pulled it into her mouth. I jumped, and she started to wail again.

"Lord," I whispered to her. "What the hell is going

on?" I put the half empty bottle on the shelf. She continued to cry, and I was desperate, not because I was afraid of my mama's wrath, but it hurt me thinking the baby was scared. I grabbed the tubers out of my pocket and wrapped them in my handkerchief. "You can't eat them, but here, feel them."

I unwrapped her blanket and looked for a sturdy-enough place to lay the handkerchief. She was so tiny. Her chest was smaller than the breadth of my palm, and the width of her tiny legs was smaller than my finger. The last tether to her mother, her umbilical cord, was almost dried up and laid on her stomach like a withered stem. I took the little packet of tubers that looked like a necklace when laid out flat on the ground and placed it on her stomach. She didn't stop crying right away, but soon her breaths were even, and she fell asleep. Her mouth was open a tiny bit. I felt her tiny body through the blankets, and her body felt warm.

"Good, she's asleep. Come in the kitchen." Mama's feet shuffled on the floor. Even from behind she looked bone-tired. The tie to her apron was a knot that sagged in the back. Miss Cora, Mr. Ashby, and Trask stood in the kitchen facing Mama and me. I swallowed hard. *Please don't anyone ask me why this little bird baby has a dirty handkerchief laying in her blanket*, I begged silently.

"Socrates, pull her blanket back on her right side so we can look at the mark," Cora said. She shifted herself so she could see out of the side of her eye. Everyone leaned in as I dropped the blanket from her arm and held the rest of her clutched to me. The tubers felt like a hot pack. "I've caught many babies, but I never saw that before."

"So she's mine," Trask interjected.

"Well," Cora said, taking her finger and pressing

lightly on the red, flower-shaped mark that covered most of her shoulder and upper arm. There was a whorl pattern in the middle and flecks of red turning to pink all around the center. "Annie, you were there too. After Mrs. Ashby died, the doctor wanted to get the baby out fast so she wouldn't be without air. He used these big metal spoons to pull her out." Miss Cora looked up at me. Her eyes were like a blue sky with restless, white clouds. There was no bottom to them. "Socrates, your mama said you knew what those spoons were called."

"Yes," I said, uncomfortable. Instinctively, I pulled the little fragile bird to me turning the birthmark away from their eyes. "They're called forceps. Doctors use them to help take the baby out when it gets stuck."

"Poor thing," Cora said. "She was so little one of the spoons pushed on her arm too hard and left a bruise that won't go away for a while." Her eyes flicked at Mr. Ashby. "Maybe not ever."

"You sure?" Trask asked. He stood with his hands hanging at his side and palms open. I think he didn't touch her because he was afraid if he felt a connection, a spark, the knowledge that she wasn't his would confirm Mrs. Ashby's feelings for him were a lie.

Miss Cora looked down at the sleeping bundle. "Yes, Mr. Trask. This is an Ashby baby. I've delivered them before. I delivered that one," she said, pointing to Mr. Ashby.

"All right." Trask went to his room and came out carrying his suitcase. "I'm going to drive the truck with Claire and make sure she is treated with respect when she is put on the train. I'm going north too. I'm taking her back to her mama. I need to do it."

"Now that is just ridiculous," Mr. Ashby mumbled his

cigar in his mouth again. "William can take the casket to the train and make sure it is loaded."

"Timothy!" Trask's shout filled the room with anger. "You told her to call you Mr. Ashby. She told me she never wanted to call you Timothy. She said she'd rather have some distance between you. She called me Edwin." He tipped his head at me. "Tell him. Tell him you heard her call me Edwin." His eyes, looking at mine, held hope not hatred.

"I think I heard her say it once." I kept my head down.

"That doesn't mean anything," Mr. Ashby retorted. "Claire was always taking on some hopeless case, thinking she could fix a person." I felt the room change. No one had their heads down anymore. He puffed fiercely on his cigar and stalked out to the front porch.

"Good luck, Trask. Send us a note to make sure everything got there safely."

"Her name is Eleanor Claire, and you must call her Ellie." I'd spoken up loud enough for both men to hear the name and realize there was a part of Mrs. Ashby that had been held back from both of them. "That's what Mrs. Ashby wanted to tell me. That's why she wrote the note. Her best friend was a woman named Ellie. It is important that the baby be named after her." My voice carried through the house to the back stoop and to the truck where Trask was tightening the rope around the end of the casket.

"Ellie," I heard Trask practice out loud. "When I visit Claire's grave, I'll talk about Ellie. Her family will let me, right, Annie?"

My mama looked Trask up and down just like she had a million times hating his guts, believing he had violated her charge. His pants were clean now, and when his shirt was ironed, he looked almost like a man who'd walk down the center of the sidewalk. When he looked you right in the eye, his birthmark didn't matter so much. It was like seeing both of him—the clean and the unclean, the evil and the good.

"Mr. Trask, yes they will," she said firmly. "You keep that nice haircut, remember to polish your shoes, have a good woman iron your shirts, because you know a man doesn't have the patience to iron his own shirt, and say, 'Yes, ma'am, and yes, sir,' to her parents, and they will like you just fine."

I saw her ponder whether she should mention wearing underwear was a good idea and using a tissue to blow his nose instead of the side of a house, and working on his grammar might help, but my mama knew she could only go so far.

"I need someone to ride in the truck to the train station with me to bring the truck back to the farm. I know it is the long way around because the bridge is out, but I'd appreciate the company." He shuffled his feet and held his hat in his hands.

"Of course," Mama announced. "I will go with you. I will figure out how to get the truck home. William's been teaching me. I'd like to see Claire all safe on the train. And you need someone from Jackson County to wave goodbye to you." My mama's worn hand trembled on my arm.

"Miss Cora? You'll make sure that woman comes to feed her?" My mama put her hand on the side of Miss Cora's cheek. "You'll help this here little girl?"

"Yes, Annie."

"Ellie," we heard Mr. Ashby say from the front porch. "She didn't know an Ellie."

I watched the truck make its way carefully down the

farm road. When it went over bumps, I saw the casket shudder on the stiff floor of the truck. Knowing her dead body was shaking in the wooden box despite the mountain of quilts Mama had placed around her to diminish the harshness of her journey, their protection did not nothing to stop the pain banging in my chest.

Chapter Twenty-Six

The men from the sawmill delivered wood to the opposite side of the creek from us. As the pile grew, I knew that our false sense of safety would be over soon. As soon as the Jackson County farmers and store owners from Gideon set to work repairing the pilings and laying the planks for the single car bridge, life would return to normal for everyone but us.

"William, what will the bank do?" Mama was rocking the baby, who had not yet figured out when to sleep and when to wake. She finally gave us some peace with long naps during the day, but we laid in bed for hours at night, listening to her cries and Mama's low singing to calm her. The night was long. Come to think of it, the day was long too. Ellie had yet to open her eyes more than a crack, and I believed that is why her day and night were mixed. Either that or she inherited Mrs. Ashby's fiendish delight in creating chaos.

"Hmm," Daddy said with his elbows resting on his knees. "Most of the pickers are gone. They must have got word to family or somebody. In the night, I heard couple of trucks and a few wagons pull up on our side of the road. The others?" Daddy rubbed his face with his hands. "They're like us. Lived here a long time. Decided to have faith a job will work out here is better than a job they don't have somewhere else."

"What is your plan?" The only sound was the rocking chair brushing the carpet. "Mama, Daddy"—I looked at each in turn—"you have to start thinking about yourselves. This house is part of the farm. Another family will buy the farm and live here. They might bring their own pickers, or they might not grow cotton at all," I said, thinking of Jubal Ridge. "You think of this farm as an idea, but it is land, a house, a barn, and a bunch of picker shacks. They can be bought by anyone. The new owner is not going to owe you anything for living here for three generations."

"Four," Daddy corrected. "Ellie is the fourth generation."

I chose not to respond to him. He and Mama saw themselves as Ellie's auntie and uncle, and there was no changing their minds. "You can go somewhere and get jobs. Mr. Ashby has no skills. Where is he going to live?"

"Socrates." Daddy blew air from between his lips in frustration. "That is the problem. We'll have to convince him to come with us. We're the only family he has." Daddy frowned. "The Jeffersons thought this farm was their home, and it turns out it is, only if it is an Ashby farm first. That's a reason right there you have to leave, Socrates. You can break this. You can own something of your own someday, but you need an education first."

"If Mr. Ashby goes with you, he'll just weigh you down." I slammed the front door shut and jumped off the front stairs. Mr. Ashby was sitting in his chair in the middle of the empty porch. It was a warm fall day, and I realized he had heard every word of our conversation.

"Socrates," I heard Mr. Ashby's voice behind me as I walked to the barn. "I need your help." He swallowed a lump in his throat. "Please."

"I have to clean Lean's stall." I shoved the pitchfork deep into his pile of straw and manure. Without Walker around, all his chores had been added to mine. Mr. Ashby followed me into the barn.

"Wait a minute, I have to get his gate shut. He might knock it open." I pushed on Lean's broad chest and I felt him lean back against me. "Damn horse," I puffed.

"No, leave him, Socrates. I want to take him out for a ride. Help me get him ready." Mr. Ashby's tiny hand reached up to grab Lean's mane. The horse shook him off, and Mr. Ashby bumped the side of the stall.

"Mr. Ashby, he might...kill you. That's how bad an idea this is," I protested, lifting a saddle onto Lean's back.

"Just because I am vertically challenged doesn't mean I can't ride him." He pointed to the stirrups. "Shrink those up, Soc." I shortened them so there were only a few inches between the foot and the leather.

"I'm going to get Walker," he said panting with exertion. Everything stopped in the barn. The other horses lifted their heads up to stare at Mr. Ashby. It was as if every living thing on the farm heard his pronouncement and wanted to believe him.

"How?" I asked, incredulous, helping him onto a stool. From there, I boosted him onto the back of Lean. Lean shivered with anticipation.

"I got my rainy-day fund here." He patted a bag he was carrying. "Put it in the saddlebag for me, please?"

It was the second time he had said please to me, which

was two times more than he had in my entire life. I hefted the heavy bag of coins rattling against one another and stuffed it in one of the bags on Lean's left haunch.

"Don't tell Annie and William. I have to make sure it works out. I'm taking Lean because Grindall thinks I am a fool. I'm not, Socrates. I'm talking about Claire and the farm. I'm talking about all of it. I've just been scared since I was a boy. If I show you all I can ride Lean, you'll see I'm not scared any longer."

He looked down at me from his perch high on Lean's back. His legs stuck almost straight out from either side of the saddle, and it would be impossible for him to bring the horse under control if Lean's natural instincts took over.

"Open that drawer." He pointed to a deep, narrow drawer at the bottom of the tack station. "Reach way in the back," he instructed. "It won't hurt you. Pull it out." I reached in past my elbow and felt something hard and leather. As I pulled it out by its black leather handle, the long end slipped from my grasp and spun in a twirling blur at my feet. "I've known it was there for years, and I've never touched it. It's time to get this evil thing off the farm. I have a daughter now, and I don't want her ever seeing something so vile." He reached down for it. "Thank you, Socrates."

"Where are you putting it?" I asked, handing over the whip that still held my father's skin caught in its surface.

"You know that section in the Low Field where the land slopes and all the privies flow there?" I nodded yes. "I don't know how deep that sludge is, but it is at least deep enough to hide this awful thing of my daddy's." Mr. Ashby stopped looking ridiculous on the back of Lean, and Lean sensed it as well. He walked out of the barn and obediently turned to head down the hill to the fields.

"What the hell was that all about?" Daddy asked, joining me outside the barn.

"Hard to tell, Daddy. But he asked for help, and I gave it to him. He even said please twice and thank you once."

Later that afternoon, Lean emerged from the longleaf pine forest between us and Jubal Ridge, carrying Walker, who rode behind Mr. Ashby with his arms around Mr. Ashby's waist. They picked their way across the pine needles until Walker jumped off Lean's back. I could see he wanted to run to us, but instead he picked up the reins and led Mr. Ashby home with patient footsteps and an exhausted smile on his face.

Our own Walker William Jefferson was home.

Mama was busy hugging on Walker's neck and praising the Lord. Daddy walked up to Lean, roped his reins in his fist, and held him tight while Mr. Ashby slid down the saddle grabbing the stirrups to ease his way down.

"Thank you, Timothy, for bringing our boy home." His eyes were still distrustful as he gazed on the man who had never given him a reason to trust him.

"I used up my rainy-day fund. I had a hundred silver dollars, and Grindall was angry he had to take them, but there was nothing he could do. You should have seen him spitting mad. It reminded me of when you made that beehive drop on his head."

"You know, Timothy, there were times when that money would have come in handy to fix the radio or the battery..." Daddy's voice trailed off.

"It was my Mama's money. She hid it from Mr. Sir in case she needed to leave. I thought I better save it for a

special time if I had to go somewhere, but when I heard
you and Annie were willing to take me with you, I knew
what I had to do. I knew Walker needed to come home."

We walked through the pasture back to the barn
where Walker took Lean's reins and disappeared through
the sagging, paint-speckled doors. I expected him to look
back at me, make a funny face, or whisper something just
out of Daddy's hearing, but he kept his attention on Lean,
removing the saddle and sliding the bridle out of his
mouth, and loading his feed bin with oats. He was gentle
with the big horse, brushing him with long strokes of the
brush and walking him quietly back into his stall. Walker
had changed.

Chapter Twenty-Seven

"Somebody's coming," I cried, running out to the porch.

A sleek, black car followed by a truck with several men riding in the back pulled up in the drive next to the barn. Mr. Carr stepped out of the car and adjusted his round hat's velvet brim. He waved to the truck to wait for his instructions. Walking to us, he stretched out his hand to Mr. Ashby. "Hello Timothy." He looked uncertainly at my daddy. "And..."

"You've met my farm manager, William Jefferson, before, John."

"Yes, I remember the last time I was here." Mr. Carr rubbed his hands on his arms. He was wearing his heavy overcoat, but it didn't seem to be keeping him any warmer than it had cooler in the summer. "Should we go inside?" He turned to go into the house.

"No, John. The baby is asleep. I don't want my daughter disturbed. We can talk here," Mr. Ashby's voice carried to me in a huskiness I had never heard.

"My son, Socrates, heard you, Trask, and Grindall having a conversation in town on the Fourth of July. He said the three of you were trying to swindle Timothy out of his family's farm." Mr. Carr's chin trembled in an already weak jawline at Daddy's words. "I talked to Edwin before he headed north, and he said he backed out of the deal, but he wasn't sure about your friendship with Grindall."

"So what about you, John?" Mr. Ashby asked.

"Well, I don't know what you are talking about, and I am not friends with that vile man," he gasped.

"You told Trask he wasn't good enough to even talk to Mrs. Ashby. I was sitting on the other side of the car. Trask pushed you against the boot." I stood next to Daddy with my hands in my front pockets like I was a grown man.

"Well," he said nervously, "anything that had to do with Trask is over. The Federal Farm Bureau has agreed to accept a lower payoff if it can be accomplished today. Of course, I am a neutral party in all of it."

"Of course, you are, John. We've only known each other since we were boys, haven't we?" Mr. Ashby smiled largely at Mr. Carr, not caring that his missing tooth left a sizable hole between his lips.

John Carr looked down the farm road to see if there was dust indicating any approaching vehicles. No dust whatsoever. The men sat in the truck, waiting for instructions. He slumped. "I do have some news. Although, Timothy, the bank is foreclosing on your farm, there are two interested buyers. I am waiting to see which one puts the money together the fastest. The better offer, the one that puts some money in your pocket, requires selling another property before purchasing this one. The second offer doesn't provide you with any funds, but it does come with an offer for you to rent the house. It's my opinion those are two bright spots in a sad situation. What do you say?"

"Who is it who will rent me my own house?"

"Well, before I tell you, just remember it means you could raise your daughter where you grew up." Mr. Carr adjusted the collar of his coat around his neck.

"Who?" Mr. Ashby was blunt.

"Grindall," John Carr said with a rush. "You won't get any money from him, but he offered you the house…"

"Hell no, not if hell freezes over, never in hell will that happen." Mr. Ashby spat out angrily. Daddy put his hand on Mr. Ashby's arm.

"There's another offer, remember, Timothy? We can start over. That's what the first generation did. We'd be like them," Daddy proposed.

"No, it wouldn't be like them, William. Not at all." His eyes were hurt that Daddy tried to mollify him. I could see him trying to make it be known that he was a man now.

A cloud of dust lifted into the air as we heard the rattling of tires cross the new boards of the bridge. Two trucks charged up the yard road their engines straining. The lead truck pushed the gas pedal and thundered toward us. I recognized the truck behind it with its rusty running boards.

"Maddie," I said under my breath. Her groaning truck pulled up even with the first truck. I could see her set lips and blue-and-brown eyes glaring in her face. She jerked the wheel to the left and drove her truck on the slant of the road. She blew the horn repeatedly. She stuck her arm out the truck's window, and a piece of white paper struggled in the wind.

Maddie pulled herself out from under the steering wheel and jumped to the ground. She was wearing her working overalls, and her thin arms looked lost in the denim.

The second truck pulled up, and I saw Grindall adjust his hat on his head before he smoothly stepped out of his truck. "Good morning, everyone," he called. His tall black boots glowed, and the silver on his heels shone like they had been polished too.

"John, here is my best and final offer." He handed Mr. Carr a folded slip paper.

"And here is mine, you lily-livered spectacle of a man, Mr. Carr. You're just lucky I found out the offers were being decided out here." I scooted over to Maddie to try to catch her eye. Calling Mr. Carr a lily-livered spectacle probably didn't help the situation.

The papers trembled in Mr. Carr's hands, and I saw him look around, searching for a place to hide. "Congratulations, Miss Porter." He handed her an envelope. "Your offer pays off the Federal Farm Bureau loan and the mortgage held at Gideon Bank. I wish you every success. You own the property free and clear. Here's the deed to the property."

"Are you kidding me? This dame bought me out? Where'd she get her money?" Grindall was livid. "What are you doing Carr? We had a deal." Grindall's neck was taut with thick, red tendons that looked like rooster spurs wheeling in the sun when they were particularly disturbed by a ruckus in the barnyard.

"There, it's done. I sold my restaurant for the farm." Maddie wiggled her way between Daddy and Mr. Ashby. "It's the best restaurant in town. They paid me a pretty penny for it. Said they go higher if I gave them my biscuit recipe. Like that was ever going to happen." Her eyes crinkled.

"I'm sorry, Grindall," Mr. Carr said. He held out the two sheets of paper. "Here are the two offers. You can see yours is much lower. There is no way I could accept it. Perhaps there is another property that might suit your needs."

"Bastard." Grindall spit in the dirt at Mr. Carr's feet. "I told the bank in March I would be buying this farm. You!" He jerked his finger at Maddie's face. "No one ever wanted you. That's the only reason you had money."

"Hey, don't talk to my sister like that." Mr. Ashby shoved Grindall's stomach with his little hands. Grindall leaned toward Mr. Ashby, and Maddie tucked in next to her brother. They looked like children standing up to Mr. Sir.

"Thank you, Timothy," Maddie said, putting her hand on Mr. Ashby's spindly shoulder. "I appreciate your nice words. Now, for your information"—she pointed at Grindall—"this old dame is a good businesswoman who knows how to bargain. I got money left over. This farm is going to be like it was when we were children. You will envy it, you fool, you good for nothing Northerner as far as I can see no one ever wanted. Now git off my land. And"—she looked around for my mama—"somebody hand me that sweet little baby with our Ashby blood in her. She's my kin, and you don't have any. Git!" Maddie stomped toward Grindall while Mama came out of the house with the baby.

Mr. Carr motioned to the truck filled with the men to go back down the farm road to the highway. "We're done here." He climbed back into his car and drove away at a snail pace looking for holes in the road. He hunched over his steering wheel and stared straight ahead as his large, black car crawled passed us like a roach fearing it had been spotted.

"Socrates Bravo, you come here and talk to me." I scooted over, trying to stay as compact as possible in case I had to make a run for it. She grabbed my chin in her hands. "What you said opened my eyes like I was wearing your glasses. I went to bed with hate in my heart for you until I realized you were right. Thank you for making me see."

"Of course, Maddie, we want you here."

"Good, because you are stuck with me now. I have nowhere else to live." She patted me and shouted loud as she could. "Sweet, sweet girl, I'm your auntie," Maddie said and lifted the baby out of Mama's arms. The dust of the Ashby farm drifted in a haze and lit in tiny bits on the shoulders of the Ashby's and the Jefferson's. Maddie pulled back the blanket to look at her niece. Ellie sneezed, and her eyes opened wide for the first time. The blue eye was light like the early morning sky, and the brown eye was the color of the spring hills before the cotton comes.

"Look there, Timothy. Eyes just like us. I told you that. You didn't have to worry." She shook her head with a smile. "Look here. No one has eyes like us. Come with me. I want you to sit down when you hold her. You are a man. We can't take the chance you'd trip or something."

Mama and Daddy dragged more chairs out onto the porch, and Mama made a fresh pot of coffee. "Timothy, you sit next to me, and I'll let you hold her," Maddie suggested. It was the first time little Ellie had been lowered into his arms.

He held her up, inspecting her like she was light shining through a beautiful window. "Maddie, am I doing this right?" He leaned over so his nose touched hers. "I don't know where that name came from, but Socrates must be telling the truth."

I edged my way toward the barn where I had options if my name was shouted by one or more of them. As I snuck toward the silent barn, I saw Mr. Ashby tuck Ellie into his chest and look up at his family.

"Claire did love Socrates the best, didn't she?" He fussed with Ellie's blankets. "Is she cold, Annie? Can I give her bottle? She's hungry. I can tell."

At Mr. Ashby's words, I suddenly felt weepy. I missed Mrs. Ashby something terrible. Her absence had left my life gray and white, and I could not see colors; I wanted the red and yellow of the autumn trees in the hills beyond the cotton field to glow with life as they did each year, but my brain struggled to accept her death, and I found myself looking for her at every turn. I would have given anything to see that scary-looking bird's nest hair with a pencil peeking out the top. It hurt to breathe.

"Hey, Soc," Walker said from inside a horse stall, "I'm catching up." He saw my face and heard the laughter from the porch. He dropped the shovel and placed his arm around my shoulder. "It's okay. You can cry. I won't tell anyone."

So I did. I cried until my breathing was jagged and my eyes hurt from the salt tears flooding my face. I gulped for air, and Walker looked scared.

"Whoa, Soc. Maybe not so much crying. Mama's going to think I punched you or something. Drink this." He held up a tin cup full of water. "Lean can just wait." Usually when we said his name, he'd stomp a foot or neigh loud enough to spook the other horses, but when I looked into his stall, he was calmly standing in place just as well as old Blaze.

"You're different, Walker," I said, my hiccupping slowing to a stop.

"Yeah, working for Grindall does that to you. That's why I hid out here while all that yelling and carrying on was happening. I didn't want Grindall to see me and go berserk."

"While you were there, did you think you were ever going to get home?"

Walker shook his head no. "Did I tell you about Archie?" My swollen eyes closed. I knew he needed to say it, so somewhere, someone would feel they had been heard. "He was there too. He was real slow, like somebody beat him up and he hadn't come out right. He told me he wished he could be me. I was stupid; I thought he was talking about baseball. But Archie didn't even know I played. He only knew about tapping trees. He said, 'Walker, you are better than me, because I got to check every tree to see if it is still alive. You at least get them when you know for sure they're dead. If the tree's still a bit alive, I have to tell them to kill it again with more cat whiskers.' He cried all the time, Soc because he was worried he'd find a tree that was still alive." He wiped his arm across his eyes. "Damn your crying, Soc. You got me watering too."

"Poor Archie." I blew air out from my lips.

"Poor Archie," Walker replied. "I got a second chance, Soc. I'm going to be a good person around here, I promise."

"You are a good person, Walker. You just got stuck between Grindall and the umpire."

"Let's not talk about baseball, Soc. I'm done playing, and it hurts too much to talk about it."

"Socrates," I heard Maddie yell from the porch. "Make

yourself useful for once. Get your Auntie Maddie a glass of water."

"Socrates, come in the house." It was scary, but I could barely tell the difference between Mama and Maddie yelling for me.

"I think I used to be gone so much they forgot I am here now. Let's keep it that way. It won't last forever," Walker pushed me gently. "Go. Mama's calling."

"William, you too. I need help with this bottle." Mama began banging pots together.

"I'll be right there," I called. "Thanks for letting me get all snotty and crying."

"Don't do it again." He shook his finger at me, and one of his radiant smiles broke across his face like a summer sunrise. It made me catch my breath; it was so unexpected and stunning.

"What did I do, Mama? Why are you yelling at me?" I said when I got to the kitchen. "Am I supposed to get Maddie some water or make a bottle? I'm confused."

"I don't know why I am here at all," Daddy said with an uneasy face. "I'd rather not be a part of this conversation, whatever it is about."

Mama grabbed my collar. "Once and for all, who is Ellie's daddy? Can it be both? I felt terrible sending Trask off like that."

"Mama, she can't have two daddies." My head was beginning to throb with a headache. I'd have to come up with some way of living with Mama and Maddie together.

"Are you sure there can't be a little bit of both?" she asked her eyes wide.

"No, Mama. She is an Ashby. The different-colored eyes are inherited. The red birthmarks can't be passed down. It's just a freak of nature that she got both. Something that can't be explained."

"Let it go, Annie. Sometimes, it is better to just accept even if you don't know why." Daddy was calm as he stroked my mama's arm.

"You mind your daddy. He's wise even if he is a man." Mama kissed him and handed me a glass of water. "We're good and done with all of this. She is an Ashby. It's good and done," she repeated. "We won't talk about it again. Timothy is going to be a better man every time he sees those eyes. He gets another chance, Socrates. How many of us do?"

I carried the glass of water out to the porch following my parents. Maddie got up, carefully gripping the arm rests of her chair. She stood and ripped the deed to the farm into two pieces. She handed one half to my parents.

"As long as we keep the two pieces together, we own this farm. It's time the Ashbys and Jeffersons owned this together. We're doing what should have been done in the first place." She reached for Ellie, and Timothy held her close. "Oh no, you don't. We got years of stories to share. There's holes in our lives that need filling. Let me hold our baby girl."

"And then there were Four," I said.

Daddy was the first to smile. "This is right. It makes Mr. Sir gone for good."

Maddie cleared her throat. "Well, it is time to talk business. The Four own this farm, and it is going to be run right. Now, I'm not in charge since Timothy and I own half, and Annie and William own half, but I learned a lot from running a restaurant. Like business ideas. Is that okay with you Jeffersons?" Mama and Daddy clutched their ragged half of the deed between them. They nodded yes.

"And me, Maddie? We're the Ashby half. What am I now?"

"Timothy, I'm going to just say this right up front. You have the reputation of being too poor to paint and too proud to whitewash. We got to change that. Do you understand?"

"Yes," he replied, ashamed.

"You got money coming to you from the sale, and I think that is right. I hope you want to invest your money."

"I do."

"Good, because you will be investing it in your daughter. Schooling, books, teachers, she's going to be the smartest girl in Jackson County. So you gotta make your money last, you hear me? You're also helping out with everything we got going on. First job for you? Finish the voice pipe. It's a good thing, and I am going to be in that kitchen, listening to you talk."

Mr. Ashby's eyes got shiny. "Thank you, Maddie. I will finish it this week."

"Good!" Maddie scooted her chair in closer to the group. "This is how I see it. First, we're going to make this farm look like it is as good as it can be. You hear me?"

The others leaned forward.

"I have some extra money. Let's call it seed money. We're going to paint this house and shore up the barn. We're going to sell the horses—all but two because every farm should have a horse or two in its pasture in order to look prosperous. We're going to burn that old wagon. It's from long ago, and we're in a fresh start." Then she looked over at me. "Socrates Bravo, if you keep sitting there with your mouth hanging open like you don't believe all this is going to happen, then we'll be changing the name to the Five, and you're going to be working all day and night just to make your keep. Drive my truck into the barn and unload those rags. We'll use them to clean the windows tomorrow." She stopped and frowned at me. "Do you know how to drive a truck?"

"Yes, Maddie."

"Fine then. You can fill it up with gas. Use the can in the back. It's full."

"Yes, ma'am." I took my time carrying in boxes of rags, and I flooded the clutch a couple of times as I strained to hear her describe the farm's new way of working.

"Of the pickers, who are left?"

"The young ones left, but the ones our age with children decided to stay." Mama's voice was guarded. She knew she wasn't a picker in Maddie's eyes, but the past was hard to let go.

"If there are pickers born on this ground, they're going to get a little piece of land. Everyone should have a piece of the world that is their own. It keeps their feet rooted in the ground and gives them respect for themselves."

"Why are you giving pickers land?" Mr. Ashby pushed his chair back, the legs digging painfully into the worn porch boards.

"We're changing, Timothy. We're going to do tenant farming." Mr. Ashby tensed up. "We'll let a little family buy forty acres on credit, and they'll work harder for themselves than they will if they don't have a stake in it. They'll pay the farm a percentage. A Negro family is not going to leave a plot of land they own. Stability, that's what it is."

I missed Maddie's description of my parents' role, but I was certain it was pretty much the same as they were doing now, but there would be no more hat holding when my parents talked to Mr. Ashby. In fact, I had not heard one 'mister' or 'missus' pass from their lips since Mrs. Ashby died. They were equal as far the acres stretched, the equipment worked, and the house stood.

I walked to our old home. I needed time alone and to think. The Four stayed out late, clustered on the porch, taking turns holding the baby, watching the parade of stars go by, and little Ellie slept for the first time through the whole night.

I opened the bag where I kept my school papers safe. I slid the typewritten pages out of the leather pouch. It felt heavy in my hands. The War of 1812, the hybridization of dahlias, the postulates of Euclidean Geometry, the deceit of Lady Macbeth. I packed them back in the stiff, new bag Maddie bought me and secured the latch. I felt unsettled, and I couldn't place my finger on why.

Chapter Twenty-Eight

It was the first week of October, and I was due to leave for Parson University Preparatory School in a few days. A stretch of sunshine and low humidity popped the casings of the final bolls on the bushes, and we were all hurrying alongside the pickers to bring the crop in. Mama and Maddie, their dresses tucked into their waistbands, picked cotton, tossing the bolls over their shoulders into their bags while vigorously debating the merits of peach pie versus peach cobbler. Daddy walked along rows stripping the bolls from the plants and tucking them in a bag slung across his body. Whoever happened to be nearby was gifted an armful of dirty white down.

About half the pickers had left when Daddy suggested the bridge washout might be a good time to leave the farm, but the fifty or so people left picked with a new intensity, eyes focused not only on the green and white in front of them, but also the rows next to the sky on the horizon. Daddy and Maddie had met with all families eligible to become tenant farmers, and there was going to be a drawing for twenty forty-acre plots. While learning about how tenant farming worked, many of them came back several times to clarify their understanding.

"We rent your land?"

"Yes,"

"We buy our own seed and tools?"

"Yes."

"You take one third, and we get two thirds?"

"Yes."

Joseph Sutter went to Maddie on his own and explained that his father didn't trust the system and thought the Ashbys were going to screw them over like always.

"Do I look like I screw anyone over, or do I look honest?" Maddie's face was inches from Joseph's, but he was brave enough to keep his chin from quivering. She admired his grit and, later that night, went to their shack for a little "educatin'," as she called it.

She was going to keep her eye on Joseph, she said. He was a boy going places. "Not on a train bound for boarding school, but maybe to help your daddy out as a salaryman someday. Don't tell him, I said that," she said, pinching my ear. "He is a man, and it would go to his head, and then he'd be useless."

I assured her I would not breathe a word, but not for the reason she thought. I didn't tell him because I feared what his father would do to him. Better let him grow up a bit more before he had to tangle with a man as mean as Mr. Sir.

The farm felt new and fresh. We spent weeks painting the big house, and it turns out Walker was a hard worker when he set his mind to it. He was up and down ladders, carrying buckets of paint with his brush between his teeth. He cut the grass around the house, put the dahlia stakes away until spring, and turned over the garden for the winter. He was so busy working we didn't notice he wasn't playing baseball.

"The team won't take me back, Soc." He shoveled Lean's manure into the wheelbarrow. He still hated all chores involving cow pies, horse dung, and Mama's compost heap where creepy crawly bugs liked to appear out of a smoking pile of rotting cabbages. "It's okay. It's not like Maddie doesn't inform me ten times a day I'm a man now, and it's time to look for my future. This is my future. Maybe I'll have a wife someday. Maybe. But you don't know in the beginning if they're going to turn out like Mama and Maddie a month later, so I'm still on the fence on that one."

"Walker, I believe you are going to play baseball again. That's all I want to say on the subject because I don't want you getting angry at me, but I am entitled to my own opinions." I scurried away as I felt the air shooshing toward me with a large shovelful of horse shit flying off the end.

WALKER AND I WERE NEARING THE END OF A ROW WHEN something white and round dropped into the dust in front of Walker. It was a baseball. He picked it up and chucked it back in the direction it had come from. He sidled his eyes my way, but I waved him off. I didn't know where it came from. I heard a whizz in the air, and this time, it tapped in the middle of Walker's back.

"Hey, knock it off, it's not funny." He scowled at me.

"Sorry," I heard a voice behind us. "Just pulling a funny one on you. I'm looking for someone named Walker Jefferson. I thought it might be you." A tall, lanky man wearing a baseball hat pulled just off center came around the end of the row and walked toward us. He was skinny with ragged cuffs on his pants and shirt, and he was eating a large peach. He stuffed the remainder in his mouth and spit the pit. It hit the center of the tarp at the end of the row like it was a bullseye target.

"LeRoy." He extended a hand that was delicate and strong at the same time. His knuckles, I noticed when he lifted his finger to scratch his nose, were calloused. "Hot one," he observed, pulling his hat off and wiping his forehead with his arm. "Got somewhere to talk?" He dropped his bag in the dirt, and it landed heavily, sinking into the dust.

"I'm picking the rest of the day. I don't have time for messing around." Walker bent over and pulled three bolls loose. One of the casings tore a red line across his fingers.

"That's got to sting like a son of a gun when you're tossing," the man noted, pointing to Walker's hand. "You got a woman around here who'd give me a drink of water?"

"Wait!" Walker and I both yelled.

Walker jumped over a bush and scooped the ball up in one smooth motion. "You can't put it that way around here. We've got mean women on this farm."

The man hooted. "Try me. Women love me. Even my wife. Come on, fellows. I'm spot on thirsty."

Walker and I dragged our bags through the rows, struggling to keep up with the stranger, LeRoy, who seemed to float just above the bushes. "Don't look back. Something might be gaining on you." He chuckled again and took off running, carrying his bag aloft. Walker and I looked at each and dropped our bags. We couldn't think what would happen if he ran into Mama or Maddie before we had time to prepare him ahead of time.

"Who are you?" Maddie asked, coming out of the barn. She was dressed in her new work pants she bought from a man's store in town, and her hair was sticking out from her handkerchief. Cobwebs gathered in clumps woven though her braids. She was sweating heavily. "No one runs around this farm as long as I am too tired to run. Who are you, and where are you from?"

Walker and I looked at one another. We had never seen Maddie do anything faster than a shuffle, but when she wanted you now, her dragging feet seemed to move awfully fast.

"Name's LeRoy, was born in Mobile. My parents had twelve kids, and they couldn't remember if I was the one born in '06 or '07, so I'm not quite sure of my age. I like to think it's more important to remember no man can avoid being born average, but no man got to be common."

Maddie nodded her head in agreement. "I agree with you there, LeRoy. Come to the porch. Best we can do is a glass of water, though."

"That's fine by me. Thank you, ma'am." My shoulders bunched up as I remembered the moment she almost boxed my ears when I called her ma'am.

"Why'd you throw this at me?" Walker tossed him the ball, watching it as it left his hand.

"I need to practice. I got a game tomorrow in Nashville, and I need a little warming up." LeRoy spun the ball and tossed it back to him. "Play a little catch?" He pulled a worn glove from his bursting bag.

"What all you got in there?" I asked. "It's awful full."

"This and that. Lots of uniforms. Depending on who I'm playing for. I'm a barnstormer."

"Man," breathed Walker taken by surprise. "Who do you play for in the regular season?"

"Barons. Birmingham." His answer was brief. He knew it spoke volumes to Walker.

"Maddie told me we had a visitor." Mama pushed the screen door open with her back end. She was carrying two plates of food—a piece of peach pie and a slice of peach cobbler. "Why you don't you sit a spell and try our peaches?"

I raised my eyebrows to Mama, but she ignored me. "Maybe you'll like one more than the other."

"What's a barnstormer?" I asked.

"We baseball players got to make a living in the off season, so people put together exhibition games, charge crazy money, and ask us to put on a show."

"What do you mean?" I tried to pick some crumbs off my Mama's cobbler, but LeRoy snatched it away and bit into it with large teeth.

"They make me throw the ball over a match box five times in a row, pitch to live batters with the infielders sitting down behind me, tell me to throw a pitch and a toss to first ball at the same time, you know." He shrugged.

"They make you act like a clown." Walker glared.

"No, Walker Jefferson, because when I stand up and pitch the way I want to, I get the first nine batters out without anyone getting on base. Then," he acknowledged, "I have to let a few on for entertainment value."

"Who do you play?" Walker edged closer to LeRoy and laid his fingers on the baseball lying next to the pie plate. LeRoy rolled it back to him.

"Everybody. We put together different teams every night. The biggest draws are when we play the Major Leaguers. Six out of ten times we beat them." He took a big bite of pie. "We beat them every time I'm pitching." He swallowed the last of the cobbler. "Y'all got any milk at this fine house?"

"Yes, sir. I'll get it for you." I went into the house where Mama and Maddie were both squeezed in next to the door trying to hear for free. "Hey, mind your own business." I smiled at the pair.

"I'm packing his bag," Mama whispered, crushing my face between her hands in glee.

Maddie grabbed some dish towels. "I'm getting the pie and cobbler wrapped up."

"How did you know about me?" Walker stood with his back to LeRoy, tossing the ball in the air.

"Word got out a special Negro pitcher was bound for the major leagues until he had a Lefty Grove ripped out of his hands." LeRoy drained the glass of milk I put by his elbow.

"Yeah," Walker said bitterly. "'Bout ruined my life."

"Look, kid, we'll toss so I can see for sure, but my mind's pretty much made up. I'm taking you to Nashville. We need another one like me. I hear you can throw a knuckleball. That had me upset for a minute, seeing how it was my pitch." Walker's entire body flushed red.

"I'll throw it all day if you want, but my slider is like a wicked old woman sneaking up on you, my curve breaks your heart when you aren't expecting it, and my fastball disappears in the air for a moment before it reaches the plate."

"I heard," LeRoy giggled. "You know you can't go off on an umpire right?"

Walker dropped his head. "I know, sir."

"We only have one ride on the merry go round, so if you leave this pretty place with me, you'll have to work like you don't need the money, love like you've never been hurt, dance like nobody's watching, get it?" Walker's bouncing head about bounced off.

"Home plate don't move. Never let your head hang down. Never give up and sit and grieve. Find another way."

"Yes, sir."

"Well, let's go throw a bit and give your mama time to pack your bag." LeRoy stood up and stretched.

Mama threw the screen door open. "Done." She thumped it down on the table.

"We wrapped supper up for you too." Maddie followed her out. "Front pocket."

After calling the rest of the family in for the goodbyes, Walker William Jefferson walked down our farm road, crossed the bridge, and headed north for the state of Tennessee. He didn't look back, but we didn't expect him to. Satchel Paige was schooling him on the ins and outs of playing exhibition ball to prepare him for the Negro League in a year's time. Even from a far distance, I could see Walker's rapt face looking into the purple sunset clouds as he spun the baseball in the air and caught it in his sure hands each time.

Chapter Twenty-Nine

"Are you sure you have everything in this suitcase?" My mama and Maddie stood next to the truck with their hats and gloves on. I could tell their church shoes pinched their feet. They shifted their weight back and forth, and rolls of skin were bursting out the top of their shoes.

"Yes, I have all my clothes, papers, pencil, everything. I have the letter from the school, and I have the train ticket Mrs. Ashby bought for me. I'll be fine." I shrugged my shoulders in my huge shirt. I was wearing Walker's church shirt, and it was ridiculously long on me.

"Where is your paper? Did you forget it?" Mama grabbed for the satchel, and I held it tight.

"It's fine Mama. The paper is fine. It's where is needs to be."

"Wait there, Socrates." Mr. Ashby came down the steps, juggling the baby and a black bowler hat. "A gentleman always wears a hat during the day. Here, put it on." He pushed it firmly on my head. It was too small, but he kept cramming it over my hair.

"Thank you, Mr. Ashby. I appreciate it. I bet the other

boys at school wear them too." My head began to sweat, and the straining ribbon dug into my skull. I climbed into the back of the truck. Daddy walked up to the side of the truck and put his hand on my shoulder.

"I hope it's okay with you that I let them take you to the train station. I think it is better. Maddie's letting your mother practice her driving. You okay?" His eyes had a softness, a calmness I'd never remember seeing. It was as if he could let his shoulders rest as he looked at the rows of dirt leading to the Appalachian hills and know they were his to nurture.

"I'm fine. Thanks. I'll see you at Christmas. I'll save up for a train ticket. I'm pretty sure I can get a job making biscuits somewhere." I tried to make him laugh, but I could see he was holding back tears.

"I did have some money saved if your mother and I had to leave, but thankfully, God made sure we could stay. He handed me a bag with coins sliding against one another. They had more heft than the bag of marbles I discovered months ago. He patted the hat. "You better take that off soon. It's going to strangle your head."

"I think it might blow off in the wind," I suggested.

"Better not, those two will make you get out and find it," he advised.

"I love you, Daddy. I'm not going to spend the money. It will come back to you."

"You know, Socrates, there's a time when a boy grows up and has to meet himself coming and going. When you come upon the boy you used to be, you'll be proud of him, just like I am. It's up to you now to create the one you haven't met yet. Make us proud."

The truck lurched forward, and my head banged against the back of the glass. Daddy waved to me and turned to go to the barn. My daddy was a man who could meet his younger self and the one he is now and know that he'd done a good job both ways.

"Socrates, move, your mama has to see out the window," Maddie called. I scooted over, and we started rolling. The farm flew away from me as the truck shifted gears and gained speed. The large bodies of water that covered the field during the rain were gone, and the dirt looked fresh. A few parasols still skipped along the roads in front of the shacks, and picker children were laughing as they waved goodbye to me. The dahlia patch was out of my view, but the necklace of tubers was safe with daddy who hid them in a special drawer filled with straw in the barn. I warned him to keep them out of Lean's view.

I said goodbye to my childhood home.

"No, Socrates, we are staying until we can put you on that train ourselves." Maddie was emphatic. We were standing on the train platform, and I was trying hard to make them leave.

"Listen, you need to get home before dark because you left Daddy and Mr. Ashby watching Ellie." I chose my words carefully. "Being men and all, they might make the bottle too hot, and I am sure they will forget to burp her. That would be upsetting to her stomach. You don't want that to happen."

Mama looked at Maddie. "He may be right," she conceded. "Yes, we better go."

"He's a man now. He can get on the train by himself. You know where you are going, right? Macon County," she said, holding up a piece of paper where she scrawled *Maken*. I hugged them both and held on tight to Mama.

"You better come home too, Socrates." She smiled largely at me. "I hated that name to start, but then it was you, and I learned to like it. You've always been mine." She hugged my neck. "Take that ridiculous hat off as soon as you can."

"I will." I motioned to them to scoot. "You don't need to go fourth gear, Mama, third's enough." I heard them cackle as they ran to the truck, their feet struggling to hold them up in the shoes. When they reached the battered old vehicle, they both reached down and took their shoes off. They tossed them in the back of the truck and pulled their hats off. The last thing I saw was the two of them waving madly to me out the windows as Mama spun the tires in the dirt leaving the train station.

I stood on the station platform, holding my suitcase of clothes and satchel of books. I looked like a schoolboy, a little small and stringy, but it was not a stretch to imagine me boarding the train to Macon County and arriving at Parson University Preparatory School.

I settled into the window seat and looked straight ahead. I wanted Gideon behind me for many reasons— mostly the confusion it caused Negros trying to decide where to stand on the sidewalk, how far to the front they could lay their blankets in the courthouse square, and could they use the automatic soda machine like Walker had? It was also the town I visited as a child, one that gave me my first job, and the place I met the Violin man. My emotions were as mixed as biscuit dough, but I felt deep down they would come together in that magical moment when dough peas become something solid by mixing it all together.

"Psst," I heard behind me. I whipped around.

"Joseph Sutter, what are you doing here? The train's about to leave."

"Don't worry. I'll jump off before anyone sees me."

"What do you want?" I asked.

"I wanted to say goodbye and tell you something."

"What? It better be good," I said irritated.

"A guy who works for Grindall pushed the copper still over with all the turpentine in it. When it spilled, it caught the grass on fire and burned the still down. It didn't make it as far as the trees, though. Grindall's leaving. He says he hates the South. I'm gonna find the guy and thank him."

Archie. I'd get word to Walker somehow.

"Hey, can I have your hat?" Joseph caressed the rough, black top where Mrs. Ashby's heel punctured it the day of Mr. Carr's visit.

"It's yours," I said, handing it over. "Just don't let Mr. Ashby see you wearing it."

"Nah, I never go up to the big house." He settled it on his head.

"Maybe you will someday," I said, thinking of Maddie's plans.

"Don't know if I'd want to, Soc. Take care. The train's moving now." Joseph scampered down the aisle and out the side door. I would never forget him. Life was his school, and I think he was going to do well.

The train picked up speed. It left Gideon and headed for Macon County. My ride would take a while, but I had the scenery and Percy Bysshe Shelley's book of poetry to keep me company. When I was choosing which books to add to my already heavy bag, I crossed paths with the book of Shelley's poetry that Mrs. Ashby and I had not picked up again after my accident.

I cracked the book open and turned to his poem, "Adonais." Two lines caused me to catch my breath, and a sudden rush of affection for Mrs. Ashby blinded me for a moment. Shelley wrote, "Thy extreme hope, the loveliest and the last, the broken lily lies—the storm is overpast."

When Mrs. Ashby had drawn the heart onto the table's surface the morning we hatched our chaos-into-order plan, I believe her scheme was bigger, grander, and meant to transform. It was her extreme hope, to quote Shelley, to save the farm but also to save all of us, change all of us. Like Lady Macbeth, she ruthlessly took power away from Trask and Mr. Ashby as they lay in her arms and opened their hearts to her. In the meantime, the pickers looked to Daddy for leadership while Mama saw herself as more than the help. Mrs. Ashby let me go to find Maddie and begin my education in becoming a man. That must have been the hardest for her to bear.

I can only imagine how becoming pregnant took her breath away. It might have changed all her plans or made her more determined to succeed in her goals. It brought her relationship with Ellie Ely to the surface, and, by telling me their story, it ensured their love would not be forgotten. I would tell their tale to Eleanor Claire someday.

Although Shelley did not know Mrs. Ashby, she was indeed the loveliest and the last, the broken lily. It was by her brokenness that Trask felt worthy, Mr. Ashby found courage, Daddy felt heard, and Mama knew she mattered. Me? I was the baby bird pushed out of the nest, certain that my wings would fan open and carry me through the sky.

The train passed fields of yellow flowers, and I thought of the Four at home arguing over the temperature of the baby's bottle, putting up a new and bigger porch swing, Daddy and Mr. Ashby wisely refusing to choose between peach pie or peach cobbler, and Lean out in the pasture wreaking havoc. Then my thoughts wandered to Peola Porter's train ride to Gideon so long ago. Wherever she was, I hope she looked down at the family she'd had a part in creating. Peace was hers after all these years, and I had faith Maddie would tell stories about her mother and keep her name alive. Peola and Mr. Sir were the ties that bound the Four together, and that was the hardest to understand. Paraphrasing Maddie, 'that is why there is a mystery and we are only who we are.' Perhaps the people most conflicted—the ones with the unmatched eyes—see from a different window than the rest of us. Whether they see a landscape wide and shallow, or narrow and deep, is unknown.

The strangeness of my name had set me apart from others in my childhood, but it also led me to the train ride I was on where every turn of the wheel took me farther from the farm. Mrs. Ashby knew that I had to go to school and learn the knowledge of the world. I was not a boy who longed for a picker's bag, or a violinist who took his talent down empty country roads, or a ball player willing to follow others' instructions to have his own place in the sun. She wished for me to be more than my namesake. The Socrates of ancient Greece taught others how to find truth through questions and she wanted me, Socrates of Gideon, Alabama, to find the answers.

The End

Acknowledgments

I would like to acknowledge the people who made this novel possible.

My husband, Paul Klenk, never wavered in his commitment to this project or the length of time it took to complete it. He accepted my wandering around the house looking for the perfect writing spot. He did not complain when I finally parked myself in our bedroom and holed up there for weeks.

My mother, Virginia Thompson, was one of my greatest cheerleaders, and my brother, Mike Thompson, encouraged me and offered plotting and thematic suggestions. My father, Ted Thompson, died in 2011, but he would have delighted in my use of baseball as a metaphor for race in America. I am 100% certain he would have agreed with me that Babe Ruth could not have stretched a single into a double, because it was documented that the "Babe" overindulged in both hot dogs and beer.

My best friend, Belinda Fricker, demanded I send her my manuscript when, during a low period, I told her I wished I had never met Socrates Bravo. The writing was difficult. I was lost in other issues, and she said, "I'll keep it safe until you are ready to write again."

My children, Connor, SarahKate, and Dane, have been supportive of all my writing projects over the years and did not complain about the many times they ate pizza for dinner because my brain was busy living in other places with other people. Be assured, children, I love you dearly.

Karen and Ray Klenk, Paul's parents, never failed to ask me how my novel was coming along in our phone conversations and during our trips to their farm. Their kindness and acceptance of me as a daughter over the years means everything.

Fritz Greenlee read my novel with a careful eye towards sensitivity issues in the depiction of racial experiences as represented by the characters in the story. Not only did he open my eyes to experiences blacks faced in the early twentieth century (and later), but he also gave suggestions to fine-tune one of the characters in a way that improved the final version of the novel.

I thank Pam Blohm, the artist who painted *"Summer Cottonfield"* and gave me permission to use it as my book cover art. It thrills me every time I see it.

Thank you to everyone, who helped me get *How Socrates Bravo Got His Name* out of my head and onto the page. So many people encouraged my journey, and I appreciate it.

Lesley Klenk
Olympia, Washington
Spring 2021

Book Group Questions

How Socrates Bravo Got His Name

1. What impact does Socrates Bravo's name have on himself and others?
2. Why did the author start the novel with Socrates's accident?
3. The author uses the stylistic device of backstory to provide more information about the characters. Which backstory did you find most interesting?
4. What do you think about the role of the pickers in the novel?
5. Are there ways the novel represents social struggles between the North and the South?
6. How are Maddie, Annie, and Mrs. Ashby the same? How are they different?
7. How did getting a job change Socrates?
8. Why did Walker make a bet with Grindall?

9. What was the most shocking event in the novel? Why?

10. Is the story of Peola important? What does it add to the novel?

11. Will Mr. Sir's actions continue to impact life on the farm?

12. Were you surprised to find out about Mrs. Ashby's relationship with Ellie Ely?

13. What do the dahlias symbolize?

14. What do the wild hogs symbolize?

15. Describe Trask's personal qualities at the beginning and end of the novel.

16. Why does the Violin Man's music create a temporary equality between the white citizens and black citizens of Gideon?

17. What stories do you think the Jeffersons and the Ashbys will tell Ellie as she grows up?

18. By the end of the novel, Socrates Bravo is no longer a boy. What event(s) changed him?

Made in the USA
Monee, IL
07 August 2021

75133333R00204